Cursed with a poor sense of direction and a propensity to read, **Annie Claydon** spent much of her childhood lost in books. A degree in English literature followed by a career in computing didn't lead directly to her perfect job—writing romance for Mills & Boon—but she has no regrets in taking the scenic route. She lives in London: a city where getting lost can be a joy.

Born in the UK, **Becky Wicks** has suffered interminable wanderlust from an early age. She's lived and worked all over the world, from London to Dubai, Sydney, Bali, NYC and Amsterdam. She's written for the likes of *GQ*, *Hello!*, *Fabulous* and *Time Out*, a host of YA romance, plus three travel memoirs—*Burqalicious*, *Balilicious* and *Latinalicious* (HarperCollins, Australia). Now she blends travel with romance for Mills & Boon and loves every minute! Find her on Substack: @beckywicks.

Also by Annie Claydon

Winning Over the Off-Limits Doctor
Neurosurgeon's IVF Mix-Up Miracle
The GP's Seaside Reunion
The Doctor's Italian Escape

Also by Becky Wicks

Tempted by the Outback Vet

Valentine Flings collection

Nurse's Keralan Temptation

Twin Baby Bumps miniseries

A Daddy for Her Babies
From a Fling to a Family

Discover more at millsandboon.co.uk.

MISTLETOE KISS TO HEAL HIS HEART

ANNIE CLAYDON

CHRISTMAS WITH HER RIVAL

BECKY WICKS

MILLS & BOON

First published in Great Britain 2025
by Mills & Boon, an imprint of HarperCollins*Publishers* Ltd,
1 London Bridge Street, London, SE1 9GF

www.harpercollins.co.uk

HarperCollins*Publishers* Macken House, 39/40 Mayor Street Upper,
Dublin 1, D01 C9W8, Ireland

Special thanks and acknowledgement are given to
Annie Claydon and Becky Wicks for their contributions
to the Royal York Hospital miniseries.

ISBN: 978-0-263-32523-2

11/25

FSC
www.fsc.org
MIX
Paper | Supporting responsible forestry
FSC™ C007454

This book contains FSC™ certified paper
and other controlled sources to ensure responsible forest management.

For more information visit www.harpercollins.co.uk/green.

Printed and Bound in the UK using 100% Renewable Electricity
at CPI Group (UK) Ltd, Croydon, CR0 4YY

MISTLETOE KISS TO HEAL HIS HEART

ANNIE CLAYDON

MILLS & BOON

CHAPTER ONE

CHRISTMAS! THE BEST time of the year… Dr Eliza Chilton modified the thought. It was the best time of the year along with the promise of a New Year, the first day of spring and the warmth of summer. Closely followed by leaves scrunching beneath her feet and fireworks parties in autumn. But right now, Christmas was less than two weeks away, and she was going to make the most of it.

She'd come into work early, after manoeuvring two large bags onto the bus. The Royal York Hospital was already abuzz with the spirit of Christmas, and the ENT department was following suit. Not quickly enough for Eliza, several of the decorations that were taken every year from the box in the department's admin cupboard hadn't survived, and some of them were beginning to look a little tired. But there was an easy answer to that. She took the Christmas cookies from one of her bags and found a place where the receptionist, Sarah, would see them. She could be trusted to offer them around and when they ran out, Eliza had more to refill the Santa Claus tin.

Good start. Eliza began to unpack the decorations from her bag, laying the ones she'd earmarked for the reception area out on the desk.

'Eliza!' Dr Beckwith, the head of department, had

given Eliza permission to spruce up the decorations a little, but clearly hadn't expected her to go so far. 'I thought you were planning on bringing in a few more paper garlands.'

'It's not too much…?' Eliza shifted a little uncertainly, but Dr Beckwith was smiling.

'It's great. Thank you. We can always depend on you to cheer the place up. I can ask someone from the office to give you a hand.' Dr Beckwith looked at his watch. 'When they arrive.'

'I'm fine, thanks. I'm just going to put these up now, and then finish off with the rest after work.' Eliza reached into the second bag. 'Would you like a snowman for your desk? Or I have a few Santa Clauses…'

Dr Beckwith chuckled. 'I'll take the snowman if I may. And a cookie, to have with my morning coffee?'

'Yes, of course.' Eliza opened the tin, and the scent of yesterday evening's baking added to the rapidly growing atmosphere of good cheer.

Dr Beckwith chose a Christmas tree-shaped cookie. 'Thanks, Eliza. You've brightened up a very grey morning.'

That was the general plan. Smiles and good cheer went a long way in a hospital, and Dr Beckwith had no hesitation in placing them alongside cutting-edge technology and dedicated staff, as an important part of caring for their patients. And where Christmas cheer was concerned, Eliza reckoned that she was the woman for the job.

'By the way, do you have five minutes this morning? We have a new patient who I'd like to talk to you about.'

'Yes, of course. I'm free until ten. The patient I was going to see at nine has cancelled.'

'Perfect. I'll be in my office all morning. Come and see me when you've finished here.'

Eliza nodded. 'What's the patient's name?' Perhaps she could look them up on the system and come prepared.

Dr Beckwith smiled. 'It's just an *in principle* enquiry at the moment. I'll explain later.'

That sounded slightly mysterious. But meanwhile, a glittering tinsel garland was ready to be fixed over the reception desk. There was a small table in the corner that would do just nicely to help her reach the ceiling, and she pulled it over and climbed up on it, reaching back down for one end of the garland. She could hear the main doors to the department opening and then closing behind her, as people arrived for work, wanting to get an early start to the day. And she was dimly aware that someone had stopped behind her…

'Morning, Eliza.'

The deep-voiced New York accent was unmistakable. Max Russo. The ENT department's very own Christmas Grinch. Any Christmas fairy would baulk under his gaze and retreat elsewhere to spread some sparkle. Since Eliza didn't have the advantage of wings, she was going to have to make other arrangements, but they didn't include turning around to face him.

'Morning, Max.' She threw the words over her shoulder, keeping her gaze on the end of the garland as she taped it above her head. It was probably a little unfair to call Max a *Christmas* Grinch, because as far as she knew he didn't have anything against Christmas in particular. He'd maintained the same level of unsmiling detachment ever since he'd arrived in the department in March.

'Are you okay up there?'

Eliza doubted this was an offer of help. Max was a talented surgeon but he had no truck with magic. She guessed that he'd probably already carried out a health and safety assessment of the situation and decided that Christmas decorations weren't worth the risk involved in putting them up.

'I'm fine.' Eliza remembered to smile. Even if Max couldn't see her face, he'd hear it in her voice. 'This table's as solid as a rock.'

He could go now. If a perfectly sturdy table suddenly *did* collapse beneath her, Eliza reckoned that landing in his arms would be the worst possible outcome. She'd take her chances with the floor.

In retrospect, she probably should have taken her chances with a cold and rainy evening four months ago. It hadn't really been Richie's fault; they'd arranged to meet some friends for an evening meal on the outskirts of York and he'd said that he would drive. Eliza probably shouldn't have taken it for granted that he would bring her back home again, and when the evening came to a close had turned down several offers of lifts. Then she'd found that Richie had already left, along with several of his mates who were going on to a wine bar that stayed open late.

She'd looked for her coat, and then realised she'd left it on the back seat of Richie's car…with her phone zipped into one of the pockets. That had been an awkward end to a nice evening, but she could get the bus home. And then it had started to pour with rain…

She was halfway to the bus stop when the car had pulled up beside her. Eliza had pointedly ignored it, and then breathed a sigh of relief when she saw the window wind down, and Max leaning across from the driver's seat. He'd been nice, hadn't cared that she was wet through and was likely to drip all over the upholstery, and even put the heater on, because she was shivering. When he'd asked her what she was doing here, alone and in the dark, Eliza had made the mistake of telling him the truth.

And Max had told her what he thought. Of course he had, because he wasn't one to mince his words in the face of an unfortunate situation. He'd called Richie a waste of space, and wondered aloud what on earth Eliza was doing with him.

Eliza had corrected him, hearing an edge of annoyance creep into her tone. It hadn't been Richie's fault and if Max was going to be like that, she'd get out of the car and walk. That had shut Max up, and he'd apologised for speaking out of turn and not said another word on the subject. Which only made everything worse, because it was perfectly obvious what he was thinking. And if Eliza was honest with herself, she'd wondered whether Richie might have thought to mention he was leaving and made sure she had a lift back home, even if she wasn't going to admit to it.

It didn't help that Max was difficult to ignore, even when he wasn't saying anything. The precise, clean lines of his body and his close-cropped dark hair gave the impression of a man who knew what he wanted and would get there by the shortest possible route. By contrast, his deep brown eyes had a warmth, a softness about them, which was hard to ignore. Eliza reminded herself for the hundredth time that eyes didn't necessarily mean anything; they were just a confection of refracted light and genetics. The things a person chose to do and say were much more accurate windows to their soul.

'Give me a call if you need anything, then. I'll leave my office door open.'

Max didn't sound too enthusiastic about that, either; maybe he was still wondering if she was going to fall. Perhaps she should remind him that sitting in a draught might give him a stiff neck.

'Thanks for the offer. No need, though.' Eliza turned to face him, with a smile ready, in case she sounded as exasperated as she felt.

But Max wasn't there to see it. He was already walking away, giving her a backward wave to indicate that he'd heard her. There was little she could say to change his trajectory, and nothing that he could do to change hers. She puffed out an irritated breath, and returned to the decorations.

When Eliza tapped on Dr Beckwith's open office door, he looked up and beckoned her in. She closed the door and sat down to face him across his desk.

'Thanks for dropping in. We have a new patient that I'd like to discuss with you.'

Eliza nodded, waiting. A new patient didn't usually involve a conversation with the head of department, and there was clearly another reason why Dr Beckwith wanted to talk to her.

'She's eight years old, and was admitted to the children's ward here with bacterial meningitis. As she began to recover, it became clear that she wasn't responding to sound, and preliminary tests have indicated that she has profound sensorineural hearing loss in both ears.'

'So there's a lot to think about in very little time.' Every person, every family, had a different approach to hearing loss, and part of Eliza's role was to help patients make meaningful and informed choices. It was a process that took time. But quick intervention was required when hearing loss was due to bacterial meningitis so that every option could be kept open.

Dr Beckwith nodded. 'As you know, I think that two doctors working together on these cases is of paramount importance, to make sure that all issues are addressed immediately and nothing's missed. And of course with Christmas fast approaching, we have to consider staff leave over the holidays.'

Eliza wasn't going anywhere this Christmas. It went without saying that when Richie had broken up with her, she wouldn't be spending Christmas with his family as planned. Eliza hadn't mentioned that to anyone at the hospital, in case it got back to Max and he even thought that he'd told her so, let alone said it.

'I'd be happy to partner up with another doctor on this case.' Another thought struck her. 'Who did you have in mind?'

'This patient is already on Max Russo's list.' Dr Beckwith waited for a moment, as if to gauge Eliza's reaction, and she automatically gave him a smile to hide her dismay. 'I know that you two have very different approaches. But you're both exceptional doctors and I've learned to expect great things from you as individuals. I'm sure that you can achieve even more together.'

Whatever that was supposed to mean… Most people in the department would agree that Max Russo might benefit from smiling a little more. Did that mean that Eliza was going to learn to smile a little less?

'So Max will be in the lead on this?'

'Nominally yes, he's the lead physician on the case. But don't let him walk all over you. I'll be making it clear that both of you are working together on an equal basis.'

It would have been nice if Dr Beckwith hadn't thought he needed to say that. Eliza could hold her own with Max if she needed to.

'I'm trusting that you can work out what that means in practise, and that I'll be learning something from you both about how to implement future partnerships of this kind.'

Eliza smiled at him. 'Are you telling me that we're your guinea pigs?'

Dr Beckwith chuckled. 'I prefer groundbreakers. You're two very talented people who haven't worked together a great deal, and I'm looking forward to seeing innovative solutions. And remember that my door's always open for you to discuss any reservations you have about anything. Off the record, of course. I'm not interested in making life difficult for any member of staff in this department.'

If only Eliza had as much confidence that Max had the same attitude towards making life difficult as Dr Beckwith did. 'Okay. You'll let Max know?'

'I'll give him a call right now and tell him the same as I've just told you. Are you happy with that?'

'Yes, I'm happy with it.' Max was going to be a challenge, but maybe he would surprise her…

Christmas decorations weren't Max's thing. Smiling at everyone, as if everything was okay and life didn't come with any dark clouds, wasn't his thing, either.

But somehow, and he wasn't sure why, Eliza *was* his

thing. She was so sweet, so kind to everyone and always seemed to gleam with good humour. She wore the same practical clothes as most of the doctors here, comfortable slacks and flat shoes, but her choice of brightly coloured tops always complemented the shine of her white-blond hair. Coming into work and finding her perched on a table had brought sparkle to an otherwise gloomy morning, and it was no surprise to find her in the waiting area of the small procedures suite after work, putting up more decorations.

She outshone all of them, dragging Max back to a time when Christmas held nothing but happiness and good cheer. A time when aching loss didn't throw a dark shadow over everything. Eliza had a way of creating moments that allowed Max to forget the past, if only fleetingly.

The way she'd climbed into his car, shivering and wet through, but still managing to find a smile for him from somewhere. He and Eliza operated in different worlds: hers full of shiny magic, and his based on a more clear-eyed approach to the realities of what might happen next. He could look—he really couldn't help looking at her sometimes—but that night when he'd found her walking by the side of the road, soaking wet, had shown him that he shouldn't make observations about what he'd seen. Max had made the mistake of speaking his mind, and Eliza had been offended.

It had added a distinct air of reserve to their working relationship, which Max had done nothing to dispel. Reaching out wasn't his thing, either. When it was necessary, he and Eliza worked seamlessly together in the operating theatre, relying on each other's professionalism and expertise. And everywhere else…he made sure that he hardly saw her.

'Thanks for emailing me with the notes for Daisy Yates. I'm looking forward to working with you on her case.'

Eliza's determination to think the best of everyone was stubborn enough—or maybe just crazy enough—to extend to him, and she gave Max a sunny smile that made tingles travel down his spine. He'd sought her out, determined to mend whatever fences he could, for the sake of their patient. But actually, smiling back didn't seem such a difficult thing to do.

'You'll be able to join us at nine tomorrow morning?' Eliza had probably already emailed him back about that; she never let anything go unanswered. 'I haven't had a chance to check my mail since lunchtime.'

'I'll be there. I was thinking that I should adopt a watching brief for the first meeting, so I can get a feel for what's going to be needed. Then we can discuss how we're going to divide up our responsibilities.' The softness in her grey eyes belied the professionalism of Eliza's tone. She'd clearly made up her mind that this partnership was going to work, just as Max had.

'I'm looking forward to your input. In every aspect of the case.'

'Thanks. That's good to know.'

Eliza turned, surveying the decorations that were neatly laid out on a group of tables and chairs. She picked up a felt wall hanging, walking over to the wall where she'd already fixed up a group of decorations to make a Christmas frieze. This time she'd found a sturdy stepladder from somewhere, and she climbed to the top of it, holding the felt reindeer and sleigh at a jaunty angle at the top of the frieze.

'Here?'

That one word made his heart begin to melt. Max took a step back, considering the question.

'Bit less of an angle, I'd say. It looks as if the sleigh's about to take the roof off some of those houses and crash land into the trees.'

She chuckled, straightening the sleigh slightly. 'Yeah. I don't want it straight, though. It looks as if Santa's going to just fly past and miss someone out.'

'Over to the left, then. And a bit straighter. Let him come in for a gentler landing.'

Eliza nodded, moving the sleigh. Max nodded back in approval and she felt in her pocket, puffing out an exasperated breath.

He was already there, despite his resolve not to get involved with Christmas decorations. Max caught up the roll of easy-peel stickers that she'd left alongside the pile of decorations, and walked over towards her, peeling one from the backing tape.

'Thanks.' She gave him a grin, fixing the tape to the wall and pressing the felt sleigh down on top of it. Max peeled off another sticker and handed it to her. 'This'll cheer the place up a bit…'

Now was definitely one of those times when he needed to keep his thoughts to himself. In Max's view, the best way to cheer patients up was to make sure they didn't spend too much time in the waiting room, but he had to admit that the two equations had nothing to do with one another.

She couldn't possibly know. That once upon a time,

fixing the decorations—putting everything where his little brother Mikey told him it should go—had been one of the best parts of Christmas. And Eliza couldn't know that since Mikey had died, his family's decorations had stayed in their boxes, waiting for a time that never came, when they would no longer provoke sad memories. If she had, she would have undoubtedly been kind and tactful, hesitating to accept any offer of help from him. But Max no longer wanted kindness or tact; he wanted to put the past behind him, and England had seemed far enough away from New York to allow him to do just that.

'You're going to put the moon and stars up here?' He gave in to the inevitable and gestured towards a pile of sparkly silver decorations laid out on the table.

'Yes, I thought so…?' Eliza effortlessly involved him in the question and Max couldn't help smiling.

'That's the place for them, definitely. It'll finish the whole thing off nicely.'

Eliza moved the steps while he gathered up the moon and stars, ready to hand them up to her one by one.

This wasn't all about decorations; they were just flimsy scraps of colour and sparkle. Mikey's doctors had been unswerving in their optimism over his medical condition, and that had left his family unable to prepare for his death and incapable of processing it. His parents had been submerged in a wave of grief that had carried them away from their surviving son. He'd learned how to ignore the pain of losing his whole family by throwing himself into his studies and then his work.

Max had learned how to be cautious. How to keep his relationships with other people casual and at arm's length, so that loss couldn't bring his world crashing down around him a second time. And that made Eliza his number-one threat at the moment. Working with her effectively involved getting to know her, and it would be so easy to allow himself to give in to the smiles and the sparkle that she scattered in her wake. But he dealt in hard facts, not impossible dreams.

'Put that star a little farther away from the moon…' If they were going to do this it may as well be scientifically correct, and the glare of the moon would make stars that close invisible to the naked eye.

'Like this…?' She leaned precariously to her left, moving the star a couple of feet.

'No, less than that. Six inches.' Telling her that she might fall hadn't gone down too well this morning, and he was supposed to be winning Eliza over. All the same, he couldn't help stepping forward, just in case she *did* fall.

She shot him a knowing smile and straightened herself on the ladder. 'Okay?'

'Much better. That looks great.' Working with Eliza *was* going to present challenges. But Max was all about meeting challenge head-on and overcoming it.

CHAPTER TWO

DAISY ARRIVED FROM the ward, fully dressed with her hair newly braided into cornrows. She was clutching a tablet computer to her chest, her father manoeuvring her wheelchair while her mother walked alongside, smiling encouragingly to her daughter. This was a big day for the family.

And Eliza was seeing a different side of Max. That was natural enough—wordless concentration worked well when patients were under an anaesthetic—but this consultation wasn't just about the battery of tests that needed to be performed to gauge the exact level of Daisy's hearing and how the meningitis had affected her cochleae. It was about getting a feel for what her wants and needs were, along with those of her parents.

He'd already met Mr and Mrs Yates, and introduced them as Sam and Iona, telling them that Eliza would be acting as joint lead for the ENT team. That hadn't been entirely necessary. Daisy was Max's patient and remained his responsibility, but Eliza appreciated the gesture.

She watched as Max squatted down on his heels in front of Daisy's wheelchair, all smiles as he took his identity tags from around his neck and gave them to her so she could see his name. The little girl solemnly examined them, her gaze moving from the photograph to his face and then back again. Suddenly, Daisy was the most important person in the room, not someone who'd be ignored because she couldn't hear what was being said.

Eliza moved towards Sam and Iona, who were naturally concerned for their child after having been through all of the worry of her recent illness and the sudden onset of hearing loss. This was what *she* did best, calming fears and answering questions about the tests and treatment options that Daisy had ahead of her.

Max had coaxed Daisy from her wheelchair and let her pick her own seat from the circle of comfortable chairs that was arranged around a low table in the consulting room. He waited while she switched her tablet on, watching to see what she was doing.

'She's been typing what she wants to say on the screen. Although she *can* speak...' Iona murmured, anxious to help. 'But she shouts a bit sometimes and Daisy noticed that one of the other children on the ward was putting her hands over her ears whenever she spoke and it embarrassed her. Now Daisy just types what she wants to say.'

Daisy was already learning how deafness could make her world smaller. Therapy would help her to regulate her own voice, but right now Max was concentrating on finding out how the little girl preferred to communicate and giving her an opportunity to make herself heard.

'That's fine. Max is assessing how Daisy's coping now. Shall we join them?' Eliza motioned Sam and Iona over to where Max and Daisy were sitting. Max could have waited and relied on the social worker's report to tell him all this, but it appeared that he wanted to find out for himself as well.

And Daisy *was* responding. Max was using a combination of gentle gestures and smiles to reinforce the words typed on the screen, and Daisy was becoming less guarded with him. But when he took his otoscope from his pocket, she shrank back, silently wrinkling her nose.

'She makes a fuss with those. Tell her it'll be over and done with soon.' Iona stiffened, leaning forward. Max clearly wasn't going to tell Daisy anything of the sort, and he put the otoscope down on the table, sliding it out of his reach, and gesturing for the tablet. Daisy shook her head in response to his typed question.

'Let's try it another way.' Max smiled at Iona. 'I'll need your help.'

Iona shot to her feet and Max stood, letting her sit down next to Daisy. He fetched a box of surgical gloves and a packet of reusable ear tips, and perched himself on the edge of the table opposite them, going through the process of replacing the otoscope's head piece and then handing the instrument over to Iona, so she could take a look at it.

It was all done without a word. Iona found the light control buttons and tried them out, and Daisy leaned towards her, watching. Then Max gestured towards Iona's right ear and she handed the otoscope back to him. Max took his time examining Iona's ears, and then pronounced them *very good*, typing his words into the tablet for Daisy to see.

'Smart man,' Sam murmured. Both Daisy and her mother seemed a lot more at ease now. Max turned, grinning.

'It's your turn now.'

Sam chuckled, and he and Iona changed places. Daisy

shifted over onto her dad's knee, wanting to try out the light on the otoscope for herself, before Max examined Sam's ears. He typed a few words into her tablet, and Daisy chuckled. Apparently, her father had a small buildup of wax in his left ear, but that could be dealt with by a visit to the chemist. Then Eliza saw all of Max's patient work come to fruition, as Daisy leaned forward, tapping her left ear in a sign that Max should examine that one first.

Then he was all quiet professionalism, taking his time. Daisy sat uncomplainingly, waiting for him to type a few words of encouragement into her tablet. There would be more tests carried out this morning, which would assess how the various parts of Daisy's ears were responding to sound. But now that Max had won her confidence, they'd be much less stressful for her.

Daisy was a great kid. And Max had discovered—yet again—why he loved his job. When he'd accompanied Daisy and her parents to the ENT department's testing suite, he'd felt Daisy tug nervously at his sleeve. He'd bent down to reassure her and when Daisy was introduced to Jeannie, the technician who would be performing the first of the tests scheduled for this morning, the little girl had reached for Jeannie's name tags all on her own and then typed a *hello* on her tablet.

'Been working your magic again, Max?' Jeannie murmured and Max shook his head.

'Just making everyone's life a little easier.'

Jeannie raised her eyebrows. 'Yeah. This is my *pretending-to-believe-you* face. You'll have the test results in your inbox by lunchtime…' She turned away from him, walking across to Daisy's parents, and Max hesitated.

Jeannie was good at her job, and she had a little magic of her own to share with the parents and children she worked with. Daisy was in the best of hands, and Max had other patients to see this morning. He had nothing to add to Daisy's care right now, and he should be going.

Then Daisy waved to him. He gave her a wide-armed wave back, along with a thumbs-up sign, and Daisy grinned.

So what if Jeannie's shoulders seemed to be shaking with amusement. She knew as well as he did that children who visited the hospital deserved the very best of everything. If that included a little bit of their hearts as well as their medical skills then so be it. And if Max didn't want to admit to the loss of a little piece of his heart to every child who left his consulting room to embark on this journey, there was no reason he should.

Daisy had been given a mild sedative for one of the tests she'd undergone, and her parents had taken her back to the children's ward to sleep. When Max had ushered them back into the consulting room, he could see that they were no longer hiding the strain that they were under.

Eliza had arranged for some tea, and had brought a plate of Christmas cookies with her to their meeting. Iona waved them away, shooting Eliza an apologetic smile.

'Daisy took one from your receptionist earlier and said they were really nice. I'm not sure I could eat anything at the moment, though.'

Eliza nodded and Max wondered whether Daisy would be finding any more of the biscuits by her bedside later on. It was just the kind of thing that Eliza would think of doing. But in the meantime the thing her parents most needed were facts.

'You have a list of questions?' He'd seen Iona take a hard-backed notebook from her bag and hand a carefully folded sheet of paper that was clipped between the pages to Sam.

Sam nodded. 'Thanks. Yes, we have a few questions.'

'That's great. I'd like to hear them, but first I'll summarise the situation as we see it now. Eliza and I have seen Daisy's medical reports from the children's ward, and they indicate that she's recovering well from the meningitis.'

'Yes, they're talking about letting her come home soon,' Sam agreed. 'She still seems to be sleeping quite a lot, though. Wouldn't it be better to assess her hearing later?'

'It may improve…' Iona added quickly, and Sam took her hand.

Hope was one of the things a hospital ran on. Max knew that false hope could be corrosive, though. Dashing Iona's hopes for Daisy was hard, but it had to be done before they could go forward.

'I'm sorry to have to be the one to tell you this, but the tests we've done this morning indicate that Daisy isn't going to recover her hearing.' Max paused for a moment to let the information sink in. Iona's pen was poised above a blank page in her notebook, and she laid it down on the table, her eyes filling with tears. If he could only make this easier for them…

But he couldn't. The doctors on the children's ward might well have explained this to Sam and Iona already, but they hadn't heard it. Eliza reached for the box of tissues that sat on the table, pulling one out and giving it to Iona. Her small gesture of kindness made him feel like an executioner.

'They said…' Sam's voice was choked with emotion. 'They said as much. We were hoping that it might be a bad case of glue ear.'

That had been a possibility, although the more likely one had always been that Daisy's deafness was caused by the meningitis. 'I'm sorry to say that's not the case. You might like to write this next part down, Iona. I'll give you some internet addresses so that you can read a bit more later.'

That seemed to be twisting the knife, but it often brought people a feeling of control in these situations. Sam nodded. 'Yes. That's a really good idea, love.' He picked up Iona's pen and she turned to him, taking it from his hand.

Max waited, giving them both a little time. He could see Eliza shifting in her seat, no doubt aching to tell them that everything was going to be all right. But before you could make everything all right, you had to know what was wrong.

He went through everything with them, stopping to let Iona write it all down, and spelling a few words for her. The tests showed that Daisy had sensorineural deafness, which was the type of deafness caused by bacterial meningitis. The infection had spread to her cochlear, and the damage done to the cells there was permanent. Sam was reading over her shoulder, and he wiped his hand across his eyes.

'Our little girl… Daisy's usually such a bright, outgoing kid. She does well at school and I always thought that she could do anything she wanted in life…'

'She still can, Sam,' Eliza broke in, with the words that were on the tip of Max's tongue. Maybe she thought he was the bad-news guy and wouldn't say them. 'Our aim is to help Daisy do anything she wants to.'

'We can do this for her, Sam.' Iona glanced in Max's direction. 'Or maybe I should say *with* her. Daisy's very determined and usually knows exactly what she wants.'

Max smiled. 'That's a very good way of looking at it, Iona. She'll be dealing with things differently, and she'll need lots of encouragement and help with that, but working *with* her and letting her find her own solutions where possible is a really good way forward.'

'Encouragement isn't going to be a problem.' Sam glanced at Iona and received a nod back. 'What's our next step, Max?'

'I know you've had to make some big decisions for Daisy recently, and this all seems to be going very fast. The reason we're doing this now is that when a child has hearing loss of this nature, there's a risk of excessive bone growth in the cochlear, which continues after they've recovered from meningitis. It's called ossification and it makes surgical implants more difficult and potentially less successful. So we fast-track the assessment of children in Daisy's situation in order keep the surgical treatment option open.'

Iona was scribbling everything he said down, and Max waited for her to catch up with him. She and Sam had a lot to think about, and if taking notes helped them to process all of this new information, that was fine.

Iona paused, rereading what she'd just written. 'You

said *keep the surgical treatment option open.* Isn't a cochlear implant Daisy's only option?'

That was the ten-thousand-dollar question. Max glanced at Eliza, and her thoughtful look showed him that she wasn't going to rush into answering, either.

'Someone like Daisy, who has already learned how to respond to sound and has recently become deaf, can benefit significantly from a cochlear implant. She has almost no residual hearing now, in either ear, which is a result of damage to the cochleae, which again means that she's a candidate to receive cochlear implants. But it's important that you have realistic expectations of how they can help her, and that you understand that there's a lengthy post-operative rehab process, which will teach her how to use them.'

Sam and Iona stared at each other. 'I thought that a cochlear implant would just...make her hear again.' Sam voiced their confusion.

'They won't restore normal hearing. They're a way of giving Daisy access to sound again, and she'll have to learn how to interpret what she hears. It'll take time and commitment from you all. One of the appointments you'll be offered within the next week will be a home visit, where you'll be taken through all of your options. I believe our speech therapist also has a collection of videos from young people who've made different decisions, talking about their experiences...' Eliza had been very quiet and Max turned to her, wondering if she had something to add.

'We know it's a big decision, and it's one that's usually taken over many months. Our aim is to support you and

Daisy through that, so that you can make an informed choice about what's right for her.'

'What else is there?' Sam asked.

'I'm sure you're aware that some people prefer to use signs rather than listening with a cochlear implant. There are a lot of people who use both, according to the situation they find themselves in.' Eliza shrugged. 'How they feel on any one particular day, even.'

'You mean finger spelling?' Iona looked a little perplexed. 'Doesn't it take ages to spell out everything you want to say?'

Eliza smiled. 'Finger spelling is the British Sign Language alphabet. BSL uses signs for each word and it's much quicker. Daisy may want to learn BSL, and research has shown that it won't stop her from getting the most out of a cochlear implant if that's what you decide on. It's a rich and visual language, which reflects the deaf culture, and has regional differences as well. American Sign Language incorporates a few words that are the same as BSL, but it's largely completely different.' Eliza's smile held a hint of mischief as she turned to Max, making the sign for 'chips.'

Max could feel her infectious good humour tugging at the side of his lips. 'Do you mean chips? Or French fries?' He signed back both words in ASL. 'A guy's liable to get confused.'

This wouldn't do. There was a lot more to get through and although Max was determined to give Sam and Iona the time they needed, there were only so many hours in the day. He slid the sheet of paper he'd prepared before the meeting across the desk towards Sam and Iona.

'This is a summary of everything we're going to try

to achieve in the next two weeks, as long as Daisy is well enough. I've ticked off what's been done today, including going through all of the test results in more detail, which I'm about to do.'

'Thank you.' Iona was clearly in charge of list-making, and she snatched the paper up, reading it carefully. 'It looks a lot…'

'Yeah. The meetings will be an opportunity to ask questions and raise any concerns you have, but if there's something you need to talk about then my mobile number is at the bottom of the sheet. I don't answer when I'm working with patients, but you can leave a message and I'll get back to you. Early mornings or evenings are a good time to get me.'

Sam nodded. 'Thanks. We'll try not to bother you too much, but it's good to know that we can contact you if absolutely necessary.'

'That's okay. There's a lot to do, and it's important that we keep you in the loop, to give you an opportunity to make informed decisions. Call me if you feel you need to.' Max turned to Iona. 'Okay…what's on the list for the test results from today?'

Iona consulted his list, running her finger along the first entry. 'Tympanometry.'

'That's done to find out how the moving parts of the middle ear are working. You remember the one where Jeannie held an earpiece to Daisy's ear?'

'Ah. Yes.' Iona wrote the name of the test down on her pad, underlining it.

Questions had been asked, explanations given, and Max was pleased with the way the meeting had gone. Sam and Iona both shook his and Eliza's hands, and Iona had mentioned that she was feeling much more equal to this than she had first thing this morning.

'Good meeting?' Max wondered if Eliza realised that he'd shut her down on a couple of occasions when the conversation seemed to be wandering. 'Did I miss anything?'

'No. It's a great start. They'll have plenty to think about.'

In other words, he'd told Sam and Iona what they needed to know. Maybe Eliza would have done it a little differently, but they were two very different people and everyone played to their strengths when talking to patients and their families.

'You knew that Iona likes a list…' Eliza murmured, thankfully keeping any hint of a question from her tone.

Of course he did. Max imagined that when Eliza dealt with patients who were already in the hospital, she, too, went to the simple precaution of asking the staff on the ward how best to approach the parents. 'I think that Iona's notebook is helping them both get their heads around everything that's happening.'

Eliza nodded in agreement. 'They're a great couple, aren't they? I have no concerns about Daisy.'

'None? I always have concerns about my patients.' He knew that Eliza did, too. Her meticulous approach to surgery didn't just appear out of nowhere.

She rolled her eyes at him, smiling. That was about as far as Eliza ever got towards disagreeing with someone in general conversation.

'You know what I mean, Max. No *extra* concerns. Do you?'

Since they'd clarified their terms of reference, he could

agree with her. 'No, I don't.' His words didn't provoke Eliza's usually sunny smile. 'What are you thinking?'

She shrugged. 'Nothing from a medical point of view. Just that it always breaks my heart a little when I have to give parents the news that their child's hearing loss is permanent.'

And she thought that it didn't break *his* heart a little, too?

He was quite sure that Eliza broke that news to parents in exactly the same way he had—professionally and as kindly as possible. But he had feelings, just the same as she did, and the thought that she might not have seen that hurt a lot more than it should.

'What makes you suppose that I'm any different?' A sudden craving for Eliza to understand him loosened Max's tongue.

Her cheeks flushed red. 'Did I say you were?'

Max didn't trust himself to reply. He knew what Eliza wanted to hear, but he'd spent half his life pretending that his heart was incapable of breaking. He wasn't sure he even had the vocabulary to explain, now. He walked over to the table, gathering up his papers.

'I'm going to get going. I'll see you in theatre at two?'

Eliza pressed her lips together. 'Yes. Of course. I'll see you then.'

There were things he should have said, and maybe a few things that Eliza might have said, too. But it was too late now. Max tucked the files under his arm and made for his office.

CHAPTER THREE

SHE'D REALLY DONE IT NOW. Eliza knew that Max's approach was different to hers, and that they both got the job done in different ways. But she hadn't been able to help searching. Looking for some glimpse of proof that deep down they were fundamentally the same, when she should probably just accept that he saw life differently from her.

It made sense that they'd both be heading towards the cafeteria, as they had a full operating schedule this afternoon and needed some calories to burn. When she caught sight of him, she deliberately made for a table where she'd be hidden from his gaze, even though Max seemed lost in the pages of a journal that lay open beside his plate.

She was hungry, but Eliza was having difficulty in taking any interest in the plate of pasta bake in front of her. Sam and Iona had some difficult choices to make for Daisy, but they'd left feeling much more positive about their daughter's future. She and Max had agreed that they'd made a good start. Why hadn't she been satisfied with that? Had she really needed to keep talking?

'You're a people-pleaser, Eliza. You can't rest until the people around you are happy and sometimes it's just exhausting.'

Richie's words sounded in her head. She'd been upset and angry, and had ignored him, but it occurred to her now that maybe he'd had a point.

'After meeting your mother, it all makes sense. She doesn't function unless everyone around her is validating her own view of the world.'

Richie had had a point there, too. Eliza was quite aware that she'd developed her people-pleasing skills at a young age, in response to her mother's moods.

That was just making her feel worse—as if everything was her fault. Richie had always been very good at suggesting that, very free in attaching blame to everyone else but himself. When he'd left her behind at the pub that night, it had been because she'd been talking to someone and obviously didn't want to be interrupted. *'Look what you made me do...'*

And when he'd wanted out of their relationship, he hadn't just left. He'd sat in her living room, drinking coffee from her favourite mug, and enumerated all of the reasons why this was her fault. Her job was too demanding, and she should be there for him instead of having to work late. Her house was too tidy. She was a people-pleaser, and she should be pleasing *him* not everyone else…

All of it was true—to a point. Her job *was* demanding, but her work gave her deep satisfaction. Her house *was* tidy, but she liked it that way and had never reproached Richie for his untidiness. And Eliza didn't see any harm in trying to spread a little happiness. In a rare display of self-defence, she'd waved away his suggestion that they were still friends and if she ever wanted to talk about it he'd be there, and told him it was time for him to leave now.

She hadn't wanted anyone to pick her life apart then,

and she didn't much want to think about it now. In the month since Richie had left she'd come to the conclusion that she might not be perfect, but her one big mistake had been to go out with him in the first place. And her second mistake had been to believe him…

'Eliza. Could I have a word?' The newest doctor in the ENT department had approached her with a worried look on his face and what looked like a list in his hand.

'Sit down, Kieran.' She gestured towards the seat opposite her, thankful for something else to think about. 'You're organising Santa's visit this year?' The ENT department dealt with a lot of families on a long-term basis, and one of the first things that Dr Beckwith had done when he became head of department was to put a visit from Santa on the Christmas calendar. The kids loved it and it made them feel that going to the hospital could be fun. And it allowed parents to get together and talk, which was often very beneficial.

'Yes, actually. How did you know?'

Eliza smiled. 'The latest recruit to the team always gets to do Santa's Christmas visit. Don't take it personally. Next year you'll be passing it on to someone else and sitting back to enjoy the fun.'

'Ah. That doesn't sound so bad…' Clearly, Kieran had been under the impression that something he'd done had resulted in his being given the job. 'Well, I have a few ideas. Maybe ring the changes a bit. I have you on my *will almost certainly say yes* list.'

Fair enough. Eliza *was* always up for Santa's visit. 'Okay. Yes, then.'

'Marvellous.' Kieran grinned at her, planting a tick onto his list. 'I was thinking that perhaps we could theme it. Make a few references to what everyone does here at the hospital. I heard that some of the air ambulance team came last year, so I called them this morning and asked whether they might consider coming as helicopters.'

'What did they say?'

'Uh… I think I'll call back and speak with someone else. I got Teddy Vaughan and he wasn't in a very good mood.'

'Teddy? He's a really nice guy. He loves a children's Christmas party.'

'So I heard, but I gather that he's been up for the role of Lead Flight Paramedic. And the word is that an external candidate might be getting the job. Maybe I just caught him at the wrong time.'

Eliza really should keep better tabs on the hospital grapevine. She could see that going for a job you were very well qualified for and not getting it, and *then* being asked to dress up as a helicopter, would rub the kindest of souls up the wrong way.

'Would it be presumptuous of me to offer a word of advice, Kieran?'

'No, I wish you would. Sarah's given me several lists, and I've been trying to think of something that'll make everything go really well…' Kieran shrugged. 'This is turning out to be harder than I'd thought.'

'The thing you have to remember is that Santa, with elves and reindeer, isn't very original, but it's what the kids have come to see. What we want to do here is reassure them and make them feel that the hospital can be fun.'

'Yes, I suppose so. I didn't think of it like that. What about presents? I've got a budget and I thought perhaps

I might get the same for everyone. I don't want the kids to squabble.'

'You could take Sarah for coffee. Her favourite is double caramel and hazelnut latte, and it's well worth the expense because she's a gold mine of information. She knows most of the families and could probably steer you in the right direction with presents. Or if you're speaking to any of the parents, and they say they'll be coming, you could ask them.'

'Won't that spoil the surprise?' Kieran asked.

'Generally speaking, the one thing that most parents want is to see their child smile. *You* might get a surprise in finding how many of them offer to contribute to your budget.'

'Gotcha. My girlfriend's a primary school teacher so she'll help me with the shopping. She'd like to come along, as well. She rather wanted to dress up as a Christmas fairy. Will that be all right?'

Kieran hadn't been here for very long, so maybe he didn't know that the Christmas fairy was usually Eliza's territory. Although maybe this year she'd move on to something else. 'That's really nice of her. She'll be very welcome. She should definitely come as the Christmas fairy if she'd like to. The children will love it. Give the air ambulance team a call back and tell them that you've changed your mind about the helicopters and you're leaving it to them to decide how to dress up. As for everyone else, just print out a couple of flyers with the date and time and give them to Sarah. She'll make sure everyone sees them and knows what to do.'

'Thanks, Eliza. That makes everything so much easier. I really appreciate the help.'

Eliza grinned at him. 'Pass it on, will you? Next Christmas you can sit the new person down and take them through everything.'

'Yes, I will.' Kieran's pencil was hovering over the paper, as if there was one last thing that puzzled him.

'Anything else?'

'Dr Russo...'

'Ask him if he's coming. He's not going to bite your head off, Kieran.' She'd noticed that Max was always polite and helpful towards junior members of staff, which was more than some surgeons managed to be. If Max *was* going to bite anyone's head off he usually confined himself to people who could answer back.

'Right. I've been overthinking this, haven't I?'

'Just a little. That's a great deal better than not caring, though.'

'Thanks again.' Kieran grinned at her. 'I hope your lunch hasn't gone cold.'

'No, I don't think so, but I really should get on and eat it. I'm in theatre this afternoon.'

Kieran took the hint, picked up his list and left Eliza to her thoughts. Pasta bake *was* even more unappealing cold than it was warm, but she had a busy afternoon ahead of her and she needed to eat something.

If Richie had taught her one thing it was that rehashing conversations, in an attempt to do better in future, was fruitless. Maybe she should remember that the next time she tried to overthink her differences with Max.

The one thing about Max was that he bore no grudges. When Eliza met with him after lunch, their earlier conversation seemed to be forgotten. That page had been turned, and a new, blank sheet of paper stood before them.

'Turn and turn about.' The synchronicity of the situation seemed to appeal to him. They were performing two rhinoplasty surgeries and Eliza would take the lead in one, working on the nose while Max extracted cartilage and bone from her patient's ear and elbow. Max would take the lead in the second, and they would swap roles.

'Yes. I'm counting on you, Max.' Eliza's patient had undergone cancer treatments and was now having surgery to help her breathe through her nose.

'I'm counting on you, too.' Max's patient was a little boy, born with a severely deviated septum. 'I have no concerns on that score, though.'

Was there a twinkle in his brown eyes? Or maybe Eliza was imagining it. 'Apart from the usual medical concerns, you mean?'

There was *definitely* a smile tugging at the corner of his mouth now. It really suited him. 'Yes, apart from those.'

They always worked together well in the operating theatre. Where words weren't chosen to please, they were used for the maximum of efficiency in communicating. There was only one aim here, shared amongst the people gathered around each patient, and Max's quiet concentration was no different from Eliza's.

They scrubbed out together in silence. Since Max seemed lost in his own thoughts, Eliza reckoned that if someone was going to say something it was up to her.

'I think they both went well.' She swallowed down the temptation to ask what Max thought, still caught up in the world where each of them made the best decisions possible for the person in their care.

He nodded. Eliza would have added a *thanks to you* or mentioned the way they'd dealt with a particularly difficult moment with Max's patient, but she supposed she'd have to make do with that.

Perhaps she should put a word in for Kieran. 'Are you going to the children's Christmas party? Kieran's organising it and he's keen on making it a success.'

'I'm very impressed with him. With a bit more experience he'll make a good doctor.'

That was Eliza's belief, too, but Max hadn't answered the question. 'So are you going?'

'He caught me after lunch this afternoon and I told him I couldn't make it. I gave him something for the presents fund instead.'

It was difficult to tell if this was a carefully rehearsed excuse, or Max actually *would* be doing something else. It would be better to stick to business.

'I'd like to go over Daisy's notes with you again. There are a few things we need to think about in regard to a possible surgery date.'

'Yeah. We're going to need to manage that decision carefully. She's still recovering from the meningitis, but if the family does decide on surgery it'll need to be done as soon as possible.' Max's brow furrowed. 'I don't suppose you have a moment now? Or do you have to get home?'

It was already late, but Eliza had nothing in particular to go home to. 'Now's good for me. Shall I go and get something to drink from the coffee shop downstairs?' Max was well known to be fussy about coffee and in his view there was only one café in the whole hospital that produced a barely acceptable espresso.

'I'll go. You'll be in your office?'

That might be a nice gesture or maybe Max just didn't trust her to be picky enough about how the barista made his coffee. Eliza decided not to ask. 'Yes. Filter coffee with a little milk for me.'

She barely had time to tidy her desk and tilt the two visitors' chairs at a welcoming angle, before Max appeared in the doorway. He was holding two large cups and two espresso cups.

'You're reckoning on a long evening?' Eliza raised an eyebrow.

'I thought that you might like to try a decent cup of coffee. The least I can do in return is to sample your chosen style of dishwater.'

'Okay. You obviously have a completely open mind on the matter.' Eliza flashed him a smile and sat down in one of the visitors' chairs, reaching for one of the smaller cups that Max had put down on her desk. Accepting that his view of life wasn't personal made things a lot easier between them.

'It's just a single shot. So take a couple of sips and then drink it down in one.' He peeled the lid from one of the larger cups, swirling the contents thoughtfully.

'Don't drink yours in one. Sip it,' Eliza batted back. His frankness *did* have a playful edge to it at times; you just had to keep your nerve to appreciate it.

'Because that prolongs the agony?'

She ignored him, taking two sips and then drinking the coffee down. The sudden shot of caffeine made her gasp. 'Oh. That's very strong.' She groped for something nice to say. 'Probably an acquired taste.'

Max sipped from his cup. 'Yeah. This must be an acquired taste, as well. Do I have to drink it all?'

'Yes, since this was your idea. Is American coffee generally this strong?'

He shook his head. 'Most *Italian* coffee is. The clue's in the name. Massimo Russo.'

It felt strangely intimate to hear his full name, when Max always introduced himself with the shorter version. Oddly friendly to be sitting here comparing coffee styles. Maybe Dr Beckwith was right, and they could both get something out of respecting each other's boundaries.

'Okay. I think I need to do something useful now, with all of this caffeine in my system. We can either go through the file and draft out a strategy for Daisy, or I'll run round the car park three times.'

Max smiled. 'I should have gotten you a double shot. It's not really coffee unless you're ready for four turns around the car park.'

They'd talked for over an hour and made a lot of progress. Different ways of looking at things did have its advantages, when Max seemed as willing to compromise as Eliza was.

He was tireless, but Eliza was beginning to get really hungry. 'I don't suppose— I'd really like to get all of this done, but could we take a quick break for something to eat?'

Max leaned back in his seat, stretching. A natural movement, after an afternoon spent in theatre, followed by a concentrated discussion, but it seemed almost primal—as if his body was aching for freedom. How had she missed the coiled strength in his usually relaxed shoulders?

'Sure. Pizza?'

Eliza thought for a moment. 'You mean we go out and get a takeaway?' She doubted very much that Max had a yearning for the rather sad, day-old mini pizzas in the cafeteria.

'I was thinking of going out and sitting down at a table. You can bring the file if you want to as long as you don't expect me to look at it while I'm eating.'

Okay. Bringing the file sounded like work-pizza, which wasn't too confronting. Eliza rose from her seat, grabbing her coat from the hook behind the door.

The now-expected group of Kyle Woodgate fans was clustered outside the main entrance to the hospital. The security officers had given in to the inevitable and erected a set of barriers for them to stand behind, to keep them out of the way. The average age of Kyle's fans rose by a couple of years as it began to get dark, when the eleven-year-olds were taken home by their long-suffering parents and replaced by older girls.

'Doctor Max…!' One of the girls saw him and waved, and the others followed suit. Max shot Eliza an apologetic look, hesitating uncomfortably.

It appeared that Kyle Woodgate, the local celebrity singer who'd been injured when he'd visited the hospital to unveil the large Christmas tree in reception, and somehow managed to pull it over on top of himself, had some competition on his hands. Kyle probably neither knew nor cared, and Max seemed a little embarrassed about it.

'What on earth are they doing?' The girls were all

reaching forward, scrunching their gloved fingers up in an obviously coordinated gesture.

'Um… They're showing off their gloves.' The girls hands moved to their heads. 'And hats…'

This was too good to miss. Eliza started forward towards the barrier and heard Max puff out a resigned breath as he followed her.

'Evening.' He gave them all a dazzling smile. 'You all look great.'

'Any news of Kyle?' One of the girls asked and Max shook his head.

'Don't you know better than to ask by now? You know as much as I do. I'm glad to see you're keeping warm.'

So there was a method to Max's madness…

'I'm wearing two pairs of socks.' The teenager volunteered the information.

'I've got my brother's hiking socks on. And a thermal vest.' Another seemed keen to outdo her friend.

'Marvellous. Shivering isn't a good look.' Max beamed at them. 'And how are you all getting home tonight?'

'Fara's dad's picking us up,' a third teenager answered. 'He's got a people-carrier. It's better than the bus. He takes us all the way to our doorsteps.'

'Good.' Max nodded, turning to leave, and the girls moved with common purpose, focusing their attention on Eliza.

'Have *you* seen Kyle? Do you know how he is?'

'No, sorry. Great artwork, though.' The placards the girls had brought were obviously home-made, and pictures of their idol, along with sparkly hearts, were featured heavily. 'I'm sure that Kyle's seen pictures of you all and he really appreciates your coming…'

She felt Max's hand on her arm, guiding her away from the group. He gave the girls a brisk wave, and they called out their goodbyes.

'Don't encourage them.'

'Trust me. I've been a teenager and there's no keeping them away. And what's all this about thermal vests?'

Max shrugged. 'I never mentioned vests. That was Lily's own enlargement on the general theme. I pointed out that they should be wearing hats and gloves if they're spending long periods of time standing around outside in this weather. They could get chilblains. Frostbite, even…'

'Max, they're standing under the awning and out of the wind. They're not going to get too cold and wet. Are you going out of your way to frighten them?'

'If I had been, it wouldn't have worked. But I notice they're all dressed a bit more sensibly now.'

At least he hadn't mentioned the part about their arrangements for getting home, although clearly he'd covered that in his off-the-cuff health and safety assessment. Eliza wasn't going to mention it, either, because she really didn't want to hear the thoughts that had been running in Max's head when he'd stopped his car to pick *her* up.

'That's not such a bad thing,' she admitted. 'But every teenage girl has her idols. Don't take all of the fun out of it for them.'

He shot her a quizzical look. 'Who was yours?'

'I'm not sure I remember.'

Max grinned suddenly. 'It's not *that* bad, is it?'

One of the things that Max really didn't get was that people-pleasing was a subtle art. Telling people what they wanted to hear was just one aspect of it—*not* telling them things was just as important. And Eliza wasn't going to admit that she and her friends had idolised a dark-eyed American rock star, whose brooding good looks just happened to bear a strong resemblance to Max's. That would make things unnecessarily complicated between them, when she was struggling to keep it simple.

'Sorry, but I really can't. There's nothing worse than admitting to an infatuation that you've grown out of.' Particularly if she hadn't really grown out of it, and Max was very definitely the type of guy she might fall for if it were just a matter of looks.

He let the subject drop, quickening his pace as they reached the hospital gates and walking briskly along the road until they reached a small, curved cul-de-sac. As they walked down it, the bright lights of a pizza restaurant, right at the end, came into view.

'Best pizza in York?' She smiled up at him. There wouldn't be any other reason to walk down this narrow, anonymous alleyway, which led only to a dead end.

'Second best, only don't mention that to them. The best isn't within walking distance.'

'You've made a study of this?'

He nodded, opening the door for her. Inside, the warm scent of Italian herbs and fresh sourdough made Eliza realise exactly how hungry she was. 'You'll be glad I did.'

The waitress greeted Max by name and told him that his regular table was free. He led Eliza to the back of the restaurant to a row of booths set against the wall and separated by obscure glass panels. Max waited for her to sit, and Eliza slid into the gap between the table and the banquette seating.

'This is nice.' The restaurant wasn't empty but there was an atmosphere of taking your time, and Eliza could imagine Max sitting and reading over a coffee or a glass of wine, as several of the other customers were. It would be very easy to become a regular here.

'I like it.' Max sat down opposite her, and the waitress offered Eliza a menu, clearly expecting that Max would already know what he wanted. 'I'll take the pepperoni, with sourdough garlic bread.'

The waitress nodded, jotting his order down on her pad. 'Aperitif?'

Max turned to Eliza. 'The house red is drinkable.' The waitress cleared her throat loudly, putting her hand on her hip. 'Sorry, Giorgia. What I meant by *drinkable* was that it's very good.'

'Thank you.' Giorgia turned to Eliza. 'Would you like a glass of drinkable red?'

Eliza chuckled. Clearly, Giorgia knew just how to handle Max. 'That would be lovely, thank you. And…how hot's the pepperoni?'

'Fiery. If you'd like flavour without too much of a kick, you could try the ham and mozzarella with black olives,' Giorgia suggested.

'That sounds good, thank you. With some garlic bread, please.' Eliza handed the menu back to Giorgia, who turned, shooting a glare at Max before she walked away.

'You and Giorgia…you don't get on?' Eliza leaned across the table towards him.

'We get along fine. They don't compromise on their standards here, and they reckon that I'm returning the compliment by expecting only the best.'

That was one way of looking at it. Eliza wondered what her mother might think of the idea. When she was a child, if she hadn't eaten everything that was put in front of her with obvious delight, it had provoked questions about whether her father's new partner was a better cook than her mother was. Which had, on several occasions, escalated into remarks that if she didn't like the current custody arrangements she could go live with her father and see how she liked that.

Her mother had been hurt, and she was doing the best she could to reconcile herself to her father's affair. But the constant battle that raged between her parents, each wanting her to choose them over the other, had been hard work and instilled a constant fear of rejection in Eliza's young heart. She'd worked hard to please them both, and the equation of having to please the people in her life or face abandonment had stayed with her.

Giorgia dispelled all of the questions and difficult feelings by appearing suddenly with two glasses of red wine, waiting for Eliza to take a sip of hers and deliver a verdict. That wasn't difficult at all.

'This is really nice! I suppose it's not good manners to ask what it is…'

Giorgia laughed. 'We don't do good manners. It's from a small vineyard near Naples. My husband drives over once a year to taste it and we import it ourselves.'

'In other words, you have to come back if you want some more.' Max's dour tone seemed to have lifted a little, and Giorgia chuckled as she turned to deal with another customer.

Max wasn't going to think too deeply about why he'd brought Eliza here. The pleasure of watching her begin to let her guard down, and genuinely enjoy a glass of wine and great pizza, was beginning to reshuffle his priorities. The second-best pizza place in York was rapidly becoming the best.

But he hadn't brought her here for his own gratification. He and Eliza worked well together in the rarefied atmosphere of the operating theatre, where medical priorities were everything and single words would do. This new working relationship was different, a matter of weighing wants with needs, and carefully assessing a solution, which would help Daisy to move forward with her life. He couldn't simply accept that Eliza was an enigma and move on; he had to understand the subtexts that governed everything she did.

In short, he had to get to know what made her tick. And in Max's experience, pizza was as good a way as any of doing that.

Over coffee, they worked their way back to the treatment schedule, speaking in general terms only as an automatic reaction to the slight chance they might be overheard.

'I'm very keen to manage expectations, and since we're dealing with an accelerated timetable we'll have to be very clear about everything,' Max observed and was surprised to see Eliza nodding emphatically.

'Very much so. Although managing expectations doesn't mean that we need to frighten everyone with all the things that *might* go wrong. It's important to give people confidence in their chosen solution.' Eliza softened the statement with a smile.

'Instilling confidence is what I want to do, too.' Max paused for a moment, struggling to make what he had to say as neutral as possible. He'd upset Eliza once by speaking his mind and he didn't want to do so again. 'I feel that we should avoid any suggestion that this is going to be easy, though, because encouraging false hopes is one way to break someone's confidence.'

He could tell, from the thoughtful look on Eliza's face, that he'd given a little too much away. Max didn't want to talk about the false hopes for Mikey that he and his parents had been encouraged in. Didn't want to say that he'd promised himself that he'd never do that with his own patients.

She held his gaze for a moment, and then stared down at her empty coffee cup. That was about as likely to give her the answer as he was.

'Okay. I don't disagree with you. This is really a matter of emphasis. I'd like to think about it overnight if that's okay with you?'

That was Eliza all over. He'd brought the subject up and now she was asking if it was okay for *her* to take some time. But she did it with such charm that it was impossible to disagree with her.

'I'll think about it, too. Are you ready to go?'

She nodded and when Max signalled to Giorgia for the bill, she reached for her handbag, pulling out her purse. He frowned at her and she blithely ignored him.

'I'll spring for it.'

'No, it's *my* treat.' Eliza snatched the bill from the table, mischief dancing in her eyes. 'If I pay this time, then maybe you'll have to ask me back here again, so that you can pay.'

The only way to combat Eliza's unrelenting cheerfulness was to give in gracefully. Or maybe not so gracefully…

'Okay, thanks. You might find that I'm the kind of guy

who lets a woman pay and then doesn't reckon he needs to return the favour.' That would have prompted a very lengthy talking-to from his father, and Max was gratified at Eliza's disbelieving chuckle.

'I'll take my chances. Shall we go back and finish off our schedule? It shouldn't take too long.' She took some notes from her purse, weighing them down with a generous tip, and reached for her coat.

'Fine with me. But it's getting late. Is someone picking you up from the hospital tonight?' He didn't like the idea of Eliza going home on the bus at this hour.

She pursed her lips, maybe thinking about that waste-of-space comment that Max rather wished he hadn't made. 'No, I'm… Richie and I have split up.'

'I'm sorry to hear that.'

'Don't you mean, *I told you so*?' Eliza's mask slipped a little, and then she shook her head and smiled in an invitation to let the matter drop.

Max wouldn't get another chance to say this, though. 'I'm sorry that I spoke out of turn about him, because it wasn't my business. He was your choice, and clearly things didn't work out the way you wanted them to. I'm sorry to hear that.'

She nodded. 'To tell you the truth I'm more *not sorry* than sorry. He was the one that ended it, but I should have done it a while ago. I'm going to give dating a miss for a while. I need some space to find out what I really want.'

It was no surprise that Eliza would have given the waste of space the benefit of the doubt, letting him dictate when their relationship would end. Max was in no mood to risk saying that, even if he felt angry that she'd been hurt, and hated the way she made excuses for the person who'd hurt her.

He pulled on his coat, thanking Giorgia for the meal, and waited while Eliza checked under the table to make sure she'd left nothing behind. Max held the door open for her, and Eliza gave a little nod in acknowledgement, breezing through onto the street like a princess.

'It won't take long to finish off the schedule.' He turned his collar up against the icy chill of the wind. 'Then I'll call you a taxi home.'

'Thank you. That's very kind.' She shivered, stuffing her hands into the pockets of her coat. 'I hope that the Kyle Woodgate fans have gone home by now. It's turning cold.'

'So do I. If they haven't, I'll leave it to you to break the news to them that he's warm and safe in his bed, and they should be as well.'

CHAPTER FOUR

MAX HADN'T JUST called a taxi, he'd waited with her outside until it arrived, and then opened the passenger door for her to climb in. The driver had the heating on full, and Eliza loosened her scarf a little before she suffocated.

Sorry but not sorry. What on earth did that mean? For that matter, what did *I agree with you but I don't agree with you* mean? It was all very well to acknowledge that she and Max thought a little differently about things, and to open up channels of communication for Daisy's benefit—Eliza felt they'd made a good start on that. But speaking in riddles wasn't going to help.

She'd seen something more in him tonight, though. His grumpy-guy persona had slipped a little, and underneath there was a decent, caring man. There were a few things that Max obviously wasn't saying, but that was fine. There were things that Eliza wasn't saying as well, and they didn't need to be confidants to work together effectively. She couldn't help wondering who, or what, had hurt him, though.

Or…maybe she was falling into the same trap that she always did. Starting to like someone and then making excuses for them, when all Max really needed to do was lighten up a bit.

'How much?' She leaned forward as the taxi came to a halt outside her house.

'It's okay, the gentleman gave me enough for the fare. And a tip.' The taxi driver grinned at her.

'Oh. Thanks, I didn't see him do that… Would you mind staying until I get to the door please?'

'Of course, miss. On a night like this, I always wait until my fares are inside.'

Eliza smiled a thank-you and hurried to her front door, fumbling with her keys. She got the door open and turned to wave to the cab driver, who flashed the lights of the cab in return and drove away. Alone. Finally.

The house seemed quiet and cold. One thing about Richie was that she always knew that he was there, because the heating was turned up to full and he'd left a jumble of his possessions in the hallway for her to trip over. That wasn't a reason to hold on to someone, though, or to spend time regretting that they were no longer around. By the time she'd taken off her coat and made herself a drink, the small house would be starting to warm up. And the large box of Christmas decorations in the sitting room was the only company she needed this Christmas.

The new day brought a quieter heart than the one that had kept Eliza awake for an hour before she finally fell asleep. And new challenges to occupy her mind, which pushed thoughts of The Max Conundrum away.

They'd made a note to check on how Daisy was interacting with the other children on the ward, and since she was due to be discharged tomorrow morning, it wasn't much of a surprise to find that Max had the same idea about what to do with his lunch hour as Eliza did. When she entered the ward, she saw him chatting with Sam, who got to his feet and walked over to greet her.

'I'm on visiting duties while Iona goes into work. Seems that we're popular today.' Sam appeared a lot more relaxed than he'd been yesterday.

'Since she might be discharged tomorrow, we're taking the opportunity to see for ourselves how Daisy interacts with the other children on the ward. I expect Max mentioned that.'

'Yeah, he did. She seems to be coming out of her shell a bit. I'm almost sorry to be leaving.'

'Have you seen the speech therapist this morning?'

Sam nodded. 'Yes, she said that we should try to keep Daisy involved with other children as much as we can. I don't think that's going to be a problem. Iona has quite a few cousins down in London, and they're all threatening to take a day trip up to York to see how Daisy is.'

'That's great. Maybe if they visit you one at a time…?'

Sam chuckled. 'Yes, Max mentioned that. Iona will make up a schedule, no doubt, so that we don't tire Daisy out.'

'Yes, she needs to be able to concentrate on interacting with people as well. A whole roomful of visitors is just going to distract her.' Sam was nodding as she spoke. 'Max mentioned that, too?'

'Yeah. Thanks, though. These days I need to hear things at least twice before they sink in.'

Eliza smiled. 'Only twice? For most people in your situation it's at least three times. How are you and Iona doing?'

'Better… There were a few days when we thought we might lose Daisy. That's changed us…' Sam's eyes filled with tears at the memory.

'Of course it has.' Eliza chose her words carefully. 'I imagine it's hard to be faced with making these new decisions for her now.'

Sam nodded. 'Everyone's been so kind and supportive. Daisy's a tough kid, and she's beginning to see that she *can* communicate with people. The speech therapist had a finger-spelling chart on top of her bundle of papers, and Daisy picked it up and wouldn't give it back. I expect that was what she had in mind all along.'

'Yes, probably.' Eliza nodded towards Max, who was currently making a game out of helping Daisy to form the letters of the alphabet with her fingers. 'I see she's interested, though.'

'Yes, she is. I never realised that people who have cochlear implants might also sign.'

'There's no one response to deafness. Everyone has to decide what they want for themselves.'

'That's what makes it so difficult.' Sam turned the corners of his mouth down. 'But I suppose that anything worth having is difficult.'

Now was the time for a little reassurance. Eliza opened her mouth, but was interrupted by Max's quiet voice.

'Sam…'

Sam looked up into Daisy's determined gaze. Max was prompting her, finger-spelling the letters to her slowly, and Eliza stopped Sam from hurrying towards his daughter.

'Stay here, Sam. Wait for Daisy to say it…'

For a moment, the noise of the ward receded. Daisy gave Sam a little wave, and he waved back. Then carefully, silently, she called to her father.

'What did she say?' Sam was trembling and it seemed he already had an idea.

'D… A…' Eliza finger-spelled the letters to him.

'Dad. She said Dad.' A tear rolled down Sam's cheek and he sent a broad smile back to his daughter. 'I still remember the first time she said it, when she was just a baby…'

'Now it's your turn. Watch me.'

She finger-spelled Daisy's name out, and Sam carefully reproduced the actions. Daisy was watching, and Max pointed out the last few letters on her chart. Daisy looked up at Sam and waved.

'I think that little girl wants a hug…' Eliza murmured.

'*She* wants a hug? I'm pretty sure that I need one.' Sam walked over to his daughter, his arms outstretched. Max moved out of the way, leaving the two of them alone.

'I've got to go.' By the time Max reached Eliza it was as if the fairy dust that suddenly seemed to be raining from the ceiling had nothing to do with him. As if he were immune to the magic of a child breaking out of her silence and calling for her dad.

'Now? You do something like that and then you decide to leave?' Eliza was having difficulty tearing her gaze from Sam and Daisy.

'I have to be in theatre in half an hour. You'll be staying for a while?'

'No, I think I'll go run around the car park four times.' This moment was like a hundred espressos. 'I saw you with Daisy just now, Max. You knew exactly what you were doing.'

He shot her a reproachful look. 'Daisy's got a long way to go. She's going to need her mom and dad to be fully involved and helping her to learn.'

And right now, Eliza could punch him. Why couldn't he just enjoy the moment? 'Don't be such a cynic.'

He shrugged the comment off. Max was about to leave, in that abrupt way of his, but Eliza stopped him.

'Are you around later on? Dr Beckwith's sent me a copy of the staffing rotas over Christmas and it may be worth having a look at them to see how quickly we can pull an operating team together over the holiday period.'

'Sounds good. I should be out of theatre by five o'clock. Shall we talk then?'

Eliza nodded. Max turned, walking quickly out of the ward without looking back. He must have nerves of steel to be able to resist just one more over-the-shoulder look at Sam and Daisy.

'Dr Russo's such a softie. Underneath it all…' One of the nurses was passing and had noticed Sam's reaction to his daughter's finger-spelling. At least Eliza wasn't the only one who knew magic when she saw it.

'He hides it well.'

'Doesn't he just. I particularly like his habit of walking away as soon as he thinks a conversation's finished, so that you have to run after him if you've still got something to say.'

'I thought that was just me…' Eliza was reassured by the thought that it wasn't.

'He does it with everyone down here, too.' The nurse chuckled, then hurried away to another young patient, leaving Eliza to join Sam and Daisy.

'Iona will be coming in this evening after work…' Sam's hand wandered to the finger-spelling chart.

'So there's one more word that Daisy needs to learn. Then we'll let her rest for a while. We don't want to tire her out. What does Daisy usually call Iona?'

Sam smiled. 'She calls her *Mum*. If you show me as well, Daisy and I can practise again later.'

It seemed that Max had already got his point across, and showed Sam how important it was for the family to learn together. Eliza didn't need to add any words of encouragement. She nodded, touching Daisy's arm to catch her attention, and then slowly spelling out the word with her fingers.

Max could do with an early night tonight. His meeting with Eliza yesterday evening had left him with plenty to think about and he'd woken in the night, stark images in his head. How he'd come back from university to see Mikey when he'd first fallen ill. How the doctor's assurances had persuaded him to go back and resume his first demanding year of study. And then the anguished call from his father. Driving all night to see his little brother but arriving too late.

He'd pushed them away, trying to think rationally. He couldn't go back and save Mikey, nor could he regain those lost weeks, when he could have stayed to support his parents and brother. They were gone, and he had to accept it and move on. If Eliza pushed all of his buttons then that was up to him to deal with. He shouldn't try to change her view of life.

He couldn't put this meeting with her off, though. They needed to move as fast as they could with the practicalities of Daisy's case, to give the family as much space as possible to make the decision ahead of them. And…there was something that Max wouldn't acknowledge that always seemed to draw him back to Eliza. When she texted him to say that she was out of theatre and would be in her office in ten minutes, he made his way to the café to fetch two cups of coffee.

'Let's not make this another late night.' He put the cardboard beakers down on her desk.

'No. I've got some things to do at home. Washing isn't really very exciting but I was working at the weekend and it has to be done.' Eliza always seemed to feel the need to explain herself to everyone. Max wasn't sure he *could* explain why he needed to get home, and decided not to even try.

'Let's get on with it, then.' He sat down, peeling the lid from his cup.

'Well, Christmas is coming—' she flashed him the obligatory grin at the prospect '—and here's the spreadsheet to prove it. I've colour-coded it according to whether people are here, on call, or not available.' She pushed a printed sheet of paper towards him, and Max focused on it.

This was a surprise. 'You're on call next weekend as well?' The doctors in the ENT department generally took turns.

Eliza smiled, flushing a little. 'Yes, a lot of people have things to do in the run-up to Christmas and I told Dr Beckwith I was happy to do it in exchange for some weekends off during the summer.'

Max decided to ignore the idea that surely Eliza—of all people—could find something festive to do before Christmas. 'And you're reckoning on working on Christmas Eve?'

'Only if it's necessary. I'm free if I need to come in. If not, I'll just take the day to…' Suddenly, the sunshine in her face gave way to shadows. 'I don't know. Whatever comes to mind. I'm happy to come in on Christmas Day as well, if necessary.'

That sounded as if she was going to be alone over

Christmas. That didn't bother Max, but he couldn't imagine that it was something that Eliza would choose.

'What about you?' She was looking positively gloomy now. Something was definitely up.

'We need to be realistic, Eliza. If everything goes to plan then we'll have a decision before Christmas. If not… we may have to ask people whether they're willing to forgo their plans over Christmas and the New Year. But I'm not prepared to ask anyone to just give blanket assurances that they're free at this stage. That includes you.'

Maybe Eliza was going to object to his straightforwardness, but Max was tired. And he felt strongly about this. He'd seen her bend almost to breaking point to fit in with other people before.

She shook her head, puffing out a breath. 'No, it's not that… I was going to spend Christmas with Richie and his family. That's not going to happen now.'

'And your own family?' Max realised that he didn't know whether Eliza had any family of her own, and the dismayed look on her face made him wonder if he'd made another faux pas.

'Mum and Dad live too far away.'

Surely, there had to be more to it than that, to keep Eliza from all of the glitter of a family Christmas. 'I'm still getting my head around what people here mean by *too far*. This is not a very big island.'

She responded to his smile. 'Well yes, I suppose that's true. They're divorced and Dad lives in London and Mum's in Oxford. It's doable, but not that easy to work out how I'm going to spend exactly the same amount of time with each of them, let alone have Christmas dinner in two places at once. So I'm flying solo this Christmas.'

It sounded as if the divorce hadn't been amicable. Max

had asked too many questions already, and he had the answer he needed. 'I'm flying solo, too, so if it does come to it we can operate over Christmas. My parents have decided to go to Miami this year.'

'That sounds nice. Although I'm not sure I can imagine Christmas without hoping for snow.'

'They do it all the time in Miami. It really doesn't cramp their style.' Max's parents were used to the cold New York winters, and thought much the same as Eliza did. Their trips to Miami for Christmas were an avoidance tactic, which meant they didn't have to drop in on the rest of the family on Christmas Eve, or remember Mikey playing outside after an early fall of snow.

'I imagine not. I'm sorry you'll be missing it.' Eliza had cheered up a bit now, and Max decided that saying *he* wasn't sorry at all wasn't appropriate.

'Next year, maybe. How's your New Year looking?' Max hoped that Eliza would be celebrating having something to look forward to. Perhaps looking forward to not spending it with the waste of space deserved a New Year's toast.

'There's the New Year's fancy dress party…' She shot him an enquiring smile, which warmed Max's heart. It seemed that nothing could keep Eliza down for too long.

'I can definitely miss that. Fancy dress isn't really my thing.'

She chuckled. 'Yes, it's always a bit of a problem. Okay, so New Year wouldn't be completely out if we needed to operate then. I emailed a few of the people who need to do home visits with Daisy, and I've heard back from them with their availability.'

'Good. We don't want everyone going at once, so perhaps we could pencil in a few dates…'

He should let it go. A lot of people spent Christmas alone. But it was pretty obvious that Eliza didn't want to, and her uncharacteristic look of dismay at the thought had concerned him. How upset did she have to be about something before she let it show?

Max spent half an hour agreeing with everything she said, since she was perfectly capable of organising a visiting schedule without his input. They called the short meeting to a close and he got to his feet, while Eliza threw their empty coffee cups into the bin. Max got halfway down the corridor and then turned around.

Christmas was so important to Eliza, and perhaps there was something he could do to raise her spirits. He probably wasn't best equipped for the task; that would take someone a little more au fait with sparkle and magic. But Max prided himself on being adaptable, and he could give it a go.

Her office door was still open, and Eliza had retreated behind her desk, clearly having decided that there was something else she needed to do this evening.

'I hear there's a late-night Christmas Fair, not too far from here.'

'Yes, there is. It's usually brilliant.' Eliza's smile almost broke him. He guessed that it would be a very easy matter for her to involve him in all kinds of seasonal cheer, if only his heart hadn't been frozen in time when Mikey had died.

'I was thinking of checking it out, maybe the day after tomorrow. I don't suppose you're free to show me around?'

'Yes, definitely. I'll be looking forward to it…'

CHAPTER FIVE

MAYBE ELIZA SHOULDN'T have seemed quite so enthusiastic about the Christmas Fair. But everything else had been cancelled this Christmas, and an unexpected invitation to some light and sparkle was currently the highlight of her festive season. And coaxing Max into enjoying it would be the kind of challenge that easily outstripped ten-thousand-piece jigsaw puzzles and Christmas detective stories.

And he seemed to be getting into the spirit of things. When she stood in the open doorway of his office, scrunching her red-gloved fingers and tapping her red-and-white hat, he managed to crack a smile.

'You're not bringing your I-heart-Kyle-Woodgate badge with you, are you?'

'No. I think there are enough of those around already. A Christmas Fair is serious business, though, and I'm dressing accordingly.'

He nodded, shrugging on his double-breasted peacoat and picking up his own gloves and hat. When Eliza hesitantly offered him a sprig of red-and-green holly for his buttonhole as a small lift for the navy-blue theme, he unexpectedly accepted it, even allowing her to pin it securely to his lapel.

'Do you have some last-minute Christmas shopping to do?' Eliza asked as they walked through the dark streets.

'Nah. I posted everything off to the States at the beginning of November.'

'It takes that long?'

Max shook his head. 'Not really. My aunts started to send presents in October. I already have a large bag of them under the stairs.'

'How can you bear it?' Eliza grinned up at him. 'I'd be shaking them and peeling back the corners of the wrapping paper.'

'I try not to think about it too much.' Max turned the corners of his mouth down. He felt *something* but it was impossible to tell quite what. 'And my family are proponents of the theory that the more securely you wrap a present, the more fun it is. Peeling corners isn't really an option.'

'Won't you miss them all?' Eliza didn't exactly miss her parents at Christmastime. It was a relief not to have to negotiate their conflicting demands. But the thought of what Christmas *might* be like, if her parents were willing to forget their differences and negotiate, always made her heart ache.

'Yeah. I may go back in the summer for a visit.'

The conversation didn't seem to be lifting Max's mood, and she should drop it. 'So how are we going to do this? We could start at the left and work our way over to the right, so we don't miss any of the stalls.'

He thought for a moment. 'What's wrong with starting on the right?'

Max's dry humour was beginning to grow on her. 'Because the best stalls are always on the right, and we'll save them for last.'

'Okay. Or the ones on the right are always the best because you know they're the last?'

'Don't mess with the system, Max.'

He nodded. 'You're in charge.'

Not even remotely. If Eliza had been in charge he'd be asking where the hot chocolate with marshmallow stall was. Instead, as they approached the lights of the fair, he'd taken his phone from his pocket…

Eliza puffed out a breath. 'Max?'

He didn't reply, typing with two thumbs, and then staring at the screen of the phone as if waiting for a reply. He was clearly having a conversation with someone, and Eliza was beginning to lose her patience.

'Max!'

He jumped. 'Sorry. This is important…'

Important enough to break off their evening? Or maybe important because it gave him a chance to distance himself from the Christmas festivities going on around him? Eliza felt her heart sink. Maybe this was his excuse to leave?

Then Max looked up at her. 'It's Iona. She apologised for texting, but apparently Daisy's very upset. She was tired today, after the excitement of going home yesterday, and when one of the therapists visited she pushed Daisy to do too much. Daisy just shut down, and she's been in tears.'

'Iona was quite right to get in touch.' Eliza frowned.

'Yep, told her that, and that I'm going to call her in the morning to sort this out. The last thing we need is for Daisy to be under any unnecessary pressure.' Max quirked his lips down, holding his phone up to take a photograph of the stalls and the lights.

'What are you doing?'

'I said I couldn't call now, as it was too noisy here. Iona says that Daisy loved the Christmas Fair last year, but this year she's not well enough…' He smiled suddenly, seeming to have joined her in the sparkle of the here and now. 'Would you like to show her around?'

'Yes!' Eliza waited impatiently while Max typed, and then he turned his phone around. The video conferencing app connected, showing Iona sitting on a fat cushioned sofa, with Daisy beside her. The little girl was curled up, her hands over her eyes, her mum's hand resting on her back.

'Oh, Daisy…'

Daisy was shutting the world out. Alone in the dark silence, trying to escape from everything that was going on around her. Max had seen kids do this before, and no doubt Eliza had, too.

All they could do was watch as Iona gently tapped Daisy on the shoulder. Daisy flapped her hand at her mother in a clear sign that she wanted her to go away and leave her on her own. He felt Eliza move closer to him, waiting quietly, ready with one of those dazzling smiles of hers for Daisy.

The little girl was responding to her mother's cajoling. She took her hands away from her tear-stained face, shifting around to lean into Iona's arms. Max moved a little closer, holding the phone out in front of Eliza, and caught an intoxicating breath of her scent.

That came as a surprise. He'd been close to Eliza before, in the operating theatre, where disinfectant and concentration were the only things anyone smelled of. If he'd thought about it he would have imagined Eliza's natural scent as being like sunshine and flowers, but there was something more… Something sensual, passionate even. Something that made all of his instincts cry out for her. He felt Eliza's elbow nudging his ribs and focused on the screen.

Daisy was looking at them solemnly, and Eliza was smiling and waving a hello. He followed suit, and the little girl waved back unenthusiastically. Eliza spelled out Daisy's name, and when Max waved again, Daisy responded with a smile.

'Let's show her the lights…' Eliza ducked under the phone, grinning, and Max shrugged in a signal to Daisy that he wasn't sure what she was doing, either. Daisy and Iona both leaned forward, obviously keen to know what was going to happen next.

Max slipped the earpiece of his phone into his ear, so that he could hear what Iona was saying, and switched to the rear camera on the phone. Eliza was grinning and beckoning him forward, and he followed her as she led the way through the crowds, pointing at stalls and the lights suspended above their heads.

'How's she doing?' Eliza shot him a smile.

'She's got a big smile on her face and…she's singing. Not sure what, but I think it's a Christmas carol.' Iona joined in, a little more tunefully than Daisy, and he saw that she'd turned around to face her daughter, using impromptu actions to guide her through the carol. 'Yeah. Definitely a carol.'

'Oh, bless her. I hope you're recording this, Max, so I can see it later.'

'I am now.' Max found the screen recorder icon and tapped it.

When he looked back up from the screen, Eliza was deep in conversation with Santa Claus and several elves.

She turned, waving again, and Santa followed suit. One of the elves blew kisses, and another began a robotic dance. Max heard a wavering cry of delight from Daisy.

Santa turned to Eliza, and she relayed the message to Max, calling to him over the din of the crowd. Max spoke into the phone. 'Iona, tell Daisy that Santa says he's checked and she's on his list…'

'Okay… Just writing it down for her.' There was silence for a moment, and then he heard Daisy chuckle.

The elves waved to Daisy, and Santa caught Eliza's attention, clearly recognising a kindred spirit when he saw one. After a short discussion, Eliza demonstrated the signs for *Happy Christmas* and Santa clumsily reproduced them. Eliza corrected the angle of his hand and he turned to the camera, executing the signs perfectly.

'Iona, tell Daisy that Santa's signing a happy Christmas.'

He heard Daisy's wavering squeal of delight and then Iona's voice. 'Max… Max, please tell Santa that she's signing back.'

He relayed the message and Eliza thanked Santa and the elves and almost danced her way back towards him, nestling against his arm, all warmth and excitement. Max switched the camera view back onto them both.

'Thank you. Thank you…' Iona was grinning, hugging Daisy. This wasn't just a matter of making a little girl smile, although right now it seemed the only thing that mattered.

'I'll call you tomorrow and we'll sort things out. In the meantime our aim is to keep Daisy involved with what's going on around her.' He felt Eliza nudge him and ignored her. That was just as important as making Daisy forget her tears. More so from a medical point of view.

'She's *definitely* involved. When Sam gets home from work Daisy will be playing the recording back to him to show him what she's been up to today. Thank you.'

It was time to go. Daisy waved and blew kisses and Eliza followed suit. Then Iona reached forward and the screen went blank.

'Mission accomplished?'

Eliza pursed her lips. 'What do *you* think, Max? Daisy obviously loved it. And for your information, I'm satisfied that your medical goals are all intact.'

Was she making fun of him? Max put his phone back into his pocket, feeling an inappropriate swell of pleasure at the idea that Eliza was comfortable enough to make him the butt of a joke.

'Not quite. I'll speak with Iona tomorrow morning and then have a tactful conversation with the therapist who visited. I think it was one of the new members of staff, just out of training.' Max noticed that Eliza had tried not to smile at the word *tactful* and decided to ignore it. She wasn't the only one who could be tactful.

'That sounds like a plan.' She took his arm, in an indication that the matter was settled, and that any bad feelings would be buried under a landslide of glitter. 'So you're still up for the fair?'

'Of course. Where do you want to go first?'

It was odd. Daisy had taken silent pictures and filled in the gaps, adding sound and smell, the warmth of an open fire and the freezing touch of the breeze, to make her own winter wonderland. And she'd left no one in any doubt about her delight. Santa and the elves had all reached out to her in their own way, and Daisy had instinctively reached back.

But Max was having a harder time of it. He could hear the Christmas carols, smell nutmeg and roast chestnuts. Feel Eliza next to him, positively radiating warmth and goodwill. And yet, there was still something stopping him from being a part of it all.

From *letting* himself be a part of it all. Max couldn't shake the vague feeling that he might lose those precious Christmases with Mikey, if he overwrote them with new Christmas joys. Maybe his parents had the right idea in travelling away from New York City for Christmas. But they'd never asked Max to go with them…

He'd understood. Rationalised it all. But the feeling that somehow he'd lost his whole family, not just Mikey, wouldn't go away. He'd gone through the motions, spending Christmas with aunts and uncles or girlfriends. Whenever he could think of a good enough excuse, alone. None of that seemed to make up for being excluded from his parents' grief.

If Christmas was a time for remembering, then his recent memories didn't have much sparkle. But Eliza… Her brand of niceness didn't take no for an answer. She was bringing out every weapon in her arsenal—hot chocolate with toasted marshmallows, lights and sound, all the best Christmas gifts and decorations on the stalls, reaching out to everyone around her—and Max couldn't help feeling enveloped in her warmth. He was fighting it, fighting the feeling that he wanted to take her in his arms in more than just a Christmas hug. Max was beginning to see that Eliza wasn't the easy-to-please walkover he'd thought she was. Her flushed cheeks burned with a fearsome joy.

'Look! That's so cute!' She was playing with the display version of a paint-your-own wooden nativity set on one of the stalls. 'Oh—and look—you can fix lights into it to make it glow on the inside.'

'You have time to paint it before Christmas?'

'I doubt it. Do you? It would make a nice centrepiece. Or even stand on its own.' On learning that Max hadn't put his decorations up yet, largely because he didn't have any, Eliza had been concentrating on stalls that might remedy the situation.

'Probably not. I definitely don't have the paints...'

Another thing to like about Eliza was that she didn't give up easily. Max watched as she reached for one of the boxes of paints that were stacked up at the other end of the stall.

His great-grandmother's large nativity set was one of his mother's most prized possessions, and she'd put Max in charge of making sure that Mikey didn't break anything. He'd made a game out of it, and Mikey's small fingers were so careful when he played with it. This one was different, a tasteful modern design that would take a few knocks...

Still, he couldn't. Max shrugged, helplessly.

'I really don't have the time.' He saw Eliza turn the corners of her mouth down, knowing that was an excuse. The least he could offer her was a pinch of honesty. 'I'm giving decorations a miss this year. Are you going to give a guy a break...?'

Max could feel himself about to retreat away from his memories and away from Eliza. He was already looking for an escape route, through the crowds...

Then she smiled. That was all he'd needed to do, just tell her what he wanted. 'Yes. Of course. Anything and everything's okay at Christmas.'

This new glimpse of Eliza's charming and relentless

pursuit of Christmas touched even Max's heart. For a moment, it seemed a very good excuse to kiss her, and then Max reminded himself that there was a *tomorrow* when that wouldn't seem quite such a good idea.

'Have we seen everything we want to see?' Eliza looked around her, obviously checking if there was anything they'd missed.

'I have.' Max had suggested this visit as a way of getting to know Eliza a little better, and he hadn't expected it to become special to him. Maybe he could reach for one more special moment. She'd be in no peril from home truths if she got into his car tonight, and maybe she would understand that. 'Lift home? My car's in the hospital car park.'

She didn't even hesitate. 'Yes, thanks. That would be great.'

Eliza couldn't help feeling that they'd reached a new understanding. If Max wasn't up for decorations, or joining in with the fun of Christmas, then that wasn't her fault and she didn't need to try a bit harder to remedy the situation. All she needed to do was to accept that she didn't know the reasons behind his choices.

When his car drew up outside her house, he reached for the driver's door and got out, clearly about to open her door for her. The SUV was roomy enough inside for her to easily slip between the two front seats, and she climbed into the back seat, grabbing her bags, ready to get out of the car all by herself. But Max was too quick for her. As she reached for the door to the back seat he opened the door of the front passenger seat, leaning into the car.

'Were you thinking of touching that door release?' His

lips gave only the hint of a smile, but his eyes were alive and dancing with dry humour.

Eliza grinned at him. 'Never crossed my mind.'

He nodded, ducking back out of the car to open the door of the back seat. Max held out one hand, and Eliza delivered her bags into his grasp before climbing out of the vehicle.

'How was that for you?' He closed the car door, handing her bags back to her.

'Good.' She'd noticed that Max was in the habit of opening doors for whoever he happened to be with, and it was obviously a gesture of courtesy, not assertiveness. Eliza preferred it to Richie's style, which sometimes involved locking the car doors and walking away if he didn't think she was moving quickly enough.

He nodded, smiling. 'So you're happy to head for a door, while I race around the car trying to second-guess you? It has the advantage of keeping me on my toes.'

Eliza couldn't help laughing. 'I am if you are. Although you could just stay put and let me get out of the car.' Agreeing on a ritual, whatever form it took, made friendship seem possible.

'Or *you* could stay put and let me open the door for you.' Max's smile told her that this was nothing to do with who got to open doors, and everything to do with how they could compromise.

'Fifty-fifty?'

He leaned back against the car, folding his arms. 'Fifty-fifty it is. See you tomorrow?'

'You can depend on it.' Eliza turned, walking up her front path. Knowing that Max was still there, watching her safely to her door, without having to be asked.

CHAPTER SIX

It had been a tough week. The department was busy, and pre-Christmas days off and holidays meant that they were working with fewer staff members. The home visitors had reported that Daisy had been improving, but was still prone to periods of exhausted listlessness. Eliza had spoken with Iona on the phone, and they'd discussed the options for Daisy in more detail, but she and Sam were still a little way away from making a final decision.

'Is Max out of surgery yet?' She stopped at reception to ask Sarah, who was just getting ready to leave for the day.

'Yes. I'd let him be for half an hour, if it's not urgent.'

'Difficult procedure?' Sarah could usually gauge the mood of everyone who walked through reception with one glance, and she knew as well as Eliza did that sometimes the surgeons needed some time alone after the high-pressure environment of the operating theatre.

'I don't know about that. I didn't ask in case he bit my head off. He came through here ten minutes ago with a face like thunder.'

'Okay thanks, Sarah. I might just head for my office, then.'

'Wise move.' Sarah picked up her bag. 'Have a good evening.'

Or maybe her office *wasn't* such a wise move. It was too close to the closed door of Max's office, and when Eliza sat down behind her desk, she couldn't gather her thoughts.

She had a connection with Max. They were different, but they seemed to understand each other—he made her smile and she could make him smile, even if it did seem at times that he was doing it despite himself. Dr Beckwith had asked them to work together because he thought that they could get the best out of each other, and he was rarely wrong about these things.

If she thought about it too long, Eliza would reason herself out of what she was about to do. Tell herself that falling for him was a very bad idea, and the very last thing on her agenda at the moment. That would be enough to stop her and…

Eliza was already on her feet and making her way to his office, before she could listen to her own good sense. She pressed her ear to the door and heard him moving around restlessly. Maybe pacing. She'd knocked before she could talk herself out of that as well.

'Not now,' Max's voice sounded.

'Yes. Now, Max.' She waited for his reply and got none. When she opened the door, Max was standing with his back to her, his hands in his pockets, staring out the window. He'd obviously dressed in a hurry; his white shirt was creased and tucked hastily into his dark trousers, and his short dark hair was slightly less immaculate than usual.

'What happened, Max?' Eliza sat down on the other side of his desk, in a signal that she wasn't going anywhere until he answered her.

He turned. Raw emotion showed in Max's face, and his body seemed to be holding all of the suppressed fury of a tiger locked in a cage. 'Give me ten minutes, Eliza.'

'You've already had ten minutes, Max. I very much doubt that another ten is going to make any difference.'

The room seemed to be buzzing with his anger. Passionate and forthright, it made her heart beat a little faster. Max seemed to be struggling to keep it under control, but she'd really rather he didn't.

He sat down, his elbows on the desk in front of him, his hands wiping his face as if he were trying to rub the emotion from it. That was the last thing she wanted him to do, because Max was generally so forthright in his reactions. It was uncomfortable at times, but she'd come to like that about him; it was a world away from her mother's spider's web of manipulation and long-held grudges that left Eliza feeling that she was responsible for the happiness of everyone around her.

'Christmas fairies have a hard job, you know. You have to be pretty tough to dispense glitter at times.' Eliza generally didn't consider her main function here to be the dispensing of glitter, but she was well aware that was the way some people saw her.

Max shook his head, the ghost of a smile playing around his lips. 'So I gather.'

'I'm not afraid to hear this from you, Max.'

Shock registered on his face. 'Afraid? I really hope *that's* not what you're feeling.'

His dismay made Eliza catch her breath. Richie had no hesitation in making the people around him feel that they were walking on eggshells, if it suited him, and there had always been an element of anxiety involved in choosing her words carefully. Max was different.

Eliza leaned forward, catching his gaze. 'That just goes to show that wishes *do* come true, then.'

He held up his hands. 'You win. I'll never doubt that glitter can be strong medicine again.'

Max seemed to be swallowing his anger, and they were veering perilously close to flirting, but that wasn't what she wanted from him. Not right now, at least.

'Well, now we have that sorted out… This is how it's going to go, Max. You're going to talk about it and I'm going to listen. And if you're thinking of telling me that it's nothing and to forget it, don't waste your breath.'

Max had just wanted to be left alone. To get out of the hospital without seriously upsetting anyone. Then take himself down to the sports centre and hit a few baseballs in one of the batting cages. Maybe it would take more than a few to make him forget what had happened this afternoon.

But Eliza had changed all that, walking into his office with her own brand of irresistible fire. He'd glimpsed it already a few times, even wondered if he could resist if she ever chose to direct its full force at him. Now he had his answer.

'Young guy, thirty years old, who had a small hole in his eardrum after being hit on the side of the head with a squash ball…' He saw Eliza wince. 'Yeah. Ouch.'

'You were doing a myringoplasty?'

'Yep, he was having ongoing ear infections and there was some deterioration in his hearing. He was referred here and I examined him and passed him for surgery.

We'd been through all of the regular health checks and procedures. He turned up this morning with his fiancée and was prepped. He was first on my list for this afternoon. Simon Townsend was the anaesthesiologist, and he said that the patient had shown quite a high resistance to the anaesthetic, but nothing outside the bounds of normality.'

Eliza nodded. 'Okay. And then?'

'Simon stopped me a couple of minutes in, because the patient was starting to vomit. We repositioned him and Simon applied suction and stabilised him. We both knew that something wasn't right and decided to discontinue the operation. I closed my first incision as quickly as I could, and Simon started to wake him up. Which wasn't as straightforward as we'd hoped, but we got there…'

'Do you know why this happened?'

Max nodded. 'Yeah. We ran blood tests afterwards and found a high level of alcohol in his system.'

From the look on Eliza's face, Max didn't need to go into details. She knew all about the dangers and difficulties involved, and the set of her jaw told him that she wasn't going to try to placate him by saying that everything had worked out fine in the end. She understood the emotional fallout when something like this happened in theatre. The grim silence and the wordless handshake that he and Simon had exchanged afterwards.

'How is he now?'

'Not well. He's being cared for and… I'd like to say that he'll be okay, but I think it's more a case of getting away with it this time.'

'And you?' Eliza dismissed Max's shrug with a wave of her hand. 'You're the one in my field of vision right now.'

'Wondering if I could have spotted it sooner. Maybe I'm losing my edge.'

Eliza's eyes widened. 'Max, I… I know how easy it is to doubt yourself when this kind of thing happens. I've been there and done that. But from what I've just heard, you and Simon did everything right.'

'I thought we did.' Max knew that Eliza wanted more from him than that; she'd seen his anger. 'Mike did all of the pre-op checks. You know how meticulous he is. Everything was signed and in order. I went back to my notes of the first consultation and I'd asked all the usual questions about alcohol consumption and written down a couple of glasses of wine at the weekend and nothing during the week. But drinking before a surgical procedure and then lying about it is an obvious red flag. How could I have missed that?'

'People who have an addiction can become very good at hiding it, Max. And we have to rely on what our patients tell us. You said that your patient came in with his fiancée. Did you speak to her?'

'Yes, she told me she had no idea how much he drinks, but that he's out every night during the week and comes home smelling of alcohol. She's put the wedding off twice because of it and then he promises he's in control of things and he'll cut down.'

'Well, it sounds to me as if she has some idea that he has an alcohol problem, but let's not go there. I know you're good, Max, but you're not a mind reader. Tell me one thing more you could have done.'

The Christmas fairy seemed to have fluttered off somewhere else for the time being, and Eliza was giving him the unvarnished truth. Max could feel the dark anger, directed mostly towards himself, begin to lift.

'I guess I could have explained the risks more carefully.'

'You asked him about alcohol consumption, and he lied. That's not on you.'

'I might have been a bit more approachable.' Max knew that there was a part of himself that distanced himself from everyone. 'You would have…'

Was that anger in her eyes? This was a side of Eliza he hadn't seen before and it felt like a privilege. As if she felt the same about him as he did about her, and that he deserved a piece of her mind.

'So…what? You think that I get everything that I want just by smiling at people?'

'I didn't say that, Eliza. I just meant…you have a way with people. You bring out the best in them.'

Eliza puffed out a breath. 'Do I? People like waste-of-space partners?'

That had turned into a no-go area. Maybe it shouldn't be. Max leaned back in his chair, waiting, resisting the sudden impulse to tell her that everything was okay and that they didn't need to talk about it when he saw a tear in the corner of Eliza's eye.

'You're going there, Eliza?'

Yes. Eliza was going there. Not really of her own accord, but suddenly it seemed that she had no choice, because she was in free fall. Arms and legs flailing, seeing the ground rush up towards her. Wondering if Max might catch her, and hoping he might.

'Max, I believe that making people smile, giving them a little hope, is important. It makes me feel good, too.'

'I know.'

'But that's not all there is to it. Sometimes I just feel a need to keep everyone happy and…that's not always a good thing.'

He didn't reply. That was probably a good move on Max's part; she knew that he didn't have much time for the people-pleasing side of her nature, and Eliza hadn't reacted well in the past when he'd called her out on it.

'I was six when my parents divorced. It was messy—my father was having an affair.'

His face darkened again, but this time his focus was all on her. 'You were caught between them?'

'Yes. Mum wanted me on her side, and Dad wanted me on his. I stopped being their child and had to grow up very quickly. You know the kind of thing?'

Max nodded. 'Yes and no. My parents had a lot of problems but they stuck together.'

'What happened?'

'It's a long story. It happened when I was eighteen and already at college so I didn't bear the brunt of it the way you did. And this isn't about me. I want to hear about you.'

Max's focus was entirely on her and it sent tingles down her spine. How often had she wished that her family would forget about their own needs for ten minutes and concentrate on hers?

'Mum wanted me to validate everything she did, and… Dad wanted me to have much more fun with him than I did at home. The only way to stop it tearing me in two was to try and please both of them.' Eliza said what Max must be thinking. 'It's become something of a habit.'

'One that you're thinking of breaking?' His eyes were dark and thoughtful.

'It depends what you mean. There are a lot of good things in life, and I don't plan on losing sight of them. Maybe I'll just…' Eliza frowned. 'I don't know. Maybe try not to feel that it's my job to fix the bad things. Although I suppose it *is* my job to fix some of the bad things.'

'Let me know if you find the answer. To what we *can* fix and what we can't.'

It was honest, but it didn't help. Maybe she and Max *were* struggling with the same questions, but they were different people, staring at each other across an impossible divide. Eliza felt drawn to him, but he wasn't the answer to any of her fears and doubts, or any of her hopes and dreams, either.

'Pizza?' He broke the silence. Pizza wasn't going to fix anything, but it was at least something that they had in common now.

'Your shout?' Eliza grinned as he shot her a querying look. There were times when she and Max didn't even speak the same language. '*Your shout* means that it's your turn to pay this time.'

'Do you imagine I'd forgotten?' He got to his feet, seeming ready to leave everything else behind. But there was still some trace of the angry man who was looking for answers. A hint of the passion and uncertainty that was so different from his usual measured outlook on life. As he passed her, Eliza couldn't help reaching for his arm.

He felt it, too. That electric sensation of reaching past the moment and into something dangerous. All of the what-ifs of the past few days, melting into one delicious solution, which shouldn't work but somehow just fell into place and made perfect sense.

Max's fingers brushed her elbow, and she could feel their warmth through the fabric of her blouse. Had he moved a little closer, or had she?

Or perhaps the space between them had just collapsed in on itself, leaving only the feel of his body against hers. That first brush of her lips against his seemed inevitable. And then, in the warm safety of his gaze, Eliza kissed him.

No… He must have kissed her, because this was beyond anything that she could have imagined. His softness, his scent. The hard swell of muscle across his shoulders that reacted to even her most hesitant touch. She gazed up into his eyes and found all of the courage she needed. Enough to take what she wanted, pulling him down for another kiss. Max was confident, commanding even, but tantalisingly unhurried. Forcing her to take what *she* wanted.

'You are…intriguing.' He dropped a kiss onto her cheek, and Eliza shivered.

'What does that mean?' She was sure it was something good, from the look on Max's face.

'Beauty and brains goes without saying. Intriguing is the kind of person you'd want to know a great deal more about.'

That was a really nice compliment. Eliza tried to think of one that was just for Max.

'And you are…' She kissed him again. Pouring all of her wants and needs into that one action. Hoping he'd understand, because she really didn't have the words for this heady connection between them that seemed to overwhelm all the odds.

He got it. Max's gaze held hers fast, wrapping her in an emotional warmth that gave the physical a whole new depth. What would it be like if they made love in this tender embrace?

This was leading everywhere, fast. Maybe Max would lock the door and… No. It was a tempting thought, but she knew enough about him to realise that it wasn't his style. He'd take her home and wait for her to invite him in. They both knew exactly what would happen next; the heat between them didn't lie.

But it was fragile. He held her tight in his arms, and Eliza felt a subtle change. Max was no longer searching; he was finding a way back. Slowly enough to allow her to gather her scattered thoughts; but when he stepped away from her, Eliza still felt embarrassed and naked.

'What is it, Max?'

'I'm sorry. I think this is…uh…'

'A mistake?' Eliza shot the worst word she could think of at him.

'I think it would be. To take things any further…'

Nothing hurt quite as much as someone agreeing with something you didn't want to say. Somehow, Eliza managed to summon a smile.

'Yes, it is. This isn't right for either of us.'

'I'm so sorry, Eliza.' Max turned away from her, walking back to the window to stare out it.

Way to go, Max. No one walked away from their own office and slammed the door, but he'd just done the next best thing. He was as far away from her now as if he *had* walked away. Eliza pressed her lips together, determined not to give him the satisfaction of a response to his rejection. She walked out of his office, closing the door quietly behind her.

Not too fast. Max might hear her footsteps if she ran away from him. Not too slow, either, because she needed to be alone. Eliza made it to her office, closing the door quietly behind her and locking it. Then she walked over to her desk, bending forward and planting her hands on it, trying to take a few deep breaths.

That didn't go too well. It was more a case of gasping for air, to fuel the whimpering sounds that didn't seem to be coming from her own throat.

Max had called a halt, and even though she'd wanted to go on she had to accept it. That was written in stone; there was no such thing as an agreement made between just one person; it took two.

It was the way he'd done it. It felt as if she'd done the wrong thing, and Max had turned his back on her. Eliza had coped with her mother's rejection every time she even hinted that she might have her own feelings about her parents' divorce. She'd dealt with Richie's rejection, even decided that he'd done her a favour. But Max was her here and now. Walking away, smiling and holding her head high to disguise how she really felt, wasn't easy when she was supposed to be building a good working relationship with him.

And it wasn't what she wanted, either. He'd called her *intriguing* and that was exactly how Eliza felt about Max. Not just handsome and clever. Not even just heart-stoppingly attractive. He was someone whom she felt drawn to and wanted to know a great deal more about.

That elusive someone who might make love to her as if they belonged together.

'Breathe. Breathe...' She whispered the words, forcing herself to take one breath and then the next. It wasn't helping the pain yet, but it would make her strong enough to bear it.

Clearing her mind of everything made Eliza feel a bit more in control. She'd wait until there was no danger of bumping into him on her way out of the building, and then go home. Find something to do over the weekend that involved a clear goal, physical effort and not too much thought. Max wasn't going to be the guy who would rock her world, but he might just be the one who facilitated a deep-clean of her whole house before Christmas.

CHAPTER SEVEN

A MISTAKE? REALLY? Max turned to sit back down behind his desk and then changed his mind. He'd just heard the door to Eliza's office close, and he reckoned that she wouldn't be leaving until she was sure he was out of the building. He shouldn't keep her waiting.

He'd wanted Eliza so completely, so urgently, that he'd forgotten himself. Forgotten that he was the guy who didn't get too close to people, and who'd moulded his emotion into a fierce resolve to do his job in the best way possible. When he'd needed someone to shake a little good sense into him, Eliza had been there. Not just been there—she'd forced her way into his office and then into his heart. Listened to him in a way that his mom and dad had stopped doing years ago. Challenged him in a way that he'd stopped accepting from anyone.

He pulled on his coat, sinking his hands deep into his pockets. Trying to ignore the sweet reverberations of Eliza's kiss that were playing languidly with his nervous system, sending shivers down his spine and making his fingertips tingle.

She was right. They were *both* right. This had been a mistake and it was something that neither of them wanted. It was a cruel trick, played by nature, endowing them with the kind of physical synchronicity that Max had heard spoken about, but never entirely believed could happen.

Not to him anyway. Relationships had come, and then gone, withering away under the pressure of his indifference. Eliza wanted something more than that, and Max believed that it was within her grasp. Acknowledging their connection would turn it into a weapon, another broken relationship with a waste-of-space boyfriend. He was a man who couldn't change, and the only thing he wanted more than Eliza's touch was to protect her.

He'd go home, have something to eat—probably *not* pizza—and get some sleep. Put the weekend between him and those dazzling kisses, and try to forget about them. If Eliza had any sense at all she'd be doing the same.

His phone rang, and when Max looked at the call display, he realised he probably wouldn't be going home just yet.

'Max Russo.'

'Dr Russo, Dr Patel here from A&E. I think we need your assistance, if you're free.'

The guy either *did* need his assistance, in which case Max would go down to A&E, or he *didn't* and Max would go home. He reminded himself that voicing that thought would only pass his own bad day onto someone else, who was probably having an equally bad day, and took a breath.

'You have a preliminary diagnosis?'

'Yes. Pinna haematoma.'

'Okay. I'll be right down…' Max put the phone down. Maybe slamming his office door on the way out would make him feel a little better… He decided against the measure, since Eliza was sure to hear and might come to the erroneous conclusion that it was all her fault.

The A&E department was busy. The young doctor attending the patient Max had come to see was clearly a bit rattled, but his notes left nothing to be desired. He'd missed nothing and given his patient a thorough check to make sure there were no other injuries.

Max took a moment to digest it all and then nodded. 'Good. Thank you.'

'It's not good at all.' The man propped on the couch was in evening dress and clearly his night had been spoiled by a blow to the head, which had caused a haematoma to form in the upper part of his ear. 'Do you know how long I had to wait? And then there was nothing but messing around. When's someone going to look at my ear?'

'I'm sorry for the wait—' Max glanced at the notes '—Mr Trubshaw. I'm Dr Russo and I'm an ENT surgeon.'

'That's all anyone says. *Sorry for the wait.* You could die in here, and no one would notice. They're all too busy drinking tea.'

Max must have missed the tea parties on his way in. Maybe he should go and see if there was any cake; he was feeling a bit peckish…

'We've been dealing with several very serious cases, Mr Trubshaw.' Dr Patel had the weary air of a man who was saying this for the nth time.

'Yes, all right, you already gave that excuse. I thought everyone was supposed to be seen in order, or am I wrong?'

He was wrong. Max looked again at the notes and saw that Dr Patel had already checked for any head injuries or alcohol use that might account for Trubshaw's belligerence.

'Patients with less serious conditions may have to wait longer, and I see from the notes that you were triaged shortly after you arrived. May I take a look at your ear now?'

Trubshaw scowled at him. 'Get on with it, then. I'm supposed to be presenting an award at the International Player of the Year dinner this evening. Since I won it last year.'

Whatever award he'd won, it was clearly not in the good manners category. Dr Patel was rising in Max's estimation by the minute. 'I'm afraid we may not be able to get you out of here in time for that, Mr Trubshaw.' One glance at the large haematoma had told Max that it would have to be drained, which was a surgical procedure.

'It's probably too late already. I should have stayed where I was.'

'It was right of you to come.' Max glanced again at the notes, wondering if it was possible to get his examination underway. 'I see that you were injured on the way in to the function you were attending. You tripped and fell against one of the press barriers.'

'Yeah. I dare say there'll be a picture of *that* in the papers tomorrow.' Trubshaw waved his hand at Dr Patel. 'Can't be helped now with all this fiddling around he's been doing. Don't you know who I am?'

No. But then Max was a baseball fan.

'Mr Trubshaw's a well-known snooker player,' Dr Patel murmured, and Max gave him a nod. He didn't like reprimanding a patient, but he'd had enough of the repeated jibes that Trubshaw had aimed at Dr Patel.

'I know now. I see from the notes, Mr Trubshaw, that Dr Patel has already examined you for several serious conditions that needed to be ruled out before we considered treatment to your ear, which is a relatively minor injury. Are you happy to proceed with that now?'

Maybe something in his tone stopped Trubshaw in his tracks. ‘Yes, all right, then. Thank you.’

He submitted quietly to Max’s careful examination of his ear. ‘As Dr Patel has already rightly concluded, you have what’s known as a pinna haematoma, which is where blood collects between the skin and cartilage at the top of your ear. If this is left untreated, it can result in infections or ear conditions such as cauliflower ear. So our next step will be a minor procedure, done under a local anaesthetic, to drain and splint the ear…’

Max had asked one of the nurses to phone ahead and arrange for someone from the ENT department to assist him and he’d heard Dr Patel puff out a sigh of relief as two porters arrived to take Mr Trubshaw to the minor surgery suite.

‘You’re new here, aren’t you?’ He knew most of the faces in A&E.

‘My first week. Thanks for coming down, Dr Russo.’

‘Max.’ Max stretched out his hand and Dr Patel smiled, taking it.

‘Binul.’

‘I see that you missed something in the notes. You didn’t document Mr Trubshaw’s derogatory comments and attitude. I’ve rectified that omission and perhaps you’ll countersign it.’

Binul glanced through Max’s additions to his notes. ‘Thanks. There’s no need. I dare say his ear was hurting him…’

There had been every need. The staff here had a hard job and they performed it with care and good humour. The vast majority of patients understood that, but one Trubshaw could cancel out a hundred thank-yous.

'In my experience, patients who are in serious pain don't generally have the energy to behave as he did. Is he *really* that well-known?' Something made Max take a moment to ask. A young doctor who'd done everything he could for his patient, despite his attitude, had his respect.

'I recognised him. I read the sports pages for the football.'

'Yeah? Football's a bit beyond me. I'm more of a baseball fan myself.'

Binul chuckled. 'You don't know what you're missing. Come down to the Red Lion when there's a Yorkshire team playing.' Binul's soft Yorkshire accent made it very clear where his allegiances lay.

'I'll do that. As long as you'll join me at the Green Dragon when they're screening a baseball game.'

'Deal.' Binul held out his hand and Max shook it, ignoring the small puff of fairy dust that had just drifted down from the ceiling. It was probably just a trick of the light…

Max stretched his shoulders as he walked back into the ENT department. It occurred to him that he'd just found a friend, and that it hadn't involved a single smile on his part. Then he walked straight into the searing heat of Eliza's smile…

Which wasn't directed at him. She'd already changed into scrubs and was sitting next to Trubshaw in the deserted waiting room of the minor surgery suite, going through the consent paperwork with him. Trubshaw was doing exactly as he was told, quietly reading through the forms before he signed them. Maybe Max's firmly worded advice, that he wouldn't be tolerating any displays of temper towards the ENT staff, had worked. Or maybe

Trubshaw was just another victim of the light that Eliza carried around with her.

She gathered up the paperwork, checking it through and then getting to her feet to join him at the reception desk. Max braced himself for what was coming. He'd been hoping for a weekend's grace, anything that might allow him to look at Eliza without feeling the full force of that kiss jolting through his senses.

'Shouldn't you be on your way home?' Something about the emptiness of her smile really hurt. Max didn't want this, and he was sure Eliza didn't, either. Surely, there was *someone* else available to assist him.

'The night staff are all busy.'

In other words, it was this way or the highway, but Eliza wouldn't say that. 'Okay. Thanks for staying.'

'It's fine. I didn't have any plans for this evening.'

As Max remembered it, there had been a moment when they'd both had very specific plans. He didn't need to think about that, because it wasn't going to happen. Ever.

'Let's get this done, then.'

They got it done with minimum fuss and maximum efficiency. Max changed into scrubs, washed his hands and pulled on a pair of surgical gloves. They both wore masks and clear plastic face shields, but somehow she managed to get a sheepish smile out of Trubshaw as they positioned him on his side.

Beauty and the beast. Now that he knew how much Eliza's smile had cost her, it seemed all the more luminous. And Max couldn't help wondering whether he was one of the beasts she'd encountered today. Maybe that wasn't such a bad thing; a little pain now would stop them from making the same mistake in the future.

She injected the local anaesthetic, then watched as he made an incision around the rim of the ear and drained the blood, talking to Trubshaw and encouraging him to keep still while Max worked. He splinted the wound with cotton rolls and then dressed it.

'I can stay,' she murmured quietly to Max, after they'd wheeled Trubshaw, along with his belongings, through into the recovery room.

No. His concentration had driven other thoughts from his head but now their quiet, overly polite professionalism was agony. Whatever Eliza thought was hidden behind her smile.

'You go home. I've got some things to do here.' Drink coffee, maybe, although that was only going to lend an edge to the feelings that he was trying to ignore.

She nodded, turning her gaze onto Trubshaw. 'We'll need to keep you here for another couple of hours, but Dr Russo will be available. Everything looks good and that's just a precaution. Is there someone I can call to pick you up?'

'Yes, thanks. I gave the number.'

Eliza nodded, glancing at the notes. 'Okay, this is your…?'

'Personal assistant.'

It was no particular surprise that Trubshaw didn't have a friend that he could rely on to come and fetch him. Max saw Eliza's fleeting look of commiseration, as Trubshaw turned his attention away from her.

'Could you tell that doctor in A&E… I didn't mean what I said?' he asked Max.

'He'll have gone home by now, I imagine. If you want to thank Dr Patel, then perhaps you could leave a note.

I'm sure it would be much appreciated.' Max couldn't help feeling a stab of sympathy for the man.

'Yes. Thanks. I…don't have any paper.'

'Just rest for a while. I'll go and get some and be back in a minute.' He followed Eliza out of the room, almost bumping into her outside the open doorway.

'The nurse who called said that he was a difficult customer,' she murmured quietly.

'Yeah. He gave the doctor in A&E a very hard time.'

'You must have set him straight. He was all right with me when they brought him up.'

Max had been wondering whether his own habit of being direct put him into a Trubshaw category at times. But the look of approval on Eliza's face placed him firmly back on the side of the angels.

'Good. Glad to hear it.'

'I'll make that call and get off home, then.' Eliza clearly didn't want to stay any longer than she had to and that came as a relief to Max. Maybe losing her wouldn't hurt so much on Monday, and they could get back to normal.

'Thanks…' Max couldn't let her go without one more word, and Eliza's gaze suddenly met his. Her empty smile was an impenetrable barrier between them, something that she was hiding behind. He wondered whether Eliza knew that, and decided she was far too self-aware for it to have escaped her.

'You're welcome.' She turned on her heel and walked away.

'What have you *done* to him?' Sarah called to Eliza as she was going out for lunch on Monday.

Eliza froze. She'd spent the whole weekend going over

the events of Friday evening in her head, despite all of her resolutions not to. How foregoing the most memorable kiss she'd ever experienced, and going out to eat pizza with Max, would have saved a great deal of embarrassment and heartache. How she might have been a little more friendly and less polite afterwards, because Max had been obviously upset, too.

But maybe she cared enough about Max to be as angry with him as she was with herself. The irony of that idea wasn't lost on her.

None of that mattered, though. Now was the time for damage limitation.

'Done to who?' Eliza walked over to the reception desk, somehow managing to pretend that she didn't know what Sarah was referring to.

'Max. I heard all about Friday night.'

Sudden terror gripped Eliza, and then rational thought kicked in. Unless someone had Max's office bugged, the only two people who knew about the kiss were her and Max. She hadn't mentioned it to anyone, and even though Max had hurt her she still trusted him enough to know that he wouldn't have said a word about it.

'You did?'

'Yes, the awkward character with the cauliflower ear. Apparently, Max made him apologise to the A&E doctor.'

'Well, he doesn't have a cauliflower ear now. And Max didn't actually *make* him apologise. He did it of his own accord.'

'I heard from the A&E receptionist that Max had been pretty firm with him. And he bought me a coffee this morning.'

'Who? Mr Trubshaw?' In her relief that the conversation had nothing to do with kissing, Eliza was beginning to lose the thread of it.

'No! Max. He went downstairs for his own, as usual, and brought me back a double caramel and hazelnut latte. I asked him what that was for, and he said nothing, he'd just noticed I looked a bit tired. Which I am. We were up late last night wrapping presents after the kids went to bed. It took me and Joe over an hour to wrap our Bobby's skateboard. The wheels are really fiddly.'

So many questions. Had Max mentioned that he considered Sarah's favourite brew to be overly sweet dishwater, or had he kept quiet about that? Why was he buying Sarah coffee anyway?

'Didn't the skateboard come in a box?' Eliza decided to go for the least contentious one.

'Yes, it did, but we had to take it out to wrap it. My little lad's a terrible worrier. He'll be sneaking downstairs to feel the parcel to make sure we got the one he wanted, and if we leave it in the box then he won't be able to do that.'

'Oh. Okay, so why…?'

The phone rang. Sarah held up one finger in a gesture that intimated more answers would be forthcoming if Eliza waited a minute, and picked up the receiver.

Max was obviously up to something. She'd been blaming herself for everything, but maybe he was doing the same and… Eliza wasn't sure how the obvious next step would be a double caramel and hazelnut latte, but Max could be hard to work out sometimes.

'Okay, hold on a moment, I've got her right here.' Sarah looked up at Eliza, covering the mouthpiece of the phone with her hand. 'It's the urgent care centre. Apparently, they have Sam Yates down there with his daughter.'

'Daisy? Is she all right?'

'Yes, there's something the matter with her father. Can you speak with them?'

Eliza nodded, and Sarah transferred the call to the other phone on her desk. 'Eliza Chilton.'

'Hello, it's Ranjini from urgent care. We have Mr Yates and his daughter Daisy here. I understand that Daisy is deaf?'

'Yes that's right, and she's recently recovered from meningitis. Is Sam okay?'

'He has a cut on the side of his head. The bleeding seems to have stopped but the triage nurse said he'll need a couple of stitches. And there's an hour's wait. I was wondering if ENT has any facility to take care of Daisy while her father's being treated.'

Not really. Childcare wasn't their speciality. Eliza suspected that wasn't what Ranjini was asking. She'd identified a potential problem and was trying to find someone who had the authority to solve it.

'Okay. I'll be right down.' Eliza put the phone back into its cradle and turned to Sarah. 'Got to go. Hold the thought about the coffee. I'll ask you later…'

CHAPTER EIGHT

When she arrived in the waiting room of the urgent care centre Eliza realised what the receptionist had been up against. Any cases that were severe or life-threatening would be escalated to A&E, but there were a few very unwell people here and the waiting room was full. She could see Sam, sitting in a corner with Daisy, trying to shield his daughter from the constant activity going on around them.

Eliza leaned forward to see the receptionist's name badge. 'Thanks, Ranjini. I appreciate you taking the initiative to call me.' She hurried over to Sam, who looked up at her, stress etched into his face.

'Dr Chilton, I'm so sorry to bother you. When I gave your name to the receptionist, I didn't mean for her to ask you to come yourself.'

'That's okay.' Eliza signed a hello to Daisy, who was staring up at her, trying to gauge what was going on. 'I don't think we can do anything here. Let's go somewhere quieter, shall we?'

'If there's somewhere for Daisy… I have to stay here, or I'll lose my place in the queue.' Sam was holding a wad of gauze to the top of his forehead, and Eliza could see blood starting to seep through it as he spoke.

'I'm a surgeon, Sam. Cuts are my speciality.' Eliza smiled as reassuringly as she could, when she was constantly being jostled by people passing behind her. 'Wait here. One minute.'

There was a bank of wheelchairs next to the reception desk and she hurried over and grabbed one. Sam hesitated, telling her he didn't want to jump the queue, and she practically had to order him into it. When he settled himself down, Daisy silently took off her coat and spread it over her father's knees as a makeshift blanket.

'Well done, Daisy.' Eliza gave her a smile and a thumbs-up. 'Hold on now.' She took the little girl's hand, curling her fingers around the armrest of the wheelchair, and Sam smiled, covering his daughter's hand with his. As they passed the reception desk, Eliza signalled that she was taking Sam and Daisy, and Ranjini nodded. Hopefully, she'd be doing whatever paperwork was required for kidnapping patients from waiting rooms.

The lift was empty, and Eliza took a moment to bend down and smile to Daisy, willing her to understand that everything was going to be okay. As they passed through the ENT reception she called to Sarah.

'Does the minor surgery suite have a free room, Sarah?'

'Yep, it's empty at the moment, until after lunch.' Before Eliza had a chance to ask for someone to assist her, Sarah had picked up the phone. 'Finding someone to give you a hand…'

The waiting room was empty, and Eliza wheeled Sam into one of the surgery rooms and parked the wheelchair. 'We'll wait until a nurse comes and they can stay outside with Daisy.' Eliza sat Daisy down next to her dad, bringing a chair over for herself, and the little girl leaned across against her arm.

'What happened, Sam?' She put her arm around Daisy's shoulders, feeling her snuggle in against her.

'I fell and cut myself. I was worried about being home on my own with Daisy. My head was really throbbing. Iona's out seeing a client for work this morning and she'd switched her phone off, and I couldn't get my sister, either. So I got into a taxi and brought Daisy with me. I'm sorry…' Sam was obviously distressed, but he didn't seem confused, which was a good sign.

'That's fine, Sam. If your head's throbbing after a blow, you shouldn't be looking after a child on your own. You did the best thing and found a safe place for both you and Daisy. I'm just going to take a quick look at the cut now, to find out what's happening there.'

Sam nodded, and Eliza got to her feet, walking over to the cupboard to find some gauze and turning to pull a pair of gloves from the dispenser. Daisy was standing right behind her, her hands reaching up. She must have seen doctors and nurses regularly donning gloves when she was a patient in the children's ward.

If she wanted to help and that kept her happy, Eliza wasn't going to argue. She pulled another pair of gloves from the dispenser and gave them to Daisy, sitting her back down and then placing her own chair in between Sam and his daughter. Daisy had already pulled on the gloves, her fingers reaching about halfway into them, and was looking at her expectantly.

Okay. She could hold the gauze. Eliza put the box of gauze pads into Daisy's lap and Daisy curled her hands around it.

'Looks as if you have a budding doctor on your hands here, Sam.' She smiled at Sam and he nodded. 'Let's have a quick look…'

Making sure that she was obscuring Daisy's view of the wound, she peeled the gauze that Sam had been holding pressed against forehead. The bleeding had stopped, but there was a two-inch cut and it was deep. 'All right. You'll need a few stitches, but… I think that's going to be straightforward. It should heal well.'

'Thanks.'

'I'll just get a fresh piece of gauze for you to hold over it.' She turned and saw that Daisy was busy trying to extract one of the packets of gauze from the box on her lap, hampered a little by the gloves. For a moment, she wondered whether Daisy could have heard what she'd said to Sam.

Then Daisy slid the packet out of the box, holding it in her hand. Waiting. Eliza smiled to her, gesturing that she wanted the gauze and Daisy handed it over with a flourish, clearly pleased that she'd anticipated Eliza's needs correctly.

'Correction, Sam. She's showing an aptitude for surgery.' Eliza opened the packet then placed the clean piece of gauze over the cut and concealed the old piece in the torn wrappings. 'Can you keep the pressure up there please? We don't want it to start bleeding again.'

'You wanted some help?' A voice sounded from the doorway.

Eliza froze. 'Um. I wanted a nurse…' No, that sounded like a rejection. 'I meant that I just needed a little nursing help. I didn't intend for Sarah to bother you, Max.'

'But I'll do?'

Eliza couldn't think of a reply that sounded even vaguely professional. Then Daisy came to her rescue, sliding down from her chair and running over to Max to give him the box of gauze pads. He grinned, squatting down on his heels in front of her.

'Thank you, Daisy.' He tugged at one of the fingers of her gloves. 'You've been helping?'

Daisy got the gist of what he was saying and nodded. Max gave her a thumbs-up and she finger-spelled the word *Dad.*

Max nodded. 'Yeah, we're going to sort your dad out.' He got to his feet, taking Daisy's hand and leading her back to where Eliza was sitting.

'Dr Chilton says I have a young doctor on my hands.' Sam was looking even more apologetic now that both Eliza and Max were in attendance.

'Looks like it, doesn't it? Perhaps she'd like to do a little doctoring from the waiting room?'

Eliza breathed a sigh of relief. There was a trace of a smile hovering around Max's lips, and he didn't seem quite so stiff as he'd been on Friday evening. Perhaps he was taking this as an unfortunate coincidence, which was exactly what it was.

'Yes, thanks, Max.' She grabbed Daisy's hand and Sam reached inside his jacket.

'Take my phone. Daisy knows where the cartoons are.'

'Great. Thanks, Sam.' Eliza took the phone, leading Daisy out into the waiting room and then closing the door behind her. Daisy slipped her hand from Eliza's and emphatically opened the door again.

'That's okay...' Max turned the wheelchair so that Daisy couldn't see the cut on the left side of Sam's brow from the doorway. Eliza led Daisy over to the Christmas frieze that Max had helped her fix to the wall—that seemed like a hundred years ago now—and helped Daisy climb up onto a chair to touch Santa's sleigh.

That was only going to keep her occupied for so long. Daisy examined the frieze and then slid back down from her perch and went to sit outside the treatment room. Eliza gently turned her chair around so that her father was out of her line of view, and sat down next to Daisy, holding the phone out in front of her.

That worked. Daisy took the phone, swiping through several pages of icons. There was a whole list of cartoons for her to choose from, and she scrolled through it until she found the one she wanted. Two minutes later, she was engrossed in the small screen, happy to leave Sam in Max's care.

'How did you fall, Sam?' Max was talking to him as he checked him over for any signs of concussion.

'I was in the kitchen and I… I just closed my eyes for a moment. Fell off the stool I was sitting on and hit my head on the way down. Daisy was in the other room, watching TV, so she didn't know what had happened, thank goodness. I picked myself up and cleaned up a bit…'

'Okay. Did you lose consciousness?'

'I fell asleep.'

There was a pause and then Max spoke. 'Pretty tired, eh?'

'I haven't had a good night's sleep since Daisy first went into hospital. It's…just the way it is.'

'Yeah, I can understand that… Watch my finger.'

Eliza wondered whether she should be listening. But both Sam and Max knew that the door was open and she was sitting outside. Putting her fingers in her ears and la-la-ing would be a bit over the top.

'I know that you need to take care of your wife and child, Sam. But in order to do that, you need to take care of yourself.'

'Daisy and Iona are everything to me…' Sam's voice broke, and Eliza put her arm around Daisy, who looked up at her, unaware of what was going on. Eliza leaned over, staring at the cartoon on the small screen, and Daisy took the hint and followed suit.

'I've seen firsthand what happens when a family has to face something like this. Everyone's tired. Silence seems like a better option than saying something…' Max paused, seeming to be in the grip of an unknown memory. 'I know you want to be there for Iona and Daisy, and you have been. But Daisy's out of danger now, and we're doing all we can to help her towards a future where she can thrive. You need to keep yourself in good shape and be there for that future.'

What did he mean? Eliza was straining to hear every word now. Max seemed so certain, so committed to what he was saying. Was *this* what lay behind his refusal to hope for the best?

'I want you to take a couple of days off work. I know you've probably taken a lot of time off recently, but I think it's important and I can write a note for your employer…'

'That's okay. They've told me to take whatever time I need.'

'Then take it. Try and get some sleep, and go and do something for yourself. Make sure you have something to give because… I'm no expert, but you seem to be close to running on empty at the moment.'

'Yeah, I am… I'll think about what you've said.'

'Thanks.' A quiet clatter of instruments sounded. Max would be preparing to stitch the wound about now. 'I'm going to numb the area before I put the stitches in. Sharp prick.'

'No sharper than the advice?' Sam had obviously retained his sense of humour, and that had to be a positive sign.

Max laughed. 'No. No sharper than that.'

Max had stitched the cut on Sam's forehead, and he seemed none the worse for his fall. Eliza watched as Daisy ran into the treatment room, inspecting the dressing that Max had put over Sam's cut. She solemnly tugged at Max's arm, giving him a hug when he bent down to see what she wanted.

'Thanks, Max.' When he joined her in the waiting room, Eliza had just finished speaking to Iona. 'I got through to Iona and she'll be here in an hour to pick Sam and Daisy up. I'm working here this afternoon and they can make themselves comfortable in the waiting room.'

He nodded. 'You've had lunch?'

'Sarah's offered to go down to the cafeteria and get us something. I expect that Daisy's hungry.'

'Good.' Max looked at his watch. 'Gotta go…'

Max did what he always did. Once he'd dealt with whatever was on hand, he moved on to the next thing. No looking back, no turning to throw a smile.

Why should he, just because Eliza wanted him to? Max was… Max. She was supposed to be the people person of the two of them, but Max had found his way to the underlying reason for Sam's injury very quickly. Maybe she should think about that the next time he turned and walked away.

* * *

The end of another long day. Saturday and Sunday had been never ending, and Monday… Eliza seemed to have thawed a little, and Max had been making an effort, too. It would take work—quite a bit of work on Max's part—but they could file the kiss under never again and forget about it.

Or…maybe not. At six o'clock, Max returned to the ENT department from the operating theatre and found Eliza sitting at the empty reception desk.

'Max. I was hoping to catch you.'

Something caught in his chest, and he felt his heart begin to beat faster. The tension in Eliza's tone told him that whatever came next wasn't going to be easy.

'Can it wait?' He tried not to meet her gaze.

'Yes, I suppose so. Can we talk tomorrow?'

Tomorrow was no good, either. Max didn't want to talk; he'd said all he knew how to say. Any more was just going to make things worse.

Then he looked at her. He should have done that sooner, instead of seeing only his own preoccupations. Eliza was clearly nervous, but he was starting to recognise that determined look in her eyes. And she was wearing her coat, buttoned up, in the warmth of the hospital. That was a clear message that she didn't want to talk here, but somewhere away from the hospital. Away from his office, which was a considerable relief. He'd almost choked on the sweet memories that had come crowding in on him when he'd arrived at work this morning.

'Perhaps now would be better. Shall we go for coffee somewhere? Or a glass of wine perhaps?' He heard the tenderness he felt for her mirrored in his voice.

Eliza nodded, getting to her feet. 'I'd like that. I'll see you downstairs by the main doors?'

'Give me ten minutes.'

Max got changed and swept the files he needed to look at for tomorrow into his bag, making it down to the main entrance of the hospital in five. For a moment he wondered whether Eliza had thought better of meeting with him, and then he saw her outside, talking to the Kyle Woodgate fans. She was animated and smiling, and they clustered together on the other side of the barrier, showing her their placards and receiving Eliza's obvious approval.

She was so sweet. So nice. Max didn't often use those words to compliment people. He usually favoured *determined* or *effective*. But Eliza gave sweet and nice a determined and effective edge. She'd obviously had a tough time of it when she was a kid, and she'd ended up with a waste-of-space partner who'd taken advantage of her good nature. Hanging on to the warmth and light that she dispensed so freely took grit.

She saw him on the other side of the glass and waved, quickly opening her bag and passing something over to an older woman who was standing with the girls. There was a little flurry of activity as the woman handed out the contents of the bag that Eliza had given her. When Max hurried outside, the girls cracked their glow sticks and waved them at him, instead of the usual gloves-and-hats salute.

'You just couldn't resist, could you?' Max waved back at the girls as Eliza walked towards him.

'Everybody likes glow sticks.' She gave him an impish grin that made Max's heart lurch. 'That's Lily's mum with them. The parents have got themselves organised into a rota.'

A group of nurses had followed him outside, and the girls waved their glow sticks in their direction. Lily's mum leaned towards her daughter, and Lily called to the nurses.

'Thank you for looking after Kyle…and everyone else!'

The nurses waved back and went on their way, smiling.

'Are we done here? Where would you like to go?' Max asked.

Eliza shrugged. 'Somewhere quiet? Where we can talk.'

That was a tall order this close to Christmas. Max thought for a moment. 'How about a glass of drinkable red?'

He was hungry and he imagined that Eliza was, too, but a meal meant that she'd be obliged to either stay and finish her food or walk out on him if the conversation she had in mind didn't go well. A glass of wine was more companionable than coffee and it could easily be cut short at any time. Max wondered if he was overthinking this, but Eliza smiled.

'Yes. That would be nice.'

They turned out of the hospital grounds, and she followed him to the pizza restaurant. Giorgia was busy with another customer, but his usual table was free and she waved them towards it. By the time they'd taken their coats off, she'd hurried across to them.

'Just a couple of glasses of wine please, Giorgia.' Max handed over a note from his wallet to add to his tab.

'Coming right up. House red and some nibbles?' Giorgia looked questioningly at Eliza.

'Thanks. That would be great.'

Eliza's worried air had been chased away by the glow

sticks, but now that they were alone it had returned. Max let the silence between them roll for a while and then decided he needed to help Eliza along a little.

'You wanted to talk. I'm listening.'

'I just wanted to say...' Eliza seemed to be searching for the words. 'Dr Beckwith said that one of his reasons for putting us together to work on Daisy's case was that we have different approaches to our patients.'

Max nodded. 'Yes, he mentioned that to me, too.' Maybe Eliza had decided that they were *too* different. He wouldn't blame her, and if she wanted to go to Dr Beckwith and tell him so, Max wouldn't try to talk her out of it. Even if an unexpected feeling of dismay had settled around his heart.

He leaned back as Giorgia arrived with the drinks and a plate of mixed appetisers, fresh out of the oven. Max thanked her and took a sip of his wine, which did nothing to brighten his mood.

'We do have different approaches and...' Eliza hesitated, and Max braced himself for the rejection. 'Dr Beckwith was right when he said that we could learn from each other. I really want to make this work, not just for Daisy but for myself.'

Max stared at her, and then realised that Eliza was waiting for him to say something. 'I really want to make it work, too.'

She smiled suddenly. 'That's great. We're agreed?'

'Yes. Agreed.' Right now, this was all that Max needed to know. Working through their differences would be personally challenging, and might ultimately be a foolish decision. But he knew now that he wanted a second chance.

'There's something else…' Eliza wasn't done with him yet.

'I'm still listening.'

'I think… We both do our jobs well and in the best way we know how. There's no reason for either of us to take those differences in approach personally.'

Max was confused now. There were times when Eliza could be a little too tactful. 'You mean…? Are you going to give me a list?'

She shot him a dismissive look. 'No. My ex made me well aware of how bruising that kind of thing can be.'

Max had no right to be angry, when he was the one responsible for the hurt that Eliza was feeling now. He slipped his hand under the table before Eliza could see his fingers clench into a fist.

'You're not just talking about the way we do our jobs, are you? Eliza, I know I can be abrupt at times. That's my own failure, not yours or anyone else's.'

She nodded. Took a sip of her wine. 'I know that I tend to cover everything up with a smile. We're not aiming those things at each other. We're just doing what we do.'

'So we'll call a truce?'

Eliza smiled. 'Yes. Accept that we're different and stop fighting back.'

The idea was both comforting and a little disappointing. It gave them a way forward, but it shut down the possibility that they'd ever take on the challenge of resolving their differences and becoming more than friends.

That was okay. It was something, and that was preferable to nothing. Max raised his glass.

'I'll drink to that. Just as long as you don't run away

with the idea that I'm the only one capable of a bit of straight talking. You're not so bad at that yourself.'

She laughed, touching her own glass against his. 'Only when I'm driven into a corner.'

'I had the distinct impression that you drove *me* into a corner this evening.' Max took a sip of his wine to seal their agreement, and Eliza did the same. 'But we did need to talk.'

'Yes, we did. And while we're on the subject of stepping on each other's territory…' Eliza's grey eyes flashed with humour. 'What's this I hear about buying Sarah coffee? She was very impressed, by the way.'

'It occurred to me—you said that you were tired of it being your job to fix everything.'

Eliza shot him a querying look. 'You *were* listening.'

He'd heard every word and thought about each one of them over the weekend. 'I may not always act on what I hear, but no one's ever told me I don't listen. I've always considered that it's my job to do big things. Being the best surgeon I could be. Making a name for myself.'

'And you've succeeded. That's something to be proud of, isn't it?'

He'd felt that it was all he had, when Mikey had died and his family had started to disintegrate. 'I want more, though. You're so good at the little things, a smile or a cup of coffee, and they mean a lot to the people around you. I was thinking to myself that Sarah looked tired and reckoned I'd try it out.'

Eliza chuckled. 'And how did that go?'

'Well, I think. This isn't a complete turnaround, just a few minor adjustments.'

'Yes, I get that, Max. I wasn't planning on stopping

wanting to fix things, if I can. I hope you didn't tell Sarah that she has terrible taste in coffee, though.'

She never failed to make Max want to smile. Maybe he should do that a little more often. 'No. I save those observations for you.'

'Very wise. I know you don't really mean it.'

'I do mean it. That stuff you drink *is* like dishwater.'

'Max! Just for that you can order me a large cup of dishwater when I finish my wine. And maybe some more snacks. These look really nice and I'm not sure one plate's going to be enough…'

The world had started turning again. They could use their differences to hurt, or they could use them to heal. However improbably, he and Eliza might be very good at being friends.

They'd worked their way through a glass of wine and a cup of coffee each, along with two shared plates of mixed appetisers. It was still early, but Eliza didn't feel she needed to hang on to the time they had together because tomorrow was more firmly fixed on the horizon now.

Not the tomorrow that her reckless thoughts had imagined. They'd both failed to mention the kiss, and Eliza was sure that Max had been as careful in that regard as she had. It was one thing that she wouldn't have minded revisiting, but she'd resigned herself to the idea that it shouldn't happen again. Even though he never talked about it, Max was clearly working through some baggage of his own. They could turn their backs on the past and their differences and be friends, but if they took the step of becoming lovers… That would unleash more than Eliza reckoned either of them could handle.

'Do you feel like some fresh air? We could walk through the grounds of the museum to the next bus stop.' Max had pulled on his coat, smiling and stepping out onto the pavement, when Eliza reached the door of the restaurant first and opened it for him.

'Yes. That would be nice.'

The parklands attached to the museum backed onto the hospital, and the path that ran behind the museum was a brightly lit and well-used shortcut. Max slowed a little, and when he offered Eliza his arm she took it.

'I'd like to say one more thing. It's been on my mind.'

'Yes?' Clearly, it wasn't anything bad, or Max wouldn't be walking so close.

'What happened on Friday… That wasn't a mistake. We were wrong to call it that.'

This was dangerous territory. But instead of stepping away from him, Eliza found herself instinctively clinging more tightly to Max's arm. He was her safe place.

He put his gloved hand over hers. 'The only thing I regret about it was that it made things uncomfortable between us. But we were right to stop. It would have made things far too complicated.'

Complicated. Good word. Accurate in this context. 'Yes, it would have been complicated for me.'

'For me, too…' He frowned, letting out a sigh.

'And you don't want to talk about it.' Eliza took a not-so-wild guess.

'No. Not right now. Rain check?'

They'd slowed almost to a halt, and Eliza stopped, turning to face him. Stripping off her glove, she pressed her fingers to her lips then reached up, transferring the kiss to his cheek. 'Is that a better ending?'

'Much better.' Max's eyes were dark in the lamplight as he caught her hand, pressing her fingers to his lips. The gesture was formal, respectful and quite electric. And it lasted five whole seconds longer than it should, in a clear signal that the kiss on Friday evening *had* meant something to him.

She slid her hand back into the crook of his elbow and they started to walk again. So close in the darkness, as if defining what they *weren't* going to do, had made everything else okay. They dawdled their way to the bus stop, and Max took his phone from his pocket, opening the bus app.

'Yours is in five minutes. Mine's six.'

'Isn't the one that's heading towards us now your bus?' Eliza nudged him and he looked up.

'Nah. The one in six minutes is mine.' He grinned at her, propelling her towards the bus shelter, out of the wind.

Max's bus shot past them, and she stood a little closer to him for warmth. Maybe this was his impeccable manners at work, telling him that you didn't leave someone alone at a bus stop. Or maybe Max was finally getting his head around the idea that a goodbye was always better than just turning to walk away…

CHAPTER NINE

ELIZA NOTICED THAT Sam was looking more rested when he arrived with Iona and Daisy on Wednesday afternoon. Max didn't say anything about their conversation on Monday, but his enquiring look when he shook Sam's hand, and the nod he received in response, was enough.

'First, the good news.' When everyone was settled in the comfortable seating in the patient conference room, Max lost no time in getting started. 'You'll be glad to hear that there isn't any bad news.'

Iona nudged Sam, and both of them relaxed visibly. Max hadn't followed up with an *as far as I know* and Eliza wondered whether this sudden burst of optimism was part of his new life plan, or just a slip of the tongue.

'We've had the reports in from different people who've seen Daisy, and the results of all her tests.' Max laid his hand on the bulging file that was on the empty seat next to him. 'She passes all of the criteria for a cochlear implant, she has no inner ear abnormalities and her cochlear nerve is intact. In addition to that, several of the therapists have mentioned that she has excellent family support, and that they expect her to do well. So I'm happy to tell you that we'll be offering Daisy that option.'

Iona's hand strayed to Sam's. 'That's really great. Thank you.'

'I'm afraid we can't relax yet, though. The risk of ossification in Daisy's cochlear means that we need a decision from you about how you want to proceed as soon as possible. I know that the department's family liaison officer has spent some time with you going through all of the options, and Eliza and I will be happy to answer any questions you have.'

'We know what we want to do,' Iona spoke. 'Daisy would like to tell you, if that's all right?'

'Splendid.' Max flashed his most irresistible smile at Daisy, taking his file from the seat next to him and beckoning for her to come and sit there.

Daisy took a piece of folded paper from the mini-handbag that was strung across her chest. Clearly, Iona had thought ahead and was making sure that there would be no misunderstandings. Max was maintaining an air of intense interest, although he must be able to see that the paper contained the signs that Daisy wanted to remember for this important conversation. Daisy looked around the group and smiled suddenly.

That was just what everyone wanted to see. Daisy had been very ill, and was now isolated by sudden deafness, and yet she felt in charge of what was happening to her. Max could rationalise that all he wanted—an eight-year-old was capable of understanding the basics of how a cochlear implant would work, and Daisy's own commitment would help her to adapt to one. But there was something in his demeanour that gave Eliza the distinct impression that he was just enjoying the moment for what it was.

Maybe he *was* allowing himself to connect with small pleasures a little more.

Daisy consulted her aide memoir and started to sign. 'Want sign language.'

'You want to sign?' Max nudged Daisy's arm, signing the words back to her. Then he added an 'okay', and Daisy nodded.

'Want cochlear implant.'

'Okay,' Max replied to Daisy and then smiled up at Sam and Iona. 'And this is your decision, too?'

Sam replied for both of them. 'Yes, it is. We were very impressed by your point that this doesn't have to be an either/or situation. The social worker who came to see us last week put us in touch with someone who runs a club for deaf kids and we went along there at the weekend. It was a good evening, wasn't it, Iona? None of the kids waited to be told. They came up to Daisy and said hello, and made it clear that they wanted to play with her. She came back home with a few new signs for me to learn.'

Iona nodded. 'It was great. We got a chance to speak with several of the parents, some of them deaf themselves and some hearing. We've always taught Daisy to be proud of herself and who she is, and this community made her feel at home and that she should still be proud of herself.'

'Many of the people there had cochlear implants but some didn't, and everyone signed,' Sam added. 'We learned a lot—and this is something we want for Daisy and for ourselves.'

Max leaned back in his seat. 'I think we have a decision, then.' He plucked at the corner of Daisy's piece of paper, and she handed it over to him, looking over his shoulder as he signed it then wrote his own name in capital letters underneath. He gave her his pen, and Daisy wrote her name under his.

He wasn't just humouring her—keeping her quiet so the adults could talk. Eliza had noticed that Max's interactions with Daisy were all on the basis that he worked for *her.* The agreement he'd just made with Daisy was just as binding to him as the forms that they'd be asking Sam and Iona to sign later, and Eliza felt a rush of warmth building in her chest.

It was too bad. Eliza knew all about going for the wrong kind of guy, and now that she'd found the right kind of guy, she didn't know how to deal with him. She'd locked her own needs away for so long, beneath a veneer of what everyone else expected to hear, that they were like strangers who couldn't be trusted.

Now wasn't the time to think about that. Max was steadily going through all of the things that Sam and Iona needed to know before they signed the consent forms, and Iona had a question for him.

'What about Daisy's hair?'

'Unfortunately, I'll need to shave a small area just behind each of her ears for the surgery. That should grow back, though. I think you're asking about how the magnets which hold the receivers in place will work with Daisy's textured hair, though?' Iona nodded, and Max took a leaflet from his file, handing it to her.

'Both Paulette and her daughter have textured hair and when her daughter was fitted with a cochlear implant, Paulette couldn't get any answers to the question you're asking now. So she set up a chat group which has evolved into a website and advice line. The ENT department here has worked with her on many occasions and Paulette's someone who can answer any questions you have from personal experience.'

'Thanks.' Iona opened the trifold leaflet, glancing at its contents. 'That's really useful.'

'Perhaps you could read that later, because I need to talk to you now about the risks of the surgical procedure we're going to be performing. Some of these risks are ones which are inherent in any surgical procedure, and the first thing that you should know is that all we do here is designed to reduce risk as much as possible.'

Max glanced at Eliza and she nodded in agreement. Max was absolutely correct, but hearing him say it with such obvious commitment was making her feel slightly disoriented.

Then Daisy sneezed.

Max looked round in time to see her wiping her nose with her hand and Iona frowned, taking a tissue from her bag and waving it at her daughter.

'Does Daisy have a cold, Iona?' The sneeze seemed to have stopped Max in his tracks, and Eliza asked the question.

'No, I don't think so. She was fine this morning…' Iona fell silent suddenly, her hand over her mouth.

'It's okay, there's nothing for you to worry about. It's very rare for bacterial meningitis to recur and Daisy doesn't have any of the risk factors associated with that. But just to be sure, we'll check her over thoroughly.' Meningitis was often mistaken for a cold or flu in its early stages, and Iona clearly needed some reassurance.

'Okay. Thanks.' Sam nodded, putting his hand protectively over Iona's.

They were trying so hard. But underneath Sam's and

Iona's delight over Daisy's recovery and the way that she was tackling her deafness, there was a great deal of fear. They were already tired and stressed, and they knew that there was more ahead of them.

'Eliza's right.' Max's tone was direct and authoritative. 'Our one and only concern is that if Daisy has a cold, that might affect our decision over a date for her surgery.'

'Sam. You shouldn't have brought her here on Monday,' Iona murmured and Sam took his hand from hers.

'What was I supposed to do? You were at work and had your phone switched off.'

'We agreed to take equal turns looking after Daisy. You switch your phone off when you're at work and in a meeting.'

'What about your sister's family? I distinctly heard Maisie coughing when they came up for the day,' Sam shot back.

When Iona turned away from Sam, shaking her head, she must have seen the worry on Max's face. 'Sorry. It's nothing. We're both a little jumpy.'

It wasn't nothing. Daisy couldn't hear the argument, but she knew what was going on and had shifted in her seat, turning her back on her parents. Eliza wondered how many more of these quickly patched-up altercations she'd witnessed.

Sam got to his feet, lifting Daisy out of her chair and taking her on his lap, hugging her tightly, and Iona leaned over to kiss her. The silence in the room blocked out everything that really needed to be said. All of the stress that Sam and Iona were trying so hard to hide.

Then Max spoke. Eliza noticed that a pulse was beating at the side of his brow. 'Let's take a break, shall we?

We should take a look at Daisy and see whether she really does have a cold.' He shot Eliza a questioning look.

Good idea. Find out what was going on with everyone. 'I'll take Daisy to my office and check her over. Maybe you can rustle up some tea, Max?'

His raised eyebrow told her that he didn't think that tea—or coffee—was going to be enough in this instance, and Eliza was inclined to agree with him. But maybe separating everyone, breaking the silence that was hanging over them, would help.

Sam nodded and lifted Daisy from his lap. Eliza picked up Daisy's tablet and beckoned to her, taking her hand and leading her out of the room.

She had to admit to a quiver of relief at having escaped the more difficult issues that she'd left Max to deal with. But maybe some of his straight talking was exactly what was needed.

Sam and Iona were trying so hard, but they were as much in need of care as their daughter. It was up to Max to convince them of that.

There was a lot he might say to them, but he wanted to hear what they had to say. He fetched the tea and Sam and Iona accepted it gratefully, drinking in silence. Max was going to have to get the ball rolling.

'In many ways, making sure that you have the care you need is just as much a part of my role as looking after Daisy.'

Silence. Sam looked at Iona but she kept her gaze on the table in front of them.

'I'm a very long way from having all the answers. Help

me out here.' The one thing he probably should have said to his parents, but never felt able to. *Help me out.*

'What you said on Monday…' Sam was the first to say something. 'It made a lot of sense to me and when I told Iona… She's been telling me that I need to take a step back for some time.'

'That's what Sam's been telling me.' Iona twisted her mouth, finally looking at her husband.

'How do you feel about taking an evening off sometime, going out somewhere together? Do you have someone that you trust who'll look after Daisy?'

'There's Sam's sister. Adele's really good with Daisy, and she's learning to sign as well. I don't want to take too much of an advantage of her good nature, though… And I'm not sure we could *both* just leave her…' Iona looked questioningly at Sam.

'Yeah. Remember when she was a baby, and we went out together for a meal for the first time. Adele was babysitting and she was splitting her sides when we got back.'

Iona smiled. 'Yes, half an hour early, after having eaten practically nothing. *And* we'd been sitting in the car outside the house for half an hour, watching for lights going on and off.'

'It got better,' Sam remarked. 'And we've had to leave Daisy with the doctors and nurses here at times.'

Iona nodded. 'That was tough. But you're all so good with her. And Daisy loves coming to see you and Eliza. You've both done so much to bring her out of herself and boost her confidence.'

There were times when a well-meant piece of praise could be very confronting. Max didn't want to think about how good Eliza was with children, although that was indisputable. The idea that they might be good *together.* That was in the too-much-to-bear category and needed to be left well alone.

'Look, I'm not the one to help you with all this. But I can refer you on to one of the counsellors here, and I think they will be able to help. Will you consider that? It's not a sign of failure. It's a sign that you want to do everything to help Daisy by helping yourselves.'

Do-as-I-say was a great deal easier than do-as-I-do at the moment. Max knew all about the consequences of smothered feelings, though, and that lent some authority to what he was saying.

'I'd like to give it a go. What do you reckon?' Sam came to a decision.

Iona nodded. 'Yes. I think we should, Sam. Thanks for giving us a push in the right direction, Max.'

'I'll get in touch with them, and they'll be emailing you later today. And getting back to Daisy, I think the thing to do is wait a day, and I'll call you tomorrow. If she's well then we can move forward and set a date for her surgery, and if she does have a cold then we'll just wait until she's better.'

'Does this mean she may not be able to have the surgery at all? Because of the...ossification thing?' Sam asked.

'We can get a very good picture of the extent of ossification of her cochlear with a high-resolution CT scan. So far the levels are too low to impact implantation. We've made very good progress up till now, which gives us some time to spare, although of course I'll be monitoring the situation very carefully.'

'So...we have every reason to hope, then?' Maybe Iona

would be better off asking Eliza that. But looking at all of the facts, Max felt qualified to hazard an opinion.

'Yes. We do.'

They found Daisy and Eliza playing a computer game in Eliza's office. She pronounced Daisy fit and well, apart from some very minor swelling of the nasal mucosa, which might indicate a developing cold, but might resolve of its own accord. An arrangement was made for a video consultation at eight in the morning tomorrow, and Sam and Iona said their goodbyes.

'Good talk, I see.' Eliza closed the door, motioning him towards one of the visitors' chairs.

'You were listening at the door?'

'No. My knight in shining armour was too busy being vanquished by Daisy's dragon, I didn't have time to listen at doors.'

'You got beaten?'

'Of course I did. Never trust an eight-year-old with a dragon, however easy a game appears when they show it to you in demonstration mode. I'm assuming that you had a much better time of things. Iona had the look of a woman who sees a light at the end of a tunnel.'

Eliza had an almost uncanny ability to assess the mood of those around her. Maybe her watchful childhood had something to do with that, but she was genuinely interested in people.

'I think that this new uncertainty was the last straw. If we can just reassure them, get them through the next few days…'

Eliza nodded.

'I'm referring them on for an emergency session with

one of our counsellors. They were talking about taking some time out and going out for a meal together. That's not going to be easy for them.'

'No, probably not. It's a good idea, though.'

'We'll keep a close eye on Daisy. I've arranged a video call for tomorrow morning. We'll find a way.'

Eliza pursed her lips thoughtfully. There was something she wasn't saying.

Suddenly, he had no patience with it. No patience with himself.

'Come on, then. Out with it.'

She shrugged. Perhaps Eliza wasn't going to come and save him this time.

'I think…' She paused, obviously choosing her words carefully. 'You know all about what they're going through.'

'I can imagine…'

Eliza dismissed him with a wave of her hand. 'You're *not* imagining. You have an investment in all of this and I can't work out what it is.'

It would be so easy to cite clinical excellence, best outcomes… Max *was* invested in those things, but that wasn't what Eliza was asking. A straight question deserved a straight answer, and the one he wanted to give was tugging at him mercilessly.

'I have…had…a little brother.' The change in tense wasn't lost on Eliza, and he saw grey clouds forming in her eyes. This was what he'd been running from, the shock and the sympathy. The awkwardness that seemed to mock the darkness he felt inside.

'What was his name?'

No one ever asked that, and Max hadn't spoken his

brother's name out loud in years. There was something comforting in Eliza's assumption that death wasn't the most important thing about Mikey.

'Michael Alesandro Russo. We all called him Mikey. He was born when I was twelve, and I suppose that could have gone two ways. I might have just ignored him as being far too young to take any interest in. But Mikey didn't take too well to being ignored. As soon as he could walk, he'd try to follow me out of the house to meet my friends or go to baseball practise. In the end, I gave in and used to take him with me, riding on my shoulders. He loved baseball, and whenever I started to run I'd hear him hollering from the touchlines.'

'He sounds great. I wouldn't have been able to resist him.' Eliza was smiling and Max realised that he was, too. It had been a long time since he'd thought about Mikey and smiled.

'You and the rest of the girls at my school. He had an eye for cheerleaders, the ones that none of us dared approach, and used to wander up to them all big brown eyes and baby curls. Before we knew it they were bringing him back and introducing themselves. I think most of my girlfriends secretly liked Mikey more than they liked me.'

'Don't put yourself down. There's something very attractive about a guy who's kind to kids.'

Max shrugged. 'I'd noticed that he used to put his hand on his chest sometimes, when he was talking. All of my friends reckoned that was just Mikey's signature move, but I told my mom she should get it checked out.'

'That's sensible,' Eliza murmured. 'Was it anything serious?'

'The hospital were very thorough, and told us that what

Mikey was feeling were ectopic heartbeats and that they were harmless…'

Eliza nodded. Max didn't need to explain to her that ectopic beats usually *were* harmless and that regular monitoring was all that was needed.

'I came back home after my first term at medical school, and after Christmas Mikey became unwell. He was listless, lost his appetite. Started holding his chest all the time. Mom and I took him to our family doctor, and he reckoned that he had an upper respiratory infection, and that he was just noticing the ectopic beats a little more. He was probably making an extra fuss over my returning to college, and it would be best to just reassure him that I'd be seeing him again soon for the Easter holidays…'

Max felt the familiar lump rise in his chest. Heard his own voice break.

'So, naturally, you followed his advice and started the new term.' Eliza made that sound as if it was the obvious thing for Max to have done. One small drop of the guilt he carried evaporated.

'Yeah. Two weeks later, I got a call from my dad. Mikey was in a critical care ward. What he'd been feeling wasn't the ectopic beats. It was a cardiac infection. The antibiotics he'd been given were enough to suppress it for a while, but it had flared up again when he stopped taking them. I got into the car and just drove, but I was too late. Mikey was gone by the time I got back to New York. My dad said he'd been crying for me before they put him on life support. I guess he thought that might be some comfort…'

The silence in the room was somehow comforting.

Everyone who'd known what had happened had tried to find something to say, and Max hadn't been able to hear any of it. Every time his parents looked at him they saw Mikey, and their grief seemed to fill the house, pushing him away.

Finally, Eliza spoke. 'I'm so sorry, Max. You know, don't you, that Daisy's going to be okay.' Her audacity in making that promise made Max smile.

'Yes, I do. But…'

'But you've seen your own family fall apart. You can't even go back for Christmas.'

'Christmas is always tough for them, and going away somewhere that doesn't hold any memories of Mikey is my mom and dad's solution to it. They don't want me there.' Max shrugged. Trying to make out that didn't hurt was probably more for his benefit than Eliza's. 'When I saw Sam and Iona starting to buckle under the pressure, it just… I guess it pushed a few buttons.'

'That doesn't surprise me. You might not want to hear this, but I think you've done as much as you can for them. You've understood what they need, and acted in a very compassionate and sensitive way to meet those needs.'

'Why wouldn't I want to hear that?'

She saw through him so easily. 'Don't be smart with me, Max. It's not easy for you to get close to people, and I see why now.'

'You mean us?' There was no point in waiting for Eliza's answer; he knew she did. 'My family had always been there for me, and then suddenly they weren't. Friendship suddenly started to look like a much more permanent option.'

She nodded. 'And it still does?'

'Yeah. It still does.'

Eliza thought for a moment. Max almost wanted her to challenge him but this time she didn't.

'I so wish I could help you change what happened to Mikey, but we both know that's not possible. But maybe I can learn something. I automatically try to defuse a situation, and that often works. It's harder for me to challenge people the way you did Sam and Iona, but sometimes that's what they need.'

So many people had asked what they could do, and some had suggested what Max might do. No one had considered shouldering a process of learning and change for themselves. It was too little and too late to make any difference for Mikey, but somehow it felt that Max had just taken a little piece of his brother back.

'You challenge me.' This was the first time he'd sat down and told anyone the full story, beginning to end. 'I was mistaken when I thought that was a fairy sitting on your shoulder. It's a dragon.'

That made her laugh. 'Do you mind?'

'No. It's a good thing. Maybe you should get a little more used to it.'

Eliza thought for a moment. 'I might need you to give me a few challenging lessons.'

'Something like… We're both due in theatre in half an hour?'

'What?' She sprang to her feet, turning to look at the clock. 'No, it's forty minutes, Max. There's plenty of time…'

CHAPTER TEN

WHEN ELIZA HAD said *challenging lessons* it was intended as a joke. It appeared that Max was taking it seriously.

'How do you feel about baseball?'

Eliza shrugged. 'Baseball? I'm neither for nor against it.'

This morning's video call with Sam and Iona had proved both encouraging and disappointing. Encouraging because the counsellor had offered them an early appointment and in the meantime they'd arranged to go for coffee together, while Sam's sister looked after Daisy. Disappointing because it seemed that Daisy still had a runny nose, and she was saying her throat hurt. After a busy day at work, Eliza was wondering whether she should go home on time tonight and try to get some sleep.

She saw Max's lip curl. He could cope with some kind of opinion either way, but apathy always seemed to confuse him slightly. 'You've never seen a game on TV?'

'No.'

'You didn't play softball at university?'

'Yes, in the summer.'

'You'd like baseball, then. I help coach a kids' team and they're playing tonight. It's a great way to let off a bit of steam.'

'Just watching?'

'No, you jump to your feet and you cheer for all you're worth. They really like that. Or you can join in if you like, as long as you make sure you don't run any faster than they can. It's at a sports centre on the edge of town. We have two teams of ten-to-thirteen year olds, and assorted parents. I could pick you up if you like, save taking two cars.'

Not a date, then. Of course not; they'd already fallen at the first hurdle along the road to intimacy, and now that they were talking to each other again, Eliza guessed that Max wasn't going to risk a replay any more than she was. Two colleagues letting off a bit of steam sounded well within their boundaries, and the thought of screaming at the top of her voice was suddenly very appealing.

'Sounds great. What time?'

'I'll pick you up at seven.'

'Thanks. What do I wear?'

He shrugged. 'Whatever you normally wear in the evenings.'

Something told Eliza that sheepskin slippers and a fluffy blanket weren't going to be de rigueur for a kids' baseball match. Jeans and trainers were going to have to do.

She'd added a warm jacket and scarf to her ensemble, and was waiting behind the curtains in the sitting room, trying to see outside without being seen herself, when Max arrived at seven on the dot. He was wearing a baseball jacket and cap, and his stride seemed longer and more fluid, as if he'd shaken off the confines of the hospital already.

'Do you play?' Eliza relaxed back into the passenger

seat of his car, not bothering to notice exactly where they were going. One thing she knew for sure was that she'd have a lift back home tonight.

'I played in a varsity league, but I had to give that up when I went on to a surgical rotation. The club organises regular games for adults during the summer, and I always try to make those.'

'You don't worry about injury?'

'No, I do more watching than playing these days. *Should* I worry about injury?'

'You worry about girls standing in the cold without their hats.'

He laughed. 'I believe in being prepared for the job. I wouldn't field without wearing a glove. If your chosen pastime is waiting around in the cold for a glimpse of your idol, then you come prepared with warm clothes. And a placard of course, although I dare say you know a bit more about the logistics of that than I do.'

'That was a long time ago. And I'm still not telling you who it was.'

Max chuckled. 'I can wait. It's only going to take one tiny slip of the tongue…'

The indoor baseball pitch was in a sprawling facility on the edge of York. Inside, there was a large synthetic turfed area, with a bank of seats to one side. Max waved to the group of parents and kids who were watching another two teams finish their game, and headed for the netted batting cages.

'Max. You made it this week.' A spry, white-haired man, who'd been watching an older boy pitching to one of the youngsters on the team, walked out of the batting cage to greet him.

'Yeah. This is a colleague, Eliza Chilton. Eliza, this is Greg Valdez, head coach. He and his wife came here from Boston thirty years ago, on a twelve-month sabbatical.'

'We decided to stick around for a while, and we're still here. Hey, Eliza.' Greg held out his hand, shaking Eliza's warmly. 'Are you a fan?'

'I'm looking forward to being one.'

'Good answer. We'll do our best with that.'

'How's Thomas doing?' Max nodded towards the young boy in the batting cage who was valiantly swinging his bat, despite never making contact with the ball.

'Still trying his best. He'll never make much of a player but he likes it here and he's not short on determination. You want to go and help him hit at least one pitch? Laura's here somewhere… Come and meet my wife, Eliza.'

Laura Valdez was in the middle of the group of waiting children, ticking off names from a list and checking that everyone had brought their kit with them.

'You came with Max?'

'We're colleagues. At the hospital.'

'Ah.' Laura turned as a loud cheer sounded from the batting cages. 'Oh, thank goodness. Thomas has hit one…'

Max was inside the cage, applauding the boy, who was jumping up and down, his arms flailing. Eliza watched as Max bent down, adjusting Thomas's stance and carefully guiding him through several swings with the bat, before stepping back to bowl a slow, underarm ball. Thomas hit the ball a second time and dropped his bat to execute another dance of joy.

Greg strolled back towards Max, handing him a bat and a helmet. Max shook his head and Greg ignored him, shepherding Thomas out of the nets to watch and fiddling with the pitching machine, before Max took up his position.

'Left shoulder, Max,' Laura murmured under her breath. Almost as if he'd heard her, Max stretched his arms above his head, loosening the muscles of his shoulders, and then resumed his position.

Laura nodded. 'Better.' She turned to Eliza. 'He always says that he's not here to play, but put a bat in his hand and he suddenly loses the ability to say no.'

An impossibly fast ball shot from the pitching machine and there was a sharp crack. The net plumed outwards as it stopped the ball, and Thomas shrieked with approval.

'Nice.' Laura turned to her, a thoughtful look on her face. 'I can't help thinking that this is when he gives us a glimpse of the *real* Max.'

Eliza couldn't help agreeing, but it was probably better just to smile and say nothing. The baseball part of it all was a little beyond her, but she hadn't missed the smooth, graceful flow of Max's body or the sheer power in his shoulders and arms.

Maybe distance made it permissible to wonder what his body might have done with hers, if they'd taken leave of their senses for long enough to find out. It was all in the past, and wasn't going to happen again, and perhaps that made it okay to watch as Max got ready for a second shot.

Pure poetry. Only poetry didn't make heat rise in quite the same way. The ball shot towards him and Max's movement was smoother and stronger than last time. Full of the freedom and joy that no one at the hospital ever saw in him. Eliza caught her breath.

A buzzer sounded and Laura huffed out a sigh. 'Just as he was getting into his swing. This is our hour now.'

The players on the pitch were picking up balls and equipment, and jogging towards the gap in the barrier. Laura called to her charges, telling them to wait, they'd be able to claim their territory for the next hour soon enough.

'I don't suppose… We're one short, and I can't put Greg in to even up the teams. He had a hip replacement three months ago. He's recovered very well, but his physiotherapist has told him not to bat for a while.'

'I imagine they're cautious about the twisting movement.'

'Yes, that's right. And Max…he can't help himself. He wouldn't be able to hit a ball that any of the kids could catch if he tried. Do you know how to play?'

'Not really. I used to play softball but…' If Thomas could do his best, despite not being able to play well, then so could she. 'I suppose I'm around the level of the average ten-year-old when it comes to hitting a ball.'

Laura smiled. 'That's the spirit. I'll put you in to bat last, so you can watch and get a feel for the rules.'

Greg was refereeing from a chair on the sidelines, and Max ranged up and down on the other side of the pitch, calling out instructions and encouragement. Twenty minutes later, Eliza wasn't so sure that she could match the average ten-year-old. These kids were good, and anything that they lacked in skill, they made up for with courage and teamwork.

'Ready?' Max had jogged over to one of the kitbags and selected a helmet and bat. He waited as she buckled the helmet under her chin, putting his hand on the top of it to check it was secure. 'This bat should be about the right weight for you. How does it feel?'

Eliza pursed her lips, not sure how to answer. 'How's it *meant* to feel?'

'It's all about balance…' He moved a little closer and for a moment Eliza wondered if he was about to coil his arms around her, adjusting her stance. Max had every excuse to do so, and Eliza would have every excuse to let him.

But Max took the bat from her, demonstrating a slow swing. 'Like this.'

'I'll keep that in mind.'

'Don't hit the ball too hard. Give them a chance to catch it.'

'You're assuming I'm going to hit it at all.'

He shot her a reproachful look. 'You'll hit it. Just keep your eye on the ball and relax your shoulders.'

Recipe for life. 'Okay.'

'Don't step out of the batter's box.'

Eliza nodded. 'That's about as much information as I can handle at the moment. I'll be back in thirty seconds.'

'And think positive…' He threw one last piece of advice after her as she walked onto the pitch.

The child who was bowling spun the ball at her with surprising force, and Eliza swung her bat, missing it completely.

'Not out. Stay where you are, Eliza,' Greg called. Apparently, the catcher, standing behind her, had missed the ball as well.

Breathe. Loosen your shoulders. Eliza imagined Max's smooth rhythm as the bowler spun the ball towards her. She felt the shock of an impact travel down the bat, and watched open-mouthed as the ball curved away.

'Run, Eliza!' She heard Max's voice. 'First base… Over there.'

Eliza dropped the bat and ran. She reached first base and stopped, unsure of whether she was supposed to continue or not.

'Keep going… Get a move on…' Max's voice rose above the general hubbub. Clearly, he'd forgotten the part about running like a ten-year-old and Eliza ran as fast as she could, making it to second base and then third.

'Yes! Go!'

She reached home base and saw Laura leading the cheer from the seats. Eliza picked up her bat, wondering how long this was going to go on for. The ball curved straight past her and this time the boy behind her caught it.

'Out,' Greg called and Eliza breathed a sigh of relief. She hadn't totally messed up, and now she could go and sit down again.

'What did you think?' Max waited until they were in the car and on their way home to ask.

'I had a great time. This was just what I needed. One whole hour when I didn't have the opportunity to think about anything to do with the hospital.' Everyone needed some time out, an opportunity to shout at the top of their voice and to run as fast as they could, and Eliza had done that this evening.

'They're good kids.' Max smiled.

'I had fun with the baseball, too. I could become a fan, with a bit of practice,' Eliza teased him. 'Laura said that I was welcome to come back any time I wanted.'

'You are. We can always do with more volunteers. I don't get down there every week, but I make it as often as I can.'

Max's approval of the idea was the only thing Eliza

needed. 'I'll make sure to give Laura a call after Christmas, then.'

They couldn't be lovers, but tonight had very firmly dragged them over the line that lay between colleagues and friends. New friends could turn into old friends over the years, and they might even get to the point where their one kiss was an innocuous secret, the kind of thing they might laughingly admit to at dinner parties as the most unexpected thing that either of them had ever done.

It was all a matter of choosing their futures. Eliza had become someone she didn't much like in too many relationships—needy and dependent on her partner's moods. How could she trust herself not to repeat the pattern with Max? And Max… He'd paid a terrible price for believing in the future, and hope wasn't part of his vocabulary any more.

They could both choose to accept that and be friends. If Eliza couldn't believe that her need for Max would ever entirely fade, then she was open to proving herself wrong.

Max stared at his image in the mirror over the bathroom sink, rubbing his hand thoughtfully across his head. Automatically reaching for the hair clippers, he adjusted the guard to an inch, ready to trim his hair back under control.

After Mikey had died, it had been agony to look in the mirror and see his brother's dark eyes and curly hair reflected back at him. As if he was a ghost. He couldn't do anything about the eyes, but Max had taken a pair of clippers to his hair.

If he'd thought that his parents would be able to see him again, rather than the son they'd lost, that was too much of an ambition. They'd barely noticed his shorn locks. The hurt over no longer having a place in his own family had faded over the years, and his hairstyle had become a little less severe, although he'd never let it grow enough to betray his curls.

He could see no trace of Mikey in his face now, though, not even the man that he'd imagined his brother would grow into. Eliza's steady gaze had only ever seen him, his memories and his emotions. Someone who'd forged his own path, working relentlessly to become the person who stared back at him now.

Everyone changed their style from time to time, and maybe now was the moment to change his. Max put the clippers back into the bathroom cabinet, then reached into the shower to turn it on.

CHAPTER ELEVEN

IT WAS CHRISTMAS EVE. Daisy's symptoms had disappeared after two days, without developing into a full-blown cold, and they'd waited another couple of days to make sure that she was well. After a very thorough examination, Max had pronounced her fit for surgery. Iona and Sam had cried a few tears together, and even Max and Eliza had permitted themselves a sigh of relief.

The operating theatres were being used only for urgent cases this close to Christmas. Several of the team had been called at home last night, and had given up part of their holiday to be here. Daisy had been lifted carefully into the special bed, which had Christmas sleigh sides attached for a child's journey down to the surgical suite. Her father would be accompanying her, there to hold her hand and lull her to sleep while the anaesthetist did his job.

It was all a familiar, well-rehearsed exercise and everyone slotted effortlessly into their roles. It was natural that some patients should stick in his mind more tenaciously than others, and when Max looked across the operating table and into Eliza's eyes it seemed that Daisy would be one of those patients they'd both remember.

'Thanks, everyone, for making this happen.' Everybody here understood the urgency, and knew what this meant for Daisy, but a thank-you at the start of a procedure that could last as long as six hours never hurt. Eliza nodded, clasping her gloved hands together in a gesture that looked a lot like love.

Then detached concentration kicked in, as it always did. After the first thin, flexible wire was successfully implanted, Max knew that a short break would equip him for the delicate, careful work that was still ahead of them, and Eliza took over while he stretched his shoulders. He knew when she'd step back for a moment, too.

'Very nice.' When the second lead went in, she allowed herself the equivalent of jumping up and down and cheering, and Max granted himself a smile. They weren't finished yet, but the part of the procedure that had concerned everyone the most had gone seamlessly.

Finally, they both stood back. The operation had taken four and a half hours and while Daisy still needed to be woken up under the supervision of the anaesthetist, their work was done.

'Great work, everyone, thanks. Make sure you stop off and see Sarah on your way out, and have a happy Christmas.'

Eliza waited until they were scrubbing out together to ask. 'Sarah?'

'I dropped by the pizza restaurant and got some boxes of *Tartufi al Cappucino*, and since Sarah's dressed as an elf, I thought she'd be the one to hand them out.'

Eliza's eyes widened. Watching her appreciate chocolate was one of the really good things in life. 'Do I have to hurry?'

'No. There's a box for everyone, I left yours in your office.' Max wondered if that sounded like a Christmas present. He purposely hadn't wrapped it, although the boxes had come complete with a festive bow.

She smiled up at him. 'A whole box? We can have one each when we're finished here this evening.'

He purposely misunderstood her, because coffee and hazelnut truffles seemed a little too much like the food of love at the moment. 'I kept a box for myself back, too.'

Sam and Iona would be waiting for news, and it seemed natural that he and Eliza should go together to see them. They were alone in the family waiting room that adjoined the children's ward, and both sprang to their feet as soon as Max opened the door for Eliza.

One thing about her smile was that it cut down considerably on the amount of time it took to reassure waiting families. Max didn't need to open his mouth before Sam heaved a sigh of relief.

'She's okay?'

'Yes. She's in the recovery room, and she won't be too happy with life when she starts to wake up. But the implantation went very well, and she's going to be fine.' Eliza spoke for both of them.

Sam grabbed Max's hand, shaking it. 'We thought it would take longer. We were just saying we only had another couple of hours to wait...?'

'It takes as long as it takes, Sam. That's got no bearing on how well a procedure's gone.' Max answered the implied question.

'It's just better if you rely on the longer estimate.' Eliza was grinning from ear to ear now.

'We'd have been climbing the walls if we'd thought it was taking longer than it's supposed to.' Iona was standing next to Sam, a slightly dazed look on her face. She reached out suddenly, enveloping Eliza in a hug.

'I'll take you through to the family room, and you can wait for her there. It won't be too much longer before you see her. She has bandages around her head and you should be prepared for an uncomfortable night. But Max has done an exceptional job with the implants and she'll start to feel better tomorrow.'

An exceptional job. Max knew that he'd worked hard, and anything other than excellence had never been an option for him. But the warmth in Eliza's voice, the way that he saw it reflected in Sam's and Iona's faces, made it feel real. A presence in the room that reminded him what he was doing here, that *exceptional* wasn't just a score on a piece of paper, but something that could change a person's life.

'You've got your bags with you?' Eliza gestured towards the tote bag that sat on top of a small suitcase in the corner of the room. Iona was clinging to Sam now, weeping with emotion, and Sam's arm was tight around his wife's shoulders.

'Oh. Yes. Nearly forgot.' Sam left Iona for a moment to fetch the bags, and Eliza held the door open for them, shepherding them out of the room.

Something inside Max broke. Sam and Iona's relief and joy was very evident, and even Eliza had surreptitiously wiped a tear from her eye. Max had no such access to his emotions, and the feeling that they were beating against his chest, clamouring to get out, made him wish that he did.

It was all good. Sam and Iona had exchanged glances when they'd first seen Daisy, but they were prepared and ready to gently comfort their daughter. Eliza had made sure that Daisy was settled, and pressed the call button into Sam's hand, in case they needed anything.

The waiting room door still stood open, and when she looked inside she saw Max. He'd drawn back one of the curtains and was standing, hands in pockets, staring out the window.

'Penny for them?'

When he turned, he was smiling. 'Just making sure there's a space in the car park for Santa.'

'He's landing on the roof, Max. I left some mince pies and carrots up there.'

It took him a moment to laugh. 'You're joking, aren't you?'

'Yes, of course I am. Do you suppose that Santa and his reindeer need any incentives to call at a hospital on Christmas Night?'

Max nodded. 'I'll be listening out for any unexpected landings.'

That sounded as if… 'Are you telling me that you'll be staying here tonight?'

'I'm doing the non-resident on-call shift. I may as well stay here at the hospital, and I can pop in on Daisy to see how she's doing. That way I'll be here in the morning to discharge her if she's well enough. Getting hold of someone else to do that might take a while and it'll be good if she can spend at least part of the day at home.'

That seemed logical. The hospital wasn't such a bad place to be on Christmas Night, and if you were alone… 'Wait a minute. I was planning on being on call for tonight.'

'I told Dr Beckwith I'd do it. He's gone home, so it's too late to change things now. Don't you have chestnuts to roast? Mince pies to make?' Eliza thought she saw the ghost of Christmases long past glimmer in his eyes.

'Don't you? Dr Beckwith's not going to mind if we swap, as long as someone's available to come in if needed.'

Max shook his head. 'Let's settle this. Close your eyes.'

'Why? What are you going to do?'

He gave her a look of hurt innocence, placing his hand on his chest to emphasise the point. Eliza closed her eyes.

Whatever Max was up to, she was in control of her reactions. She felt him take her arm, his fingers pressing lightly on her sleeve. Somehow, Eliza managed not to shiver with delight.

'Take three steps forward… Another one…' She felt the fingers of her outstretched hand against the cool of the window. 'You can open your eyes now.'

Eliza caught her breath. 'Max! It's snowing!' Before she knew it she'd flung her arms around him.

Daisy's procedure had gone well and the little girl was going to have the opportunities she wanted. Max was returning her hug. It was Christmas Eve and there was snow on the ground outside. This could all be so perfect…

No. They'd both made their feelings far too clear when they'd kissed. The decision about whether to take things forward had been made and it wasn't going to change. She looked up at him and he was smiling.

'You're going home now? If you don't hurry, you might miss your chance to make a snowman.'

Max let her go with just enough regret in his eyes, just enough finality, to let her know that a friendly hug was okay at Christmas, and maybe if she ever managed to hit the ball out of the park in a summer baseball game. But he always would just hug her and then let her go.

'Yes, I'm going home. I'll send you a picture of my snowman.' So what if there was only a light covering of snow on the ground. Eliza had worked with less.

'Looking forward to it. Want some help digging your car out?'

She chuckled. 'No, I think turning on the windscreen wipers will be fine. You stay in the warm and look after Daisy.'

'Yeah. I might even have a chocolate.'

The snow might be gone by tomorrow and Eliza wasn't going to miss her chance. She'd promised Max a snowman, and he was going to get one.

In the light from the patio windows at the back of her house, she gathered up handfuls of snow from the garden and built a snowman, all of two feet tall. He had twigs for arms, some buttons from her sewing box for eyes and a mouth and a small, red flowerpot, decorated with tinsel, for a hat. She fetched the light-up baby penguin from the family group in the corner of the patio, and put it down next to the snowman. The two were about the same size, and the angle of the baby penguin's head made it look as if they were holding a conversation. Eliza took a photograph, sending it to Max.

You and Frosty?

His text came back as she was boiling the kettle for a cup of tea and Eliza chuckled.

He's my new boyfriend.

Eliza added a few laughing emojis to the end of her text, just to make it clear that she was joking.

He'll be gone in the morning…

When applied to a two-foot-tall snowman, Max's relationship advice made her smile.

Don't burst my bubble. How's everything there?

Since Max hadn't told her, Eliza was going to have to ask.

Absolutely fine. Daisy's sleeping. Happy Christmas.

You get some sleep too. Happy Christmas.

Eliza laid her phone down on the kitchen counter and made the tea. Was this all there was ever going to be? She loved Max… *Really* loved him.

And she was going to make a mess of things if she didn't accept the realities of the situation. Max was a good man, but he couldn't love her back. Thinking about a rose-tinted future was going to destroy what they had—all the things that Eliza wanted to hold on to.

Maybe some of Max's hard-headed ability to forget all about hope and concentrate on certainties was rubbing off on her. He didn't believe that wanting something enough would make it come true, and perhaps if Eliza had taken that approach to some of her previous relationships, she wouldn't have been hurt so badly. It was a hard lesson to learn, but a good one.

CHAPTER TWELVE

CHRISTMAS DAY. ELIZA HAD been up early, and was in her car by nine-thirty. She'd worked everything out in her head, the wards always centred around the revolving routines of mealtimes, doctors' rounds and visiting times. Although Christmas Day would be a little different, Max would move Daisy's day forward at that regular pace. She'd wake, the family would have breakfast together, and then at about the time she entered the hospital he'd be assessing Daisy to make sure she was ready for discharge. By the time she'd entered the ward and wished everyone a happy Christmas…

She saw Max leaving the family room right on cue. He caught sight of her and walked over, smiling.

'Why am I not surprised?'

It wasn't hard to smile back up at him. The difficult part was not throwing her arms around him.

'I very nearly didn't make it. We're under siege at the moment by a whole army of eleven-year-olds and their parents. With presents for Kyle Woodgate. It's going to take him until March to open them all.' Eliza changed the subject before Max could ask again about the identity of her own teenage pop idol. 'What doesn't surprise you?'

He shrugged.

'I didn't think you'd be able to stay away, and wearing a Christmas sweater goes without saying. I never would have expected reindeer antlers, though.'

'Too much?' Eliza really liked the red headband, which had two glittery reindeer antlers fixed to it.

'It's very cute. Works well with the sweater.'

Cute! Perhaps Christmas was getting to Max. Or maybe he was just humouring her. 'I thought I'd just drop in.'

'Of course you did. I haven't written up the notes yet. Would you like a verbal report?' He didn't wait for her answer because they both knew that was what she was here for. 'Daisy didn't have a great night. She was sick a couple of times and it took Iona a while to settle her back down to sleep.'

'As expected.'

Max nodded. 'But she's a lot better this morning. I had her walk up and down a bit and there are no signs of dizziness. There's minimal swelling around the sutures and she's not in any pain, although she has had analgesics this morning.' He handed over a symptom-checker sheet that the ENT department used with a set of flashcards, so that children could understand and answer their doctor's questions. Max would have assessed Daisy's answers carefully, but Eliza couldn't help scanning it.

'Good. Everything looks great.'

'You'll sign her discharge sheet?' Max grinned suddenly.

'She's your patient, Max.'

'*Our* patient.' He extracted the paper from a bundle under his arm and put it into her hand. 'I'm going to go down and get her medication from the dispensary.

It might take a while if I leave it to the system. What's that smell?'

There were a lot of different smells in a hospital, but he was looking straight at the bag she had slung over her shoulder. 'Mince pies. I made them this morning. Want one?'

'Thanks. I didn't get any breakfast. I was called down to A&E at seven this morning.'

Eliza propped her bag on a nearby trolley, then took out the box of mince pies and wrapped one in a serviette. That would be enough to keep Max going for a while, and he could grab a coffee to go with it on the way down to the dispensary.

'You'll be glad to hear that Santa managed to land without incident last night.' Max delivered a final status update. 'Daisy's just unpacking her stocking.'

'Shall I leave them to it?'

He gave her a pained look. 'Iona was disappointed that she'd missed her chance to wish you a happy Christmas last night. And doesn't every kid want a reindeer in attendance on Christmas morning?'

She'd been wondering whether every doctor might. But not all wishes came true, and it seemed that Max was more intent on practicalities. But it was Christmas Day and when she'd looked out onto the patio this morning, Frosty had survived the night. Nothing was going to spoil her mood.

Sam and Iona were sitting beside Daisy's bed, watching her carefully extract presents from a stocking. Iona looked up, grinning at her.

'Eliza! We didn't expect to see you today. Happy Christmas! I love the antlers.'

Daisy obviously did, too, and was pointing at them and giving her a thumbs-up sign. There was no time like the present, and Eliza put down her bag and signed back. Antlers in BSL didn't need a great deal of explanation and Daisy tried it out, turning to Sam, who did the same.

The little girl went back to her stocking, taking little wrapped presents out of it one by one. Sam was watching her intently and Iona smiled. 'She's always done this. Give me a Christmas stocking and it's unpacked in about thirty seconds flat. Daisy likes to take her time.'

Sam looked up. 'Yours is at home, sweetheart. It's great to see you, Eliza. I hope we're not dragging you away from anything.'

No. Eliza didn't have a stocking waiting for her. 'Dropping in to see how you're all doing is one of the really nice parts of my Christmas.'

She busied herself unpacking the box of mince pies, and hiding the card and the little present she'd brought for Daisy behind it on the console that stood on the other side of the room, so that nothing would divert her attention from her parents' presents.

Sam turned. 'Are they mince pies?'

Iona shot him a reproving look. 'Sorry. We've been up for a while. Daisy woke at five this morning, fretting… We got her back to sleep and she's much better now.' Sam and Iona clearly hadn't managed to get any more sleep.

'I brought them to have whenever you were hungry. Shall I go and get some coffee to go with them?'

'I'll come with you.' Iona got to her feet and Eliza shook her head.

'You're on stocking duty. You take milk and sugar?'

By the time Max returned from the dispensary, holding a bag of medication, Daisy had worked her way down to the toe of her stocking and accepted a corner of Iona's mince pie to eat. Daisy signed a *happy Christmas* and he laughed, signing back.

'Any more mince pies?'

'We saved you some. Have you had breakfast?' Iona glanced at the cup of coffee in his hand, which Eliza reckoned was probably his second cup of the day, picked up on the way back from the dispensary.

Max nodded, and went to fetch himself another mince pie. 'What's this?' He picked up the card and the present.

'Just a little something for Daisy.'

'That's so kind…' Iona got to her feet, fetching the present and putting it into Eliza's hands. 'Why don't you give it to her now?'

Suddenly, she was a part of all this. The warmth of a family who could work out their problems by talking to each other, and which functioned the way it was supposed to. Eliza laid the card and present onto Daisy's lap. *'Happy Christmas, Daisy.'*

The little girl carefully opened her card first, looking at the smiley Santa on the front and then passing it to her mum and dad to see the greetings that Eliza had written for the whole family inside. Then she opened the present, looking carefully at the photograph of a young girl, wearing a cochlear implant transmitter, that Eliza had taped to the lid of the box.

'What have you got there, Daisy?' Sam craned over as his daughter opened the box and took out two plastic bags.

'They're covers for her transmitters, when she gets them in a few weeks' time.' Eliza's explanation was lost on Daisy because she seemed to have already worked it out. 'One pair matches her hair colour, so they'll make the transmitters a little more inconspicuous. The other pair is if she ever wants to show off a bit.' The pink, sparkly covers were Eliza's personal favourites, and Daisy was already taking them out of the bag.

'Those are such fun.' Iona clearly liked the pink sparkly ones as well and picked up the box, taking the leaflet out of the bottom. 'Where can I get some more of these?'

'One of the dads in our parents' group has a 3D printer, and he makes them up. We've worked with him on getting the patterns correct, and he only charges for the cost of the materials, so it's less expensive to get them from him.'

'This parents' group? Who are they? I think I need to get in touch with them. See if there's something *I* can do to help,' Sam said.

Max chuckled. 'I'm sure they'll find something for you to do. They're always on the lookout for volunteers. They meet once a month at the hospital and generally spend about an hour with us, comparing notes on what everyone needs, then go off for a meal together.'

'The number's on the leaflet here.' Iona tucked the leaflet safely into her bag. 'We'll wait until the New Year, Sam, and call then. People are busy…'

It was time to leave. Max had removed the bandage from around Daisy's head and applied smaller, sticky dressings, and Iona had helped her into her clothes. Their bags were packed, and Sam took them down to their car, bringing it round to the patients' pickup point, where Iona was waiting with Eliza and Max. She got Daisy into the car, and then turned.

'Thank you so much. I know we have a way to go still, but this feels…' She shrugged, her eyes filling with tears.

'Like a milestone? That's exactly what it is.' Max prompted her gently and Iona nodded. 'Enjoy it, won't you?'

'We will. I can promise you that.' Iona took Max's hand between hers, and then turned to Eliza to hug her. Sam waved from behind the steering wheel, and Eliza watched the family drive away.

They'd both brought their coats downstairs with them, and Max had handed over to the doctor who'd be covering the day shift a few hours ago. There was nothing more to do here and on a crisp, clear morning, a Christmas alone didn't feel quite as appealing as it once had.

She and Max had been so close in the past few days. Eliza knew what she wanted; would it be so terrible to ask?

'I don't suppose… Since we're both flying solo this Christmas, why don't you come over to me for some lunch?'

'Thanks, but I think I could do with a few hours' sleep right now.' Max *did* look tired and had clearly been awake for longer than he'd admitted.

'You could come over to me afterwards, if you want. I'll put lunch forward a bit. Or we can eat and you could get a few hours' sleep this afternoon. I have a very comfortable sofa bed in the spare room…'

She fell silent. Max hadn't moved an inch but he was retreating from her, his face expressionless and his eyes focusing through her into the distance. She'd got carried away and pushed too hard.

'I'm not great company at the moment. I really need to sleep. I'll see you in a couple of days. Have a happy Christmas, won't you?'

He turned. Max was going to walk away, and this time it was all her fault. She and Max had made an agreement, and Eliza had changed her mind and wanted more.

'Happy Christmas…' she called after him and he raised his hand in acknowledgement.

However hard she stared at his retreating back, she knew Max wasn't going to turn. He wasn't going to stride back and take her in his arms. Why would he, when he'd already told her that he found it impossible to commit to a relationship? Daisy was going home now, and there was no reason for her to work so closely with Max any more. Dr Beckwith could tick the experiment off his list and mark it down as a success.

A tear rolled down Eliza's cheek. She'd picked the wrong guy, again. And what made this time worse than all the others was that she loved Max. But even that couldn't make him into the right guy for her.

She couldn't stand here moping. Someone was going to find her, sooner or later, and that would just make everything worse. If she was going to cry, then it was better to do it in the comfort and privacy of her own home.

CHAPTER THIRTEEN

MAX HAD DROPPED his bag and coat in the hall, and barely managed to take most of his clothes off before he was in bed and asleep. He woke up with one leg sticking out from under the duvet, and beginning to cramp with cold.

He'd been asleep for three hours, and the light outside would be fading soon. It wasn't time wasted, though; his sleeping brain had been able to get on with ordering and cataloguing his thoughts, without his intervention. And it seemed to have come to a solid conclusion.

He'd fought so hard to convince himself that all he and Eliza shared was random chemistry, and that it would fade if he ignored it for long enough. But he couldn't deny it any longer. Eliza was the one, and he was done fighting, done trying to persuade himself that all they could be was friends.

Max walked to the bathroom, wondering if a shower might add a different perspective to it all. But all it did was to get him closer to the point where he could do something practical about putting his thoughts into actions.

He hadn't just been a fool, he'd been cruel. He'd known what Eliza was offering, and it wasn't just a good lunch and a pleasant afternoon. Max had taken fright and walked away from her. He couldn't expect anything from her now, but the least he could do was to tell her that he was sorry and hope against hope that there was still something there for them.

He got dressed and drove to Eliza's house, stopping outside to wonder whether he might just drive away now, but knowing he wouldn't. When he rang the bell, and saw Eliza's shadow behind the obscure glazing in the top of the door, the agonised and unfamiliar feeling of hope was almost too much to bear.

'Max!' Eliza was wearing a pair of sweatpants with red fluffy slippers that matched her oversize Christmas sweatshirt. Her blond hair shimmered across her shoulders and…her eyes were heavy, as if she'd been crying. He didn't dare expect anything of her now, and it was a tribute to Eliza's unflinching good nature that she didn't slam the door in his face.

'I…um…' He remembered the plan and decided to stick to it. 'I was just passing and I wanted to apologise. You made a generous offer and I was dismissive.'

Eliza stared at him, her cheeks reddening. 'That's okay. You were tired. You needed to get home. Have you slept now?'

'Yeah. Don't make excuses for me, though. I don't deserve them.'

She looked him up and down, as if trying to work something out. 'Is something up? You're needed back at the hospital?'

'No, everything's fine,' Max answered before he realised that Eliza had just outwitted him. 'When I said I was passing, that was—'

'An excuse?' Eliza raised her eyebrows.

'I was going to say that it's the kind of term you use

when you don't want to say you've made a special journey. *Excuse* is a bit more concise, though.' Standing on the doorstep, being bedazzled and twisted into knots by Eliza, was rapidly turning into the best part of his day.

'Come in, Max.'

'I don't want to interrupt whatever you're doing. I should go…'

She raised her eyebrows. 'You mean you don't want to be late for whatever you weren't on your way to do? It's freezing standing here with the door open, and I'm not coming outside to get you in my slippers.'

It wasn't difficult to give in to her. 'I didn't bring anything…' Just a heart that so desperately wanted to belong to Eliza.

'You brought yourself, didn't you?'

The cliché seemed to really mean something on her lips. Max took a step forward and Eliza reached out, grabbing the arm of his jacket and pulling him inside.

'Take off your coat. Can you bear another mince pie?'

Max realised that he was hungry. 'Sounds great.'

'I'll make some sandwiches as well. I didn't feel like cooking so I'm going to have my Christmas lunch tomorrow. Would you like coffee? Or something else?'

'What are you having?' Max reckoned that Eliza might be preparing something a bit more Christmassy for herself.

'Hot chocolate?'

'Sounds nice.'

'Hot chocolate for two, then.' She waited while he took his coat and boots off and then propelled him into the sitting room. 'Just ignore the decorations if they're a bit much.'

There was a Christmas tree in one corner of the room,

carefully decorated with glittering glass ornaments. Lamps and a comfortable-looking sofa gave the room a welcoming look, and fairy lights around the picture rails gave it sparkle. The empty hearth of the period fireplace was filled with an arrangement of Christmas greenery and there was a line of home-sewn Christmas stockings hanging from the mantelpiece. The only thing that could have been better was if his and her names were on two of those stockings.

And…a patchwork quilt lay rumpled on the sofa, as if Eliza had been sitting wrapped up in it. It half concealed a box of tissues.

'Have you been crying?'

She reddened again. 'No, I don't think so. If I was it was probably the Christmas weepy that I was watching on TV. It doesn't matter. Sit down and I'll go and put the mince pies into the oven.' Eliza whirled out of the room, and suddenly it felt colder and darker.

Max couldn't let this go. He followed her through to the kitchen, leaning in the doorway.

'It *does* matter. I hurt you and I have no excuse for that. I'm so sorry, Eliza.'

There was a light in her grey eyes as she walked back towards him. 'I was the one who broke our agreement, Max. I wanted more and you had every reason to say no. We'll just have something to eat, and then I'll let you go.'

She looked up at him, her face suddenly creasing in embarrassment. Eliza reached up, plucked a sprig of mistletoe from the greenery that decorated the top of the door frame and hid it behind her back. 'Sorry. You didn't see that there. It's only plastic so it doesn't count.'

Max knew exactly what he wanted now. And unless

he was very much mistaken it was what Eliza wanted, too. He grinned down at her. 'You and Frosty?'

'No, you had him sussed. He was gone by the time I got back from the hospital. I think he must have run away with the penguin.' She was laughing now, twirling the plastic mistletoe between her fingers, and Max didn't have to reach around behind her to close his hand over hers.

'It's Christmas Day. Isn't that magic enough to make anything real?'

Eliza stared up at him. 'Do you want to make it real?'

He took the mistletoe from her hand, and reached up to reattach it over their heads. 'Yes. Do you?'

She stepped towards him, melting into his arms. So soft and warm. Max's whole body was screaming for her, but he was going to take this slow. He had to be sure, because there was no coming back from this.

He allowed himself to brush his lips against hers, just once, and felt her shiver in his arms. This was real, something that he wanted desperately to hold on to. And there was only one way to do that.

'Are we going to renegotiate?'

She reached up, winding her arms around his neck. 'You say the nicest things, Max.'

Max was a great deal braver than she was. They'd both known that they felt something for each other and that it had ended this morning, but he'd been the one to slice through all the obstacles. The one who'd taken the step that she so wanted, but was so afraid of asking for out loud.

And he knew how to make it real. Give everything they felt a chance to grow and flourish.

'Tell me what you want, Eliza. Anything. Everything.'

He brushed a tender kiss against her cheek. 'Or—maybe you should tell me what you *don't* want.'

That was easy. 'I don't want you to regret this. You don't have to stay forever but you can't turn your back and walk away from me in the morning.'

'I'm done with that, I promise. I tried so hard to pretend that it was just friendship I felt for you and I failed. If you make me your lover, I won't let you down.'

Max was an honest man, and he didn't say pretty words to get what he wanted. This was set in stone now.

'I don't want you to stop speaking your mind.' Max opened his mouth to protest and she laid her finger over his lips. 'Note that I said *stop* speaking your mind.'

He smiled down at her. 'I'm not entirely sure why you felt you needed to include that. I'm not thinking of undergoing a personality transplant. Can I rely on you to tell me what's on *your* mind?'

'That's why I asked. Because you've made what I think important to you, and that means a lot. I want you to tell me what you think, and to demand the same of me.'

'I won't stop telling you what's on my mind and demanding you do the same. It means a lot to me, too. Anything else?'

'I want you to have time for me. Because I have time for you.' Their wants—needs—were the same. She and Max weren't so different, after all.

Max chuckled. 'I have all the time in the world for you, Eliza, and that's not going to change.'

'And you?' He must have something to add…

Max kissed her. She wanted that—more than ever. Because now she knew that it wasn't just chemistry. It was a meeting of minds. All of their hopes and desires.

'I have just one thing to ask.'

'Ask.' She smiled up at him.

'You're a beautiful, strong woman, Eliza. Your capacity to smile and hope for the best dazzles me and I want you to share that with me.' He grinned at her. 'Will you be my Christmas fairy?'

That wasn't difficult at all. A piece of glitter had transferred itself from her sweatshirt onto his sweater, and when Eliza brushed at it with her fingers it stuck fast. 'Consider yourself well and truly sparkled, Max.'

It was hard to break the magic of these moments, kissing here under the mistletoe. Those precious promises that bound them together and gave them the space they needed to love each other. But when Max's kisses became more insistent, Eliza hadn't been able to bear it any more. She'd taken him by the hand, leading him upstairs.

His body was beautiful. Smooth olive skin and a tantalising smile. He undressed her slowly, making each moment more exquisite than the last. Capturing each sigh and turning it from arousal into desire. When he finally laid her down on the bed, Eliza couldn't wait any longer.

'Max…come here!'

'Is that an order? I've got to tell you your bossy side is far more enchanting than I'd ever imagined.'

'It's an order. You get to call the shots next time.'

'Really.' He grinned. 'You're quite sure about that?'

He was playful, incredibly sexy, and he wanted her as much as Eliza wanted him. Max made lovemaking feel like something new and bright, something that broke her and then remade her, stronger than before.

The best moment took its time in coming, though. It

waited, through the long hours of the evening, through dozing and waking in each other's arms, talking and raiding the fridge and then making love again.

Max stilled for a moment, gazing into her eyes. Their connection was so strong now that it felt his emotions had the power of a physical caress.

'I love you, Eliza. With all my heart.'

Joy burst through her senses. 'I love you, too, Max. My heart belongs to you now, so be careful with it.'

A tear streaked his cheek. Something honest and precious that she couldn't bring herself to wipe away. 'Always. You have mine in return.'

Max held his nerve, letting the impact of their words feed their climax together. It was more than Eliza could ever have imagined, and the shocked look on his face told her that he hadn't expected this, either.

He was gentle in the quiet moments that followed. Maybe he knew that Eliza had never been this vulnerable before, and he curled his body around hers protectively, holding her tight.

'What happened?' she heard him murmur.

'I don't know. Something special.' Eliza couldn't put it into words yet.

'Yeah. Something very special.'

Max was the coffee guy. He always made sure he was awake and showered early, and that he brought a lover coffee in bed. It was good manners, wasn't it?

But Eliza had stripped him of everything. What he *should* say to a lover, all the things that he should do. It was possible that she'd deprived him of part of his brain, and that the next time he walked into an operating theatre, he'd have to think twice before he could tell one end of a scalpel from the other. The only thing he knew was that he loved Eliza, and she loved him.

He felt the bed move as she slid carefully from his embrace. Max reached for her, and she pushed his arms back under the covers.

'Go back to sleep. I won't be long.'

'Yeah. Five minutes, and then I'll make breakfast for you.' If he could work out where the kitchen was.

Max felt Eliza kiss his cheek and then she was gone.

It seemed that he'd only just closed his eyes when he felt something nudge his shoulder. Then he smelled the sweet scent of Eliza's soap, mixed with the aroma of coffee.

'What's the time?' He rubbed his hand across his face, trying to come to his senses.

'Midday. We both slept for a long time. Have some coffee.'

He heard the clatter of a cup on the bedside table. Max opened his eyes and promptly forgot all about coffee. Eliza was standing beside the bed, wearing a white cotton nightshirt and a luminous smile. There was a crown of tinsel on her head, and she had a wand in her hand. A pair of sheepskin booties gave a practical feel to the outfit, as if she might need to keep her feet warm while travelling across the snow to find him.

'My Christmas fairy.' He grinned at her. None of the playfulness of last night had been lost, and its passion was beginning to stir again now. 'Dare I ask where you got the wand from? Or were you just born with it in your hand?'

'A fairy never tells.' Eliza examined the star at the tip of the wand. 'You like it?'

'More than you could possibly imagine.' Max tried to play it cool, reaching for the small cup on the bedside table. There was a thick crema on the top of the coffee and when he stirred it in a little and took a sip, the brew was strong and aromatic. 'Where did you get this from?'

'I have coffee beans. It's just a matter of grinding them differently and not putting so much water in, isn't it?'

Not always. But everything that Eliza touched seemed to turn to gold. Max downed the rest of the coffee, feeling wide-awake now. He got out of bed, and Eliza's eyes widened.

'Max! We used up all the condoms last night!'

'Time to improvise, then.' They'd done a fair bit of that, and it hadn't turned out badly.

He reached for her and she dropped the wand, dancing a few steps back. Max advanced and she retreated, laughing. He caught up with her on the other side of the bed and gathered her in his arms, guiding her back against the wall. As he fell to his knees, she pulled at his shoulder.

'Max… What about you?'

'Did you forget something about last night? The part about your pleasure being mine?'

Eliza was still, suddenly. 'And yours being mine? No, I haven't forgotten that, Max.'

He slid his hand up her leg, gathering the nightshirt as he went. That was enough to make her gasp, and he felt her hands gripping his shoulders as Eliza steadied herself. 'I'm going to get you back, Max.'

'Yeah. Sure you are.' Last night had taught him that Eliza liked slow, and this was going to take a while.

CHAPTER FOURTEEN

New Year's Eve. They'd been together for a week, and it felt as if Eliza's whole world had been turned upside down. Max was the man she'd always wanted, someone who was strong enough to respect that she had thoughts and opinions of her own. Gentle enough to love her, and who somehow just got her, the way she got him.

He'd asked if she wanted to go to the New Year's Eve party that most of the hospital would be attending, and Eliza had said yes. So what if they'd be going public with their relationship, when it was still so very new. One of the good things about amazing sex was that it left them with nowhere to hide, and several people at the hospital had guessed already that they were together now. The only problem had been getting something to wear, as the party was fancy dress.

They'd spent several hours phoning around, and several more in the car. Eliza had rejected space suits, and Max had drawn the line at being a Regency beau, and finally they'd settled on something they both liked. Max had said that he'd dress at his place, leaving Eliza to curl her hair and wriggle into her dress in peace.

At nine o'clock the doorbell rang and Eliza ran down the stairs, still not sure that her hair was going to pass muster. Max was standing on the doorstep, grinning, and Eliza realised that this was the moment he'd wanted. Meeting at the door, all dressed up for their first proper night out.

'You look wonderful! Very handsome.' His 1920s-style suit fitted him perfectly and he wore his fedora hat tilted back on his head.

'And you look just swell, ma'am.' His American accent became broader to match their speakeasy costumes.

'I'm not sure about my hair. Do you think I should wear the hat?' Eliza had arranged her hair in sleek curls, held in place by diamanté pins. Her costume had come with a cloche hat, which didn't fit her well, but it would do.

'Your hair's heart-stoppingly beautiful. I was going to move on to that when I'd finished appreciating your red lipstick.' He gave her a wolfish smile and came inside, shutting the door behind him. 'Do you think a kiss, right here, would complete my outfit?' He pointed to his cheek.

'How serious are you about coming clean to the whole hospital that we're together?' Eliza shivered with pleasure. Max never held back with his compliments, and having someone who was so obviously proud to be with her was a new experience.

'Very serious. You?'

'Me, too.' She placed a careful kiss onto his jaw, and Max looked into the mirror, admiring the mark left by her lipstick. Eliza reached up, teasing one of the dark locks that escaped onto his forehead into a curl.

Max chuckled. 'Nah. It's not going to stay like that. It's still too short. Give it another few weeks.'

'So you're not going to cut your hair after tonight?'

They'd talked about so many things in the past week, and Max had told her how he'd cut off the curls that were so like Mikey's.

'I'll leave it for a while. See whether it still suits me after all these years.'

Eliza thought it would. Max stepped away from her, smiling.

'Will you give me just one twirl? Before we go?'

Showing herself off was a new pleasure, too. Eliza turned full circle and the beads at the hem of her shimmering 1920s flapper dress spread out around her legs. She'd never tire of the way that Max spoke his mind, when all of the things she'd always wanted to hear were what preoccupied him.

Max didn't usually take much notice of New Year celebrations, because they generally involved hope. But Eliza had changed all that.

She'd changed him. The man who was only confident about expressing his fears was one who could now share his hopes with her. Maybe tonight was the night when he'd be able to show her just how serious he was about those hopes.

He loved the way that she walked a little closer to him as they entered the exclusive wine bar, giving their names at the door to gain entry to the private party. How she allowed him to help her out of her coat, and then took his arm, holding on to it possessively as if it belonged to her. It did, along with the rest of him.

Sarah had left her husband chatting with one of the ENT nurses and her partner and was making a beeline for them, pushing her way through the press of people.

She straightened her Regency bonnet, and gave them a very un-Regency grin.

'Is this…what I think it is?' Her finger waved back and forth suggestively between him and Eliza.

'Depends what you're thinking,' Max replied and felt Eliza nudge him. 'Yes. It is.'

'I *thought* you two were looking a bit cosy when you came back to work after Christmas.' Sarah liked to be the first to know everything that happened in the ENT department.

'We couldn't fool you…' Eliza told her exactly what she wanted to hear, and Max found himself laughing and nodding in agreement.

He caught a passing waiter with a loaded tray, taking a glass of sparkling water for himself and one of champagne for Eliza. She turned her mouth down. 'Perhaps we should have come by taxi.'

'No. I'm the one who's taking you home tonight.' Max wanted tonight to be perfect, and having Eliza wait shivering on the pavement while he tried to hail a taxi at the end of the evening wasn't his idea of perfect.

She laughed suddenly, pointing to the far side of the space and leaning close so that he could hear her over the heavy beat of the music. 'We could have saved ourselves the trouble of dressing up.'

Ash Dhillon, a surgeon from orthopaedics, was standing next to the dance floor, wearing scrubs—his only concession to the party being a string of tinsel decorating the stethoscope that was draped around his neck. 'Nah. We have a life outside our work, remember? And I'd have missed being able to appreciate how gorgeous you are tonight.'

'Charm will get you everywhere, Max.' Eliza's hand flew to her mouth. 'Oww. Don't do it… No, she's done it, look.'

A woman, dressed identically to Ash, was walking towards him. 'Who's that?'

'Serena Fleming. She's one of the physiotherapists from the hospital. Now we have *two* people in scrubs, standing right next to one another.'

Ash and Serena had started to talk, and Ash refilled Serena's glass from a bottle of champagne he'd been holding. Max dismissed the thought that he might have been the third doctor attending the party if Eliza hadn't added her imaginative sparkle to his life, and gave Ash and Serena the benefit of the doubt.

'They must have been working late.'

Eliza nodded. 'Yes, I expect so. I hope they're not feeling the urge to talk shop…'

Something about their body language told Max that they weren't. 'Yeah. That would be taking things much too far.'

He saw Dr Beckwith dressed as a Roman senator, with a woman on his arm who was obviously his wife, circulating smoothly in their direction, and felt Eliza move a little closer. Max put his hand protectively on her back.

'Happy New Year.' Dr Beckwith turned to his wife, who had chosen a gladiator costume, somehow managing to make it look both fierce and ladylike. 'Darling, this is Dr Max Russo, one of our most talented surgeons.'

'Caroline Beckwith.' Max found his outstretched hand gripped in a businesslike handshake.

'Caroline, you look wonderful.' Eliza smiled at her. 'That's not a *real* sword, is it?'

'Sadly not, or we might have been noticed a little sooner by the waiters,' Caroline replied. 'You look gorgeous, as always, Eliza. I see that life's treating you well?'

The veiled comment provoked a grin from Eliza. She was shining tonight, in a way that only she could. 'Very well.'

'Seems I did one thing right this year.' Dr Beckwith shot them a glance of quiet approval.

'You sure did, sir.' Max tried out the speakeasy accent again, and everyone laughed.

Max never tired of watching her. Eliza had moved from his side a little, talking animatedly to friends and colleagues. He wanted this. Her confidence, the way she knew he'd always be there for her and didn't need to hold on to him. The way she outshone even the Christmas lights, and how she made him feel when they were alone together.

His hand strayed again to the small pocket of his waistcoat. All of his hopes for the future. He'd never dared entertain them before, but now… The difficult thing about starting to hope was that it was almost impossible to stop.

He left Eliza chatting with two of the theatre nurses and went to speak with the attendant who was standing at the bottom of the staircase that led up to the roof terrace. Then he made his way over to the cloakroom to fetch their coats.

'Come with me.' Max waited until she was alone for a moment, and whispered the words into her ear. Eliza smiled, taking his arm.

The stairs had been roped off until later in the evening, when people would be allowed up to the terrace to see

New Year's fireworks going off across the city. The attendant let them through, as promised, and as they walked up the carpeted stairway, Eliza leaned towards him.

'What's going on, Max?'

'I just wanted to be alone with you for a moment. There's a New Year coming soon, and we haven't made our resolutions yet.' They'd walked past the door that led to the upper level of the wine bar, and reached the top of the stairs. Max helped Eliza into her coat and opened the door that led onto the roof terrace. Hand in hand, they walked out into the chill air.

Suddenly, anything seemed possible…

Max had something on his mind. Eliza wasn't sure what, but he was focused on a mission of some sort. He turned his back on the bright lights of the city, drawing her beneath an awning to shelter them from the wind.

'What do you think, then?' he asked. 'About our resolutions.'

Eliza thought for a moment. 'You give me your pizza recipe?' Max had made her the best pizza she'd ever tasted, and laughingly refused to give up the secret family recipe.

'I don't know…that's a very serious commitment.'

'Okay. I like a challenge, so my resolution is going to be that I'll get it out of you somehow.'

He chuckled. 'I'll look forward to it. My resolution is to plan a trip to take you somewhere with snow next winter.'

'New York? I'd really like to go to New York and see where you grew up.'

'New York for starters. It might not be snowing there so we'll have to take a road trip to Lake Placid or the Adirondack Mountains. Wherever it is, we'll find it…'

That sounded wonderful. 'I'd love to chase the snow with you, Max. That's a definite resolution.'

'I have one more.' His eyes were bright with the possibilities that the year in front of them held.

'Tell me.'

'I want to share my hopes and dreams with you, Eliza.'

Hope meant so much to Max. He'd been deceived by it, but they were here together, making resolutions because Max had had the courage to hope again.

'If you'll hope, then I trust your dreams. For the both of us.'

'I have big hopes. A lot of dreams.'

'The bigger the better.' She smiled up at him. 'I don't want to be a passenger in my own life any more, Max. I want to share it with you.'

A thrill of excitement hung in the air between them. Time had stopped, and the twinkling lights of the city seemed to be holding their breath. Waiting for something to happen. Max must have felt it, too; when he drew her close she could feel his limbs trembling, his heart beating fast.

Maybe this exquisite moment would pass them by, carried away in the freezing air like a playful sprite. They'd dared so much in the past week. Could they really hope for more?

'I love you with all my heart, Eliza. I'll always respect your wishes, and… I want to make a loving home and a family with you, the kind that you didn't have when you were little, and that I lost.'

Eliza caught her breath. When Max dreamed he didn't do it in half measures. 'A family…?' That was a huge step for him. He'd seen firsthand how the loss of a child had broken his own family.

'If that's what you want?'

'You need to ask?'

'Yeah, I do. I *really* do.'

'Max, I… I want that, too. I didn't expect you to feel that way so soon. I hoped…' She felt tears spill down her cheeks. 'Max, I'll always love you. Big hopes always come with some fears, but we'll face them together. When the time comes…'

'The time's now.' Max let go of her hand, reaching inside his coat for a moment. When he closed his fingers over hers, she felt something nestling against her palm, still warm from his own body heat. 'Will you marry me, Eliza?'

Eliza caught her breath. This was so soon, but time never seemed to matter with her and Max. Once they'd stopped fighting it, and realised that they were made for each other, everything else had fallen into place.

She tried to blink the tears back and failed. Max smiled, seeming to already know what her answer would be. It was the only answer she knew how to give him.

'Yes, Max. I'll marry you.'

Those few words were enough to change everything. And then Max kissed her and everything changed again. Their new reality became more substantial, no longer a dream, but something solid that she could always depend on.

'What do I have in my hand, Max?'

'I hope you like it.' He cupped her hand in his, and she opened her fingers. Eliza gasped.

'It's beautiful!' One square-cut diamond, sparkling

in the fairy lights. Held fast by a golden circle of their dreams.

Their hands were trembling, and Max fumbled as he slipped the ring onto her finger. It fitted perfectly.

Then it happened. Max swung her round suddenly, out of the shelter of the canopy, and Eliza felt something against her face. They looked up together at flurries of snow dancing above their heads, both laughing in delighted disbelief.

'Did that *really* happen?' The wind had blown it all away as quickly as it had appeared.

Max brushed a few melting flakes from the shoulder of her coat, and moved closer to whisper in her ear. 'When magic's in the air, don't question it.'

That sounded like a good solution. Eliza nestled into his warmth, unable to put her cold fingers into her pockets, because she wanted to look at the ring.

'It's so pretty, Max. When did you get it?'

'Yesterday. When I went out to get our lunch.'

'You chose a ring, which just happened to be gorgeous and exactly the right size. *And* bought two rounds of sandwiches, in half an hour?' Eliza was chuckling, unable to resist the tide of joy that was washing over her.

'I'd been on the internet and had already chosen one. And I measured your finger, while you were sleeping.'

Eliza raised her eyebrows in mock outrage. 'I hope I wasn't snoring. That might have spoiled the moment…'

'No, you weren't. You kept trying to put your hand back under the duvet, though, so I had to chase it around for a while.'

He curled his hand around hers, sliding it into the pocket of his coat. People were beginning to filter up onto the roof terrace now, to see the New Year's fireworks going off across the city. Eliza pulled Max into the shadows, not ready to share him with anyone just yet. She could ignore the chanted countdown and the sudden eruption of noise as fireworks exploded above their heads. Max was kissing her, and it was all she could feel or see.

'You want to come home with me and light up *my* sky?'

That was better than fireworks any day. 'Yes, Max. Let's go.'

EPILOGUE

Four weeks later

THE FIRST FOUR weeks of a New Year. The dark evenings and cold weather usually made this the time of the year when Eliza had to work her hardest for smiles, but they came so easily this year. Whenever she had a moment alone at work, and all the time at home. Max smiled whenever he shooed her out of the kitchen, saying that the family recipes would be all hers on their wedding day. When she told him how much she loved watching him smiling in his sleep, he confessed to watching her do the same.

Five weeks after her cochlear implant surgery, Daisy was due in for her 'switch on' appointment. Today the speech processors would be fitted and tuned, allowing Daisy to hear sounds for the first time in almost three months.

'You told Sam and Iona not to expect too much, didn't you, Max?' He was striding along the corridor and Eliza had to jog a few steps to keep up with him.

'Yep.'

'And Daisy knows that, too?'

'Yep.' He stopped suddenly, stepping quickly to one side before Eliza bumped into him. 'Whatever did you see in me, Eliza?'

'You *know* what I see in you. What's that got to do with it?' Then Eliza realised what he meant. 'You mean how did I put up with you always expecting the worst?'

'Yes. It's maddening.'

'I guess you weren't quite as good at pessimism as you thought you were. And I'm so excited, I can't bear it. I'm trying not to expect anything, because I want so much for Daisy…'

'Better. You had me worried for a minute. If you could manage to stop dancing on the spot, we'll go and see our patient, shall we?'

Eliza hadn't been aware that she *was* dancing on the spot. She nodded, following Max into the comfortable, quiet room where Daisy was sitting with her parents.

Now that they were looking better, Eliza realised how gaunt Sam and Iona's faces had been when they'd first met. Max signed a hello to Daisy, before greeting her parents.

'Is she ready for today?' Max asked and Iona nodded.

'She keeps telling us she won't hear us properly, but that she's starting out. That's her thing at the moment. She's had a few different starting-out days recently. She went back to school for the day last week, and she was very tired afterwards, but we told her that now she'd got the first time over and done with, the second time would be more fun.'

Max nodded. Eliza knew that he'd been monitoring Daisy's recovery carefully, to make sure that she wasn't overstressed by too many things happening at once. Now the implant surgery had been successfully completed, they could afford to adopt a more relaxed timetable and wait until Daisy was ready for today's appointment, which would take more than an hour.

'Okay, I just need to take a look to check that she's

maintained the progress I saw last time.' Max signed to Daisy, and she scrambled up into the examination chair. Eliza went to sit down with Sam and Iona.

'We can't thank you both enough.' Sam turned to her. 'We were so confused, so stressed out, when Daisy first came to you. But we all feel that we're ready for whatever happens next now.'

'That's really good to hear, thank you. I imagine it's difficult to stop Daisy once she's made up her mind that she wants to do something.'

Sam chuckled. 'Tell me about it...'

Max showed Daisy the external parts of her new implants, and fitted the sparkly pink covers that she'd brought with her onto the speech processors. Then he carefully fitted them, along with the receivers. Iona had braided Daisy's hair around the magnets that would hold the receivers in place, and she craned around anxiously to see whether Max was having any difficulty with them.

'You've done a really nice job with Daisy's hair, Iona. The receivers will be very easy for her to put on, even when the areas I had to shave grow out a little more.' He swivelled his stool around to face her.

'The lady you suggested, Paulette, came over and showed me a few ideas. She's been great. She gave me advice on products as well.'

'Yeah, as long as you're careful not to put hair products actually on the processors, you should be okay. I'll add a few extra filters onto your prescription, just in case you need them.' He got to his feet. 'Why don't you come and sit here, with Daisy. The processors are connected via Bluetooth to that computer over there, and Eliza's going to be sending sounds across to see whether Daisy can detect them. I'll be staying out of everyone's road.'

Actually, Max would be watching Daisy carefully to see whether she was reacting or not. Eliza took her seat behind the desk, starting off with very low levels of sound, which Daisy couldn't hear. But as she increased the volume, Daisy began to react, pulling at her mother's sleeve and waving both her arms above her head at Max.

'No need to shout, Daisy.' He grinned, giving her a thumbs-up. 'She'll wear herself out if she does that every time. Iona, see if you can get her to just give an *Okay.*'

Iona signed to her daughter, and Eliza returned to the careful process of tuning each processor so that they wouldn't be too loud for Daisy, but she'd have plenty of chances to react to audio stimulation. It was an hour before she'd finished, and by that time Sam and Iona were smiling. Daisy was reacting to sounds, and her head turned towards Sam when he called to her.

'You're too loud, Dad.' Daisy put her hands over her ears at the sound of her own voice, but she already knew how to speak and her confidence in doing so had improved a lot recently.

Max went through some of the main points contained in the bundle of fact sheets that he'd handed over to Iona. 'It's important that Daisy wears her cochlear implants as much as possible, so that she can learn to process the different type of sound that the cochlear implant produces. But don't force her. If she doesn't want to use them on a particular day, then try to respect that choice. And keeping background noise to a minimum will help her to focus on hearing the sounds she wants to hear.'

Iona nodded. 'It says here that she's more likely to pick up sing-song noises.'

'She may well do. Try that out. Every child's different.'

'That'll be Iona's job,' Sam added. 'No one wants to hear it when I sing, but Iona's in the church choir.'

Iona started to sing a familiar melody, a child's song with accompanying hand movements. Daisy reacted, mimicking Iona's actions in time to the song.

Tears were dried and hands shaken. Daisy signed a *see you later* and when Max cupped his hand behind his ear she said the words, only wrinkling her nose a little at the way her voice sounded.

He turned back into the consulting room, closing the door. Max was grinning broadly as he sat down, his hands behind his head, swinging the office chair back and forward. 'Happy ending?'

'You think so?' Eliza perched on the desk in front of him, unable to resist leaning forward and running her fingers through the thick curls that covered his head.

'Don't you?'

'Well…' She pretended to think. 'There'll be regular appointments for the next year, to fine tune Daisy's implants. As she grows, we'll need to see her at least once or twice a year. We'll watch her learn how to hear again and we'll hear all her news. Boyfriends, exams at school. Pop idols, hopes and dreams. Going away to university, maybe…?'

'A few broken hearts, but she'll get over that and find *the one*…' Max chuckled.

'Yes. She'll have her own children and Sam and Iona will be such proud grandparents. And she'll still be coming back once a year to see us. If we're still here of course, and haven't gone back to New York.' They'd talked about that and decided to keep that possibility open, along with all the other futures they might have.

'If we move away, she can always write. At Christmas…'

Eliza nodded. 'Think of all we'd be missing out on if this was the end.'

'True. We'll call it a *happy*, then. You have to go now? Or do you have time for coffee?'

Eliza looked at her watch. 'Got to go. I have a new patient in ten minutes. I'll see you later.'

When Max came to find her, Eliza was sitting on the bed, dressed in a nightshirt and thick socks, a blanket around her shoulders. She was also wearing a frown. Max took off his shoes and joined her, leaning against the pillows.

'I've written the letter and sent it off, and in one month's time I'll be officially homeless,' he announced.

Eliza caught her breath in an expression of mock horror. 'Oh no! Whatever will you do, Max?'

'I'll find a bed for the night somewhere. We'll save up and buy a house with a few extra bedrooms for the little lodgers.'

Eliza's elbow found his ribs. 'You are *not* to refer to our children as *little lodgers*. They'll be arriving on a permanent tenure.'

He nodded. Nothing about his future was fixed now, apart from the one golden fact that he wouldn't be facing it alone. That was an iron-clad guarantee that everything *wasn't* going to work out in the worst possible way.

'I'm really looking forward to meeting them. Do you suppose they'll be interested in baseball?'

'Not for a little while. Give them a couple of years before you start trying to explain the rules to them.' She dumped the pile of brochures and paper on her lap to one side. 'Although we have to get the wedding over first. At this rate the children will be grown up and planning their own weddings before we get this one on the road.'

He kissed her. 'There'll be a wedding. If I have to kidnap you and take you off to a deserted beach, where there are only sea turtles to witness it.'

'Mmm. That sounds like paradise at the moment.'

Eliza's parents had reacted as expected to their news. Her father was thrilled, and wanted to walk her down the aisle. Her mother was also thrilled, but had hung up on Eliza when she'd told her that she wasn't going to exclude her father and his wife from the day. Silences and tears had followed, as Eliza had tried to negotiate her way through an impossible situation.

'It's not what you want, though. You want to get married with all of your family and friends there. Then go to New York and do it all again, because we had such a fabulous time the first time, and *then* we'll go find our deserted beach.'

Eliza sighed. 'That would be lovely. I've come to the conclusion that it's not going to happen, though. We're going to have to grit our teeth and maybe break up a few arguments that look as if they're about to descend into fisticuffs. We'll escape to America, and… I don't really know how that's all going to go. It's not easy trying to arrange something at arm's length. I like the deserted beach part of it all, though, just as long as we're not too exhausted to enjoy it.'

'I'm going to propose a deal. It's important we start as we mean to go on, because we're not going to pass these family dramas on down to our own kids. They'll be having birthdays and Christmases and I won't have them negotiating their way around all of the things we've had to.'

Eliza smiled at him. 'I love it when you put your mind to a problem. I can almost believe that this deal of yours is going to fix everything.'

'Just give it a fair hearing. I'm going to take over all of the arrangements for the UK. Invitations, venue, flowers. Who does what. Your dad will walk you down the aisle, and your mom can organise a mother-of-the-bride evening. I'll give her a fixed date, about three weeks before the wedding, to give you some time to get over it. If anyone has a problem with anything, then they'll have to come to me. There'll be no point in applying any pressure on you because you won't know what's going on. That's what they'll think anyway. Actually, I'll be asking you exactly what you want, every step of the way.'

Eliza was staring at him. 'You'd do that, Max?'

'Yeah. You're the love of my life and that includes taking on your family if I have to. It won't all be hard work. We'll have a platoon of friends between your mom and your dad and his wife at all times. Everyone at the hospital's very used to defusing difficult situations, if I happen to be otherwise engaged.'

'What about my dress?' Max knew that Eliza was set on surprising him with her dress and he was looking forward to that moment as well.

'Like I said, you'll be my secret ally in all of this. You pick your dress. We just won't let your mother know about that, in case she arms the bridesmaids and organises a coup d'état.'

Eliza laughed. 'You think you're joking…'

Max shrugged wearily. 'Not so much. I've seen the way she's treated you up till now over it all, and it's going to stop. What do you think?'

She flung her arms around his neck. 'I think you just saved our wedding day. I love you.'

'Wait…' Max disentangled himself from her kisses. 'You don't know what your side of the deal is yet.'

'Tell me…' Eliza sat up straight, grinning. 'I can't think of anything I wouldn't do in return.'

'For the New York ceremony… I was talking to my dad on the phone the other day, and he told me that Mom's been sneaking out to all the big stores, looking around at the wedding displays.'

'Yes, that's right. She's been so nice about it all. She emails me and asks me what I think about everything, and she has really good taste. I don't want to ask too much of her, though.'

'Well, it appears that's exactly what she's thinking. She doesn't want to ask too much of you, either. She reckons that it's your day and you'll be wanting to do it your way. But this is a big thing for her.'

His parents had greeted the news of their engagement with polite and appropriate congratulations, which had upset Max. If they couldn't show a little enthusiasm over his wedding, then they truly *had* forgotten him. But Eliza had kept the lines of communication open, organising regular video calls. Over the weeks that followed, his mom had seemed to come out of her shell, diffidently suggesting small ways in which she might help.

'I think… When Mikey died we were all so caught up in our grief that we forgot how to hope. Now that Mom and Dad have got to know you, and seen how things are between us, they've found something to look forward to. If we'd talked a bit more…'

'What's done is done, Max. We can make things different in the future. Would you like me to contact your mum and ask her to help arrange everything?'

'Do you mind? I know it's a lot to ask, but Mom's really good at that kind of thing. She used to organise a party at the drop of a hat when I was young. Nice venue, lots of food and three hundred people up on their feet and dancing… She made it look effortless.'

'Three hundred? Can we afford that?'

'Probably not, but my dad's offered to make up the difference if mom takes us over our budget. He's been missing the parties. There's been too much silence around them for too long. I'm not sure that we have a bigger family than anyone else. We're just in the habit of keeping up with everyone, and I'd like it if they all came.'

'Max, that sounds wonderful.' Eliza's face was shining. 'It's not a lot to ask at all. It would be my privilege to share the day with your mum. I'd really like it to be *her* day, too.'

Max felt tears rise in his eyes. He hadn't realised quite how much this meant to him before Eliza had agreed to it. 'I'd love that. Do we have a deal?'

'Yes, we do. I can't wait to get started with your mum. Do you think she'd mind looking at some venues?'

'Try stopping her.' The tears were relentless, and Eliza brushed one from the side of his face.

'Shake on it now, Max. I've got the easier side of the bargain and if you agree to it then I'm going to hold you to it.'

'I'm pretty sure *I* have the easier side of it. Mine's a piece of cake. I just channel my grumpy persona and lay down the law a bit. You're going to have to look through a million brochures and catalogues.' The best part of all of this was that it was easy for him to do something for Eliza, and she found it easy to do something for him.

She slipped her hand into his, squeezing his fingers tight. 'Deal.'

'Yeah. Deal.' He kissed her to seal the bargain.

She tipped the pile of brochures from the bed onto the floor. 'Since we have that sorted, is there anything else?'

'Yeah. There is, actually.' The laws of arithmetic didn't allow any improvement on 100 percent, but he and Eliza seemed able to flout them on a daily basis. Max kissed her again, his hand sliding beneath the comforter around her shoulders.

'And what would that be?' She tugged his sweater over his head, and started work on the buttons of his shirt.

'There's so much more for us to do.' He rolled her over, feeling his heart burst with emotion as he kissed her. Eliza knew. A tear appeared at the corner of her eye as she smiled up at him, her face shining.

'Better get started, then…'

* * * * *

Look out for the next story in
the Royal York Hospital miniseries
Christmas with Her Rival *by Becky Wicks*

And if you enjoyed this story, check out these other
great reads from Annie Claydon

The Doctor's Italian Escape
The GP's Seaside Reunion
Neurosurgeon's IVF Mix-Up Miracle

All available now!

CHRISTMAS WITH HER RIVAL

BECKY WICKS

MILLS & BOON

To all the doctors, nurses and medical professionals who choose to work over the holiday period for the benefit of their patients. You are all Christmas angels.

CHAPTER ONE

ANGEL FLORES BLINKED and sat bolt-upright as her phone vibrated loudly by the bed. 'What?'

Scrambling to answer, her sister's name blazed at her in the darkness and she blinked again, sighing and ramming a hand through her mussed-up hair.

'*Kumusta*, Ate,' she said into the phone, her voice still thick with sleep. 'Merry Christmas.'

'Angel!' Her sister's voice crackled through the line, bright and cheery, no thanks to her being eight hours ahead in the Philippines. Ate was there with their parents, who'd flown over from their home in Scotland for the festive holiday.

Ugh: holidays.

Ate started talking a million miles an hour and Angel did her best to sound enthused as she stared out of the bedroom's frosty window at the ice-dusted rooftops of York. As usual, the ancient Minster loomed in the distance like a silent sentinel, eerily devoid of birds for such an early hour. Not only was it the holidays, it was Christmas Day.

It wouldn't be entirely fair to label it the worst day of the year so far, because she'd only been awake for less than five minutes. But, whereas her small flat in the heart of the city provided a postcard-perfect view and cosy vibes, today it already felt alien and isolating, and Ben lingered at the back of her thoughts like the Ghost of Christmas Past.

The glowing screen of her phone illuminated her face in the pre-dawn darkness as she held it to her ear, glancing at herself in the dressing-table mirror opposite the bed. 'That's great, Ate,' she responded absently, feeling guilty that she wasn't being entirely present, but she really needed coffee. And, now that she was awake, she might as well get on with the day. It wasn't going to be easy but she'd just have to put on her brave face and hope that everyone at her new job wouldn't harp on about all-things-Christmas all day.

Even before Ben had left her at the altar, exactly one year ago today, the Christmas holiday had always stirred up a whirlwind inside her. She usually felt torn between two worlds. Her Filipino roots ran deep, nurtured by her sprawling family, so much so that Glasgow—the place of her birth—sometimes felt like a distant backdrop rather than home. Well, it *had* been home, before she'd upped roots for Yorkshire in the hope of finally putting the Big Ben Disaster, as her sister called it, behind her.

'*Maligayang Pasko!* How are you feeling about your big day?' Ate asked her now.

Angel's stomach twisted in apprehension. It felt like a whole lot more than just another Christmas Day in the UK. It even felt like more than three hundred and sixty-five days since her would-be husband had decided not to show up for their Scottish Christmas wedding. Today held a bigger purpose and promise that she would do her best to focus on as soon as she was fully awake and functioning.

'I'm a little nervous,' she admitted, padding across the room, her bare feet cold against the hardwood floor.

'You should be excited!'

Cradling the phone between her ear and shoulder, she

began pulling her new uniform from the wardrobe and laying out her clothes. 'I am! It's a huge opportunity, as you know, Ate, but I just… I don't know; I can't help feeling like I'm stepping on a few toes.'

Her sister snorted indignantly. 'You earned that position, Angel. Don't let anyone make you feel otherwise.'

Angel's fingers traced the embroidered patch on her flight suit: *Royal York Hospital Air Ambulance.* A thrill of pride surged through her, quickly followed by another wave of anxiety. She hadn't met any of her opponents in the interview process, but on her last visit she'd overheard a few whispers. Someone internal had gone for the team-lead position and clearly hadn't got it. She couldn't recall the name of the candidate, but it sounded as if, whoever they were, they were very well liked and very much admired.

'I know, but…' She hesitated, biting her lip. 'You know how these teams are—super-tight, usually; close-knit. They have each other's backs and I'm coming in from the outside, a total newbie. What if that person resents me for taking the job they wanted?'

She couldn't help the paranoia. Annoyingly, it had started around this time last year, when she'd dressed like the perfect bride for Ben, who'd sadly turned out to be decidedly less than perfect for her. She still didn't know why exactly he'd changed his mind, why he hadn't said anything sooner, why he hadn't voiced any doubts, fears or concerns, why he'd just…failed to show up. *Coward.*

'Then that's their problem, not yours,' her sister said firmly. 'You just keep your focus on being the best Lead Flight Paramedic you can be.'

Angel nodded, even though her sister couldn't see her. 'You're right. I've trained for this. I'm more than ready.'

'That's the Christmas spirit, sis!'

She cringed. 'Can we not use that word?'

Holding up her shirt, she started looking for her shoes and let Ate tell her all about their day so far. The excitement was palpable in her voice and, while she was glad to be away from their sympathetic condolences and questions, it made her miss her distant family hugely. 'We woke up early for Simbang Gabi, as we always do.'

'Mmm, I can almost smell the freshly brewed Barako coffee.' Angel closed her eyes for a second as her memory recovered its bitter fragrance mingling with the scent of bibingka and puto bumbong: delicious, traditional Christmas foods back in the Philippines. The warm, glutinous rice cake topped with butter, grated coconut and muscovado sugar was one of her mother's specialties and Angel missed it deeply, especially on cold days like this.

'After Mass,' Ate continued, 'We all came back here and started preparing for Noche Buena. Lola spent ages making her special lechon again—it's roasting right now.'

The mention of their grandmother's famous roast pig still had the power to make Angel's mouth water, even at this early hour. Lola's lechon was something else, its crispy skin perfectly covering the succulent meat inside infused with lemongrass, onion, garlic and other secret ingredients the proud woman had never revealed, despite the dozens of visits Angel had paid her over the years. Her parents had worked hard to keep the family ties all tied up tightly since they'd chosen to relocate to Scotland, just before having Kuya, Ate and Angel.

'And Kuya was on fireworks duty yesterday,' Ate added with a giggle. 'You remember how he loves making a spectacle.'

Indeed, she remembered. Their elder brother was used to lighting up the sky with a rainbow of colours that danced over their small town in Cavite every Christmas Eve and New Year's Eve. It was hard to believe it had been two entire years ago that she'd had taken Ben home to celebrate the holiday the Filipino way, with her family. She'd been so proud, showing him off, and showing off her ring too. They'd had so much fun in the kitchen, cooking up a storm with her aunts and singing out of tune until their voices had turned hoarse. Now...well, tonight she would be all alone.

Still, there was no need at all to infect Ate with her bad mood. Laughing wistfully, she perked up her voice. 'Sounds like you're having a fantastic time; give my love to everyone.'

Then she tried not to imagine where Ben was now. Was he with someone else already, spending Christmas with a new lover?

Ate passed the phone around the family, which took about twenty minutes and gave Angel time to make a pot of coffee and re-iron her flight suit, even though it didn't need another iron. Everyone sent their love. Her mother, tipsy already, went one step further, of course, and told her not to be lonely today, promising her she would find true love eventually, reminding her that Ben was a 'bad and undeserving man' and that Angel shouldn't feel as if she'd been left on the shelf...or whatever the Filipino version of that was. The meaning of her local dialect was loud and clear and most definitely not lost in translation.

Despite feeling flatter than an unbaked gingerbread man, when Angel hung up she at least knew her family cared unconditionally. She could always count on them, even if she'd never get too close for comfort with a man again. *No thanks.* She was done with that for...well, for ever.

Fastening up the last button on her uniform, she gave her reflection a once-over in the mirror. Her thick, dark-chestnut hair looked shiny, neatly tied back in a black band. She straightened her shoulders and lifted her chin. The woman staring back at her in the crisp, navy suit looked capable and professional—everything a Lead Flight Paramedic should be.

'You've got this,' she whispered to herself, forcing herself to believe it. 'This is the new Angel Flores: confident; in charge. And nobody in the Royal York Hospital Air Ambulance crew will ever know you were a jilted bride.'

The crisp winter air nipped at her cheeks as she stepped out of her car, locked it behind her and surveyed the Rufforth air ambulance base. First impression: cold. Second impression: windy.

She'd expected nothing less. The squat, utilitarian building stood like a grey, hulking concrete mass against the rolling Yorkshire countryside surrounding it. The moors were covered in a frosty white layer on this freezing cold Christmas morning, their craggy layers looking like an icing-sugar-coated cake. Angel squared her shoulders, doing her best to project confidence as she strode towards the entrance, though from a distance she could already see someone had strung up tinsel in the doorway.

Inside, the base was buzzing with quiet activity. Dr Samira Patel, a woman in her mid-forties with kind eyes and salt-and-pepper hair, looked up from a medical chart. 'You must be Angel,' she said warmly, extending a hand. 'Welcome aboard.'

Angel shook her hand firmly. Already, she liked her. 'Thank you so much, Dr Patel. I'm looking forward to working with you.'

'Call me Sam,' the doctor insisted with a smile. 'We're a pretty tight-knit crew here.'

As predicted, Angel thought to herself, looking around for anyone in this tight-knit group who might *not* look particularly pleased to see her.

A lanky man with a shock of ginger hair bounded over. 'Hey, you're the new lead, yeah? I'm Ollie, your fellow paramedic and resident comic relief.' He grinned and held out his hand, but as Angel shook it she detected a hint of wariness in his eyes. This was not a role that held much time for comic relief, but she'd take it where she could. 'Merry Christmas, by the way,' Ollie said, causing an icy chill to shoot up her spine.

Instead of visibly grimacing, she nodded politely. *No one knows; you're fine.* 'Nice to meet you, Ollie.'

Angel was briefly introduced to the pilot, George Abara. George was a broad, bearded forty-something local man who had a mischievous glint about him, despite seeming very serious and focused. She also met blonde-haired doctor Kate Johnson, a mother of two in her late thirties who was equally professional, but put her at ease with her friendliness, albeit with another, 'Merry Christmas' she could have done without.

Then, Sam led her on a tour of the base, showing her where everything was located and explaining various procedures and protocols. As they walked, Angel couldn't help but notice how clean and organised everything was. This was clearly a close-knit team that took its job extremely seriously, and she couldn't help another twinge of pride at landing this role. She'd always been extremely detail-oriented herself, especially when it came to her work. And wedding planning, she thought with another twinge that was definitely not related to pride.

Despite willing them to stay buried, memories of last Christmas rushed back at her like a speeding wave when she pictured herself this time last year, getting ready to walk down the aisle. The church had looked so beautiful. It had all been decorated with poinsettias and twinkling lights. She'd felt like a Christmas princess in the lacy bodice and flowing white skirt, a dress she had so carefully chosen with Ate during a long afternoon spent getting tipsy, over-excited at spending for ever with her Scottish hunk, Benjamin Faraday.

She would never forget how it had felt, standing in the church: the growing unease as the minutes had ticked by; the whispers; the pitying looks. And, finally, the crushing realisation that Ben wasn't coming. His version of for ever had already ended, and his future didn't include her.

'What do you think?' Sam asked her now, pulling her back to reality.

'I think this is impressive,' Angel commented as they passed by the fully stocked medical supply room, but in a heartbeat she found her gaze drawn to the helicopter, standing on the forecourt just beyond the open doors.

'Ready for the checks?' Sam asked, following her line of sight.

'Absolutely,' Angel replied. Its sleek lines and emergency markings filled her with both excitement and trepidation as she took in its shiny red-and-white exterior. There was something about being at one with the sky that had drawn her to this particular line of work: the freedom; the thrill of hovering high above a scene, seeing what no one from the ground could see. Being part of a team of professional risk-takers, who could reach people first in often-terrifying predicaments.

Stepping outside, the winter sun remained stubbornly hidden behind the clouds, but for a moment Angel was completely dazzled. A male figure leaning against the helicopter drew all of her attention and stopped her clean in her tracks. He was tall, broad-shouldered with dark hair ruffled by the wind, and he cut a very impressive silhouette against the frost-dusted landscape.

Who…was…this?

The man turned slowly, and Angel had to do a double-take. There was simply no other word for it—he was gorgeous. Beyond gorgeous. His piercing blue eyes met hers and his gaze stole all the breath from her lungs. Who *was* this? Pushing down the unexpected reaction, Angel straightened her spine.

'Angel, meet Edward Vaughn, flight paramedic,' Sam said, before she quickly excused herself, leaving Angel alone with the gorgeous man.

'They call me Teddy round here,' he said, his vivid blue eyes taking her in from her boots right up to her slicked-back hair. His tone was perhaps a touch cooler than she'd anticipated. He slid the phone he'd been talking on back into his pocket, and she noticed how he crossed his arms and kept one shoulder against the helicopter, as if he was propping the chopper up, and not the other way round. And then, it hit her.

Oh no. Angel's stomach dropped. *This* was the internal candidate she'd beat to the position. It had to be. Suddenly, the day ahead looked far more complicated than she'd anticipated. She'd only beat the hottest looking man she'd ever seen.

'They call me Angel Flores,' she replied anyway, taking him in, in return.

He nodded, a hint of a smirk playing at the corners of his mouth. 'An angel who loves to fly,' he noted dryly. 'Welcome to the team, Lead Paramedic Flores.'

Angel found she was trying pretty hard to keep her expression in neutral as she held out her hand, despite his tightly crossed arms. 'Thank you, Mr Vaughn. I look forward to working with you.'

After a pause that lasted too long for comfort, Teddy took it, his grip firm, his fingers cold from the frost in the air. He continued to eye her carefully, as if expecting her to do or say something untoward. Her mind suddenly spun on empty, and she was acutely aware of a treacherous flutter in her chest. She withdrew her hand too quickly.

'OK, Ed… Teddy. How about these pre-flight checks?'

Angel tracked him everywhere he set foot, whether behind her, on the opposite side of the forecourt or under the chopper itself. She focused intently on her tasks with Sam, listening as she and George explained everything. When she was sent to check the exterior with Teddy, she knew he'd been tracking her movements: he only explained the things he hadn't seen the others explain yet.

'So, Angel Flores,' he said casually as he inspected the rotor blades. 'What made you decide to join our little team here in York?'

Angel hesitated, not quite sure how much to reveal. 'I was ready for a change,' she finally answered. 'The opportunity to lead a team like this doesn't come along very often.'

She eyed him sideways, half-expecting a snide response—something along the lines of, *I know, this was supposed to be my role.* But Teddy merely nodded, eyes on the blades, his expression unreadable. 'It's certainly a demanding position. I trust you're prepared for the challenges ahead of you.'

OK, *ther*e it is, she thought, smirking herself now: the razor edge of bitterness. Or resentment…? She straightened, meeting his ice-blue gaze and holding it. 'I assure you, I'm more than capable of handling whatever might come at us out there.' If he was going to try and challenge her, she would challenge him right back. 'I hope you are too.'

A ghost of a smile flitted across Teddy's face and he bit down on it, almost as if he hadn't expected her reply but had rather enjoyed it. 'I don't doubt you're capable. You wouldn't be here if you weren't the best.'

The compliment caught her off-guard, and she felt a flush creeping up her neck, which thankfully was covered by her uniform. She turned away, ostensibly to check the medical equipment, but really to gather her composure.

Angel's mind raced as they completed the checks. She'd prepared herself for all kinds of scenarios on her first day, but this unexpected attraction to a colleague—and potential rival—had not been one of them. There was also the fact that, on one of her visits last week, she had heard a couple of the nurses mention that she'd been up against 'the hospital hottie'. There was no doubt in her mind now that they'd meant Teddy.

She took a deep breath, reminding herself of her goals. She was here to lead, to prove herself, to rid her brain of Ben—nothing else. This was her fresh start, and she was not about to let anything, or anyone, derail it —especially a 'hospital hottie' bad boy.

CHAPTER TWO

TEDDY GESTURED TOWARDS the supply room. 'Let's go over inventory procedures.'

Waking up on Christmas morning, prepping the giant turkey feast he planned for himself and Bruno—with inevitable, plentiful leftovers for the children's ward tomorrow—he had done his best to ignore the lingering sting of not landing the lead position. But, the second he'd turned round and met Angel Flores's imploring green eyes, another feeling had taken over, equally as profound. Now, to his immense irritation, he found himself battling *two* quite overpowering emotions: jealousy *and* attraction. Not ideal in any sense, especially when both surrounded one criminally beautiful colleague.

As he entered the cramped space with Angel, he was acutely aware of how close to her he was forced to stand. He hadn't expected to be half this floored by the woman who'd swiped 'his' role right out from underneath him, but his heart had completely betrayed him the moment she'd stuck out her hand and her chestnut hair had caught in Yorkshire's excuse for sunshine.

Her tone had been even more disarming as she'd met his gaze head-on and told him, in not so many words, that she was every bit as suitable for the lead role as he was. Maybe even more so; who knew? If he wasn't so annoyed by the injustice of it all, he'd probably have been amused.

Teddy reached for a clipboard. 'We keep narcotics in this locked cabinet,' he explained, tapping the metal door. 'Access codes are changed weekly.'

Angel nodded, crossed her arms, then bit her lip, which he guessed meant she was itching to counter something he'd said.

Sure enough, she offered, 'Wouldn't it be more efficient to use biometric locks? Less chance of compromised codes.'

Teddy looked at the floor. 'We've never had issues with our current system,' he told his boots, as well as her. When he looked up, she was staring right at him.

'Just because something's always been done one way doesn't mean it's the best way.'

He clenched his jaw tightly, fighting the instant urge to snap back. He never snapped. In fact, he prided himself on keeping his emotions in check. That was how things got done— diplomatically, empathetically, with kindness. Growing up at boarding school, he'd had to figure that out for himself, but it had never steered him wrong. Still, she was kind of putting him on edge, here. Not only was Angel Flores far too pretty up close, with those hypnotic wide-set green eyes, pale skin and almost-black hair, he wasn't used to having his methods questioned, especially by someone so new to the team.

'Look,' he said, 'I appreciate your input, but let's focus on getting you up to speed with our existing protocols first. There's a lot that Sam didn't cover.'

Angel lowered her chin to the floor, her entire posture radiating the kind of disapproval that reminded him for a split second of his mother—not a great start.

'OK,' she said, finally. 'What's next?'

He silently cursed himself for letting her get under his skin so easily. He'd always been pretty quick to take offence, no thanks to an upbringing chasing his parents for approval and rarely getting it. But the prickly tension between himself and Angel was not about to disappear any time soon, not if she was going to keep trying to fix what wasn't even broken.

'These trauma kits need restocking after every shift,' he told her now, gesturing to the row of red bags in front of them. 'As I'm sure you know, every second counts. That could be why we don't change things up very often. We know what we know, and we know what's where.'

Angel looked as if she was about to say something, but then thought better of it.

He cleared his throat, glad of the tiny victory. 'So, Ms Flores, what made you decide to transfer here? I think they said you were up in Glasgow before this? You don't sound like you're from around here anyway.'

Angel laughed softly. 'You're smarter than you look,' she said, and he rolled his eyes behind her back. Confident and a little cocky—great; just his type.

Angel paused, her hand hovering over a box of gauze. 'I was ready for a change,' she said simply. 'New challenges, new team.'

'New everything; I get it.' Teddy nodded. Something about her tone told him there was more to the story but he knew better than to push. Sometimes the best thing to do was seal the past up in a box, hide it where it couldn't torture you and start something new from scratch. Still, what ghosts was Angel running from? She had ghosts, he could tell.

'Yorkshire Air Ambulance was looking for new paramedics, so I thought I'd give it a shot.'

'So you packed it all up, came down here from Scotland and landed your dream job.'

She looked at him sideways, and Teddy regretted the slight bitterness that had crept back into his tone at the mention of 'dream job'. Yes, this *was* supposed to be *his* dream job, but Angel was probably entirely capable of doing it, from what little he knew of her so far. It was always going to sting, knowing *anyone* had been chosen over him. He had never handled rejection too well, even though he kept that fact to himself.

You are going to have to prove yourself, he thought, watching her inspect a lock on a cabinet. Then, almost as if she'd heard his unforgiving brain whirring, she turned to him.

'I know you went for the role too, Teddy. Sorry if you were disappointed.'

Teddy felt like a beetle under scrutiny all of a sudden. Her green eyes seemed to see far too much.

'I wasn't too disappointed,' he said, clearing his throat. Why did he suddenly picture his parents shoving him off to boarding school when he was kid instead of involving him in their plans? Now, that had been disappointment personified. He *knew* disappointment. 'We're a team out there, that's how I see it. Don't you worry about me.'

'OK.' She frowned at the boxes still on the floor. 'If that's how you see it, Teddy.'

His turn to frown. What was that supposed to mean—that they weren't a team? That she was planning to pull rank at every turn? She was clearly skilled, but their personalities seemed destined to clash. Well, as long as they could set aside their differences when it mattered most—out in the field, or rather, out on the dangerous moors—then maybe they'd be able to work together.

Angel's gaze shifted to him, curiosity replacing the guarded expression she'd worn moments ago. 'What about you?'

Teddy felt a familiar tightness take hold of his chest. 'What about me?' He checked his phone, then put it back into his pocket, trying to appear nonchalant.

'Well, let's start with why you're working on Christmas Day.'

'Someone has to. I'm here for the same reason you are.'

'I doubt that,' she said, too quickly. She laughed almost bitterly before catching herself, and his curiosity spiked. Then she changed the subject again and started asking about the fire extinguishers. The strange tone in her voice and the look of vague vulnerability on her face just now struck a chord in him. As he showed her the ways of the wonky cabinets and the refrigerator that sometimes had a stuck door, he was hit by a sudden wave of loneliness that he usually managed to keep at bay.

Images of his family flashed through his mind. What were they all doing today?

His sister Jules would already have called in to their mum and dad's from another of her snooze-some law firm Christmas parties. His brother Matt would already be over his City bonus celebrations. Whatever they had to report in the lead up to going home for Christmas Day was always far more interesting than anything *he* had to report, because their careers were deemed more acceptable. By the time this day rolled round, he was usually too worked up by them all that it was better for his sanity to avoid them, and this year was no exception.

So here he was, spending another festive season flying over the moors on medical missions. He could have joined his lawyer parents, and Matthew and Jules for the day, sure.

It was always an open invite. But they'd only spend the whole time belittling his career choice. Maybe not always intentionally—they were never cruel—but it grated after a while, feeling like the black sheep. They were all about success, all of them: money, status, power.

This job…well, it wasn't exactly what his mum and dad had had in mind for him when they'd packed him off to boarding school, intent on instilling both discipline and a drive to make as much money from a career as possible, as they did.

'Where's your family?' Angel asked now, clearly curious, thanks to his silence.

'Doing their thing, probably. Same as I'm doing mine. They're scattered all over.' The last part was kind of true, he thought guiltily. They were scattered all over the place on every day, except for today.

George Abara, their pilot, hovered in the doorway, his eyes darting between them. He was no doubt already feeling some of the tension they'd filled the space with. A wry smile played at the corners of his mouth, but he made no comment.

'Just wanted your opinion on something, mate…' he said finally, stepping fully into the room and unbuttoning the front of his flight suit. Then, much to Angel's obvious shock, he did a full twirl in a reindeer-patterned jumper. The garish Christmas top was a hideous hodgepodge of bright green-and-red baubles, with a huge brown reindeer head smack in the centre. Its eyes were all googly, its nose was a shiny red pom-pom and its antlers were covered with jingling bells. At least it was lifting Teddy out of the funk he'd just fallen into.

'The perfect blend of awful and awesome, mate, as usual,' Teddy said with a genuine grin, feeling Angel's eyes on him. Like Kate, George had two kids at home to whom he'd be going back tonight, complete with gaudy jumpers, presents and songs, unlike Teddy. He'd be cosying up with his best bud, Bruno the French Bulldog, and a whole banquet of food that would last until well into January. It was a ritual he had come to prepare for and secretly enjoy, one that kept him away from his family.

But if *George* was doing this now, then he might as well… 'I mean, googly eyed reindeers are great,' he said, standing up and unbuttoning his own military-style flight suit. 'But can you really compare with this…?'

Again, Angel's eyes were practically glued to him, even more so as he lowered the top half of his suit down around his middle, revealing his worst Christmas jumper yet.

George burst into laughter. 'Oh, mate, no, you didn't put *lights* on it too?'

'Yes, I did, George. Yes, I did.'

Teddy's jumper was the clear winner here, even if he did say so himself, and even if it wasn't a competition. The neon snowmen and snowflakes all clashing and screaming for attention was one thing, but the flashing snowflake lights were quite another. He watched Angel's eyes widen in disbelief as he flicked them on and off via a tiny battery pack in his pocket, and he couldn't help but chuckle at this particularly shameless choice in festive attire.

George was almost doubled over with laughter, so much so that both Kate and Sam poked their heads in to see what was going on. Pretty soon they were all admiring their jumpers, talking about how their kids were dressing up and discussing what they were doing tonight and for the rest of the holidays.

Teddy glanced at Angel, expecting a similar response. Maybe she'd hint at what she was doing tonight, not that he should want to know. Instead, he watched as she visibly stiffened when Kate jokingly asked where her Christmas jumper was. She was still shoving gauze into boxes and he could almost see a shudder running through her body, the way everyone was talking about their Christmas plans around her. Her lips pressed into a thin line. Eventually, she mumbled something unintelligible before brushing past them all to locate the bathroom.

No one else seemed to have noticed but Teddy. His instincts were primed. What was *that* reaction all about? OK, so he didn't exactly spend the Christmas holiday like most people, surrounded by family and kids. And, being a bachelor of twenty-seven, some would say he had nothing in particular to celebrate. But Christmas was usually a time for a bit of silliness and a few laughs with colleagues, even in this line of work. What could have triggered such a visceral response from Angel?

Before he could think any more about it, the radio crackled to life on the box beside him. Ollie's voice cut through the noise from somewhere outside on the forecourt. 'We've got a situation, team. We need to move.'

CHAPTER THREE

ANGEL'S SHOULDER WAS pressed firmly against Teddy's in the cramped space as the helicopter vibrated around her. The forced proximity to this undeniably attractive stranger sent strange jolts of electricity through her body. She shifted in her seat, trying to put even a millimetre of space between them, but there was nowhere to go.

Flustered, she kept her eyes on the outside world and drank in the scenery. The stark beauty of the moors was a far cry from the urban sprawl of Glasgow she'd left behind. Here, the world seemed both vast and intimate, wild and serene all at once. The frosty morning had painted the landscape in stunning shades of silver and white, transforming the rugged terrain into a breathtaking winter wonderland.

Even a Christmas-hater like her couldn't stop picturing flying reindeer cruising along beside them up here, where the rolling white hills gave way to stark, craggy outcroppings and impossibly high peaks. In the distance, a patchwork of fields was dazzlingly delineated by dark and ancient stone walls, their lines etched sharply against the pristine white of the scene. Incredible. If only her grandma in the Philippines could see this, she'd probably cry in awe.

'Do you like the view?' Teddy's deep voice cut through her thoughts.

Angel turned to him. 'It's stunning,' she said. But just

locking her gaze onto those ice-blue eyes of his caused the reality of their mission to settle over her like another icy frost. This was not about admiring the scenery. Someone was probably hurt.

Quickly she moved her gaze back to the moors below. Somewhere out here in this harsh, beautiful landscape, a lost boy called Joe Carter was probably shivering into layers she hoped he'd had the foresight to put on, already regretting his decision to run away. Whatever it took, Angel was determined to bring him home. This was her first ever mission with the team. Failure was not an option.

Her gaze flickered back to Teddy as he started up a discussion with Kate. With her shoulder still pressed to his, she could hardly not notice or appreciate the way his flight suit stretched across his broad shoulders. The earlier conversation in the storage room could have gone better, she thought, cringing inwardly. Her cheeks burned as she recalled how fast she had high-tailed it out of that room when the topic of Christmas had caused one too many memories to jump in and burn her.

How could she explain her hatred for Christmas without revealing the absolute humiliation Benjamin Faraday had inflicted upon her on their wedding day? The wound was still too raw, too personal. But, weirdly, the more she thought about Ben now, the more his image morphed in her mind's eye into Teddy, albeit in that ridiculous Christmas jumper he'd revealed back there—all lean muscle and easy confidence. The kind of swagger only a ladies' man possessed and paraded around.

She knew his type. Teddy Vaughn was well aware of how attractive he was, and she'd do best to heed the warning bells in her gut. She was drawn to him the way she'd been drawn to Ben, an A&E doctor at the same hospital in

Glasgow. Ben had been the accident, steamrolling into her life unplanned, but very much welcomed at the time. He'd been the emergency, her lifeline to happiness, her reason to breathe. She should know this feeling. She should know to ignore it. *Danger, danger, danger!*

Still, now, squeezed next to Teddy, she felt small and fragile in comparison, which wasn't entirely awful. He smelled nice too, but she couldn't place the smell: something sweet; not cologne. Something more…edible?

'You seem a little quiet,' Teddy pressed, his eyes searching her face.

Angel eyed him sideways. She wasn't about to say she'd been thinking he smelled like something she wanted to eat.

'Was it something I said earlier? You left pretty quickly.'

She shrugged, embarrassed. 'I just… I'm not a big fan of Christmas, that's all.'

Shoot, she hadn't meant to come out and say it quite so directly, but he'd thrown her, smelling so nice and everything—

Curse him.

Teddy frowned. 'I thought it might be something like that, seeing as you didn't even wear your Christmas jumper on Christmas *Day*.'

A bitter laugh escaped her before she could stop it. 'Well, for starters, this newbie didn't get the memo.'

He was quiet, no doubt contemplating all the things she wasn't saying. 'Why don't you like Christmas? Did Santa put you on the naughty list when you were a kid and forget to take you off?'

His questions made her squirm in the impossibly tight space, five hundred feet above the ground. He was onto her. He wasn't afraid of digging hard for the details. He was probably still mad that she was here, doing the job that he was supposed to be doing, even though he'd tried to claim he didn't care, that they were a team. *Yeah, right.*

But there wasn't a hint of animosity in his gaze when she met his blue eyes. If anything, the more she was silent, he just looked concerned. For a moment, Angel was tempted to spill everything just to get it out of her, to set it free over the moors. Maybe it would blow away in the wind instead of lodging in her throat and between her bones, dictating every little reaction to anything regarding Christmas. But, of course, that was not going to happen. Instead, she stayed quiet until he got the hint and started talking to Kate again.

Angel found herself studying his profile—the strong jaw, the hint of stubble, the way his mouth curved into a mocking smile at every opportunity. She could have mistaken that smile for cockiness, but maybe it was just his dry sense of humour coming through in the ever-changing set of his lips. Oh, lord. Why was she thinking so much about this, and his lips?

She tore her eyes away, her heart racing, just as the helicopter hit a pocket of turbulence, jostling them. Angel instinctively grabbed Teddy's arm. As her fingers dug into the sturdy material of his flight suit, she got a grip of the rock-solid muscle beneath.

Oh gosh, so hard. So... Oh dear.

'I've got you,' Teddy said softly, his hand covering hers for a brief moment.

Angel pulled away, crossing her arms tightly over her chest. She had done this many, many times; she wasn't afraid of a little turbulence. Teddy was just putting her on edge for some reason. She stared straight ahead, willing her pulse to slow. This attraction, this awareness, of Teddy was the last thing she needed. She'd come here for a fresh start, not to fall for another man who would inevitably trample all over her heart the moment he got even a morsel of it. So what if he smelled like gingerbread cookies?

Yes, that was it! *Gingerbread.*

She couldn't help cracking a smile at the realisation, which he caught. 'What's funny?'

She coughed. 'Nothing, just… I was just feeling very glad to be here. And the moors look so beautiful from up here.'

Damn. She'd already said that.

Angel's breath caught as the helicopter crested a hill, revealing in full the vast expanse of the Yorkshire moors stretching out below. 'It's…not like anywhere else,' she whispered, mostly to herself.

Teddy leaned over to look out of the window, bringing his face so close to hers, his stubble practically grazed her cheek. 'It never gets old. No matter how many times I see it.'

'I've never seen anything like it. It's like something out of a fairy tale.'

As they flew over a particularly dramatic cliff face, Teddy's expression grew pensive. 'Makes you wonder what could drive a kid to run away into all this, doesn't it? Especially at Christmas.'

She nodded as the familiar pang ripped through her chest. 'Something about Christmas just makes things worse.'

Teddy's brow furrowed. 'In what way?'

Angel shrugged, suddenly aware of how much she'd revealed. 'Everyone has their own reasons for why it just all gets too much, I suppose. Some people just need to escape. I just hope this boy, Joe, is OK once we reach him.'

She could feel Teddy's eyes on her, searching, but she kept her gaze fixed on the landscape below. The beauty of the moors seemed to mock her now, reminding her of everything she herself was trying to escape. She leaned across to George. 'What's our ETA?'

'About ten minutes out,' he replied. 'The last sighting was near an old quarry. Tricky terrain.'

Angel nodded, grateful for the shift back to work, but a small part of her couldn't help thinking that, despite this new job keeping her busy today, she was just as lost at Christmas as the boy they were searching for, and Teddy Vaughn was onto her.

The radio crackled to life. Dr Kate spoke to someone, presumably back at the hospital. Then she turned to them in disbelief. 'You won't believe this—the hospital's being swarmed by fans already, at this hour. They're all bringing Christmas gifts for Kyle Woodgate.'

Angel raised an eyebrow. 'Who?'

Teddy tutted. 'Some boy-band persona…'

'Not a boy band; he's a solo singer,' Kate corrected him sternly. Something told Angel she was a fan.

'What happened?' Angel asked.

George chuckled from the front, shaking his head. 'Oh, you haven't heard? Our local celebrity hit the hospital reception area at the start of December for a gig. The idea was that he would perform under the giant Christmas tree—'

'Only it wasn't installed properly,' Kate interrupted.

'Well, we don't know for sure what happened,' Teddy added tactfully. 'He was asked to put the star on top—this giant gold thing, twice the size of his head. Somehow the poor guy wound up pulling the entire tree down on himself and his entourage. It was like pulling pop stars out of a forest for about fifteen minutes.'

'You're kidding,' Angel said, doing her best not to laugh. It wasn't exactly funny but she couldn't help picturing the scene, all those people watching, then Kyle, whoever he was, tumbling down in an avalanche of pine and tinsel.

'Wish I *was* kidding,' Kate replied with a sigh. 'Broke his right leg, tib and fib. Fractured one of his hands, which is not exactly helpful to a guitar player. Poor guy has already been operated on once but he's going to be laid up for weeks.'

'Ash Dhillon will have to do another surgery,' Teddy added. 'Dhillon's the best surgeon we have, by the way.'

Angel winced. 'That's awful. Though you have to admit, it's a bit…'

'Ridiculous?' George supplied, a grin tugging at his lips.

'I was going to say ironic,' Angel said, but she couldn't help smiling too.

'Ironic is right,' Kate agreed. 'He definitely gave his fans a show they won't forget.' She was clearly hiding a smile too.

With some relief, this time Angel found herself warming to the camaraderie. It was a welcome distraction from her earlier melancholy, at least. But their amusement was short-lived. George's voice came over the intercom. 'We're approaching the landing site, guys. Prepare for descent.'

Angel's focus snapped back to the boy. She peered out of the window, taking in the rugged terrain below. The old quarry George mentioned was visible now and it looked like an eerily perfect spot for a teenage runaway to get himself into all kinds of trouble.

'Ready?' Teddy asked, grabbing the ropes and handing a bag to her. For a moment, Angel saw past the cocky exterior and got a full glimpse of the dedication and concern that mirrored her own. She nodded at him and was glad to feel a silent understanding pass between them.

The moment the helicopter touched down, they raced across the frost-covered ground, their breath making clouds in the freezing air. As they approached the edge of a steep ravine, Angel's heart sank. There, about fifteen feet down, huddled against the rocky wall, was the teenage boy they'd come to find. Even from here she could see that his thin frame was shivering violently in a threadbare jacket, his jeans torn and caked in mud, and he was clutching his leg, whimpering in pain. Beside him, also whimpering softly, was a scruffy Border Collie mix, its black-and-white fur all matted with dirt.

'Joe?' Angel called out, her voice carrying over the wind. 'I'm Angel, and this is Teddy. We're here to help you.'

The boy looked up, his face a picture of relief through the pain. 'My leg,' he croaked.

She turned to Teddy, assessing the situation, but he was already on it, already unpacking the gear. 'We need to set up a rope system. The ground's too unstable for a direct descent. I'll anchor the main line. Will you guide me down?'

'Affirmative.' Angel kept talking to Joe, keeping him still and calm as Teddy expertly secured the rope to a sturdy tree, double-checking each knot as he went. A surge of admiration took her by surprise. This was clearly where he excelled. Behind him, the others readied a stretcher.

'Remember,' she instructed, lowering her voice for Teddy, 'The boy's likely hypothermic on top of his injuries. We'll need to move fast, but carefully.'

Teddy flashed her a quick grin and a wink that threw her off-guard. 'Fast and careful? Not a problem.'

Before she could even conjure up an appropriate response—*was* there even an appropriate response to that—Teddy began his descent. The wind did its best to throw them off-course but Angel kept a steady hand on the belay device, her eyes never leaving Teddy's form. She called out instructions, guiding him around loose rocks and ice patches, acting as his eyes from above as she was used to in these situations. Not that she'd ever worked with someone like Teddy before. He was a whole new Yorkshire species of man…and she could not afford to dwell on this right now, or ever.

'You're doing great, Joe,' she shouted down to the boy. 'Just hang on a little bit longer.'

Angel felt the spike in her heart rate as Teddy neared Joe and the dog, only to be blown sideways by another gust of icy wind. He didn't seem fazed. His two feet were firmly on the ground and she could see the gentleness in his approach, the way he spoke calmly to both the boy and the dog, although she couldn't hear what he was saying. She watched him get to his knees on the ground and place his hands on Joe's shoulders, steadying him. He checked his leg quickly before attaching the harnesses.

'I've got them,' Teddy's voice crackled over the radio. 'Preparing for ascent.'

Angel braced herself, ready to assist in pulling them up. The moment Joe and his dog emerged over the edge, she rushed forward, wrapping a thermal blanket around the shivering boy, helping him carefully onto the stretcher Ollie and Kate were holding.

'You're safe now,' she murmured, rubbing his arms to generate warmth. 'You and your dog; what's his name?'

'Bandit,' he replied through shivering teeth, reaching for the loyal dog, who did not look about to leave his side any time soon. It was clear they were going to be taking the dog back in the helicopter too. 'He went too far, and then he fell, and I couldn't… I couldn't leave him…' Joe trailed off, grimacing in pain.

His left leg was busted—she could tell that much without Teddy repeating the same in medical terms—but Angel's chest tightened at the loyalty towards his pet in the boy's voice. While she had no pets of her own, and hadn't had in Glasgow either, her family in the Philippines had lots of dogs between them. Last she'd checked, Granny Lola was feeding at least nine.

Teddy was climbing out of the ravine now and her eyes met his. Angel felt a newfound respect for her colleague and, if she was honest, maybe another jolt of attraction to him in this moment of mutual accomplishment. She held her breath as together they quickly assessed Joe's injuries. The kid's left leg was badly broken—his shin swollen and misshapen beneath his torn jeans. There was no way they could transport him safely without stabilising the fracture first.

'We've got them,' Teddy's voice crackled over the radio. 'But we need to splint his leg before transport. It won't hold during ascent otherwise.'

Angel dropped to her knees beside the stretcher, already pulling supplies from their medical kit. She adjusted the straps, then moved fast, cutting away the fabric around Joe's leg with a pair of trauma shears. The sight of the injury made her stomach tighten—not because it was particularly gruesome, but because she could see just how much pain the boy was in and it only made her want to help more. Joe whimpered, gripping Bandit's fur in his hands like a lifeline.

Teddy crouched beside her. 'Joe, listen to me,' he instructed. 'We need to straighten this out before we can get you in the helicopter, alright mate? It's going to hurt a bit, but I promise we'll make it quick.'

Joe's breath hitched, but he gave a shaky nod.

Angel met Teddy's eyes. 'I'll keep traction while you set it, okay?'

Teddy bobbed his head. 'On my count.'

She positioned her hands carefully, gripping Joe's ankle and knee, applying just enough pressure to keep the leg stabilised. 'Squeeze my hand if you need to, OK?' she told Joe.

The kid nodded again, his fingers wrapping around hers.

'Three, two…' Teddy braced his hands on either side of the fracture and applied firm, steady pressure. Joe let out a sharp, agonised cry. His body trembled in their hands like jelly, but it was over in seconds. Angel murmured soft reassurances as she quickly helped Teddy secure the leg in a vacuum splint. They tightened the straps.

'You're doing amazing, buddy,' Teddy enthused, brushing a hand over the boy's shoulder. 'The hard part's done now. We're going to get you somewhere warmer.'

Joe blinked up at him, still teary but clearly reassured. 'Bandit too—he has to come with me.'

'Of course, Bandit too,' Angel said, rubbing his arms to generate warmth. 'He's not leaving your side. I bet he never does, huh?'

Teddy stood, rolling his shoulders. The storm was picking up, and they needed to move. He reached out, offering Angel a hand as she adjusted Joe's position on the stretcher. She hesitated, only for a fraction of a second, but the weight of his gaze sent a jolt of something through her that had no place here in the middle of a rescue.

Still, she took his hand. The warmth of his grip, solid and strong, lingered even after they pulled Joe and Bandit into the helicopter. Once inside, Angel got to work starting an IV, while Teddy leaned in, adjusting the boy's oxygen mask and checking his vitals. The dog curled protectively against Joe's side, ears flicking nervously at the hum of the rotor blades.

Teddy met her gaze again across the small cabin, something unspoken passing between them. They worked well together. That was a fact. But this? This was something else.

Angel looked away first, forcing her focus back on Joe. 'You're safe now,' she said softly.

'So, Joe,' Teddy said seriously as she and Kate checked

the boy's vitals and inspected what looked to be a pretty severe fracture. 'Want to tell us what brought you out here on Christmas Day?'

Joe hesitated, his eyes darting between them as Angel helped him drink some water. 'It's complicated,' he mumbled through his pain, reaching for Bandit, who had his paws up on the stretcher.

Angel busied herself with fitting Joe an oxygen mask but kept her ears tuned to the conversation, to Teddy's every expression of understanding. 'Family stuff, huh? Been there, mate. Some people don't have it easy at home.'

Joe's eyes widened slightly. 'You…you get it?'

'More than you know,' Teddy replied with a wry smile. 'Christmas in my house was… Well, let's just say it wasn't exactly a medley of Hallmark moments.'

Angel found herself pausing, struck by this glimpse into Teddy's home life and his past. He hadn't said anything earlier when she'd told him some people just need to escape at Christmas—meaning herself, of course—and she'd thought he'd been judging her, or at least silently wondering what her problem was. But maybe he had issues of his own around Christmas. She was seeing layers she hadn't noticed till now. Maybe she'd been too quick to pigeonhole Teddy Vaughn.

Joe seemed to relax a fraction, despite his obvious pain. 'My dad…and my mum…' He trailed off, absently scratching Bandit's ears. The boy clearly had a lot going on in his head.

'It's tough, whatever it is, I can tell,' Teddy said, while Kate confirmed the boy had likely suffered a femoral fracture to his left leg. They wouldn't know for sure until they got him to the Royal York for a proper check. For now, she and Teddy kept him talking. 'But you know what, bud? You've got people who care about you, even if it doesn't always feel like it. Your mum's probably worried sick right at this minute.'

'I doubt that,' Joe said glumly.

Angel stepped closer, meeting Teddy's eyes for a moment. It was clear this boy was going through some issues at home. They'd have to tread carefully until the right people could talk to him. 'And you've got Bandit here. Looks like he'd follow you anywhere,' she added softly.

At this, Joe managed a small smile, and the dog swiped his tongue over his outstretched hand, which only made Angel feel more homesick for her family and its menagerie of animals. They were celebrating in the sunshine now, or maybe the twilight, seeing as they were eight hours further into their Christmas. Being around their sympathetic glances and whispers was never any fun but at least they cared. She tried not to think about the single can of beans and three-day old loaf of supermarket bread waiting for her back at her flat. She hadn't bothered to go shopping. The Christmas food, decorations and supermarket staff all wearing their silly hats only annoyed her and sent her spiralling backwards.

Her hand brushed Teddy's as they both went to adjust the IV at the same time. A spark of warmth travelled up her arm that had nothing to do with the physical exertion of the past twenty minutes out there on the moors. Then, the dog swiped a lick at Teddy's hand, making Joe and him laugh despite the situation. She couldn't help joining in with their laughter. In this moment she would do anything to make this boy smile and it seemed as if Teddy was on the same page.

For the first time today, she was truly glad to have Teddy as her partner, even if she was going to have to watch her heartbeat around him. He was exactly the kind of maddening man she could see herself falling for. Maddening in the way he didn't seem to take himself too seriously, even when they were both knee deep in the middle of a crisis. Maddening in that his gorgeous grin appeared at exactly the wrong moments—when she really needed to focus—and maddening in how he made her laugh despite herself, disarming her with an offhand comment or a knowing glance that somehow said far more than any words could say.

And then there was the way he cared. Not in a performative way, but in the quiet, steady kind of way that crept up before she could even think to stick up her defences. And, most of all, maddening because Teddy seemed to see through her bravado to the tired, threadbare parts of herself she normally kept hidden.

And that was one hundred percent *not* something she could afford to keep happening.

CHAPTER FOUR

THE HELICOPTER'S BLADES whirred to a stop as Teddy's feet hit the helipad. Joe was strapped to the stretcher, looking small and vulnerable. The waiting team helped lower him to the ground as Bandit jumped loyally out beside him and he stood with his tongue out, as if awaiting instruction from his master.

'We won't be able to take Bandit inside,' Teddy explained quickly, casting his eye upwards where a drone was hovering close by. Reporters had been sneaking in however they could since Kyle had arrived. Joe looked visibly distressed at this news about his dog and he scowled from under the oxygen mask.

'Don't worry, we'll make sure he's safe,' Angel assured him. Teddy flanked the gurney, their steps in sync as they headed for the entrance. True to form, George kept hold of the dog and told them he'd keep him close for the rest of his shift. There would have to be some calls made to Joe's parents, Teddy thought. They needed to get to the bottom of why this kid had run away in the first place. He caught Angel's eye, noting the determined set of her jaw, and knew she was thinking the same thing. Maybe she was also wondering about the drone.

He still wanted to know why she hated Christmas so much. He hadn't missed the hint back there that she might have run away from something herself. His hunch about her ghosts was correct, but it wouldn't do to probe her, he decided. She'd barely been here five minutes and already things were…well, not exactly normal.

The lift doors slid open, revealing the chaos inside Royal York. His ears rang at the noise as they entered the A&E reception area, where the fateful tree had been reinstated. He hoped it was attached more securely now, following the accident that had taken down Kyle. The giant pine tree towered over them from the ceiling, resplendent in twinkling Santa-shaped lights, tinsel, and trinkets that the kids on the children's ward had made.

A sea of desperate faces with outstretched arms was clamouring outside, wanting to get in. It was like a scene from a zombie movie, except the zombies were all eleven-year-old girls waving gift-wrapped parcels accompanied by their irritated and no-doubt uncomfortably cold parents. It wasn't the best weather outside for accommodating groupies, but there was no way they'd all be allowed inside.

'Please, we just want to give Kyle our gifts!' he heard one young girl pleading, clutching a teddy bear to her chest.

Teddy's brow furrowed. 'They think this is Kyle Woodgate!' he said to Angel in amusement. Someone had obviously mistaken Joe for Kyle on the way in and a game of Chinese whispers had sent word around the whole crowd. Ah, he thought, remembering the drone. Maybe they thought Kyle had been snuck out and in again by way of the chopper.

'This is crazy,' he muttered to himself.

'This is *Joe*,' Angel corrected the girl gently, her voice barely audible over the commotion. 'He's not a pop star; sorry, hun.'

A security guard ushered her backwards to the door and attempted to reason with the pleading crowd. 'I understand you're concerned, but Mr Woodgate isn't here. Please, go home and…'

His words were drowned out by a chorus of protests. Teddy felt a pang of sympathy for the guard as well as the misguided fans and journalists waving their mics around at the entrance, even as irritation flared in his veins at the unnecessary distraction. Where was…?

'Teddy, hey!'

The deep male voice made him spin around. A&E doctor Ares Petrides strode towards them, his white coat open, revealing his own ugly Christmas sweater. They followed him through the double doors as Ares barked orders and sent the boy into a nearby room, leaving the din behind. Teddy's muscles tensed as he watched the doctors swarm around Joe. He wanted to help, to do something else, but he knew he had to step back now. He'd done his part, dropping down into that ravine in the bitter wind and cold, and now his stomach was growling. Somewhere there was a whisky with his name on it, and a dog waiting for his dinner.

Seeing his obvious distress in the midst of all the fuss, Angel leaned close to Joe at his bedside, her chestnut hair in its tight up-do gleaming under the lights. 'They're going to take good care of you, OK? We'll be right here if you need us; all you have to do is ask.'

'And Bandit?' Joe asked her hopefully.

'He'll be just fine; we'll keep you posted. Maybe he'll be allowed to visit you once you're settled, right Mr Vaughn?' Angel turned to him with those imploring green eyes. Those eyes had been doing strange things to his insides all morning.

'They let therapy dogs in the wards,' he told her, not wanting to disappoint her any more than Joe at the minute. 'Maybe we could pull a few strings.'

He was slightly disarmed at the way she smiled her thanks, and stepped back again when he caught the look from Ares. It was more than impressive, the way Angel was so calm in the face of such chaos—first out there on the moors and now in here, with all the drama going on regarding Kyle Woodgate's presence. He'd misjudged her earlier, he realised with a twinge of guilt. He'd assumed that of course he was the better person for the job. They were at least equals, he thought now, congratulating himself on his own generosity. It was Christmas, after all.

They exited the room and waited outside until Ares Petrides stepped out, snapping off his gloves. 'Femoral shaft fracture, as suspected. We'll need to prepare for surgery,' he said. 'Nice job, getting him here before he froze his b… Oh, hello there, I don't believe we've met.'

Ares extended a hand to Angel, and Teddy watched her eyes narrow in appreciation as the tall, strapping doctor introduced himself. A twinge of something like annoyance took him by surprise. 'So, um, while we're here, Dr Petrides, what's the latest on our pop icon, huh?' Teddy asked him.

Ares crossed his arms and Teddy did not miss the way Angel's eyes still raked over his friend's shoulders and forearms. He'd heard one of the nurses describe Ares as a Greek god not so long ago and it had stuck with him, though Ares seemed as reluctant to hold down a relationship as Teddy; the guy was literally always working. Teddy didn't actually know if Ares had ever taken a day off in his life.

'Kyle's stable, but it doesn't stop the journalists all fishing for a tragic story,' Ares said, casting his eyes behind them both. 'Tragedy sells!'

Teddy spun round to see who he was looking at: Ruby. *Ah...of course.* Teddy smirked to himself. He had a sneaking suspicion Ares had a giant crush on A&E doctor Ruby Phillips, who in turn always seemed to be in a world of her own. There was too much gossip in this hospital to keep up with.

Angel was already heading back into the room, where Joe was processing the news about his surgery. Teddy followed her. Fear was written all over the kid's face now but Angel was as soothing as ever. 'Joe, I'm sure the doctors explained how you've broken your thigh bone,' she said. 'Did they tell you how they'll have to stabilise the bone with rods and screws?'

Joe nodded glumly, but Angel squeezed his arm in comfort. 'I know it sounds a bit scary now, but it's the best way to help you heal. Don't worry; you're in very good hands.'

'I just want my dog.'

'Like we said before, you'll see your dog soon enough. For now, you have to concentrate on yourself and get better. OK?'

Teddy watched as Joe processed the information, his young face contorted with both fear and resignation. He felt a surge of protectiveness for the boy that he couldn't help, despite the rumble in his stomach telling him to end his shift on a polite goodbye and go home. This situation was taking him right back to boarding school, when he'd been the voice of reason for the bullies intent on roughing up the new kids, himself included. He'd made friends with everyone there and kept the bullies as close as his peers. People never started on someone if they liked them. Trust was everything.

'Will…will I be able to walk again?' Joe asked him directly, fixing him with wide, scared eyes.

Angel's green eyes softened as she answered for him. 'Sooner than you think. You're strong. You've got this.'

Teddy found himself nodding in agreement. 'You'll be

fine, son,' he added. 'And, like Ms Flores said, we're here if you need us.'

He surprised himself with the depth of his commitment to Joe. Maybe it was because it was Christmas but it already felt easier than he'd anticipated, being Angel's partner. He always wanted to be committed to the people he rescued and brought here for treatment, but sometimes it seemed as if his job was just one emergency after the other. He often had to deposit one person and go back for someone else and only sometimes did he get time to check on them after.

He could make more time if he truly wanted, he supposed, if he wasn't so averse to emotional connections of any kind. It seemed as if Angel was the kind of person who gave everything one hundred per cent—everything except Christmas. Still, she was firmly making herself available for this lonely boy, and it moved him. This case had already become so much more than a routine rescue, just from being in it with Angel.

He glanced at her, and in that moment it hit him—what her presence had stirred in him, what it had unearthed. The role of adrenaline junkie, the cocky, untouchable bachelor—roles he'd worn so well and so easily—suddenly felt like cheap disguises, masks he'd convinced himself were enough. But now, standing in the gravity of something real, something that mattered, they felt hollow.

He didn't want just to be the hero who swooped in for a brief moment and then raced off again, but maybe some people saw him as that—was that another reason Angel had got the job over him?

Teddy leaned against the wall, watching as Joe's eyes fluttered closed. The stronger pain medication was finally taking effect. The teen's face was a little more relaxed now and Teddy watched the lines of worry smoothing out. He looked even younger and more vulnerable than his fourteen years at this moment.

'I hate Christmas,' Joe managed to mumble, his words slurring slightly. 'S'stupid.'

'You and me both, pal,' Angel said softly, adjusting his blanket.

Teddy's eyebrows shot up. What was up with this anti-festive attitude anyway? The vehemence in Angel's voice suggested she'd rather lock herself in a dark room until Christmas was well and truly over than involve herself in any of that.

'What did Santa really do to you?' Teddy asked her outside in the hallway, trying to keep his tone light.

She shrugged, her focus still on the window to Joe's room. 'Let's just say Christmas and I aren't on speaking terms.'

OK, he thought. *Interesting.* He wouldn't question her here, or now. If he had any sense, he would make his excuses, go home and see about cooking that three-course dinner for Bruno and him, yet somehow sense had eluded him, and he was still standing opposite Angel, arms folded.

'So,' he began, his heart suddenly pounding. 'We're both off now until tomorrow morning.'

Angel raised an eyebrow and smoothed back her already-smooth hair. 'Your point being…?'

Teddy ran a hand through his hair, mirroring her, suddenly feeling like a nervous teenager. 'I was thinking maybe we could grab a coffee? I know we might have started out on the wrong foot this morning.' He held his breath, watching Angel's face for any sign of reaction. 'Or, you can keep me on the naughty list,' he ventured.

Her eyes narrowed slightly, and for a moment Teddy was

sure she was going to refuse him. Whether she hated it or not, it was still Christmas Day, and she probably had plans.

'Coffee,' she said finally. 'I could do that.'

'Coffee it is,' he said, relieved. 'But we'll go out. The coffee here is terrible.'

Angel excused herself and headed to the staff room to change, just as he did. When they met again in the foyer, Angel was minus her flight suit, holding a thick winter coat over one arm and Teddy had to do a double-take. He knew she'd left some clothes in her locker earlier in the week, as they all did on his team, in case they started out at the air ambulance base and ended their shift back here in the city.

Like him, she'd chosen to keep jeans here, which were far more flattering than the flight suit. The denim hugged her hips and flared slightly at her ankles, where her chocolate-brown winter boots began. The cream knitted sweater had tiny, shimmering specks of gold thread woven through it, and the hemline ended exactly at her waist, showing off the slim belt of her jeans and highlighting her gorgeous figure.

She threw his mind in directions it probably shouldn't go. What a cracking figure, he thought to himself. He loved a woman in uniform but this was a welcome transformation.

Teddy felt eyes on him from across the room. Turning, he caught a passing nurse eyeing him up. For the first time in a long time, he barely offered a reaction. Usually he'd throw a grin or a wink in her direction, or at least say a casual, 'Hi there,' but today his eyes only seemed to want to fix on Angel Flores.

They walked towards the lift and Teddy couldn't help but steal a few more glances at her profile as she pulled on a black duffle coat and dragged up the zip to her neck. He tried not to stare at her in the lift on the way down, and was more than grateful when three other people entered and stood between them.

Maybe it was her everyday outfit, or maybe it was watching her with Joe just now, being reminded of himself and how he'd been at boarding school, but she was intriguing, enchanting and hot as hell. They also seemed to make a good team so far—professionally speaking. Maybe in time he'd forget that she was doing *his* job. Or maybe that was a stretch; time would tell.

Outside, Teddy matched her stride without over-thinking it, the crisp air carrying the faint hum of city life and the scent of roasting chestnuts. It was a thousand times more peaceful out here than in the hospital. Across the street, the sprawling Museum Gardens beckoned with what was left of their late-season blooms and meandering paths, while the River Ouse sparkled under the pale afternoon sun. A boat was gliding along and from here he could just make out Santa hats through the windows. An extravagant Christmas party on the water, perhaps, for a family?

He glanced at Angel as they walked, watching as she pulled her zip up a notch higher against the wind. There was a cosy riverside pub just off the south bank that he knew was open today—a perfect excuse for a detour and a coffee—but it wasn't just the promise of caffeine that pulled him along. Something about Angel Flores had hooked his curiosity, and he couldn't resist the chance to peel back a layer or two of her mystery.

'So,' he began, thinking it was best to start with something simple. 'Do you live in York itself?'

Angel nodded, keeping her gaze fixed firmly ahead. 'I have a little flat in High Petergate,' she said, and he nodded. That wasn't too far from his own house.

'Do you like it here?'

'I do,' Angel replied. 'It's different to Glasgow.'

'How so?'

'It's warmer here, if you can believe that!'

He chuckled into his thick, woollen scarf. 'I can't believe that, I'm sorry.'

Christmas lights twinkled at them from lampposts and shop fronts and a string of reindeers flashed overhead as they took an underpass, not unlike the ones on the jumper he was wearing under his coat. He noticed Angel deliberately averting her eyes from the festive displays.

'What would you like?' Teddy asked as they entered the bustling pub and approached the bar.

'Just a black coffee, thank you,' Angel said, and the silence between them descended again while they waited, louder than the buzz of conversation from all the festive pub-goers. He'd been hoping to strike up more of a dialogue. So far she was definitely more of a quiet, observant type than a talker. Unless he'd put her off earlier, shutting down her ideas for improvement. He felt a little bad about that now.

'So,' he ventured, handing her an Americano and motioning her out through the door again and onwards along the street. 'You were really good with that kid, Joe.'

Angel's lips quirked into a small smile. 'So were you. But it's sad how he felt the need to run away from home, especially today. I hope he gets the help he needs, for whatever's going on there.' She eyed him sideways over her coffee cup. 'You said holidays in your house were pretty rough.'

'Did I?' He didn't recall saying that to her but, come to think of it, he might have said it to Joe.

'Well, you definitely seemed to empathise with him over something. Did you have strict parents growing up?'

'You could say that,' he offered, feeling his cheeks warm

as he took a swig of his steaming hot pumpkin-spiced latte. He wasn't about to admit how little his parents had ever valued his decision to step away from the corporate grind. Their quiet disappointment—the pointed questions, the passive-aggressive praise for his siblings—had lingered for years, chipping away at him until he'd learned to shut out anyone who might unwittingly make him feel smaller.

He liked to think he didn't care any more; that their opinions rolled off him like water off a duck's back. But the truth was harder to ignore. Their judgment had left its mark, and had made him wary of letting anyone get too close over the years. Instead, he'd cultivated a persona, one that suited him perfectly well. Around the hospital, he wore his reputation like armour—the charming, unattached bachelor who made people laugh. It kept things simple. Women knew the score: a drink, a laugh, maybe a night or two, but nothing deeper, nothing messy. Emotional connections were for other people, not for him. He was perfectly fine relying on himself, and making sure Bruno could rely on him. He kept everything—especially his heart—under very tight control.

Teddy realised Angel was looking at him, waiting for him to elaborate. 'They shipped me off to boarding school,' he found himself explaining, trying and probably failing to keep the bitterness from his tone. 'So I guess Saint Olivier's School for Boys saw more of me than they did when I was a kid. What about you? You said you grew up in Glasgow; is that where you went to school?'

She nodded, and stopped to lean against a railing, looking out over the water. 'My family never encouraged us to travel very far from Scotland, not for anything. Well, unless it was to travel to the Philippines. I have a lot of family over there. My parents and siblings are there now, actually.'

She had a faraway look on her face as she talked, and he followed her eyes to the sparkling water and the boat full of people in Santa hats that had turned around for another cruise. 'And you weren't tempted to go with them for Christmas?'

'Nope,' she said firmly. He smiled. *OK, then.* There was definitely something more to her decision not to be with her family, the same as there was probably a very good reason she didn't like the festive holiday season in general, but she wasn't going to say it and he wasn't about to push.

Well, maybe just a little. 'Reckoned you'd stay here all alone, huh?'

'Just me and my baked beans tonight,' she said. Then she scrunched up her face. 'Gosh, that makes me sound very sad, doesn't it?'

Teddy shook his head, trying and failing to shake the thought that was building in his mind like a giant snowman. 'I'm actually planning to make dinner tonight for myself and my dog,' he started, willing himself to stop. What was he doing here, exactly?

'Your dog?' At this, Angel turned to him with interest. 'Oh, I do love dogs. What kind of dog do you have?'

'A hungry one.' He smiled. 'Bruno's a French Bulldog. I could tell you were a dog person too, from the way you were so concerned about Bandit back there.'

She bit her lip and shrugged, telling him her gran was always feeding the community dogs in the Philippines. He felt a shift in the air between them now. The initial frost was thawing, slowly being replaced by something warmer that had somehow made him step closer without realising. His sleeve brushed hers against the railing. Why not just extend an invite for dinner? What harm would it do?

He drew a breath. 'Well, Bruno is waiting for me at home,

and I know he's probably hungry because that's his standard setting. I don't suppose, if you're not doing anything tonight, you'd be willing to ditch your baked beans and come to *my* place for dinner instead?'

CHAPTER FIVE

ANGEL FELT HER eyes widen as she took in the sight before her. Teddy's home in the heart of York's Low Petergate was a complete, tinsel-clad Christmas wonderland.

'Welcome to the grotto.' He grinned, ushering her in from the cold.

'Wow.' She breathed, not entirely sure what else to say. His place was the total opposite to hers, which of course was devoid of anything remotely to do with Christmas.

'My flat is…completely bare compared to this,' she admitted, distracted for a moment by a giant paper snowman beckoning them into one of the rooms off the hallway.

'Really, you don't have anything Christmassy up at all?' Teddy looked confused by this, as if he himself had been waiting eagerly all year just to light up his place like Santa's personal refuge.

'Nothing,' she said as he took her coat. 'A friend sent me an advent calendar the other week but…' She stopped herself quickly. It would not do to admit to this man how she'd stashed it into a drawer before it could so much as tempt her to empty it of chocolates. 'This is…special,' she managed, as she watched him carefully hanging her coat on a brass hook, which was overlooked by a grinning elf, its stripey-tight legs dangling from the shelf above it.

Teddy chuckled, his deep voice sending an unexpected

shiver down her spine in the enclosed space. 'I take it you approve?' he said, leading her into the living room.

It was all she could do not to let out a gasp. A towering pine tree he must surely have either felled himself somewhere in Norway or had imported was strung with twinkling lights and shimmering ornaments. The thing entirely dominated one corner of the living room and there were already more than twenty brightly wrapped parcels on the carpet underneath it.

Soft fairy lights were draped across exposed wooden beams, casting a gentle glow over the space as he walked ahead of her to light the fire in the hearth. This was amazing. She had never before been in a York townhouse like this. The place was five times the size of her tiny flat and yet fifty times more cosy. How on earth could he afford this on a paramedic's salary?

Ah, yes: he came from money. If his parents had sent him to boarding school, that had to be the case.

Before Angel could tell him that it smelled nice in here—like gingerbread, funnily enough—a snuffling sound drew her attention towards the floor. 'Oh, hi there!'

A stocky French Bulldog waddled towards her, its wrinkled face set in an expression of curious determination as it went about sniffing around her boots. 'And you must be Bruno,' she said, crouching down to greet the black-and-white dog.

'That's my boy,' Teddy replied, and her heart swelled at the pride in his voice. 'He's the real master of the house. How are you, bud? Did you have fun with the dog walker this afternoon?'

Bruno sniffed his outstretched hand, his cute, stubby tail wagging furiously. Then without warning, he turned back and launched himself at Angel, nearly knocking her off-balance onto the hallway rug in an attempt to lick her face enthusiastically. Angel laughed hard and genuinely for what felt like the first time in ages. 'Oh, you're a friendly one, aren't you?' she cooed, righting herself and scratching behind Bruno's ears.

As she fussed over the dog, Angel felt Teddy watching her as he stoked the fire. In turn, she stole looks at him in his silly jumper and jeans. He looked pretty good in those jeans. Just now, outside by the river, she'd felt electricity coursing between them every time their sleeves had brushed, but she hadn't wanted to make it too obvious by moving away.

'He doesn't usually take to strangers so quickly,' Teddy observed. She looked up, meeting his gaze. The warmth in his blue eyes caught her off-guard and sent another jolt of electricity through her, even from a distance. So different from this morning. *Dangerous*, she reminded herself.

She quickly returned her attention to Bruno. 'Well, I'm honoured,' she said, meaning it. 'He's absolutely adorable, Teddy.'

As Bruno settled into her lap on the sofa, apparently more than content with the attention from a stranger, Angel found herself relaxing despite her earlier reservations about coming here. When he'd asked, her first thought had been, *absolutely no way,* but the thought of those baked beans had been less than inspiring, and besides, she'd thought, would it hurt to get to know her colleague? The cosy space and the presence of this lovable dog was a far cry from the lonely evening she had anticipated, and she could almost overlook all the festive cheer. Almost.

Teddy's living room was a study in understated elegance, with dark wood furniture and leather arm chairs that exuded old-world charm. The subtle touches—a neatly folded throw on the sofa, a vase of wooden tulips catching the firelight—hinted at influences beyond his own. The subtle results of a woman's advice, maybe? Or, women's…? The thought unsettled her more than she cared to admit, and a flicker of jealousy sparked before she could even try and tamp it down.

This wasn't a date, she reminded herself. Of course, it wasn't. Teddy wasn't a potential anything; he was a colleague, and this was just…dinner. Two people avoiding solo meals and filling the awkward silence with polite conversation. So why did the air in the room feel so charged? Why was her heart too aware of his easy confidence as he poured her a glass of wine? It was nothing; just a professional getting-to-know-you moment, wasn't it? So she should try and get to know him, as he'd been trying to do with her.

'I love what you've done with this place,' she fished, unable to help herself. 'I had no idea flight paramedics were paid so well.'

Teddy chuckled, the sound low and warm. 'This house is a bit of a family heirloom, you could say.'

Angel nodded, trying to quell the discomfort rising in her chest. She had already guessed that he came from money. Her own family had always been, not poor exactly, but certainly not wealthy. As if reading her mind, he asked what had brought her family over from the Philippines.

'Mum and Dad wanted a family and they wanted to give us a better life, I suppose,' she said. 'Mum was a healthcare assistant in a care home. Dad was a bus driver at first, for the city's public transport service, but after he completed his engineering training he worked in construction. What about your parents?'

'They're lawyers,' he said simply, moving to a sleek sound system, his fingers playing with the controls. Soft, jazzy Christmas music soon filled the air, adding to the festive ambiance, which she tried to ignore. She was already thinking how Ben had played this very song last Christmas when he'd invited a group of colleagues over for Christmas drinks in early December, barely a month before the wedding. Come to think of it, they hadn't really spoken much that night. Ben had been all caught up in discussing something with that new A&E doctor he'd invited… What was her name again?

'Ah, there you are!' Teddy's swooping motion jolted her from her reverie. He picked something up from the floor, then turned to her, holding out a pair of fluffy red slippers covered with white snowflakes.

'Here,' he said, his blue eyes glinting. 'We can't have you getting cold feet now, can we? Change these for your boots.'

Angel felt her cheeks warm at the double entendre. Cold feet… Was he flirting? Suggesting she might leave, rather than get comfy? She slipped off her boots and put them on, and caught Teddy watching her, his gaze lingering on her feet.

'They look good on you,' he said casually, but an undercurrent of appreciation in his voice made her blush even more, and she never blushed if she could help it. He wasn't exactly flirting, but he was admiring her, and she didn't entirely dislike his attention. Wiggling her toes, she felt oddly exposed.

'Thanks,' she murmured. The tension in the room seemed to thicken till she found herself holding her breath. 'So, um, they're lawyers?' she followed up, clearing the block from her throat and reaching for her wine glass.

As Teddy bent to put on his own pair of slippers, a blur of black-and-white fur darted past him. Bruno had snatched one of her boots in his mouth and was making a mad dash for the hallway. 'Bruno! No!'

Teddy lunged after the dog and nearly lost his balance as he scrambled across the polished hardwood floor. ‘Leave it, you little menace. I said leave it!’

Angel couldn’t help but laugh again at the sight of him on his knees, chasing after the dog. ‘Who has trained who, here?’ she asked, careful not to spill her wine as Bruno dodged around the coffee table with Teddy on his tail. The boot was still firmly clamped in the dog’s jaws and there was no sign that he was going to let go. Angel realised she hadn’t laughed this much in ages.

‘I’m so sorry,’ Teddy called over his shoulder, his face flushed with exertion. ‘He’s got a thing for shoes. Especially nice ones.’

‘It’s fine,’ she managed between giggles. ‘Bruno has good taste.’

After a few more loops around the living room, Teddy finally cornered Bruno and wrestled the boot from his grip. He returned to Angel, slightly out of breath, holding her now slightly damp boot. ‘I think it’s still in one piece,’ he said, gathering up the other one and placing them both on the shelf in the hallway beside the elf, out of the dog’s reach.

Angel looked at him expectantly as he entered the room and sat on the sofa with her, albeit at the other end. One of the decorations now dangled off his jumper but she resisted the urge to do anything about it.

‘Oh, you want details about my parents?’ He frowned for a second, sinking back into the cushions. ‘Well, it’s not that thrilling, really. They actually met in law college, back in the day. Classic, really—two ambitious types with money on their minds, vying to be top of the class, studying late in the library, arguing over case studies, trying to outdo each other at first. You know the type. Dad ended up going into corporate law—high stakes, long hours, flashy clients.

He's the kind of guy who lives for a big deal, like he gets some buzz out of beating the other side into the ground. I remember him saying it's all about strategy: "making your opponent think you're one step ahead, always…"'

Angel listened to him, and she didn't miss the slight bitterness in his tone, the same one she'd heard earlier when he'd mentioned they'd sent him to boarding school. What was the deal here?

'Mum's totally different,' he continued as Bruno leapt onto the sofa to snuggle between them. 'She's a family lawyer. Spends her days untangling messy divorces, custody battles, that kind of thing. Always saying she's there to help people through their worst times, you know? Not like *what we do*.' He looked at her pointedly, arching his brows, then shook his head.

'Not like what we do? You mean…?'

'Flying around looking to rescue people in danger. Yeah, what they do is way more important than that.'

His sarcasm fell flat, and he seemed to know it. Sighing, he swigged from his wine glass then pursed lips, a sudden darkness descending over his face.

'Sometimes I wonder if she's got some martyr complex or something, but maybe that's too harsh. Anyway, all they talk about now is work, or they don't talk at all. They've done well for themselves—big houses, nice holidays.' He gestured around him at the living situation they'd clearly afforded him. 'But when you spend too much time with them, you start seeing all the cracks, you know? They look perfect from the outside, like they've got it all figured out. But I don't think either of them is actually happy. My brother and sister are the same. Do you have siblings?'

'I have an older brother, Kuya, and a younger sister, Ate,' she said, still processing what he'd just told her. 'We're all pretty close, but I don't speak to them as much as I used to, not since…' She trailed off, stopping herself short before she could add, *since they watched me get completely humiliated on my wedding day, exactly one year ago today.* Talking to her family for too long invited too many queries as to her wellbeing, when she'd rather everyone just forget about it and move on.

'Since…?' Teddy was looking at her, curiosity all over his face. She looked down at her slippers, then at the roaring fire. She could tell him just enough, she supposed, leaving out the most humiliating part. 'Well, the thing is, they knew my fiancé…'

'You have a fiancé?' Teddy looked quite shocked for a second and she swallowed back a sudden thrill, followed by a pang of the usual embarrassment and heartache.

'No. I have an *ex*-fiancé. But, since we broke up, it's kind of been… I don't know… I guess I don't want to talk about it. They all just want to talk about it.'

Teddy was quiet for a minute, patting Bruno between them, probably letting her words marinate. 'I'm sorry, you and your fiancé broke up? Was it recent?'

'It happened last year,' she said simply, hoping he'd leave it at that. She made a thing out of fussing over Bruno again, but he was still eyeing her when she looked.

'This time last year?' he pressed.

'Mm-hmm,' she replied, swigging her wine, knowing full well he was putting the pieces together.

'So, *that's* why you hate Christmas?'

'Something like that,' she said, and she stayed silent, patting Bruno until Teddy excused himself and disappeared into the kitchen, muttering something about checking on dinner.

Angel found herself alone in the living room, her fingers

brushing the edge of the mantlepiece as she tried to steady her breathing. The faint hum of a Christmas tune and clinking dishes from the kitchen felt miles away, drowned out by the rush of her own heartbeat.

She hadn't told him. She couldn't. Some scars weren't meant to be laid bare—not to a relative stranger and brand-new colleague. Teddy didn't need to know about the dress that had never made it to their hotel room floor, the promises left unpromised or the ring that now sat buried in a drawer at her parents' house in Glasgow. But at least now he had a glimpse of why she felt so untethered.

For most of the year, she could keep it all locked away, box it up and carry on as normal. But December… This month unravelled her every time, maybe would for the rest of her life. No matter how hard she tried, the memories would always creep in—the twinkling lights, the music in the church as she'd stood there, the well-laid plans for a dream Christmas wedding that had never come to pass. All of it was a shadow, a ghost that would haunt her for ever.

Shaking herself out of the funk, her eyes wandered over the tastefully decorated space, taking in the details she'd missed earlier. Despite the warmth of the house, with all its lovely furniture and art, she noticed there wasn't a single family photo in sight. Maybe there was more to Teddy not being with his parents today than them simply just being lawyers and in a completely different professional headspace. It seemed to them vocations didn't matter. And anyway, how could they not think what Teddy did was incredible?

Angel's mind drifted to her own flat, where a single framed photo of her parents sat on her bedside table. Sinking back into the sofa, she couldn't help thinking how this evening was panning out. If she were at home now, she'd be munching on dry toast and microwaved beans, probably scrolling mindlessly through her phone before falling into a fitful sleep. This—being here with Teddy—was infinitely better, even if their conversation stirred up some pretty complicated feelings.

Angel took a deep breath, inhaling the comforting scent of gingerbread. At least he had initiated this chance to reset their working relationship on a more positive note, she thought. He was fundamentally a good man, and there weren't enough of them in the world.

Teddy reappeared, balancing a tray laden with an assortment of festive snacks, including gingerbread men, complete with little smiley faces. 'Home-made?' she asked.

'Yes, ma'am,' he said. 'I took some to the children's ward yesterday.'

Of course you did, she thought, biting down on her lip and accepting one. The rich aroma of warm spices filled the room, wrapping around her like a cosy blanket. She resisted the urge to tell him he'd carried the same scent earlier himself—no doubt from baking these in his kitchen earlier in the week. A man who baked… Fantastic; just what she needed—one more reason for this wildly inappropriate crush to spiral even further out of control.

'Don't eat too much,' he warned her, setting the tray on the coffee table. 'Dinner will be ready in about an hour.'

He settled beside her on the sofa again, close enough this time that Angel could have reached out and fixed that dangling bauble on his jumper. She tried to ignore the way her heart was thudding an entire upbeat tune at his proximity.

'So tell me,' Teddy said, reaching for a handful of nuts, 'Favourite Christmas movie—or do you hate those too?'

Angel hesitated, her mind immediately flashing to last Christmas Day evening, curled up with Ate half-watching

It's a Wonderful Life and crying into her wine glass. She shoved the memory aside, warning it not to intrude on her again.

'Um, probably *Elf*,' she lied, forcing a smile. 'You?'

As Teddy launched into an enthusiastic defence of *Die Hard* as the ultimate Christmas film, Angel found herself relaxing, despite her inner turmoil at being surrounded by all this Christmas stuff. She laughed at his arguments, momentarily forgetting the ache in her chest that had been present the entire lead-up to the holiday. He was good company. Not to mention so ridiculously hot, especially in this context, all lit by the fire. Gosh, was she getting tipsy?

'Earth to Angel.' Teddy's voice cut through the haze in her mind, pulling her back to the moment.

She blinked, shaking herself loose from her thoughts. How long had she been staring at him?

'Sorry, just... You were saying?'

Teddy's gaze softened, studying her as if he was trying to read between the lines of her distraction. But, instead of pressing, he shifted gears. 'I was wondering how you got into flight paramedicine.'

Thank God for the change of subject, she thought, leaning slightly towards him as she crossed her legs, the movement small but deliberate on her part. Somehow her body wanted to get closer.

'It was a bit of a roundabout journey, actually,' she admitted, watching the way his eyes flicked down just for a second before returning to hers. 'I always knew I wanted a job that kept me on my toes. I thought about nursing first and trained in emergency medicine. Ended up working shifts in the A&E at the Royal Infirmary in Glasgow for a while. It was...intense, as you'd expect. But I loved it.'

Teddy's expression shifted from curiosity to something

intent that sent a slow heat curling through her stomach. Was he interested in her story, or just in *her*?

'What got you into air work?' he asked.

Angel shrugged, the weight of his attention pressing against her skin. God, he was too handsome for his own good. 'I wanted to be out there, reaching people before they even got to hospital. So I trained as a paramedic with the Scottish Ambulance Service. But there's only so much you can do in a city. I wanted to see more, and more of the countryside too, from up there.' She gestured upwards with a finger.

His smile tugged at the corner of his lips, slow and knowing, and for some reason it made her breath catch.

When she turned the question on him, he ran a hand through his hair. The effortless motion was small and meaningless but it sent her thoughts scattering.

'I'd always thought about doing medicine,' he said. 'I liked the idea of helping people in a real, hands-on way, but the thought of six, seven years of study…nah. I worked as an ambulance tech for a while and got some real-life experience. Then, one day, we got called to this accident on the moors. It was rough terrain, middle of nowhere, and I just remember watching the helicopter come in. These guys just stepped out, calm as anything, totally in control of the chaos. It sounds daft, but right then I knew—I wanted to be one of them.'

Angel could easily picture it—Teddy, younger but just as rugged, standing in the wind, watching the helicopter descend. She swallowed, her throat suddenly dry. Had he always been this ridiculously attractive, or was it just the way he talked about things—with that fire in his eyes and that low, addictive timbre in his voice?

'So, I trained, did all the courses and qualified as a paramedic, then went through the extra training to fly. Yorkshire Air Ambulance took me on after that. And, yeah, it's intense. But there's something about it…being in the air, getting to people who really need you, sometimes saving lives right there in the field. It feels like you're making a difference, in a way I don't think I would have if I'd stayed on the traditional path.'

He glanced at her again, but this time it felt different. His gaze lingered. Heat prickled at the base of her spine.

'Sounds like we're in it for the same reasons, fundamentally speaking,' she said, her voice coming out a little lower than before.

'I suppose so.'

His eyes dipped to her lips—so quick she almost convinced herself she'd imagined it. Almost. Her pulse hammered. God, this was dangerous.

As if sensing the shift in the air, Teddy got up and returned with two glasses of water. She took hers, her fingers brushing his as he handed it over. The contact was fleeting but it sent a flicker of something hot and electric straight up her arm.

'The job itself is exciting enough for some people,' he said. 'But I've always been an adrenaline junkie. I don't really ever take a day off that doesn't involve something crazy.'

Angel leaned forward without thinking, drawn in…drawn to him. 'Oh? Like what?'

Teddy tapped his fingers against his knee—a lazy rhythm that somehow seemed more intimate than it should. 'Well, there's fell-running in the Dales; there's nothing like sprinting up and down those hills to get your blood pumping. And cave diving; Yorkshire has an awesome cave system. Did you know, the Yorkshire Dales National Park has one of the biggest underground chambers in Britain?'

'I did not know that.'

'I've recently got into paragliding off the cliffs at Flamborough Head, too. That's a rush.'

Angel exhaled, feeling warm in a way that had nothing to do with the fire in the hearth. Every word that came out of his mouth made him seem wilder and even more untamed. And some reckless, hidden part of her *wanted* that.

'I wish I could try something like that,' she blurted before she could stop herself.

Teddy's lips curled at the edges, slowly and smugly. 'Oh yeah?'

Angel flushed but refused to back down. 'I mean, paragliding sounds fun. I've never done anything like that.'

'Well,' he said, his voice dropping just a fraction, 'Maybe we could change that.'

The way he looked at her now, as if she was some puzzle he was enjoying working out, made her stomach tighten.

'I'd be happy to show you the ropes some time.'

Oh boy. That shouldn't have sounded as suggestive as it did, but maybe it was just the way he'd said it. Or the way his gaze swept over her, slowly and assessingly *while* he said it, as if he was already imagining it.

Her heartbeat kicked up. 'You know what?' she said, forcing a casualness she absolutely did not feel. 'I think I'd like that.'

Teddy's eyes darkened just a little, and she swore she saw his jaw tighten. But, before he could say anything, an alarm blared from the kitchen. He exhaled sharply, breaking whatever had been simmering between them like a pot, then got up with an easy stretch.

'I'd better check the oven again,' he said, disappearing into the kitchen with Bruno at his heels.

Angel let out a breath she hadn't realised she was holding. Her skin felt too tight somehow, and her hair too heavy. She reached up, tugging the band from her bun, letting her hair tumble loosely around her shoulders.

This was not how she'd expected today to go. And, if she wasn't careful, this crush, this thing growing between them, was going to spiral way beyond her control.

CHAPTER SIX

TEDDY LOOKED UP from where he was laying the cutlery. The candlelight flickered across Angel's face as she stepped into the dining room in her slippers. She'd taken her hair down. It had been up all day, tightly pinned back, but now the candles cast the kind of ethereal glow on her long, thick dark hair, that made her truly look like an angel. He almost dropped the knife he held.

Quickly, he pulled out a chair. He'd always had a thing for brunettes, and ever since they'd started talking he hadn't been able to look away from her green eyes for too long before being drawn right back into their magnetic depths. It was probably why he'd already said far too much about his family. That, and the wine.

'I hope you're hungry,' he said, clearing his throat. He was nervous and trying not to show it. 'I know Bruno is.'

It wasn't every day, or indeed every year, that he had Christmas dinner with a woman. Especially one who this time last year had had a fiancé. She seemed hesitant to share many details about what had happened, but she was here now, and he'd take her mind off it. It was what he was doing for himself by having her here: taking his mind off what bothered *him*. What a pair they were, not that this was anything more than a getting-to-know-you dinner. Angel was off-limits.

Her eyes widened as she took in the elaborately set table. He'd gone all out with the good decorations his grandma had given him years ago. In fact, he'd never used them at all until now.

'Teddy, thank you so much for this,' she said, sweeping a hand through her hair and then crossing her arms across her jumper as if she didn't know what to do with her limbs. He fought the urge to grin, feeling far too satisfied with her reaction to his efforts. 'Just wait until you taste my turkey,' he said lightly, then paused, wondering if that sounded like innuendo.

Usually, he'd lean into a line like that—innuendo was his go-to, the perfect shield to keep things breezy and detached, another way to dodge the vulnerability that always seemed to creep in when someone got too close to seeing the real him: good old cheeky Teddy.

Somehow it didn't feel right with Angel, especially not after what she'd just told him. He hurried back into the kitchen and came back carrying a dish with a golden-brown roasted turkey on it, its skin crackling under a glaze of herbs and butter. He'd set the timer to slow-cook it all day. Now that his efforts were wrapping the room with the scent of rosemary and thyme, he was very glad he'd got such a big turkey this year, just for something to do with the leftovers. It was always so satisfying, knowing people enjoyed his cooking.

'This is… Teddy! Were you going to eat this all by yourself?'

'There will be some for the freezer. But I was also planning to make some turkey sandwiches for some of the kids at the hospital,' he said, carefully setting the turkey down at the centre of the table, its juices glistening in the soft light.

He returned to the kitchen and brought out the side dishes

next, and Angel 'ooh'ed and 'ah'ed as he explained each one: creamy, garlic mashed potatoes, swirled with melting butter; honey-glazed carrots with caramelised onions; a green-bean casserole topped with crispy bacon; tiny sausages wrapped in more bacon; and two perfect Yorkshire puddings, of course.

'You even did Yorkshires?' Angel looked beyond impressed as he took off the oven gloves and finally took his seat beside her. 'This looks amazing. I honestly can't believe you did all this.'

Teddy shrugged, aiming for nonchalance, even as warmth spread like syrup through his chest. 'Just a little Christmas taster. We're having beans on toast after this, if you're still hungry.'

She covered her laugh with a hand, and he began carving the turkey, placing generous slices on Angel's plate before serving himself. As he did, he couldn't help but notice how the candlelight was performing tiny, erratic dance moves in her eyes, bringing out flecks of gold he hadn't noticed until now.

'More wine?' he offered, reaching for the bottle.

She hesitated a second.

'Oh, go on, it's Christmas,' he encouraged, and she rolled her eyes, holding out her glass.

'Go on, then.'

'We drink to remember. We drink to forget,' he said, topping up his own glass and watching for her reaction. She clinked her glass to his and bobbed her head thoughtfully, and he left it at that. Her break-up still seemed so raw; how could it not be? He couldn't actually believe she'd been engaged. Not because she wasn't beautiful, mature and smart, and more than capable of becoming someone's wife, but he'd never come close to that kind of commitment in his life.

He found it almost impossible to imagine how two people in their late twenties, as he assumed she was, could get to that point at all.

As Teddy poured, he caught a whiff of her perfume, just as he'd done today in the helicopter. It made him want to lean in closer to discern what it was. Sometimes he could get it right; it was a game he liked to play with his dates, not that they ever knew he was playing it. He resisted the urge now, focusing instead on filling their plates with the various side dishes. This was not a date, or a game.

He should be ashamed of himself, he thought, only to be pulled right back to those gorgeous green eyes again as she said, 'You really do know how to make a good Yorkshire pudding, this is wonderful!'

'Why, thank you. It was my gran's first lesson with us in the kitchen when we were kids.'

'My gran loves to cook too,' she said, tucking in. 'During the Christmas holiday in Scotland, we'd make all her favourite recipes from the Philippines—especially the years we couldn't make it back. It was our way of bringing a little piece of home to the house, even when we were miles away.'

He liked the thought of her cooking in her own kitchen, maybe wearing a cute little apron, sticking her finger into pies and stuff… God, where was his head at?

A soft whine from beneath the table caught their attention. Teddy moved out his chair, suddenly remembering his other guest.

'Sorry, boy, did we forget about you?' he said, standing up and leaning over to grab a small plate. He prepared a little taster of everything for Bruno and Angel laughed as he set the dish on the floor.

'That's definitely got to be tastier than my boots.'

Teddy nodded, settling back into his chair. 'I reckoned

he deserved a proper Christmas dinner too. Though I doubt he'll appreciate the cranberry sauce as much as we will.' He raised his glass again, meeting Angel's eyes. 'Merry Christmas, Angel.'

Angel's brow furrowed slightly. She clinked, but with less enthusiasm than he'd been hoping for, and he pulled a face. 'You really do hate Christmas, huh?'

'Sorry, it's no reflection on this dinner, but…' She set down her fork and looked at Teddy, her expression unreadable. Somehow it sent a chill through him. 'Can we not talk about it now?'

He sucked in a lungful of herby air and carved himself another slice of turkey. 'Apologies for my nosiness.'

'Apology accepted,' she said, and was silent for a moment. He hoped she was still enjoying the meal, even though he'd put her on the spot. What the hell had happened with her fiancé to warrant a break-up at Christmas anyway? Wasn't it supposed to be the happiest time of the year? He'd read somewhere that January was when most break-ups occurred. People wanted fresh starts in January; everyone's flaws seemed sharper once the New Year hit and the festive fun was a blur, behind them. Maybe her ex had spent the season pretending—holding back until he couldn't any more. Teddy had reached the end of a few relationships feeling that way; most had lasted less than six months.

'Anyway.' She turned to him. 'You seem to be the biggest Christmas fan I've ever met, Teddy. I know you said you have your differences, but why aren't you with your family for Christmas? Or anyone, for that matter?'

He paused, taking a sip of wine to buy himself a moment. It was a fair question, with a multi-faceted answer. 'Like I said before, my family are all over the place…most of the time.'

'But not today?'

He sighed, feeling his usual confidence wavering slightly. 'Not today, no, but I had to work. And, as for the second part of your question, well, I'm single by choice, Angel.'

'Single by choice?' Angel's perceptive gaze told him she sensed there was more to this story, and also that she was already on to his reputation with women. The hospital grapevine spared no one, even new starters. He sawed into a carrot, dragged it through some mash and dunked it in yet more gravy, avoiding her eyes.

She was quiet for a moment, eating her meal and watching Bruno wolf his down. 'I don't want to inflate your ego but I don't think I've ever had a Christmas dinner like this. All I can say is everyone else out there is missing out,' she said. 'They're *really* missing out.'

He grinned. 'So, you do love something about Christmas.'

She bit back a smile. 'I wouldn't go that far.'

'Admit it, I've found a crack, haven't I? Was it the mash or the green beans?'

'Stop it,' she laughed, and he did, but it didn't stop the thrill of another victory lighting him up from the inside. He'd spent years convincing himself that he preferred his independence, that the lack of family gatherings didn't bother him. But something about Angel's appreciation had snuck into his own cracks. Despite the fact that they were having fun in each other's company, her gentle observations were making him acutely aware of the emptiness he'd been trying to ignore. An empty void he was used to filling all year round with a string of beautiful women and his work.

Clearing his throat, he shifted the focus. 'What about you?' he asked her, rolling up his jumper sleeves. The now-blazing fire in the other room was heating up the whole ground floor now. 'Why didn't you head back to the Philippines with your family this year?'

Angel's eyes flickered with surprise, perhaps to know he was storing up all these little details about her and her past whenever she cared to share them. She took a moment before responding, absently twirling her fork in her mashed potatoes.

'I wanted to focus on my job,' she said finally. 'It's so new; I knew they'd be short on Christmas Day, and if I'm honest, I felt like I needed to prove myself.' She paused, then added, 'I heard someone equally talented was going for the role.'

He laughed. 'Smooth.'

She smiled. 'Plus, after everything that happened last year… I guess I needed a fresh start.'

Teddy nodded. The hint of vulnerability in her voice caused a surge of protectiveness that jarred him. He'd only known her for a day! And this was the same woman who'd stolen his job from under him…not that that was her fault, exactly.

'Well,' he said, opting for the kindness she deserved, 'I for one am glad you stayed. Christmas wouldn't be the same without you here to help me make a hundred turkey sandwiches.'

Angel sat back in her chair. 'Oh, you have me on sandwich-making duty, do you?'

'It's either that or the washing up. Bruno can only do so much of that with his tongue before he vomits on the carpet.'

The clock ticked on unnoticed as they lingered over their meal. Their conversation flowed easily. Between bites and sips of his best South African wine, they swapped stories, laughing over the quirks of various dogs they'd known and loved in their lives. Teddy surprised himself by how much he shared with her. Stories poured out of him—tales of calls out on the misty moors, the unpredictable rescues he'd endured, the beauty and danger of Yorkshire's caves and why he'd probably never stop chasing the skies.

Angel matched him story for story, painting vivid pictures of Glasgow's streets and day trips to haunted Scottish castles, and the chaotic cacophony of her family back in the Philippines, who sounded like a hoot—not like *his* family. She talked about her siblings a lot, and the culture that had shaped her, and the more they talked, the more her voice seemed to warm with affection for a million things he found himself longing to experience for himself. She didn't touch on her past heartbreak, and Teddy didn't feel compelled to peel back the layers of his own romantic errors either. Instead, they stayed firmly in the moment, discovering surprising things that connected them: their birthdays were two weeks apart.

Three hours slipped by. It felt as if they'd been suspended in a bubble. Her laughter felt like a balm he hadn't known he needed, and somewhere between her stories and the glow of candlelight in her eyes Teddy realised that he couldn't remember the last time he'd felt this light, this content—especially at Christmas, and especially in the company of a woman.

Even when they finished dinner, he didn't find himself looking at the clock or reaching for excuses to end the night. Instead, when he suggested they take Bruno out for a walk, Angel grabbed her coat without hesitation and he was glad that she wanted to join him. He was even gladder when she came back inside with him afterwards. For the first time in years, he didn't even think about being alone.

'You know, Flores,' he said later, leaning back into the sofa cushions with his feet up on a foot stool and Bruno snoozing with a full belly by the fire, 'This is a bloody good Christmas. Usually, I'm on edge around now, waiting for a call.'

'You don't like *any* calls at Christmas, Mr Holiday Enthusiast?' she teased.

Teddy realised what he'd said. She must think he despised communicating with his family, which wasn't true at all. He just avoided them as best he could.

'I just like my alone time,' he offered, handing over a plate of mince pies. She took one, saying she'd just have one more, even though they'd both devoured three each by now, half-talking about food and half-watching *Elf* on his giant TV. She curled her feet up under her on the other end of the sofa, biting into the crumbly pie.

'I hope I'm not encroaching on it,' she said, and he watched her mouth for the millionth time, imagining wiping a stray crumb from her lower lip, then forcing his hands to stay firmly where he could see them, on the remote control. 'I should probably call a taxi soon,' she added, stifling a yawn as she glanced around. 'What time is it?'

'Time you stopped worrying,' he replied with a grin. 'We'll get you a taxi when Elf makes it back to… Elf Land.'

She turned to him, mock horror spreading across her face. 'Elf doesn't live in Elf Land. Have you seriously never seen this film?'

'Nope. Mostly because people won't stop talking through it.' He tossed his crumpled mince pie wrapper her way and she dodged it with ease, her playful smirk returning as she lifted her foot to give him a light kick. But before she could connect, he caught her ankle in one swift move, grinning triumphantly as she leaned into the tug, trying her best to reclaim her footing.

That was all the invitation Bruno needed. The dog stole

Angel's warm corner the second she moved, like a seasoned thief.

'Traitor,' she laughed, nudging Bruno lightly with her elbow. Bruno just wagged his tail. Teddy leaned back, his eyes lingering longer on her mouth than they should. For a brief moment, Angel left her foot in his hands, looking at him down her nose, half in amusement and half in suspicion. Then she curled her legs back under herself, this time right next to him in the middle seat.

Teddy stretched out again, feeling a warmth that had nothing to do with the crackling fire. He tried to concentrate on the film, but his eyes flicked back to her whenever she moved until eventually he caught her stifling another yawn. Her eyelids were growing heavy, and so were his.

'Tired?' he asked.

'Mmm,' she murmured, her head gradually tilting towards his shoulder. 'Just a little. It's been a long day. I'm good, though; the film isn't over yet.'

Teddy's heart quickened as Angel's weight settled against him. He debated moving, and offering to call her a taxi right now, but the thought of disturbing this peaceful moment felt almost sacrilegious. Instead, he allowed himself to sink deeper into the sofa, his own exhaustion catching up with him. The room was so warm and cosy. His belly was full. The fire's glow created a cocoon of comfort around them that felt so delicious and snug…and Bruno snoring softly next to Angel just added to the tranquillity. Maybe he should just close his own eyes for five minutes, no more than that. Just to relax…

As his own eyes grew heavy and the noise of the film faded out, Teddy's last coherent thought was how nice this felt. For the first time in years, he felt truly at home in his own house.

CHAPTER SEVEN

ANGEL SIGHED CONTENTEDLY, burrowing deeper into the warmth. Her mind was still hazy with sleep, and it convinced her this was another Sunday morning with Ben, with his slender arms wrapped around her waist, his gentle breath on her neck.

'Mmm,' she murmured, eyes still closed. 'Five more minutes.'

But something nagged at the edges of her consciousness. The arms encircling her felt different—stronger, more substantial. The chest pressed against her back was broader, radiating heat like a furnace.

Angel's eyes flew open. This wasn't Ben.

She stirred, the weight of a solid, muscular thigh pressed intimately between hers jolting her fully awake. A large, warm hand rested across her stomach, the heat of it seeping through her shirt like a brand. Slowly, she turned her head, already dreading the confirmation: tousled dark hair; sharp, chiselled jawline; and—oh, God—a truly heinous Christmas jumper covered in grinning reindeer.

Teddy.

Her stomach flipped as the realisation hit like a brick. She had fallen asleep wrapped in Teddy Vaughn's arms. Panic zipped through her veins like hot lightning as memories of the previous day and night came crashing back. The hospital. Joe. The coffee and the drive to Teddy's place. That dinner. That wine. Talking for hours at the table, and then on the sofa…

The warmth that had felt so comforting moments ago was suddenly something else entirely. She should not be here, let alone enjoying it.

'Oh God,' Angel whispered, her throat constricting. How could she have let this happen? She was supposed to be a professional team lead—detached, starting new and afresh—not cuddling up to her impossibly handsome co-worker on day two of her employment like some lovesick teenager!

She tried to extricate herself from Teddy's embrace without waking him, but his arms tightened reflexively. Angel wracked her brains as to how she could possibly travel back in time and undo this. Her heart was pounding so loudly she was sure it would creep into her dreams like the bass from a dance track.

Just relax, she told herself silently, sternly. *This doesn't have to mean anything. You fell asleep talking and watching a film. That's all. It was completely innocent, and totally unplanned.*

But, even as she tried to rationalise it, Angel couldn't ignore the traitorous part of her that loved the feeling of being held like this. It felt like a lifetime since she'd felt safe and protected enough to fall asleep beside a man, leaning against a man! She hadn't been in anyone's arms since Ben…and, come to think of it, she hadn't been able to relax with him completely since well before the wedding.

He'd always been on his phone. He'd told her he was stressed about the wedding plans, which of course she'd understood, because she'd been stressed too. Not so stressed that she hadn't wanted to be intimate, though… Thinking back now, he'd fended her off a few times when she'd tried to get close, which had left her feeling a little rejected. This… with Teddy…well, it was lovely, actually.

She shook her head. *Nope.* This was Teddy Vaughn—self-appointed single-by-choice playboy, adrenaline junkie and colleague. The last person she should develop feelings for.

With a deep breath, Angel steeled herself and abruptly pulled away, nearly tumbling off the sofa in her haste. The sudden movement jolted Teddy awake as well as Bruno, their eyes snapping open in confusion.

'Angel?' Teddy mumbled, voice husky with sleep. 'What…?'

She was already scrambling to her feet, smoothing down her crumpled clothes. 'I'm sorry,' she blurted, completely unable to meet his gaze despite just telling herself to relax, that this meant nothing. 'I shouldn't have… Oh gosh, this is embarrassing. I should go.' She backed towards the door, looking for her boots.

Teddy sat up on the sofa, dragging a hand through his hair. It was sticking out in all directions now. His drowsy eyes widened as the realisation dawned on him what had happened. 'Angel,' he said, his voice gruff. 'I meant to wake you up, then I fell asleep myself.'

The genuine remorse in his eyes made her chest tighten. She forced herself to meet his gaze. 'It's not your fault,' she said, surprising herself with the sincerity in her voice. The last thing she wanted was for him to feel bad. She should have called a taxi after that dog walk, or during it, but she hadn't wanted the night to end.

Teddy stood. His imposing frame seemed to fill the room as he blinked himself fully awake. 'I should have called you a taxi when I saw you were sleepy. That would have been the gentlemanly thing to do.' She could see he was frustrated by the set of his jaw. 'I don't want you to think I was…'

'Taking advantage?' Angel finished for him, a wry smile tugging at her lips. 'Teddy, we fell asleep talking. That's hardly scandalous.'

He shook his head and told her he should walk Bruno. Angel was about to announce that she'd leave them to it when her eyes landed on the clock on the wall. Her heart jumped into her throat. 'Oh no,' she gasped. 'Teddy, look at the time. We're going to be so late for work!'

His eyes followed hers. 'Damn,' he muttered, already striding towards what she assumed was his bedroom. 'Give me five minutes. We can take my car. I'll call the dog walker to come early.'

Teddy disappeared to change. Angel leaned against the door, her mind popping all over the place like a Christmas cracker. How on earth could she have let this happen? She had always prided herself on her professionalism, and now she was going to be late because she'd spent the night on her colleague's sofa, snuggled up to him no less.

'Get it together,' she whispered to herself in the hallway mirror, straightening her clothes as best she could. She couldn't go back in time and change the past, but she could make sure this didn't affect their working relationship at least.

And, if a small part of her already longed to be back in the warmth of Teddy's arms, well, she'd just have to ignore that.

Angel hugged herself against the biting cold as she followed Teddy to his car. The world outside was a proper Yorkshire winter wonderland this Boxing Day, beautiful, but she bet the roads were treacherous. A thick layer of frost coated every surface.

'I should've warned you,' Teddy said, his breath forming small clouds in the frigid air. 'It's going to take a few minutes to defrost this thing.'

He climbed into the driver's seat and started the engine, which sputtered to life reluctantly. The windshield was completely opaque with ice. Angel stood awkwardly by the passenger door. Should she get in, or wait outside? What was the protocol here? Just yesterday she'd been the lead in the role she'd been hired for, her head had been clear and she'd been prepared for anything. But after last night with Teddy, well, what was she now—a dirty stop-out?

No. She'd made a mistake, that was all. She'd just told him so. At the very least, outside of work they were equals, and he was a gentleman.

'You can hop in if you want,' he called to her, his voice muffled. 'The heat should kick in soon.'

Angel slid into the passenger seat, immediately struck by how small the car felt with Teddy's six-foot-something frame beside her. She focused on rubbing her hands together, trying to generate some warmth through her gloves. If only she had a coffee, that would help. It might also clear her hazy brain.

'So…' Teddy began, trailing off as he fiddled with the defrost settings. 'Now you've seen how I look first thing in the morning—'

'It's fine,' Angel cut in quickly. 'Really, Teddy.' Then she realised he was smirking. 'Well, and you've seen me too,' she said, smoothing down her hair again self-consciously. 'Nothing like a twenty-four-hour introduction to a new colleague to make you never want to see them again.'

'Speak for yourself,' he said, and she sighed through her

nose, willing away the tingles his words sent back between her thighs. He lowered his voice, which somehow only made her wish even more that she could be back on the sofa in the confines of his solid muscles. 'No one needs to know, Flores. We wouldn't want them to talk.'

'Do they normally talk about you?' she asked, throwing him a look.

'I would hope so.'

Angel frowned to herself, not sure how to take that. She'd only been here five minutes, and she hadn't exactly had the chance to talk to many people, but then he'd said himself that he was single by choice. And he was pretty much the hottest man she'd seen in the place…in the whole of Yorkshire, to be honest…so who knew who he'd hooked up with from the hospital?

They lapsed into silence as the defroster slowly cleared the windscreen but she was hyper-aware of Teddy's movements and the scent of him, which was decidedly non-gingerbready today, and mingling with the car's leather interior. She tried to distract herself by watching the ice melt, but her mind kept drifting back to how it had felt to wake up in his arms just now.

'OK, looks like we're good to go,' Teddy announced, startling her out of her thoughts.

The drive to Angel's flat was mercifully short, but the awkwardness lingered in her hair like the faint scent of firewood and candles. As they pulled up outside, Angel hesitated before getting out.

'Thanks for the lift,' she said. 'And for…everything.'

Teddy's blue eyes met hers, and she swallowed. 'Any time, Angel. But I'll drive you all the way; come on, hurry up!'

'I don't want to make you late,' she insisted. But he shook his head.

'We're already late; come on, get your things.'

Torn, she hurried inside, her heart racing, and rushed through her morning routine at five times the usual pace. The whole time she showered and changed at lightning speed, her mind kept replaying moments from the night before: Teddy's smile; Teddy's laugh; Teddy's openness the more the night had gone on, and her own. Except for the part about what had really happened with Ben. That secret still burned inside her like an excess piece of smouldering Christmas firewood.

Ben. This was the first time he'd crossed her mind since waking up, when for just a fraction of second she'd confused him with Teddy. Angel paused, toothbrush in hand, and stared at her reflection in the bathroom mirror. 'Don't,' she warned herself. 'Don't you dare start falling for him. You know better than this.'

But, as she slid back into the passenger seat to find he'd run over the road to the coffee shop to retrieve two hot, steaming brews, she couldn't quite shake the feeling that it might already be too late.

Angel's footsteps echoed in the hospital corridor as she walked towards the nurses' station. Her heart made a leap when she spotted Teddy already there, his confident stance unmistakable even from behind. As if sensing her presence, he turned, and their eyes met for a brief, electric moment before they both looked away.

'Morning, Vaughn,' Angel said, keeping her voice carefully neutral as she reached for a patient chart. She could feel the warmth creeping up her neck, betraying her composure. He'd dropped her off near to the hospital so they wouldn't be seen pulling up together, which had been her idea. She'd had to dart off for another introductory training session, but she couldn't shake the feeling that everyone knew she'd spent the night at Teddy's place anyway.

'Flores,' Teddy greeted her pointedly. 'Sleep well?' he dared.

Angel fumbled with the chart, nearly dropping it. 'Fine, thanks, why wouldn't I…have slept well?' she managed, more than aware of the curious glances from nearby staff. She was seriously wondering about his reputation around here. He had been nothing but lovely, considerate and kind to her last night, a real gentleman, but then she'd been looking through rosy wine-coloured glasses. The man could cook! It had always been the way to her heart. He'd said himself he knew people talked about him.

Teddy put a hand lightly on her arm, steering her with him. 'We should check on Joe,' he suggested, already moving them towards the paediatric ward.

'What are you doing?' she snapped, her pulse quickening as she struggled to keep up.

'Couldn't resist,' he whispered, a wicked grin taking over his mouth. 'Secrets are fun.'

She shot him a glare, pretending to swat at his chest, but he sidestepped with a boyish smirk that made her stomach flip.

Maddening! It wasn't just his kindness that got under her skin, and last night was an example of that—it was dangerous how he didn't even seem to realise the effect he had on most people, on her. He didn't notice how the smallest gestures made her pulse quicken—a hand brushing hers, a rare, serious expression crossing his face, even in jest—and every single one of her carefully constructed walls tremble. She should be annoyed that he was enjoying this, but she couldn't deny it *was* maddeningly fun.

A passing doctor paused mid-stride, raising an eyebrow

at their antics, and she immediately straightened, her face burning. 'How's Joe doing?' she asked a little too loudly, aiming for professionalism but landing somewhere closer to flustered teenager caught sneaking out.

Teddy didn't miss a beat, but the knowing glint in his eye told her he was not going to let her forget their little accidental sleeping arrangement. 'Better than expected,' he replied. 'The surgery went well, but…'

He trailed off as they reached Joe's room. The boy lay looking small and vulnerable in the hospital bed, despite the defiant set of his jaw. A woman in a crisp blue suit and thick, brown woollen tights stood at the foot of the bed, her expression as stern as one of Angel's old Scottish school teachers. 'Social Services,' he whispered to her, by way of explanation.

That makes sense, she thought, hoping the boy wasn't too intimidated. They didn't waste much time. What a way to spend Boxing Day. She followed Teddy into the room.

'Joe.' His voice softened markedly as he approached the boy. 'How are you feeling today, mate?'

The boy's eyes darted between Teddy and the woman. 'Fine,' he mumbled. 'When can I leave?'

The suited woman stepped forward. 'I'm afraid that's not possible just yet, Joe. Hello there, I'm Ms Reeves from Social Services. We've just been discussing Joe's situation.'

'Nice to meet you,' Angel said, as did Teddy, and just as the woman excused herself, saying she'd be back tomorrow, Teddy pulled up a chair next to Joe's bed and leaned in close. 'Did she help at all?'

Something in Joe's expression cracked. 'She doesn't understand,' he whispered. 'I can't go back home. I was just telling her that, not that she cares.'

Angel's heart clenched. She glanced at Teddy, expecting to see some kind of professional detachment. Instead, she was struck by the genuine compassion in his eyes, the gentle way he placed a reassuring hand on Joe's shoulder and gave it another squeeze.

'We'll figure this out,' Teddy promised. 'Meanwhile, there's someone else here to see you, who I think you'll want to see.'

Teddy reached for a walkie-talkie and mumbled something into it. A faint affirmation responded from the other end and then the door creaked open abruptly. Joe's wariness over another visit was gone in a flash, quickly replaced by the purest joy Angel had ever witnessed as Bandit bounded into the room, his full body wagging enthusiastically as he leapt to the bed and showered Joe in a frenzy of licks and happy whimpers.

'Bandit!' Joe buried his face in the dog's neck, letting out a shaky laugh. When she joined Teddy in patting the dog, his hand found hers amongst the thick fur, and warmth spread through her body like sunshine when his fingers lingered against hers. He didn't acknowledge the contact with his eyes. Instead he kept talking to Joe, leaving Angel flushed and more flustered than ever. What was she supposed to do with this giant flirt?

A nurse followed Bandit into the room, her uniform dotted with stray dog hairs she was still trying to brush away. 'Mr Vaughn has arranged for daily visits,' she explained to Joe with a kind smile. 'Bandit will be here every day until you're discharged.'

As Joe buried his face in the dog's fur, his grin stretching ear to ear, the nurse gently pulled Angel and Teddy aside. 'We contacted his parents about the dog,' she murmured. 'Unfortunately, neither of them has the time to care for him right now.'

Angel glanced at Teddy, her chest tightening. Despite the nurse's apologetic tone, she couldn't stop the smile tugging at her lips as she watched Joe's pure euphoria. Had Teddy done this?

'He'll stay with me for as long as you're in the hospital,' Teddy said. 'I'll bring him to see you every day—how does that sound?'

Joe was beaming now, still ruffling the dog's head, and Angel nudged him. '*You're* keeping the dog? I thought George was keeping it.'

'George's daughter is allergic. Bandit will just stay with me and Bruno; it's already arranged. When I'm working, the dog sitter can take over. What's one more dog?'

Angel shook her head. Was this guy for real? He probably would have stayed up all night making those turkey sandwiches for the children's ward too if they hadn't passed out on each other, watching that film.

With a pang she realised that just yesterday she had dismissed Teddy as an arrogant playboy. But he was revealing layers of compassion and depth by the second, and she was already powerless to resist his charms. Something told her she was going to have to guard her heart very carefully around this one.

CHAPTER EIGHT

TEDDY PEERED OUT at the stark landscape below. 'What's the status of our hiker?' he asked George into his headset.

'Young woman, early twenties. Apparently she slipped on some ice and twisted her ankle pretty badly. Can't make it back on her own.'

Angel leaned in. 'Any underlying conditions we should be aware of?' she asked, trying and failing to stop her hair flailing around in all directions and swiping Teddy's face from beneath her helmet. He didn't mind. In fact, he was quite enjoying it, along with the scent of her. He was starting to enjoy a lot of things about Angel Flores.

'None reported,' George replied. 'But you know how these things go. People don't always disclose everything.'

Teddy watched the frost-laced landscape stretching endlessly across the moors below. Hopefully this poor lady wasn't too badly injured. People did some crazy stuff in this bleak expanse between Christmas and New Year, taking themselves out on long walks they weren't always prepared for. He flexed his gloved hands, willing some warmth back into his fingers. He had also done some crazy stuff lately—namely, letting Angel get to him.

'How much longer till we reach her coordinates?' she asked.

'ETA five minutes,' George replied.

As they fell silent, Teddy found his gaze drifting to Angel, then back again. It was almost impossible not to look at her. The memory of waking up with her in his arms on Boxing Day wouldn't leave him, and every time he thought about it, it sent a bewildering blend of guilt and longing back through his brain and bones. He hadn't meant it to happen, but there was no denying how nice it had felt.

'We ready, Teddy?' Angel's voice cut through him over the rotors, directly into his ear. 'I like saying that, it rhymes.'

'Adorable,' he quipped in response. Unfortunately it came out with none of the sarcasm he'd intended, because he did indeed find her adorable. She was also infuriatingly untouchable. He knew his reputation preceded him, and he knew Angel knew about it by now. But, despite the awkwardness of their unexpected intimacy, he and Angel had fallen into an easy rhythm these past few days and he'd missed her company whenever she'd been out of his sight at her induction sessions.

They had sat together, hunched over stacks of paperwork and supply lists, and several people had poked in their heads, wondering about the laughter they'd heard spilling out of the room. Between flights, their tasks were far from glamorous—reviewing patient logs, checking inventory on emergency medical supplies and making sure the oxygen tanks and defibrillators were fully stocked and in working order. All the very un-fun stuff he usually didn't care for at all. She didn't seem to mind, though, which made it all more interesting for him. He had even started to accept that some of her proposed changes were viable and beneficial.

Somehow his own routine had taken on a different rhythm since she'd joined the crew, and every night when they finished their shift, he'd fought the urge to ask her back to his place, or at least somewhere else. He wouldn't do it, though. She was not to be touched. Angel was still healing. She'd only broken up with her fiancé a year ago. Every time he caught a trace of sadness in her voice or in her eyes, he wanted to punch whoever it was she'd agreed to marry for doing whatever the hell he'd done to dim her light.

All of this was very unlike Teddy. It wasn't like him to form emotional attachments of any kind, and it was unsettling to say the least. Maybe it was all the Christmas festivities, making him all mushy. He'd spent his whole life keeping people at arm's length, convincing himself he didn't need anyone. His parents had taught him that lesson early: attachment was a risk, a trap. Love was just another way to hand someone a weapon and wait for them to use it. So why chase something that would only slip through his fingers? Why let himself believe in belonging, in the warmth of reassurance, when experience had taught him that in the end people always walked away?

And yet…here she was. And, for the first time, he wasn't sure he wanted to run.

George's voice cut through his pondering. 'We're approaching the coordinates. Get ready to drop.'

'I'll take point!' Angel told him as she swung her medical kit across her shoulders. He fell into step just behind her as they dashed across the frosty ground. The moors were uneven, unpredictable terrain, but at least the fog was clearing a little now.

They soon spotted the hiker. Her crumpled form sat slumped against a rocky outcrop. Angel dropped the supply kit and Teddy got to his knees beside her, pressing a hand to her neck, checking for a pulse. The ground beneath his knees was jagged and unforgiving, about a mile off the footpath. She must have got lost due to the frost—some of the signs were impossible to see, even now.

'Ma'am, can you hear me?'

The helicopter's rotors were overwhelmingly loud. He could barely hear himself think. The woman's skin was damp under his touch, but thankfully not as cold as he'd feared. Her pulse throbbed beneath his fingers as he moved the sleeve of her hiking jacket and, slowly, her eyes fluttered open, unfocused and glazed with severe pain.

He introduced himself quickly. 'We're here to help you. Don't panic; you're going to be just fine. I'm Teddy Vaughn, flight paramedic. What's your name?'

'Annabel,' she managed through chattering teeth.

Angel kneeled opposite him, already pulling out the thermal blanket, and he watched her trained green eyes taking in the woman's blue-tinged lips and violent shivering. It was freezing out here, and he knew they were thinking the same thing: hypothermia.

'Possible fractured ankle too. We need to warm her core, stat.'

Angel wrapped the thermal blanket tightly around the shivering woman while Teddy hurried to get a warm IV solution ready. 'You're going to be just fine, OK, Annabel?' he reassured her again as he gently inserted the IV. 'We've got you. You'll be home and warm in no time. We'll get you to hospital first, though. Ready for a sky ride?'

He felt Angel watching him as he spoke gently to Annabel while she was loaded carefully onto the stretcher, huddled into the blanket. Her condition stabilised dramatically on the flight to the Royal York, and by the time they landed on the helipad she even had some colour back in her cheeks.

'They'll need to check your ankle,' Angel told her, rubbing her hands together for warmth. They were both frozen to the bone now. Annabel thanked them both as she was helped into a wheelchair and wheeled away, even though she looked utterly exhausted and would probably sleep for a week after this ordeal. It was a good thing they'd found her before anything worse befell her out there, Teddy thought, but he was going to be late picking up Bandit now.

'If you're done,' he said to Angel, running a hand through his wind-tousled hair. 'I'm heading home to pick up the dog. Want a lift home? You're on the way.'

Angel hesitated for a moment, looking up from her file. He knew her shift was over, the same as his. Being her diligent self, though, she would stay even longer if she could. Did she have any other friends here yet besides him?

To his surprise, though, she put down the file. 'If you're sure?'

'Sure I'm sure.'

Walking with her to his car, Teddy wondered what she was thinking. He wasn't used to this—wanting to spend more time with someone beyond the thrill of a casual fling, wanting just one more conversation in the store room, just one more coffee or car ride. It was uncharted territory for a man who usually kept his connections fleeting and uncomplicated.

The traffic ground to a halt just as they reached the outskirts of York. Teddy tapped his fingers on the steering wheel, stealing glances at Angel as she checked her phone. 'Looks like we might be here a while,' he apologised.

Angel tucked her phone away, fixing her eyes on the queue of cars ahead. 'It does seem that way.'

She seemed distracted. 'Everything OK?' he asked.

'That was my sister, Ate,' she said. 'She's been filling me in on what the family is up to.' He noticed that look on her face again: the one that told him she wished she were somewhere else. With them, perhaps. Or maybe she was thinking about that guy she'd broken up with last year.

'So what are they doing for New Year's Eve?' he asked her, ignoring the honk of a horn somewhere behind him. It wasn't his fault they were stuck. In fact, now he was questioning whether the universe was playing a trick on him. This wasn't his usual terrain, this restless need to extend his time with a woman, and now he couldn't have got out of it if he tried.

'New Year's Eve is huge for my family in the Philippines,' she said. 'Everyone usually gathers at my grandma's house. We start cooking early—all the good stuff. Her lumpia is to die for.'

'Lumpia?'

'It's like…it's like a Filipino version of spring rolls. My aunts all bring something different, so the kitchen is usually total chaos. At midnight, we all jump with the kids when the clock strikes twelve…'

'Jump?' He was intrigued now, not to mention starving. 'Why do they jump?'

She smiled. 'Obviously there's no science to it, but it's supposed to help the kids grow taller in the new year. There's also no science to say jingling coins in our pockets brings good fortune either, but we do it anyway. Then… fireworks. So many fireworks…'

Her voice grew distant as she gazed out of the window. She was somewhere else again. 'I took Ben two years ago,' she said quietly, glancing back at him. Teddy's heart jolted in his chest at the name. 'I thought he loved it. He seemed to really fit in. He told me afterwards that he wanted to spend every Christmas and New Year like that. Clearly he didn't mean a word of it.' She closed her mouth and turned to him, shaking her head. 'Sorry, I didn't mean to be such a downer.'

'That's OK, I get it,' he said, trying his best to get it. He had never taken anyone home for Christmas, but he felt for

Angel. She'd obviously been deeply in love with this guy… Ben…and, despite feeling this utter loathing for a man he'd never met, he was not about to stop her talking about him if she needed to. Maybe she was still in love with him. The thought was a little uncomfortable to process, but it had only been a year. He had to ask her now what he'd wanted to ask her that whole night they'd sat talking on Christmas Day.

'Why did you break up with Ben anyway—what happened? You never told me.'

She turned to him. 'I know. Thanks for being so understanding.'

She turned away again and pursed her lips. He drummed his fingers on the wheel again to fill the silence. OK, clearly she was determined not to share what had happened with him. The details were none of his business anyway. How embarrassing that he'd asked.

'The way you are with Joe, with his dog—doing this for him…' she continued. 'I mean, you just finished your shift and now you're going all the way back again with the dog. You have a big heart under all your ugly jumpers, Teddy. Huge.'

Her words caught him off-guard and he nodded slowly at the road, forgetting momentarily that he'd tried and failed to extract more information from her on her ex. He wasn't used to such genuine compliments and praise from the people around him, nothing as heartfelt as she'd just expressed.

'I guess I've always had a soft spot for the underdog,' he admitted, thinking of poor Joe, all laid up and scared of going home for whatever reason. 'I figured out back in boarding school that kids can be even crueller than adults.'

'Were you picked on?' she said in surprise. For some reason he was glad the thought surprised her; he was anything but weak. He prided himself on his physical strength and it did not go unnoticed by the ladies. He laughed, then reined it in quickly to maintain his humble shield.

'No, I wasn't picked on…but some of the kids were. The small ones, the nerdy ones, the ones who hadn't managed to find their voices yet. I guess I kind of became their ambassador—not in a violent way. I was just pretty good at negotiating with the enemy.'

Angel smiled. 'Always the diplomat. Must be from having so many lawyers in your family!'

He shrugged as the vision of his parents and siblings crept in through the cracks, like pouring ice on a fire. He shook it off and focused on the road as the traffic started to part, but his mind was already spinning him back further, to the school yard.

'I remember this one boy called Eli. Skinny kid with glasses, always buried in some book or another. He had a lisp.'

Just saying it out loud made the restlessness stir up in him again, a tamped down version of the urge to intervene he'd felt at the time. 'He was picked on incessantly by this big guy in the year above him; his name was Jake, if I recall. Such a mean kid; I never really knew why. Not at first, anyway.'

He caught her eyes lowering to his fingers, which tightened around the steering wheel in an unconscious mirroring of his protective instincts. 'He'd trip Eli up on purpose, make him spill his own drinks on himself…all that mean-kid stuff. Eli had brains over brawn but he just didn't know how to channel it right.'

'Let me guess…' Angel cocked a smile. 'You showed him?'

'I couldn't just watch and do nothing, you know?'

'So, what did you do?'

'I decided to make good friends with Jake,' Teddy continued, flicking his gaze onto hers. 'My idea was to steer him away from tormenting Eli without making it obvious. So, I started inviting Jake over for video games. We'd battle it out on the screen, but we'd talk while our characters fought it out. You'd be very surprised what boys share when they're distracted.'

'Would I?'

He caught a smile on her mouth before she bit it back. He'd shared quite a lot with her these past few days and he still was. Angel was distracting.

'It turned out that Jake was dealing with some pretty heavy stuff at home,' he continued. 'His dad disappeared when he was a toddler and his mum wasn't coping too well with things without chemicals, if you know what I mean, so his grandparents had paid for him to attend Saint Olivier's School for Boys while his mum was getting help. He felt like no one wanted him around, so of course he was taking his frustrations out on other people. Mainly on Eli. It made him feel stronger, when everything else in his life was spiralling.'

'So what happened in the end?' Angel asked.

'I pointed out that being mean to Eli wasn't really solving any of his problems,' Teddy said, remembering the way Jake's shoulders had slumped in shame when he'd finally realised the effects and consequences of his cruelty. 'I told him how much of a difference it would make if he actually stood up for Eli instead of pushing him around. So he started doing that. I was pretty surprised, actually, at the turnaround. By the time I left that school, those kids were best buddies. Jake would jump in and defend Eli whenever anyone else tried it on with him and, in the end, he realised it made him a lot more popular, being an all-round nice guy instead of a bully. He was a lot happier after that. They both were.'

Angel was looking at him as if her heart was turning into a ball of mush and he shrugged. 'What?'

'Teddy bear,' she muttered into her scarf, smiling. The traffic had cleared and they were now rounding the corner to her street. 'I hope they made you head boy, or whatever the top role was for a student at your boarding school,' she said as he pulled to a stop outside her apartment building.

'Nope.' He shrugged. 'But I didn't care about that.'

'Well, I hope you and Bandit enjoy your trip back to hospital.'

'We will,' he said, trying to quell the disappointment that, yet again, their time together was coming to an end. But, then again, maybe it didn't have to, he thought, as her hand found the car door handle.

'Listen, Angel. I was planning on checking out the ice-rink tonight.'

She turned back to him. 'Oh? Another extreme activity, huh? You can't seem to take a break.'

'A break? What's that?' He watched in hope as her hand retracted. 'You're probably busy but, if you're free, you could come with me. It's good people-watching.'

Angel seemed to consider it, but he couldn't read her expression now. She looked intrigued, but also unsure. What was he even doing? He'd said he wouldn't do this.

'There will be toffee apples and flapjacks, loads of other stuff loaded with sugar and e-numbers and maybe even me falling on my face,' he told her anyway.

'I very much doubt it would be *you* falling on your face if I came,' she said.

'You never know.' He held his breath, waiting for her rejection. It would probably be better if she did reject him, actually, all things considered.

She returned her hand to the door handle, then sat back in her seat for a second and looked at him with narrowed eyes.

'OK, schoolboy hero,' she said finally. 'Why not? I'll join you.'

CHAPTER NINE

'ARE YOU SURE about this, Angel?' Ate's concern filtered through the phone and echoed around her tiny bathroom. 'You don't have to go if you're not ready.'

Angel reached for her mascara, willing her hand to stay steady as she carefully coated her lashes. The butterflies in her stomach refused to settle, and she had to apply her lip gloss twice. At least her reflection in the mirror didn't show her nerves.

She took a deep breath, steadying herself in the new shade of gloss entitled 'ruby bliss'. 'I'll be fine. It's just ice-skating with a colleague, nothing more.'

'But it's Teddy,' Ate pressed. 'The same Teddy you've been talking about since day one. The one with the, and I quote, "unfairly handsome and entirely distracting face, and arms that could bench-press a small car".'

Heat crept up Angel's neck and she was very glad her sister couldn't see her blush. 'It's not like that. We're just… friends. Colleagues, like I said. Nothing more.'

Even as she said the words, Angel knew they weren't entirely true. There was something about Teddy that set her pulse into frenzy mode every time she saw him now; a magnetic attraction she couldn't deny. 'Besides,' Angel continued, desperate to change the subject, 'It's not even Christmas any more. I don't know why they still have the ice rink up. All these festive decorations everywhere, it's ridiculous.'

She could practically hear Ate's eye-roll through the phone. 'Let people enjoy the holiday spirit a little longer, will you, Scrooge? You used to love it yourself, remember?'

'I know, I know,' Angel sighed, running a brush through her hair one last time. She was keeping it down tonight, so her hat would look cuter with her hair flowing out from under it. Ugh, of course; she was dressing for Teddy. 'I did love it once, you're right, Ate. Everything about it. Why else would I have wanted a Christmas wedding? I'm sorry I'm such a Scrooge these days.'

'We all understand,' she said pointedly. 'But focus on what you have right now, alright? Don't let Ben ruin anything *else* for you.'

The memories of last Christmas threatened to surface again as Ate hung up, leaving her alone in the bathroom, but Angel pushed them down and finished her make-up. Her sister was right: she was not going to let Ben ruin tonight. She might even try to enjoy the Christmas lights.

Ugh. As if.

The purr of an engine outside caught her attention. Her heart almost leapt through her jumper as she peeked through the bathroom blind. Teddy's sleek car was parked at the kerb down below, its headlights shining brightly on the pavement. With a deep breath, she grabbed her thickest woollen coat, pulled on her plum-coloured hat, being careful to arrange her hair just right, and headed out of the door. In an instant the bitter, cold evening air was nipping at her nose and cheeks as she hurried to the passenger side of Teddy's car.

'Love the hat,' he said by way of a greeting as she slid in beside him.

'Thanks, I like your hat too,' she said, by way of acknowledging the black beanie he'd pulled down almost to his eyebrows. As the compliment left her mouth, she cringed at her own words. Why the heck had she said *that*? She'd just proved to him exactly how nervous she was, going out with him. She had to keep reminding herself that they were just friends; colleagues and friends. Teddy was on some kind of mission to introduce her to new people and make her feel at home here because he was a sweetheart. A Teddy bear at the core. She still couldn't believe what he'd done for that boy Eli at his school.

The familiar backdrop of historic buildings and quaint shops gave way to a winter wonderland she'd done her best not to notice in the daylight. In the evening light, there was simply too much festive cheer and sparkle to ignore. In the heart of the city, York Minster loomed against the night sky and Teddy pulled into a parking spot. As they stepped out of the car, Angel's breath caught in her throat at her first sight of York Museum Gardens. Right in the centre was a huge ice-rink, surrounded by twinkling fairy lights and towering evergreens, all flickering with shimmering stars.

'Welcome to Yorkshire's Winter Wonderland,' Teddy said with more than a hint of pride in his voice. 'What do you think?'

Angel realised that, far from being the Scrooge she'd come to expect of herself, she was actually smiling, taking in the scene. All around them people were laughing and talking, bundled up in scarves and gloves, pulling on skates, chatting over steaming mugs of cocoa and mulled wine. The toffee-apple stall was buzzing and the flapjack guy seemed to be rushed off his feet. The air was thick with a hundred delicious smells, all carrying along on the breeze, and it was all accompanied by the gentle strains of classic Christmas carols.

'It's…beautiful,' Angel admitted. Her eyes had turned wide with wonder. She couldn't turn off the effect it was having, especially standing beside Teddy. 'I had no idea York could look like this. Maybe *New* York, but York?'

Teddy led her towards the skate-rental booth. 'New York has nothing on this.'

He looked so good tonight, she thought, taking him in while he ordered their skates. His puffer jacket looked just the right kind of snug on his broad frame, paired with charcoal-grey jeans and an olive-green scarf. His whole look made her sneak more than one glance. He knew how to dress. Ben's look had always confused her, while Teddy's was refined and casual without being too try-hard about it. His hair was slightly tousled from the breeze around his hat tonight. He would not have looked out of place in a winter catalogue.

'Ready for an adventure, Flores?' Teddy asked her, leading her to the bench.

Strapping on the skates beside him, Angel felt genuinely excited. But minutes later her enthusiasm had waned somewhat. Just as she'd feared, ice-skating was not one of her strong suits. She wobbled precariously on the ice, her arms flailing out to her sides as she struggled to maintain her balance. A nervous laugh escaped her lips as Teddy hovered, occasionally skating a full circle around her as if to ward everyone else away from this potential danger zone. She rallied onwards, acutely aware of everyone else gliding past her with effortless ease. There were children doing this better than she was.

'I think I've made a terrible mistake here,' she called out to Teddy.

'You're doing great,' he encouraged, skating backwards with infuriating ease. 'Just keep your knees bent and lean forward a bit.'

Angel did her very best to follow his advice, but her feet just wouldn't stop sliding out from underneath her. 'Easy for you to say, Mr Olympian,' she muttered, concentrating on staying upright, only to wobble again.

Teddy chuckled, his voice low and teasing. 'Here, let me help,' he offered, extending his hands toward her.

Angel reached for him but, the moment their fingers brushed, her skates had other ideas. A sharp wobble stole her balance and she gasped, her body tipping forwards. A startled yelp left her lips too fast, her stomach flipping as she braced for the cold, unforgiving ice.

But the impact never came. Instead, she crashed into something warm, solid: Teddy.

His arms wrapped around her in one swift, instinctive motion, his grip strong and steady. He pulled her against him, chest to chest, the heat of him seeping through their thick layers of winter clothing and making her heart pound.

'Steady there,' he murmured, his voice rougher now, quieter.

Angel's breath caught as she looked up. Oh, lord. His face was mere inches from hers, his blue eyes burning into hers with something she couldn't quite name but felt everywhere in every atom of her body. His breath was warm against her chilled skin, the scent of him—woodsy, masculine, intoxicating—filling her senses. Her hands, which had instinctively gripped his coat, remained there all on their own, fisting the fabric as if she wasn't sure she was even physically able to let go.

Everything slowed. The noise of the rink faded. It was just him. His fingers flexed against her lower back, holding her there, as if maybe he wasn't in a hurry to let go either. The firm press of his body, every muscle taut beneath his jacket, the way his gaze dipped, just briefly, to her lips, all spoke of his attraction, just as powerful as hers.

Her pulse was thrumming wildly in her throat. If she shifted even an inch, if he leaned in just a fraction more…

Teddy sucked in a slow breath. Then, instead of stepping back, he tightened his hold for the briefest second, as if testing something. Testing her? A slow smirk tugged at the corner of his lips. 'Are you always this graceful, Angel, or am I just lucky today?'

Angel exhaled, but it came out shakier than she intended. 'Shut up,' she muttered, but she didn't move away.

Neither did he.

A very strong part of her wanted to close this tiny distance and just give in to the magnetic pull between them but reality crashed back in like a bucket of ice water.

Angel pulled back abruptly, steadying herself on wobbly legs like a newborn deer. 'Thanks,' she mumbled, avoiding his gaze. 'As you can see, I'm not cut out for this; maybe I should've stayed on the sidelines.'

Teddy's hands lingered on her arms for a moment longer before he stepped back, finally giving her space. 'Don't sell yourself short, Flores,' he said, crossing his arms and performing another effortless twirl in front of her. 'You just need practice. And maybe a good teacher.'

Angel forced a laugh. 'Are you offering your services, Vaughn?'

'Always,' he replied. A suggestive undercurrent in his voice sent her pulse throbbing the whole way up her arms to her throat, but she did her best to ignore it. He did this with all the girls; she already knew that about Teddy single-by-choice Vaughn.

He encouraged her to keep skating, and sure enough with time she began to get a little less wobbly, a little more confident. Not that confidence equalled *good* by any means, but he took it all in his stride and made it enjoyable rather than embarrassing. Angel couldn't help thinking that, as much as she'd loved him, Ben would have given up on her by now, left her gripping the side rail and taken off like a speed skater without her.

Ben was kind, but his patience had its limits. If she was truly honest with herself, she'd felt him slipping into autopilot, especially in the final year of their relationship. Even in their intimacy, it often seemed as though he wasn't fully present—as if he was going through the motions, not out of genuine desire to connect, but because he thought it was what a good partner should do. The difference was subtle, but unmistakable, and over time it had worn on her. She'd naively hoped that marriage might change things, but deep down she'd probably been lying to herself.

Angel stumbled again and Teddy's arm tightened instinctively around her waist this time. A rush of warmth sped up her spine. 'How about some hot chocolate?' he asked.

'Yes please,' she said, grateful for the chance to catch her breath. As they stepped off the ice, Teddy's hand instinctively steadied her at the elbow. The casual touch sent another jolt through her body—what was this man doing to her?

They wandered over to a quaint wooden stand surrounded by colourful fairy lights, the soft glow overhead twinkling like stars. Teddy ordered two hot chocolates, and she turned away, her gaze drifting back to the rink, conflicted. This fresh start was supposed to be about reclaiming her independence, about proving to herself that she didn't need anyone—least of all a man. She'd set that rule very firmly, and even told her sister. But, every time Teddy's hand found hers, or steadied her in any way—ostensibly to keep her from face-planting on the ice amidst a thousand sharp blades—she found herself quietly deciding that maybe her self-imposed, not particularly exciting rules would be better broken. It was utterly ridiculous.

But, to her surprise, she hadn't felt irritated by the festive cheer since she'd arrived with Teddy. Just days ago, the sights and smells of the season would have sent her spiralling into despair. But tonight was different. Instead of replaying Ben's betrayal in her mind, she was drawn into the present—into Teddy. Drawn to the way his eyes crinkled when he laughed, the pink flush of his cheeks from the cold and the carefree ease in his smile. She realised, with a little jolt, that she'd never seen him look as devastatingly sexy as he did tonight.

'Here you go,' he said, handing her a steaming cup.

'It smells incredible.'

'Yorkshire's finest.'

They found a bench overlooking the rink, settling down close enough that their shoulders touched. Angel wrapped her hands around the warm cup, inhaling the rich smell of cocoa.

'This is nice,' she murmured, watching the skaters glide by.

Teddy hummed in agreement, stretching his arm out behind her on the bench. 'It is. I'm glad you came with me tonight, Angel.'

She turned to look at him and was struck by the sincerity in his eyes. Their faces were so close she could see the different shades of blue in his irises. Feeling her heart rate start to climb again, she looked away, taking a sip of hot chocolate to hide her flushed cheeks. But, as they sat in what should have been companionable silence, Angel became hyper-aware of every point of contact between them.

Every time their shoulders brushed, fresh tingles shot down her spine. When Teddy shifted, his hand grazed her back, and she had to suppress a shiver.

'What are you thinking about?' Teddy asked.

Angel blinked. 'Just how different this feels,' she admitted softly. 'Usually, all this Christmas stuff makes me want to hide away. But tonight…'

She trailed off. How was she supposed to explain to this man that tonight she was not thinking about the absence of Ben without sounding pathetic? Besides, now she *was* thinking about Ben again, curse him.

'Tonight?' Teddy prompted.

Angel took a deep breath. 'Tonight, I guess I can see the magic in it.'

He looked at her for a long time, until she felt like she might actually melt into a puddle on the ground and drip away into the drains at the side of the rink. Then, in a blink, Teddy was on his feet again. 'Still thirsty? I'll get us some mulled wine.'

'Um, OK, thank you.' She watched him stride to a nearby stall, his confident gait drawing admiring glances from passersby in all directions, especially the women. Was it wrong that she was proud to be with him? He was so intense, though. Those eyes… She could swear he saw right through her. He really wanted to know what had happened with Ben. He kept on asking, and he'd given up being subtle about it too. But he'd think she was a real idiot if he knew the truth. Surely she'd missed signs that something was going on with Ben? It had crossed her mind lately that Ben might have even been cheating on her with that woman from his work. She just hadn't wanted to believe it.

Teddy returned with two paper cups of sweet mulled wine and she took one, glad of the calming aroma of cinnamon and cloves. Their eyes locked as they both took a sip, and the world seemed to fade away again. 'I know you don't want to talk about it,' Teddy said, lowering his eyes to her lips. 'And that's OK, but for the record, I just can't imagine why anyone would let you go.'

Angel sighed. 'Because I'm such a good skater? I wanted to go pro, he was just holding me back.'

'Very funny.' Teddy put his cup on the floor, shifting round to face her properly. 'Don't get me wrong, I know you're coming round to my point of view that Christmas is indeed the most wonderful time of the year...'

'I wouldn't go that far,' she protested as her heart drummed like a nutcracker.

'But something extra-horrible must have happened with that guy, to make you hate *everything* about Christmas in the first place.'

'And you want to know, so you can fix me? Drape me in tinsel till I succumb and fall in love with it all again?'

Her words hung in the space between them and she realised how bitter she'd just sounded. She sighed, frustrated. Maybe she should just blurt it all out, just to stop the words lodging in her throat and making her nauseous, but she couldn't do it. It was too humiliating. Before she could stop them, tears welled in her eyes. Mortified, she pushed to her feet.

'Where's the loo?' she mumbled, needing a moment to compose herself. She tottered blindly on her skates towards what she hoped was a toilet block, her mind spinning. How was she supposed to answer a question like that—from a colleague, no less, and a man who made her pulse race every time he looked her way? But, before she could escape, a strong hand caught her arm, gently spinning her round again.

'Angel.' Teddy's blue eyes locked onto hers, instantly cutting through the chaos in her mind. His gaze was steady, intent and utterly disarming. He reached out, cupping her cheek with a tenderness that made her knees weaken, his thumb brushing lightly over her lower lip. 'Forget I asked, OK? I'm an idiot.'

'Why do you care so much?' she pressed, her lip throbbing, needing more of his touch.

He faltered. 'I don't know. I really don't know, and I barely know you, but…'

His words were gentle, but it was the way he looked at her that stole her breath. She felt her resolve falter in the unwavering blue of his gaze, the tension between them humming like a live wire. Without thinking, she leaned into his touch, and in that moment she knew. She knew exactly what Teddy was thinking—what they were both thinking.

Teddy closed the distance, his lips brushing hers with a tenderness that made her heart stutter and then threaten to stop entirely. Their kiss deepened, slow and deliberate at first, then building in heat and intensity as the world around them on the ice-rink melted away. Her hand found his chest. Her fingers curled into his jacket as she felt the steady, grounding thrum of his heartbeat under her palm, even through his clothes. In response, he pulled her closer, his arms as strong and protective as before as their bodies pressed together, drowning out everything else in sight.

Angel was dimly aware of people glancing their way, but she couldn't bring herself to care. Nothing had ever felt like this. No kiss with anyone had ever set her skin alight or made her blood hum with this kind of desperate, uncontainable energy. It wasn't just a spark any more, it was a fire, and it totally consumed her.

When they finally broke apart, Angel's heart was pounding and her breathing felt unsteady as she met Teddy's gaze. His eyes were darker now, filled with a raw intensity she'd never seen. She didn't need words to know how he felt—it was written in every line of his face, in the way he still held her close. He seemed completely unwilling to let go. And she couldn't bring herself to withdraw her arms from around his neck either. He cared about her, and knowing he cared was all she needed to let her walls fall away for a moment… Well, as low as she'd ever dared let them fall when it came to revealing the truth about herself. How had this happened so fast?

'Damn you, Teddy Vaughn,' she muttered through her tingling lips as he laced his fingers through hers and led her back towards the car park.

CHAPTER TEN

TEDDY COULD FEEL Angel watching him in the moments she wasn't scanning the landscape below for any sign of the distressed hikers they'd been sent to find. He could practically feel her green eyes burning into his cheeks.

'There!' Her voice crackled through the headset and into his ears. 'Two o'clock, near that outcrop.'

George had already seen. He banked the helicopter, bringing them closer, and soon their lost hikers swept into view. A middle-aged man in a red and yellow jacket was sprawled on the ground, his leg bent at an unnatural angle. A woman was huddled next to him, waving frantically: husband and wife. What were they doing all the way out here?

'Close as you can get, George,' Angel urged, and George manoeuvred the helicopter to a relatively flat patch of ground about fifty metres from the couple. They'd still have to hike a little. As the rotors slowed, he and Angel gathered their kits and rescue gear and soon they were on the ground.

'I'll take point,' Angel told him, shouldering her pack. 'Watch your footing—it's treacherous out here today.'

'Yes, Flores,' he replied, trying not to smirk. They'd changed something between them with that kiss, and now neither of them really knew where they stood, so she was being extra-authoritative at work. He had to admit, kissing her hadn't been the wisest decision he'd ever made for numerous reasons, but he couldn't bring himself to regret it either. And hadn't she gone in for the kiss first?

They picked their way across the uneven terrain together, the bitter wind doing its best to tangle their hair and clothes. Soon they were close enough for the woman's panicked cries to reach them.

'Help! Please, he's in so much pain!'

Angel knelt beside the man, carefully unzipping his red and yellow jacket and patting him down gently to check where he was hurt. 'Sir, I'm Angel, a paramedic, and this is Teddy. We're here to help you.'

The man groaned at her by way of reply. His face was grey and drawn with the agony of his fall. 'My leg… I slipped on some loose rock…'

Teddy crouched on the other side, unpacking splints and bandages. As he worked, his mind wandered as fast as Angel's capable hands. How was he supposed to get that kiss out of his head with her here, right in front of him? Maybe he shouldn't have done it. He'd sworn he wouldn't get involved, but that was like telling the moon not to shine at night. His lips had a whole other mind of their own; he hadn't been able to stop himself at the ice-rink. And she'd kissed him too. Neither of them had exactly pushed the other away.

Still, common sense kept nagging him. Getting involved with a colleague was risky enough, never mind the fact that Angel was still recovering from her past relationship and was clearly here for a fresh start. What was her ex's name again—Brian? Ben? Yes, Ben. He shouldn't have kept pushing her for details, but he *did* care, and he couldn't place it. He'd started to care too quickly, and yes, he did want to cover her in tinsel and make her hatred of all things Christmas disappear for good. It was his favourite holiday. He was already picturing what he'd cook for them next year because surely Christmas nights as good as that shouldn't only happen once?

'Teddy, I need the morphine.' Angel's voice cut through his thoughts.

He handed her the medication, their fingers brushing briefly. 'How's it looking?'

Her brow furrowed under her thrashing hair. 'Looks like a compound fracture of the tibia. We'll need to stabilise it before we can move him.'

They worked in tandem, Teddy supporting the man's leg while Angel carefully aligned the bone and applied the splint. The injured hiker gritted his teeth. Teddy could see the sweat already beading on his forehead.

'You're doing great,' he reassured him. 'We'll have you out of here in no time.'

As they prepared the stretcher, Angel tucked a stray lock of hair behind her ear, leaving a smudge of dirt on her cheek that he had to force himself not to lean over and wipe away. He knew better than to act on his impulses a second time.

'Ready to lift?' Angel's voice snapped him back to the present.

Teddy nodded, shoving aside his conflicted thoughts before they could torture him. 'On three. One, two, three…!'

They hoisted the stretcher up together, being careful to keep it level as they took the same route back to the waiting helicopter. The man's wife trailed behind, clutching at her husband's hand, and Teddy made sure to reassure the poor lady that everything was going to be OK. He didn't miss the appreciative glance on Angel's face when he did so, which warmed him from the inside out as usual. Why did her admiration affect him like this? Surely he should be used to women admiring him?

This all had to stop. He should abandon this complication ahead of it getting really complicated…but he already pictured kissing her again, in numerous different places. He was due to attend the mountain rescue volunteer group get-together on New Year's Eve at the indoor ski slope, and had been contemplating inviting her to try some indoor skiing…

Soon, their couple was safely at the hospital and, as they handed off the patient to Ares and Ruby in A&E, Teddy prepared to get back to his paperwork.

'Hey.' Angel's voice stopped him in his tracks. 'Want to check on Joe with me quickly? I know you guys have struck up quite a bond.'

Teddy nodded, wondering if this was her way of ensuring they had some time alone, even if it was only walking to the ward. But she kept quiet the whole way and so did he. What was he supposed to say? They'd both made this awkward now.

Joe was propped up in bed, looking marginally better than when they'd brought him in. The teen's eyes lit up over his book when they walked in, despite his affected nonchalance. 'My favourite paramedics. Did you bring Bandit?' He looked around for his dog.

'No, I'll bring him later, like I promised,' Teddy told him. 'How are you feeling today, tough guy?'

Joe shrugged. 'You mean despite my prison sentence?'

'Very funny. It's not that bad is it? The food's good, so I hear.'

'It's better than Mum's cooking, when she actually decides to make anything for us to eat these days, so yeah, you're kind of right.'

Teddy exchanged an apprehensive glance with Angel.

'Well, you're being discharged on New Year's Eve—liberation will soon be yours.'

He realised Joe didn't look particularly happy about this, so he settled into the chair by the boy's bed, aware of Angel on the periphery, checking his chart at the end of the bed. He was concerned about Joe's home situation, of course, but it wasn't his job to get into that with the kid. They had social services and a psychologist for that. Joe was going to be taken care of. *His* role was to cheer him up while he was here. 'A new year means a new start, right?'

Joe's expression sobered further. 'Yeah, if you say so. What about you two anyway? Got any wild plans?'

Teddy glanced at Angel, and caught the flicker of her eyes at him, right before she turned away again and shrugged. So, did she have no plans? Or did she simply not want to share them?

Teddy frowned. 'I'll need to bring Bandit to you before you're released. How about I bring him after my indoor ski get-together?'

Joe's face lit up at the mention of his beloved dog. Angel's gaze turned to him and he knew she was processing the new information that he was going indoor skiing on New Year's Eve. Something had caused him to inform her under the guise of informing Joe, but maybe he wouldn't think about that yet. His stupid heart was going all out lately to trick him into involving Angel. This was about Joe; a good kid who deserved someone looking out for him while he worked things out at home. Bandit was a great dog too, who deserved to be with his human when he was released and sent home.

'That's really sweet of you, Teddy,' Angel said quietly. 'Bringing Bandit here, I mean.'

'It's nothing,' he said, suddenly very interested in the pattern on Joe's blanket.

The admiring look in her eyes had caught him off-guard. He could barely resist the latest urge to pull her into the nearest secluded space and capture her lips in another kiss that would no doubt leave him wanting more. How did she do this? How did she trap him under this spell? When he looked up again, she drew her eyes away at lightning speed, as if she was struggling with the same thoughts about him.

Angel's pager buzzed, forcing her eyes away from Teddy's overly alluring gaze. If only he would just stop looking at her. Every time she felt his intense eyes on her, she was thrown right back to that kiss. The kiss he hadn't mentioned since. The kiss *she* hadn't mentioned since, either. She glanced down at the small screen, her brow furrowing. He was so sweet, helping Joe with the dog like this. But had he really meant to tell Joe about his New Year's Eve plans, or had he secretly been telling her?

'I've got to go,' she said reluctantly. 'Induction time.'

Teddy nodded, picking up Joe's book. 'Go on, then. I'll catch up with you later.'

Angel hurried down the corridor, her mind racing. How was she ever going to be able to work around Teddy again without that kiss from two days ago coming back to her? The warmth of his lips on hers in the ice-cold air, the gentle pressure of his hand on her waist as he'd steadied her, the mesmerising scent of his cologne… It all came rushing back with startling clarity whenever she summoned it, and even when she didn't.

She pushed through the ER doors, her heart pounding. Dr Patel waved her over. Today she was supposed to be brushing up on aviation safety, and an experienced retired pilot called Fergal Malone had come in to walk her through the essentials. But the whole time Fergal explained the basics of aeromedical safety, walking her through pre-flight checks, emergency egress and crash survival techniques, her responses came out on autopilot while her thoughts remained fixated on Teddy. She realised with a jolt of excitement and terror that she was barely thinking about Ben at all any more. She hadn't since that kiss. It was as if, the second Teddy's mouth had claimed hers, he'd banished Ben from her head completely. She was falling for Teddy. Hard.

'Is everything alright?' Fergal's hesitant voice broke into her thoughts.

Angel blinked, realising she'd been staring blankly at a buoyancy device for about three minutes, holding it in her hands as if she'd never seen one before. 'Yes, sorry. Just… thinking about another patient I need to check on after this.'

Fergal didn't look convinced. *How embarrassing.* She forced herself to pay attention, but eventually as they sat in a small room together to review a case study of an aviation accident she heard familiar voices outside the partially open door and couldn't help tuning into what they were saying.

'Did you hear about Teddy and that new lead paramedic?' a nurse whispered.

Angel froze, her pen hovering over the page.

'You mean Angel Flores? What about them?' another voice responded conspiratorially.

'Rumour has it they're getting pretty close—not that anyone's seen anything, it's just a vibe. You know how he is, though.'

'What do you mean?'

The nurse let out a sharp, indignant laugh. 'I know someone who went on a date with Teddy last Christmas. Trust me, she better keep her guard up—he's a total player.'

Angel's cheeks burned hot as she listened. This was excruciating! She was torn between running in embarrassment and sitting with this strange, hollow feeling in her chest that threatened to consume her with a fresh emptiness. In the end, what could she do? She couldn't leave this room without exposing herself. It was grossly uncomfortable to hear people talking about her; did they not have anything better to do around here?

'They seem pretty cute together to me,' the second nurse mused.

'Trust me,' the first voice insisted. 'Teddy Vaughn only dates totally gorgeous women, and never anyone from hospital. He doesn't even do relationships. He'll break her heart if she's not careful.'

Angel swallowed hard. She turned to Fergal, who was watching her with a deep concern in his eyes.

'Let's...let's finish up here, if that's OK?' Angel managed, flustered. Her fingers trembled slightly as she closed the book she was writing in.

The nurses' words echoed in her mind. She took a deep breath, and back in the corridor she caught sight of her reflection in a nearby window. Her hair was still a bit dishevelled from the flight and the long shift. Dark circles under her eyes showed last night's lack of sleep. She couldn't help but compare herself to all the gorgeous, glamorous women Teddy must date—women who were not about to complicate his working life—and her stomach twisted into one huge knot. She had always prided herself on her professionalism, on not getting caught up in workplace drama. But now the thought of being the subject of hospital gossip made her feel a little ill.

'I can't do this,' she muttered to herself, and then did

her best not to look like a crazy person as she parted ways with Fergal.

Walking back to the nurses' station, she tried to block those nurses' conversation out, but it didn't stop Teddy's face drifting back into her brain. That kiss with him had felt so right, so natural. And he had driven her home after, like a true gentleman. But she had completely forgotten for a moment how mortifying it was to be the centre of a scandal. Was it not enough that her ex-fiancé had left her at the altar, standing alone in her wedding dress? Was it not enough still to suffer the pitying looks from her friends and family, even now?

Never again, Angel vowed to herself silently. She could not risk her heart, not when it was still so broken and fragile from Ben taking a sledgehammer to it. And certainly not with someone like Teddy, who clearly wasn't looking for anything serious. This was supposed to be her fresh start in her dream job!

She busied herself with paperwork, trying to push every nagging thought about Teddy from her mind, trying to make a solo plan for tomorrow night—another New Year's Eve in, alone. Maybe she'd get herself the ingredients for a nice macaroni cheese from the deli down the street, and a bottle of wine. And she would not answer the phone to anyone, no matter what.

Teddy's laughter soon drifted down the hallway, and she couldn't help but look up. There he was—of course.

Teddy was chatting with a group of doctors, his easy charm on full display as he bantered, laughed and joked. For a moment, their eyes met, and Angel felt the usual lightning rod of awareness and attraction zip through her belly. But she turned away quickly, even when he raised his hand in her direction, pretending not to have seen him.

'Teddy Vaughn is strictly off limits,' she muttered to herself, keeping her head down. If only she could make her heart believe it.

Teddy stood in his living room, staring down at his phone, one hand braced against the back of the couch. The screen glowed back at him with Angel's number already pulled up on it and he re-read her last message, hearing her voice in it.

He rubbed the back of his neck, torn between typing something out and tossing his phone on the table and forgetting the whole thing.

Except he couldn't forget it. He'd seen her earlier, watching him with all those people. And then she'd pretended she hadn't seen him at all. It only made him want to be around her more.

It's just a casual get-together, he told himself. *Just a low-key invite to the mountain rescue group's meeting.* They were getting together at SnowMania Xtreme Ski, as they did every year—nothing too formal, just people swapping stories, grabbing drinks and hitting the artificial slopes to blow off steam. Still, asking Angel felt different, somehow.

Since the night of their kiss, every moment they spent together had this…weight to it, as if there was something simmering just below the surface. Inviting her wasn't just about showing her a new place or introducing her to the mountain rescue team. If he was honest with himself, it was about wanting to see her smile, to spend time with her outside of work, to see her tackle something as wild as skiing with that same spirit she tackled everything with. And to kiss her again, even though he shouldn't.

He let out a sigh, thumb hovering over the keyboard, debating how to make the invite sound casual, as if it was no big deal. It shouldn't be a big deal, he was just turning it into one.

Finally, he tapped out a message:

Hey, we're doing that mountain rescue New Year thing at the indoor ski slope tomorrow afternoon. Feel like joining? Nothing crazy, just some drinks, a go on the slopes if you're up for it.

He hit send before he could over-think it yet again.

Immediately, a barrage of nerves swarmed his insides like flies—he hadn't felt this nervous about approaching a female since he was a teenager. Seconds ticked by, and then his phone buzzed:

I'm sorry, I can't.

His heart sank. He stared at his phone for a while, letting the unfamiliar sting of rejection sink in. Then he typed:

Way to crush a man on the second most exciting day of the year, Flores.

Again, she paused and he watched the dots that indicated her typing stop and start. Then, her message pinged:

I'm quite sure there's someone gorgeous you can ask, if you wrack your brains.

Teddy frowned. Someone gorgeous? Was she completely unaware of how gorgeous *she* was? He paced the room, wondering what to say. He could say something witty and funny, or self-derogatory, or complimentary, but where would it get him? Eventually, he drew a breath and typed:

Please? I forgot to say please.

You're determined to get me into extreme sports, aren't you?

He laughed under his breath, relieved, and quickly typed back:

You were so good on the ice. It's time to get you onto some bigger blades, don't you think?

Angel replied almost instantly with an eye-roll emoji:

Alright, but just remember, I have a serious talent for making a graceful disaster out of anything. And I also have plans for after.

See you at 4pm.

Then he thought some more.

I'll pick you up, and take you home before your next big event. I'm also busy later tonight.

Angel said nothing for a few minutes. Then the dots appeared to show she was typing. Then they stopped again for good, leaving him restless. Maybe she was stopping herself from retracting her acceptance, or asking what *his* plans were for afterwards, seeing as the get-together was an afternoon plan.

Teddy didn't actually have any plans after the event. Midnight would come and go while he made a dent in the sofa with Bruno but, being a single bachelor with a reputation to uphold, he wasn't going to admit that to Angel.

CHAPTER ELEVEN

'SO, THIS IS where all the crazy people hang out,' Angel said in amusement as she looked around the bustling bar area of SnowMania Xtreme Ski. Teddy followed her gaze, but his eyes soon landed back on her. The giant blue logo sent an other-worldly sheen across her face and hair, which she'd worn down again today. She looked different with her hair down, he thought—younger.

He'd had a dream about her last night. She'd been in his parents' house, waiting for him, which was odd in itself. He'd walked in with a hamper full of food. His parents had ignored him—which was not so odd, the more he thought about it—but Angel had walked right up and taken the hamper, then had led him to the kitchen, which in the dream had become the air ambulance base. She'd gone through the hamper, which had somehow become packed full of pineapple and nothing else, and they'd eaten pineapple together in the helicopter, soaring over the bluest ocean he'd even seen...near the Philippines, maybe? She'd been dressed as an elf, a sexy elf, eating pineapple in a helicopter in the Philippines. What the heck was his brain doing to him?

The dream clung to him, stubborn and unshakable. Was it some cryptic nudge to send his parents a fruit hamper? he wondered. And, if he did, would they even care? Or was this about something deeper—about Angel slipping, uninvited yet weirdly more than welcome, into the shadows of his past?

Lately, she was everywhere. Awake or asleep, she wove herself into the fabric of his memories, rewriting them, softening the jagged edges. Was she unknowingly exorcising old ghosts, replacing them with something lighter, something good? Or was he simply becoming more open to letting her? Maybe it was a message to escape and make a break for the Philippines while he still had a shred of sanity, he mused. But Angel wasn't in the Philippines, even though he was sure she secretly wanted to be. She was here with him.

Teddy propped himself against the polished oak bar, nursing his soft drink, letting his gaze sweep over his fellow mountain-rescue volunteers. 'It's more like the place we come to feel less crazy, if that makes sense,' he told her, nodding towards the huge glass window to their left. Through it they had a floor-to-ceiling view of the indoor skiers speeding down the slopes and climbing their way back up again on the colourful chairlifts.

'A lot of the volunteers let off steam here, after their regular jobs. We get to race around with none of the pressure, no emergencies to tend to, no lives to save. We can just enjoy the thrill of the elements…'

'Without being out in the elements,' she finished, gesturing upwards to the ceiling, and he laughed.

'Exactly.'

Angel took it all in and he thought of his brother and sister, working at their own regular jobs, with no idea of what he did all day to actually help people—real people, who needed him. It shouldn't still make him angry, but it did, which was exactly why he'd established limited contact over the years. They didn't deserve a hamper full of pineapple, or a hamper full of anything.

Two familiar faces approached them now and Teddy squared his shoulders. 'Elf Angel, I'd like you to meet a couple of friends.'

'Elf Angel?' She cocked her head in amusement and he shrugged.

'You were dressed as an elf in my dream last night,' he whispered before he could stop himself. 'Guess it stuck.'

She frowned and a blush crept over her cheeks as her lashes fluttered. 'Wait, you had a dream about me?'

'Teddy!' A tall, muscular man with a shock of black unruly hair clapped Teddy on the shoulder, saving him from an awkward reply. This was Eric. 'Teddy my man, good to see you! Who's this lovely lady?'

Teddy felt a flicker of possessiveness when he saw the way Eric was sizing her up, but quickly shoved it aside. 'Eric, this is Angel. She's the new lead paramedic I was telling you about.'

Angel extended her hand. 'Nice to meet you both.'

He introduced Mira next, a petite woman with close-cropped blonde hair and bright-pink lip gloss. 'So you're the one who'll be keeping our Teddy in line on the job?'

Teddy scoffed, even as a mild flush crept up his neck. Now he pictured Angel keeping him in line with an oversized candy cane, still dressed in her elf outfit. 'Hey now, steady on. I don't need keeping in line.'

Angel raised an eyebrow in his direction. 'Oh, really?'

Eric let out a belly laugh. 'She's onto you already, Vaughn!'

Teddy shuffled on the spot. He was doing his best not to let the guy ruffle his feathers, but he didn't miss Angel looking to the floor, equally as uncomfortable. He had to wonder what exactly she'd heard going round the hospital. A couple of people had mentioned their 'chemistry' to him, but he hadn't given anyone any reason to think anything was actually going on, aside from two colleagues hanging out over the festive season.

As they chatted with the others, Teddy found himself hyper-aware of Angel's presence beside him, of the way she laughed at Eric's jokes, the subtle shift of her body as she leaned in to hear Mira over the noise of the bar. He realised he was fighting a strange and very unfamiliar urge to reach out and touch her, to just put an arm around her and pull her into him as a clear, territorial signal to everyone that he was here for *her* tonight, and she was here with *him*.

Obviously, he would not be doing that. Angel was clearly conscious of her own reputation, being so new to the job, and in town. It would be obvious to everyone that he was into her if he so much as looked at her at work, such was his own reputation—but then, he could hardly turn this attraction off just because they worked together.

After a few minutes, Eric and Mira drifted away to greet other friends. Teddy noticed Angel glancing around the room. In fact, she seemed to look everywhere but at him. 'Everything OK?' he asked, leaning in close to be heard over the music.

She nodded, then hesitated. 'You had a dream about me?'

He closed his mouth, pressing his lips together, then shrugged again. 'Sorry, I can't help how you managed to sneak in there, Flores. But yeah, I half-expected you to show up today in elf attire with a basket of pineapples. And. before you say it, yes, it's entirely possible that I've been driven completely insane by you…' He hesitated, realising his slip, and scrambled to recover. 'By you…reminding me of everything fun about Christmas…like costumes. You remind me how much I like costumes.'

He tugged awkwardly at his ski pants, as if pretending

they qualified as a costume, and immediately knew there was no undoing what he'd just blurted out.

Angel was flushing. 'What was that about pineapple?'

'Nothing.' He cringed. Why the hell couldn't he shut up just once before putting his foot in it?

'Why did you ask me here today, Teddy?' she asked, a half-smile on her lips as she looked at him.

The tension rose up again out of nowhere, thick as the snow on the *faux* Alpine cabin halfway up the slope. Her question threw him momentarily but he maintained eye contact, willing himself not to say anything else that would brand him the biggest idiot in the room. 'I told you, I saw a future extreme-sport fanatic in you, Flores.'

She drew her lips into a line and looked away, and he knew his flippant attitude wouldn't wash. 'I also didn't think you had any plans. At least, you didn't mention any.'

'I had no afternoon plans, it's true. But I have plans for after this. For midnight,' she said, looking at the clock on the wall, then quickly at her phone. It was only five p.m. now. He bit back a smirk. Again, she seemed very keen that he know this fact and take it straight to heart: that she would be unavailable at midnight, and would definitely not accept any more invitations from him after this very safe, very public outing. Fair enough. He had his own plans with Bruno, once he'd made sure Joe got to spend some time with Bandit.

Wow, he was turning into a dog freak, he thought briefly, before pushing it aside. He led Angel to a secluded corner of the bar, where a suddenly empty plush leather booth offered a modicum of privacy. Angel's fingers traced patterns on the condensation of her glass as she seemed to consider what to say.

'So, you're a mountain rescue volunteer, too. I don't know

why this surprises me. Is there anything Teddy Vaughn doesn't do?'

He considered it for a moment. 'I don't eat molluscs.'

Angel blurted a laugh. 'You don't eat molluscs? Like, no oysters, no mussels—nothing?'

'Nope.'

'Why not?'

He studied her features in the dim-blue light. 'I made friends with an octopus once, on a spear-fishing expedition in Indonesia. It followed me around all day, and again three days later, like it remembered me. I don't know; something changed in my head when I saw how smart they are.'

Angel nodded thoughtfully. 'And in your heart, you big softie. You *are* a teddy bear really, aren't you?'

He chuckled at that. 'I've been called a lot of things by women in my time but…' He shrugged. 'Maybe.'

'You know, I didn't even think octopuses were molluscs until now,' she mused.

'Well, you learn something new every day, Flores.'

She laughed, leaning closer over the table. 'So, spearfishing too… How come you're into all these extreme sports anyway? When did that start?'

Teddy felt a familiar tug in his chest at the question. They'd touched on a lot, that night she'd accidentally stayed over, but there were some things he'd kept back. He took a swig of his drink, buying himself a moment to gather his thoughts. 'I suppose you could say I've always been fortunate enough to have the means to pursue my passions.'

Angel's eyes narrowed slightly. 'I see. Your family, you mean? They encouraged you?'

He sighed, running a hand through his hair. 'Anything to get me out of the house and their hair.'

He saw the question forming on her lips, then realised

worse—she'd care. So, instead, he smirked. 'Plus, what I do is a great way to meet beautiful paramedics.'

Angel rolled her eyes. 'Smooth, Vaughn.'

'Back to my question, Flores: are you ready to show me what you've got on some bigger blades?'

'Lead the way, octopus king.'

By the time they reached the rental area, Teddy had mostly got himself back under control—mostly. But then Angel tugged on her ski jacket, smoothing it over her curves, and all that self-restraint was gone in a flash.

He told himself he wasn't staring, except he absolutely was. The fitted jacket hugged her in a way that made his fingers twitch with the sudden, dangerous urge to slide them down her waist, just to feel the gorgeous shape of her beneath the layers. Then she pulled her hair back into a sleek ponytail, exposing the elegant line of her neck, and he had to fight the instinct to lean in—to press his lips to that soft, tempting skin just to see if she'd tilt her head for him.

Instead, he cleared his throat and said, 'Looking good, as usual,' which earned him an eye roll and a playful shove instead of the kiss he might have got if he'd been more honest. Why could he never show even a trace of vulnerability around anyone, even her? She was the least judgmental person he'd ever met.

Old habits die hard, he thought to himself begrudgingly.

As they both stepped into the beginners' area, Teddy noticed Eric halfway down the diamond slope. His fellow volunteers were already carving up the more advanced runs. The familiar rush of adrenaline burned through him. He was itching to join them, but he pushed the selfishness aside. Today was about Angel.

'Alright, let's start with the basics,' Teddy said, demonstrating the proper stance. He watched as Angel mimicked his position, her determination tickling him. It was so evident in the set of her jaw.

'Like this?' she asked, wobbling slightly.

Teddy moved closer, his hands hovering near her waist before moving and steadying her hips, adjusting her posture just slightly. The second he touched her, the air shifted.

Angel went utterly still. Teddy swallowed hard, his fingers tightening against the soft padding of her jacket. Beneath all the layers, he knew she was warm, knew that if he slid his hands just an inch lower he'd feel the curve of her beneath his palms.

Focus, Vaughn.

'There. Keep your knees bent, weight centred,' he murmured, his breath brushing the shell of her ear.

Angel let out a slow exhale, and for a split second neither of them moved. Then she took her first tentative glide forward, breaking the spell. Teddy let his hands fall away, even though every nerve in his body screamed at him to keep touching her. She was determined; that much was obvious. Her brow furrowed in concentration, lips slightly parted; damn it, how was he supposed to be a responsible instructor when she looked like this? He was doomed.

'You're a natural,' he said, skiing backwards to keep an eye on her progress.

Angel laughed, but the moment made her unsteady, her arms flailing. Teddy was on her in an instant, catching her hands before she could topple over. The force of it pulled them together, chest to chest, and she stared up at him, cheeks flushed, lips inches from his. And then, she said quietly, 'I think you might be a bit biased, but I'll take the compliment.'

Teddy didn't let go.

'You should take every compliment.' His voice was lower

now, rougher. More honest than was probably good for him. 'You're a pretty amazing woman.'

Her breath hitched, and the blush that spread across her cheeks could've melted the ice beneath them.

'Always the charmer,' she managed, but then... She looked at him from under her lashes, eyes dark with something new, something dangerous. 'But, for the record, something about you has snuck into my head too, and I don't really know what to do about it.'

Teddy's stomach dropped. There it was—the thing they hadn't been saying, laid bare between them. He searched her eyes, half-expecting her to take it back or to laugh it off. But she didn't. She just stood there, caught in the same mess he was in, waiting.

His fingers twitched against hers. He could lean in right now. He could end the guessing game. Instead, he exhaled. 'That makes two of us,' he admitted, reaching up—God help him—to tuck a stray lock of hair behind her ear. His knuckles brushed her cheek and she shivered.

'But for now...' he forced himself to say, even though 'for now' felt like absolute hell. 'Why don't we just...ski?'

Angel swallowed, then nodded quickly, her voice a little breathless. 'Yes. Skiing sounds good. Let's ski.'

Teddy didn't move as she pulled away, didn't move as she turned back to the slope. He was too busy watching her, and also wondering just how long they could keep pretending this wasn't going to explode into something from which neither of them would be able to return.

Teddy encouraged her for the next forty minutes, watching her gather speed, then chicken out and slow herself right down. Whenever she fell, he helped her up, but she remained as determined as ever to improve and do it on her own. He'd seen Angel in a few high-pressure situations by this point. She was always cool and professional. But watching her completely embracing something new like this, and seeing the genuine smile that lit up her face while she did it, was exhilarating.

So, she didn't know what to do about this attraction, just as he didn't. But he had to ask himself whether it was just because they were colleagues, or whether there was something else going on on her part—something to do with her ex being so recent, the break-up being so fresh. It shouldn't matter. He wouldn't think about it now.

'I think you're ready to try something new,' he suggested now, skiing to her side. He gestured to a bigger slope and she looked at him in surprise.

'Already?'

'Well, unless you're too chicken?'

'I'm no chicken.'

They skied out together. At first, Angel was pretty good. He could see her confidence growing with every movement, and he couldn't help wondering again what had happened with her ex fiancé to have caused their break-up. They'd been about to get married. At what point after proposing to someone—a decision that must take a lot of careful thought and consideration—did someone suddenly decide it was not what they wanted? And who wouldn't want her? he thought, watching as she hit the slope again, and started gathering more speed. She was gorgeous.

Teddy's pondering was shattered in an instant. His trained eyes spotted the danger ahead before Angel even realised what was happening. She had picked up speed on a slight incline, but her novice skills were no match for the momentum carrying her straight towards the looming wall at the edge of the slope.

'Angel!' he shouted, his body already in motion. Years of mountain-rescue instincts kicked in as he angled his skis, cutting through the snow at high speed.

Time slowed down to nothing as Teddy raced to intercept her path. He could see the moment the panic flickered across Angel's face, her eyes widening as she realised exactly what was about to happen. Without hesitation, Teddy launched himself into her trajectory at full velocity, expertly manoeuvring to block her collision course with the wall. Several people around them gasped and shrieked as the impact sent them both tumbling, a tangle of limbs and skis. They rolled together, finally coming to a stop via a skid through a flurry of powdery snow.

For a moment, there was only the sound of their heavy breathing. Then, unexpectedly, Angel burst into laughter. The sound was infectious, and Teddy found himself joining in. Thank God she wasn't hurt; he didn't know what he would have done if she'd been hurt on his watch.

'Are you OK?' he asked between chuckles, propping himself up on one elbow to look at her.

Angel nodded, still laughing. 'Thanks to you. That was quite the mountain rescue, Teddy. I can see your training is paying off.'

He grinned, noticing how snowflakes clung to her eyelashes, how her cheeks were flushed with cold and excitement. 'Just doing my job. Don't scare me like that.'

Their laughter subsided. Teddy became acutely aware of their proximity, Angel's body warm against his, her breath visible in the frigid air between them. For a moment, he forgot all the people who were likely looking at them and got completely lost in wondering if her lips would be as soft as they looked and whether they'd taste as good as last time.

Reality crashed back in. Teddy cleared his throat, getting to his feet. 'Let's get you back on your feet,' he said, offering his hand down to her. 'Are you ready to try again?'

'Absolutely,' she replied, dusting down her trousers and shaking the snow out of her hair.

Teddy helped Angel to her feet, but she lingered for a moment, adjusting her jacket before meeting his eyes. The connection was brief—she looked away almost immediately—but it was enough to send a familiar, electrifying thrill through him, followed by a heavy weight of uncertainty that settled right onto his shoulders. This unspoken thing between them was undefined and fragile, and it was becoming almost impossible to ignore. Angel Flores was starting to mean far more to him than he'd ever anticipated, and it all unnerved him more than ever.

CHAPTER TWELVE

ANGEL STOLE ANOTHER glance at his profile in the driver's seat, struck by how the fading sunlight was catching his sharp jawline just right, as if trying to highlight his handsome face from every possible angle.

'So,' she ventured, 'What are your plans for tonight?' She'd been dying to ask. Personally, she had no plans. She'd just pretended so as not to sound pathetic.

Teddy's hands flexed on the steering wheel. 'I've got to swing by my place to pick up Bandit, so he's there when Joe gets discharged.'

'You really do have a thing for the underdog,' Angel said, her fingers absently tracing patterns on the arm rest between them. She hesitated, then added, 'I know Joe appreciates everything you've done for him.'

Teddy shrugged, but Angel caught the ghost of a smile on his lips. 'Kid's been through enough. Least I can do is make sure his furry friend is there to welcome him back. I hope he's going to be alright when he gets back home. Do you think I should give him my private number, just in case?'

'I think he'd like that a lot.'

Why did he have to be so gorgeous in every sense of the word? Teddy's compassion for the troubled teen never ceased to amaze her. He'd gone all out to be a rock for him ever since they'd picked him up from the moors.

The car fell silent, save for the hum of the engine. Angel's mind raced, searching for a way to prolong their time together. She found herself torn between the desire to invite him over later and the fear of seeming too forward. She should just go home and make macaroni cheese on her own.

'What are you doing after that?' she heard herself say anyway.

Teddy's reply was brief to say the least. 'Nothing much. I'm a bit tired, to be honest. Probably an early night.'

'I thought you said you had plans.'

He looked sideways. 'Oh. Yeah…well, nothing I can't cancel. You know how big groups are; they barely notice when someone's not there.'

Angel couldn't help but smile into her scarf. He'd never had any plans. He had just told her that. They'd both told a white lie. There was something in his tone, though, a kind of weariness that went beyond physical exhaustion. It struck her that perhaps Teddy's aversion to the New Year celebrations wasn't just about being tired. Maybe, like her, he had his own reasons for wanting to avoid spending the festivities in the company of others. She could tell he didn't always see eye to eye with his family—that their money and status wasn't as important to him as it seemed to be to them.

As they neared her street, Angel felt a pang of disappointment. She wasn't ready for this day to end. She had told herself not to accept the skiing invitation, knowing it was best to keep her distance, but she simply couldn't do it. He'd swayed her with one simple text message last night, and now, being next to him was making it even harder. The crazy connection she felt with him was starting to feel like delicious respite from the emptiness that had plagued her evenings before she'd met him.

Teddy pulled up to her building. Angel unbuckled her

seatbelt deliberately slowly. She turned to face him, summoning the courage.

'Teddy, I...' she began, but the words caught in her throat. How could she express this without seeming desperate or clingy?

He looked at her expectantly. Those piercing eyes always seemed to see right through her. She took a deep breath.

'I just wanted to say thank you,' she managed. 'For today. It was...really nice.'

Teddy's smile was genuine, reaching his eyes. 'I had a great time too, Flores. We should do it again some time, see if you can stay upright for longer than three minutes.'

'Ha ha,' she said, rolling her eyes, her hand on the door handle. The seconds she'd been awarded to grab this opportunity were ticking away. Stepping out of the car, she lingered on the street, then turned towards her building, fumbling for her keys. What was she doing? *Just go inside, Flores*, she warned herself. But then...it was New Year's Eve, after all. Maybe...

'Hey, Teddy?' she called out, just as he was pulling away. The car stopped with a jerk and she watched as he leaned over and rolled down the window on the passenger side.

'Yes?'

His gentle support throughout the day had already made her decision for her, really. Whatever was going on with him and his family, whatever shadows or demons lurked behind this ultimately charming facade, she wanted to be there for him, the way he'd been there for her. 'Want some company for that early night?' she asked.

Her heart pounded at her chest like a woodpecker as she waited for his response. The seconds stretched into an eternity. Maybe she was overstepping—reading too much into their connection?

'That sounds nice, actually,' he said. 'But I wouldn't want to ruin your New Year plans.'

A laugh of relief bubbled up from her chest. 'You're looking at my plans.' She gestured to her apartment building. 'I've been planning to cook something amazing all day. You can be my taste-tester.'

There was a pause, then he smiled. 'That was your big plan?'

'Hey, now. Is macaroni cheese not a plan?'

He laughed. 'Well, how can I refuse an offer like that? I'll come back after I've swung by the hospital. If it's OK, I'll bring Bruno. He's not a fan of the fireworks, and he needs my emotional support.'

'Perfect. I'll see you and Bruno then.'

Turning round with her keys, she listened to him drive off, and realised that she was actually looking forward to New Year's Eve now. But she had some planning to do. She waited for Teddy's tail lights to disappear. Then she turned round and headed for the Italian deli. In minutes she was surrounded by shelves of artisanal cheeses and imported delicacies, feeling a twinge of guilt at her deception as she dropped two of the most delicious ones into her basket.

As she perused the vibrant array of organic vegetables, her mind whirled with possibilities. She wanted to impress Teddy, the way he'd impressed her. Macaroni wouldn't cut it. Her fingers trailed over glossy aubergines and plump tomatoes, finally settling on a selection that would make any chef proud.

Back in her kitchen, Angel tied on an apron and surveyed her ingredients. The rhythmic chop of her one sharp knife against the cutting board was oddly soothing, and helped to calm her nerves as she worked. She sautéed the garlic and onions, the aroma filling the air, reminding her of lazy afternoons from her childhood when her mother had cooked up a storm utilising all the recipes from the Philippines.

As she prepared a rich tomato sauce for the eggplant parmesan, she mused about how much Teddy would probably enjoy the Philippines. There were loads of adventurous things to do there. There were rugged trails, stunning, panoramic views and challenging climbs around Mount Pulag and Mount Apo, the highest peak in the country. He could jump through canyons and waterfalls at Cebu's Kawasan Falls, or even free-diving at Tubbataha Reefs.

Why on earth…? Why was she picturing Teddy there? Only days ago, she'd been dredging up memories of Ben, sitting with his drink on her grandma's porch with the sunlight all over his stupid face.

'You're losing your mind, Angel,' she murmured, stirring the sauce without really seeing it. Her eyes flicked up to the windowsill. Ben's face grinned back at her from behind the glass of the photo frame, frozen like a relic in ice. She stilled, waiting for the sting of grief to sink its teeth in. But nothing came, just a dull flicker of memory this time.

It should have hurt. It used to.

She had left him there, where she could see him, after a conversation with her sister—a kind of self-inflicted torment or maybe a test of endurance.

'Face him,' her sister had said. 'Don't bury him, only to have him lunge at you when you least expect it. If you look at him every day, if you keep breathing through it, one day the pain won't own you any more. One day, you'll remember without breaking.'

Angel wasn't sure if that day had arrived. But tonight, for the first time, Ben's face was just a photograph. She studied it, remembering the day it had been taken—a friend's birthday party in the park, long before everything had fallen apart between them. But, instead of the usual pang of hurt and regret, she felt…nothing.

'I really am over you, you know,' she told his image, layering the aubergine with sauce. Sprinkling on the last bit of gourmet cheese, it dawned on her that she was actually hoping for more than just dinner with Teddy tonight. 'Am I really considering this?' She grinned, sliding the dish into the oven. 'Sleeping with Teddy Vaughn?'

The thought was both thrilling and terrifying and the idea hung in the delicious air, as tantalising as the food she was preparing. She busied herself tossing the salad and doing her best to sort through a thousand conflicting emotions.

'I like him,' she admitted to the empty kitchen. 'I shouldn't. But I do, and he knows it. And, after everything that's happened, don't I deserve some fun—just a little bit? Like, one night of fun?'

Stepping into the living room, her heart revved under the new dress she'd just slipped into. She smoothed the throw pillows on the sofa and adjusted a vase of flowers. Her movements were all jittery with nervous energy. As she turned to straighten a stack of magazines, her eyes landed on another framed photo tucked away on a bookshelf. In this photo, she and Ben were laughing at something off-camera, their heads pressed together in an intimate moment. She remembered the day this one had been taken—a beautiful hike through the Cotswolds countryside, just the two of them, at the start of their relationship.

It could all come flooding back in a second if she let it—the stolen looks in bustling pubs, the local delicacies topped with his kisses in olde worlde chocolate shops and cheese shops. A million memories of falling so deeply in love with Ben…

She sat on the sofa, her gaze drifting over the familiar

image, yet all she could really see now was Teddy's face, steady and reassuring, pulling her back to the present. She was just about to tuck the photo away in a drawer when the doorbell chimed.

'Oh, shoot!' Her pulse screeched into thud-mode. It was Teddy. 'Coming!' she called out.

Leaving the photo frame on the coffee table, she hurried towards the hall, stopping briefly to check herself in the mirror. Smoothing her hair one last time, she took a deep breath, willing her nerves to settle.

'It's just dinner,' she reminded herself, but she couldn't stop the flutter of nervous excitement in her stomach at the thought of what else might be about to happen.

The door swung open, and there she was—Angel, her hair tumbling loosely around her shoulders. She was wearing a beautiful, sparkly ankle-length dress in shades of green and peacock-blue that seemed to shimmer like sunlight on water. The intricate pattern traced her figure gracefully. Every detail amplified her natural elegance and it was impossible to imagine anything else suiting her so perfectly, except perhaps a wedding dress.

He blanched, suddenly. Woah, where the heck had that come from? His brain was misfiring. Maybe he should've got more sleep. She looked absolutely stunning, though, even if it *was* a bit extravagant for a night in. What else was she planning? he wondered, and the thought instantly dried up his throat.

'Hey,' he managed, his voice huskier than he'd intended. 'I brought dessert.' He lifted a box that contained a gourmet tiramisu from the best Italian bakery in town—the only stop he'd had time to make after leaving the hospital, having safely deposited Bandit with his rightful owner.

'That looks amazing,' she said with a smile.

'So do you,' he said without a beat. Their fingers brushed as she took the box, sending a jolt through his arm, and he took her in as she welcomed him inside—how her hair fell over her shoulders, how every sparkle on her dress caught the warm glow from the hallway lights. She did look slightly nervous. Did she regret asking him here? They were already on the verge of mixing business with pleasure but he wasn't about to let her down on New Year's Eve, and he didn't *really* want to spend it alone.

In the living room, Angel bent down to scratch Bruno behind his fuzzy ears. 'Hello again, handsome boy,' she cooed. The French Bulldog adjusted himself for more of her petting, his tongue lolling out in contentment. Teddy chuckled, grateful for the momentary distraction from Angel's curves in that dress.

'I hope it's OK that he's here. I think he misses Bandit.'

Angel straightened. 'I like having him here. How did it go with Joe's release; were you there?'

Teddy nodded, letting the warmth of the cosy room envelop him, breathing in the mouth-watering aroma of whatever on earth she was cooking. It really did smell incredible. 'I left just before he was collected,' he said. 'He didn't seem too happy about going, between you and me, but at least he has Bandit, and social services will check in on him.'

'And you gave him your number?'

'I did.'

Angel poured him a glass of wine, her fingers grazing his as she handed it over. The tension crackled between them like livewires, electric, and so obvious that he was sure her neighbours must feel it through the walls. She went to sit down, then bolted up again.

'Oh! The main course. I should check on it.' She hurried

towards the kitchen, leaving Teddy to follow with his glass of wine, Bruno trotting at his heels. He watched as Angel pulled on oven mitts and retrieved a dish from the oven. The scent intensified as she placed it on the work top and Teddy's stomach growled in anticipation.

'What culinary masterpiece have you whipped up?' he asked, leaning against the counter. 'Are you trying to outdo my cooking skills, Flores?'

Angel threw him a playful glare. 'Can you blame a girl for trying? It's aubergine parm.'

Teddy whistled, impressed. 'Fancy. I didn't know you were such a gourmet chef.'

'There's a lot you don't know about me, Teddy Vaughn,' Angel replied, and he didn't miss the challenge in her voice…or was that maybe an invitation?

She reached for the cutlery drawer. He noticed the slight tremor in her hands, the way her composure was slipping slightly in his presence. All of this meant something. Whatever they'd started and done their best to ignore was not about to shatter and evaporate into nothingness any time soon. She fumbled with the silverware. The clatter of metal against metal was suddenly far too loud in the quiet kitchen. Then a fork slipped from her grasp. It fell towards the floor, and Teddy's reflexes kicked in. He lunged forward, his hand shooting out to snatch the utensil mid-air, and when he straightened with it he found himself mere inches from Angel, close enough to catch the faint scent of her perfume, to note the plumpness of her kissable lips. Their eyes locked.

'Nice catch.' Angel breathed, staring straight at his lips.

Teddy straightened, the fork cool against his palm. Angel's gaze softened on his and he felt an overwhelming urge to close the distance between them and just kiss her, the way he had at the ice-rink. But, as quickly as the moment arose, Angel blinked and looked away, her cheeks flushing. 'Thanks,' she muttered, taking the fork from his hand and busying herself with the drawer again.

Teddy stepped backwards. He'd seen the spark in her eyes; he was sure of it. But then, if this was really meant to be an evening of something more than friendship, why had she just pulled away? The sting of rejection prickled at the edges of his mind but he squished it back down ruthlessly.

Angel wasn't meeting his eyes now. 'Um, could you help me carry these cheeses to the living room?'

'Sure thing.' He picked up the platter of gourmet cheeses she'd motioned to, following Angel out of the kitchen with her little pots of chutney. Lost in his own thoughts about what all this really meant, Teddy barely registered setting the cheese plate on the coffee table, but a sudden commotion snapped him back to reality. Bruno, ever the opportunist, had managed to snag a giant chunk of brie and was gleefully gobbling it down as if he'd just won the lottery.

'Bruno!' Teddy yelled. 'You little cheese thief!' His eyes darted to Angel. Oh God, this was so embarrassing; she was probably going to be upset. To his relief, however, Angel just sighed and shook her head.

'Dogs will be dogs. You have to be one step ahead, or else *they* will be. At least Bruno has excellent taste!' She laughed lightly.

'He's got an iron gut by now,' Teddy said. 'Trust me, this isn't his first cheese heist.'

Angel motioned for him to take a seat. 'I'll go grab the rest of the food. You'd better stay here, on guard.'

'Yes, ma'am. He's under strict observation now, don't you worry.'

Teddy watched her glittering dress as she retreated to the kitchen. At least Bruno was a pro at sucking any tension from the room. His gaze wandered round the room, taking in the cosy decor, until it landed on a photo frame face-down on the table. He picked it up, curiosity getting the better of him. The first thing that struck him was Angel's beaming smile. Her arms were wrapped around a man he'd never seen before. They were both laughing, all caught up in a moment. His first, overwhelming observation was, *wow, she looks so happy.*

Then the realisation hit him like a punch to the stomach—this was Ben, Angel's ex-fiancé. It had to be. Teddy's fingers tightened on the frame as he studied the photo closely. They looked so happy, so in love. Obviously it hadn't lasted. But why was this photo out? Had she been looking at it recently—tonight? Did she wish *he* were Ben?

'Get a grip, Vaughn,' he muttered, but he couldn't shake the feeling of unease, unworthiness—a beast he knew too well. Was he setting himself up for an embarrassing ending? He'd assumed they could have a bit of fun, but seeing her like this, so in love with her ex, just made him realise that for the first time in his life it wasn't fun he was after. It was strange and completely unprecedented after his string of non-starter relationships but he was falling for Angel, and falling hard. And she was still in love with someone else. She was going along with whatever this was because she didn't really want to be alone right now, as he didn't, but she'd go on to ignore him at work, as she had done the other day, and he'd have to pretend he wasn't crazy about her. He wasn't so great at pretending when he didn't like someone, especially someone as gorgeous as Angel.

The sound of her footsteps approaching snapped him quickly out of his spiralling thoughts. He set the frame back down, trying to compose himself. But, as Angel re-entered the room, her arms laden with dishes, Teddy couldn't help seeing her through a whole new lens.

'Everything alright?' she asked, catching his eye. 'You look like you've just seen a ghost.'

Teddy forced a smile. 'Yeah, just…um…' He cleared his throat, trying to shake off what he'd just seen, but it was no good; he couldn't un-see that photograph of Ben. Now he could almost visualise them together. 'Listen, Angel, I hate to do this, but I just remembered about that…um…. that I said I would meet someone early tomorrow morning. I should probably head out.'

Angel's face fell. 'Oh,' she said, slowly placing the steaming dishes on the table in the corner. 'But we haven't even eaten. And it's not even midnight. Are you sure you can't stay a bit longer?'

For a moment, when he saw the hurt and confusion in her eyes, Teddy wavered. It would be so easy to give in, to act as if he hadn't seen the photo. But the image of Ben and her kept flashing through his mind again and again, taunting him. This had to stop, right now. He was not about to invite in more rejection, especially not from the woman to whom he'd spent the last week baring his soul; the woman who had started to make him realise that maybe his non-decisive bachelor days of playing the field were not as fun as they used to be.

'I'm sorry,' he said, hating how formal his voice sounded. 'I really should go. Thanks for cooking; it really does smell great.'

'Well, wait a minute, I'll box some up…'

'No need.'

As he gathered his things and summoned a lazy Bruno, who was likely ninety-eight per cent cheese at this point, he could literally feel Angel's bewilderment radiating through the room towards him. He wanted to explain, to pour out his heart and tell her how he felt, how she'd made him reconsider a few things since they'd met what felt like a lifetime ago. But what was the point? She clearly wasn't over Ben. And he didn't *do* relationships for precisely this reason—they made him stupid and vulnerable—so what was he even thinking?

She stood in the middle of the room, arms crossed protectively over her chest. 'Well…' she said, and stopped, no doubt because her voice was cracking a little.

'Well…' Teddy replied, taking Bruno's lead from its hook on the wall. His chest ached with the need to comfort her as the dog padded behind him, looking somewhat sadly between Angel and him. He wanted to stay and make things right, but he couldn't bring in a new year like this.

'Goodnight, Angel,' he said softly, then stepped out into the cold, damp night air, just as the first early firework screamed above them and lit up the sky over York.

CHAPTER THIRTEEN

KATE'S EYES WIDENED as she lifted the lid of the container, taking a giant sniff of the aubergine parmigiana. 'Angel, this smells incredible! What's the occasion?'

Ollie and George both leaned in for a sniff, and Angel reached into her bag, pulling out two more containers of the cold dish from last night. 'No occasion. I made it to share so, here, I'm sharing.'

George grabbed a fork and started tucking excitedly into his portion. Angel felt Teddy's gaze on her from the coffee station. She refused to meet it. Little did the team know she'd made this dish to share with Teddy, only to have him walk out on her without even tasting a morsel last night. She hadn't spoken to him yet, and he hadn't spoken to her beyond a feeble, 'Good morning.' A storm that had started at some point after midnight was still raging outside, which suited her mood just fine.

George, oblivious to the tension, spoke up with his mouth full. 'Teddy, mate, you've got to try this. It's bloody fantastic! Even for breakfast.'

'I'm sure it is,' Teddy said over the wind outside, which brought with it more rain by the second. Angel's jaw clenched. She hadn't brought any food for Teddy, and she certainly wasn't going to offer him any now. He didn't deserve it.

'So, Teddy,' Angel said, finally turning to face him. 'How did your early-morning meeting go?'

Teddy's eyebrows shot up. Surprise flashed across his face before he schooled his features. 'Oh, it was…'

'Meeting?' George interrupted, swallowing a mouthful of aubergine. 'There wasn't any meeting scheduled for this morning.'

The room fell silent as everyone looked between them in confusion. Angel's cheeks burned. She'd meant to catch Teddy in his lie, to expose him for the coward he was. Instead, she'd only managed to make things more awkward amongst the team. Great. But this was all her fault anyway. She'd let her guard down, allowing herself to finally move on from Ben, and now she was paying the price for her naivety—thinking the so-called hospital hottie might be interested in a colleague, beyond that one kiss and some fun flirtations.

Obviously Teddy didn't want anything from her; he had a reputation as a ladies' man for a reason. He'd probably left her place last night because she'd got way too cosy and 'couple' with all the effort she'd gone to with the food. He'd probably gone straight to someone else's place and slept with them.

The thought twisted like a knife in her gut, but she forced herself to confront it, then shake it off. It was better this way anyway: no more illusions, no more wishing for something that clearly wasn't meant to be. *Focus on the job, Angel*, she told herself firmly, just as the emergency alarm blared through the station. Angel's heart rate spiked as Kate answered the radio, her face showing immediate concern.

'Joe's run away again. He's been missing all night.'

Angel's eyes met Teddy's. A flash of shared concern

passed between them before she quickly looked away again. 'But he was just released,' she said. 'His leg—'

'It gets worse,' Kate cut in, already gesturing to the helicopter on the forecourt. 'His parents went looking for him on the moors. They've crashed in the storm. I have the coordinates.'

The helicopter's blades whirred to life, drowning out the howling wind and creating more of its own as Angel climbed aboard. She settled into her seat, acutely aware of Teddy's presence beside her in the tight confines. She could feel the heat radiating from his body, and there was no mistaking the fact that he was still tense around her. As they lifted off, her knee and elbow brushed against his. She moved away as much as she could, even though a traitorous jolt zipped through her body at the contact. It was impossible to create any distance here; the turbulence just kept pushing them back together even closer.

Ugh, this was a nightmare. She couldn't bear it any longer. Angel stood, gripping the overhead rail for balance. 'I'm going to double-check our supplies,' she announced, then moved to the rear of the helicopter, feeling Teddy's eyes on her back as she busied herself with the medical kits.

The flight felt interminable as George fought his way through the howling wind and Angel found herself stealing glances at Teddy, taking in the tightness in his jaw, the way his hands clenched and unclenched on his knees as his gaze darted to hers in turn. What was he thinking? Did he regret leaving her house last night, or was he simply focused on the mission ahead of them: finding Joe and his parents? Why should she care about Teddy Vaughn now anyway?

Whatever had happened between them, it was over and they needed to work together now. Her job, and other people's lives, depended on their ability to function as a team and she wasn't going to let anyone down, least of all herself.

Her heart leapt to her mouth as the wreckage of a car came into view, mangled against a large boulder, the windshield completely shattered. Two bodies lay slumped inside, surrounded by twisted metal and broken glass. 'Oh, no…'

The helicopter's blades chopped through the thick grey storm-clouds, slicing them apart, finally coming to land in a nearby clearing. In minutes, Teddy was sprinting through the driving rain towards the vehicle. Angel followed close behind, her medical bag bouncing against her hip. She was getting absolutely drenched. Her hair stuck to her face in clumps like glue as she ran head-first in the rain to the driver's side of the car, where Joe's father was unconscious. He was bleeding profusely from a nasty gash on his forehead.

'Possible concussion, definite lacerations,' Angel reported, her fingers checking for a pulse. 'Breathing is shallow but steady.'

Teddy nodded, moving to the passenger side where Joe's mother was stirring weakly. 'Ma'am, can you hear me?' he called out, carefully opening the door.

'Joe,' the woman mumbled, her eyes unfocused. 'Where's Joe?'

'We're looking for him,' Angel assured her, joining Teddy. 'Right now, we need to take care of you. Can you tell me where it hurts?'

The realisation that they'd crashed seemed to sink in now and Joe's mother started to panic, crying out for her son, trying to move despite her injuries. 'It's OK.' Angel placed a firm hand on her shoulder. 'Please, stay still. We think you might have a broken collarbone and some fractured ribs. We need to immobilise you before we can move you, OK ma'am? You're going to be fine.'

Teddy was already retrieving a neck brace and backboard in the rain, and a silent understanding passed between them as they worked quickly in tandem to extract Joe's parents from the wreckage. He helped secure Joe's father to the stretcher, calmly explaining every step of what they were doing to the frightened couple. Angel wished her heart would stop reverting back to wanting those big, strong, hands on her in very different circumstances…

'Angel, start an IV on her,' Teddy called out. 'I'm worried about internal bleeding.'

In minutes, she'd inserted the needle, Joe's mother gripping her arm like a vice. 'Please,' she whispered, tears in her eyes. 'You have to find our son.'

Angel felt a lump form in her throat. 'We will,' she promised, hoping she sounded more confident than she felt. 'The mountain-rescue team is already searching. Joe's tough, remember? He'll be alright.'

As they loaded the injured couple into the helicopter, Angel caught Teddy watching her. For a moment, the tension between them seemed to dissipate. All that mattered was Joe and his family, making sure they were OK. Taking her seat, she found herself next to Teddy again, but this time she didn't move away. Whatever had happened between them, right now they were partners with an important job to do, and somewhere out here on this treacherous terrain there was a very scared, very emotionally troubled teenage boy who needed their help.

Hopefully Joe had Bandit with him, and Bandit was protecting him. In fact, they'd be better go back out on foot—at least that way they could call for the dog, and he might answer. Bandit knew them, after all.

She got to her feet again, turning to George and Kate, raising her voice over the roar of the rotors. 'Take them straight to hospital, will you? Teddy and I will continue the search on foot.'

George nodded, his usual jovial expression one of grim determination. 'Roger that. Be careful out there, you two. The weather's turning even nastier.'

She and Teddy stood beneath the helicopter, watching it disappear into the grey sky over their heads. They were alone now. And they didn't just face the elements; they faced very awkward tension between them. Well, there was nothing she could do about that.

'I'm thinking we might find him first if we call for Bandit.'

Teddy nodded, adjusting his backpack. 'Good idea. I'll follow you.'

They set out across the windswept moor, and to her disappointment the weather only became more hostile. The blustery landscape seemed intent on growing more treacherous with each step. Icy rain pelted her face and the wind howled into her ears like a wolf, drowning out any attempts at conversation he might be trying to make. Thank goodness. Angel was rather grateful for the excuse to stay silent right now. Her mind had a bigger storm than this going on inside it.

After what felt like hours of trudging through the unforgiving landscape and calling out for the dog, Teddy's voice cut through the storm. 'Did you...did you watch the fireworks last night?'

Angel's stomach clenched. She kept her eyes fixed on the path ahead, willing her voice to remain steady. 'Of course,' she replied. 'Did you? Or were you too busy preparing for your fictional morning meeting?'

Teddy fell silent, but she refused to fill the emptiness.

She scanned the horizon, squinting through the rain for any sign of Joe.

'Angel, I—' Teddy began, but she cut him off.

'We should split up. Cover more ground.'

Teddy shut his mouth and nodded. 'You're probably right. Radio me if you find anything.'

Angel felt a pang of regret but she pushed it aside. Whatever was going on between Teddy and her, it could wait. Joe was out here, alone and scared. But, just as they were about to part ways, the dog's bark bit through the wind.

'Bandit!' they cried in unison, sprinting towards the sound. It wasn't long before a bright-red object, vivid against the dull grey of the moorland, caught her eye and her heart leapt.

'Teddy!' she called out, already moving towards the spot. 'Over here!'

They drew closer, both frowning into the slashing rain now. The red object was a tent, a very crumpled, battered tent, with its fabric flapping wildly in the wind. Angel's stomach dropped.

Teddy appeared at her side, studying it.

'It's been torn away,' he said. 'Looks like he may have tried to pitch it and got into some trouble. He can't be far.'

The dog barked again and another faint sound reached her ears, barely discernible from the wind. Angel froze, straining to listen. There it was again—a low groan. 'Joe!' she shouted, scrambling towards the noise just as her foot slipped on the wet grass, almost sending her tumbling face-first down the slippery slope. She would have done if Teddy's hand hadn't grabbed her arm, steadying her. For a moment she clung to him, catching her breath before yanking her arm back. 'I'm fine.'

Joe was huddled against a rocky outcrop with Bandit at

the bottom of the incline. His clothes were soaked through, just as were theirs, and Bandit was wet through, refusing to leave Joe's side, as before.

'Joe, it's Angel,' she called down to him, starting to scramble down the slope from a lower position. Soon she was crouching beside him. 'We have to stop meeting like this.'

'I think my other foot is twisted now,' he said, wincing in pain. His teeth were chattering like mad. As Teddy radioed for extraction, Angel began assessing Joe's injuries; it was clear he was more emotionally hurt than physically hurt this time, but there was a severe risk of hypothermia considering he'd been out here all night.

'You gave us quite a scare,' she murmured, wrapping a thermal blanket around his shivering form. 'Your parents are worried sick.'

Joe's face clouded. 'I'm sure they didn't even notice I left,' he muttered, but Angel caught the flicker of doubt in his eyes.

'That's not true,' Teddy intervened firmly, meeting his gaze. 'They love you, Joe. They came out here to look for you. They got into an accident in their car. We already sent them to the hospital,' he added, while she radioed in the situation. The team had already deposited his parents and were on the way back.

For a moment, Joe's tough exterior seemed to crack like an eggshell. She glimpsed the vulnerable child threatening to escape before he looked away, blinking rapidly. 'Are they…are they OK?'

'They will be,' Teddy assured him.

Angel looked at him, holding Joe's hand, offering what little comfort he could while their crew caught them up again. Why had Joe run away again? He was lucky not to have been seriously hurt; he was still nursing his injuries from before! They had to keep him warm and sheltered until help arrived.

Handing Joe a flask of hot water, she met Teddy's piercing eyes. Her breath caught as his concern for this boy shone through, right into her. Whatever was happening or not happening with them, right now they were united in their care for this troubled kid who had somehow worked his way into both their hearts.

Luckily it wasn't long before they heard the familiar roar of the helicopter blades. She stayed on the radio, instructing Kate and Ollie to bring a stretcher, keeping her gaze fixed on the descending vehicle through the rain. Its flashing lights broke through the relentless downpour and Bandit started barking in confusion. *The poor dog.*

Suddenly, a sharp crackle and a splitting shudder raced through the ground beneath her feet. Angel didn't even have time to react as an uprooted tree tipped ominously on its side, no doubt a victim of the storm. A gasp lodged in her throat as she dropped the radio. She tried to leap away but she wasn't quick enough. The thick, wet branch struck her square in the chest like a giant baseball bat, propelling her backwards with such brutal force that she found herself flying three feet into the air, coming down with a smack.

'Angel!'

The world spun sickeningly as she crumpled onto the wet earth like a marionette who'd just had its strings clipped. *Oh my God, the pain...*

'Angel!' It was Teddy calling for her, racing towards her, getting to his haunches at her side. She was sure it was Teddy, but nothing made sense. Darkness edged her vision as she clutched at her chest, and he pulled her close to him.

Everything was moving in slow motion now as she was cradled to his wet body. The pain was so intense, though, all she could do was surrender to it and slip into the blackness.

CHAPTER FOURTEEN

IT HAPPENED SO FAST. Angel lay motionless on the ground with her chestnut hair fanned out around her head like a halo on the frosty white ground. 'Angel!' he yelled again, handing Joe over to Kate to help into the helicopter. She didn't move.

Dropping to his knees, he knelt beside her and pressed two fingers to her neck. Relief flooded through him as he felt the steady thrum of her pulse beneath his fingertips. He ran his hands over her limbs next, checking for injuries, but his touch lingered longer than strictly necessary, as if he could get her to open her eyes through sheer force of will.

'Come on, Angel,' he whispered into her ear, watching her closed eyes for any sign of a flutter. No such luck. She was out cold.

'Teddy!' Kate's sharp voice cut through his thoughts. 'We need to move!'

He called back to her that he was on it, forcing himself to focus. With the gentlest movements he could manage he lifted Angel up, acutely aware of how small and fragile she felt in his arms. He loaded her gently into the helicopter, feeling his chest and his entire body tighten with an unfamiliar ache. This woman was undoing him. It was bad enough that he'd hurt her by lying and leaving early on New Year's

Eve, but now she was physically injured—knocked out on the job, on his watch.

Inside the chopper, Kate worked on Joe's leg while Bandit faithfully looked on. The poor dog was getting used to all this, Teddy thought—first his owner sneaking away and landing them both in trouble, and then having to travel miles by helicopter. They both deserved some kind of frequent flyer points by now.

Teddy hovered over Angel. He adjusted her IV and checked her vitals, all the while fighting the urge to brush a stray lock of hair from her forehead in full view of his colleagues.

'How's she doing?' Kate asked, glancing up from Joe and patting Bandit's furry head. The boy looked with interest between Angel and him now, his pain momentarily forgotten.

'She's stable,' Teddy replied. 'Possible concussion, but no visible trauma.'

Kate's eyebrow arched as she observed his tense posture. She'd probably noticed the way his gaze rarely left Angel's face, how worried about her he was. She was putting the pieces together; he was sure of it.

'And how are you doing, Teddy?'

He shrugged, not trusting himself to speak. He busied himself with rechecking Angel's pulse, trying to ignore the way his own heart raced. Just seeing her like this was killing him.

'Teddy...' Kate's voice softened. 'Is there something—?'

'We should radio ahead,' Teddy interrupted, finally tearing his eyes away from Angel to meet Kate's. 'Make sure they're prepped for both patients. I want a full exam on her.'

Kate nodded, and he saw a trace of a knowing smile play at her lips as she turned back to Joe. Teddy exhaled slowly. Then he realised his fingers had unconsciously intertwined with Angel's limp hand. The realisation hit him with the force of a physical blow: he couldn't lose her. Not when he was only just beginning to understand how much she meant to him.

Back in hospital, the harsh fluorescent lights cast a sickly pallor over Angel's features as Teddy slumped in the chair beside her bed. He rubbed his eyes. Waves of exhaustion kept sweeping over him and seeping into his bones. He was cold and damp from being out there on the moors but still he couldn't bring himself to leave Angel.

He leaned forward, elbows on his knees, and studied her face over the steady beep of the heart monitor. Her beautiful, dark hair lay limp against the white pillow and this time he couldn't fight the urge to brush a lock of it away from her forehead.

'Come on, Angel. You've got to wake up. I need to tell you…' He trailed off, swallowing hard. 'I need to make things right.'

Suddenly, the door creaked open, and Teddy straightened, composing his features. One of the nurses strode in, her sharp eyes taking him in immediately and he knew she saw how quickly he moved his face away from Angel's.

'Any change?' she asked him, moving to check Angel's vitals.

Teddy cleared his throat and shook his head. 'Nothing yet.'

He knew this nurse a little. A few weeks ago, and in any other situation, he might have attempted some cheeky humour. He might even have innocently flirted with her, but things were different now. She kept looking up as she hummed thoughtfully, making a note on the chart. 'You know, Teddy, I never thought I'd see the day when you'd be camped out at anyone's bedside like this,' she told him.

He felt the heat creep up his neck. 'She's my colleague,' he said, aiming for nonchalance and missing by a mile.

'Uh-huh,' she replied, her tone as sceptical as the smirk on her face. 'And I suppose you'd do this for any colleague?'

Teddy opened his mouth to argue, then closed it again, shrugging instead. How was he supposed to find the words to explain the whirlwind of emotions churning inside him when he couldn't even understand it himself?

The nurse's expression softened in front of him. 'It's OK to care, you know.'

'I don't…' Teddy began, but the words died a death on his lips as he turned to look back at Angel. 'It's complicated,' he finished lamely.

'Isn't it always?' The nurse patted his shoulder gently. 'Just…don't wait too long to tell her how you feel, Teddy. Life's too short.'

She closed the door softly behind her, leaving Teddy alone with the echo of her words ricocheting through his skull. He slumped deeper into his chair, never taking his eyes off Angel's face. For years he'd walked away from anyone who threatened to get too close. It was easier that way—safer. Shielding himself from the ache of rejection or, worse, the cold sting of indifference from the people who mattered most had, over the years, become almost second nature. His life since boarding school had been a series of fleeting encounters, surface-level flings that hadn't held any real substance at all, and to think he'd told himself he'd enjoyed it. Maybe he had enjoyed it for a while, but wasn't the eventual loneliness the reason he'd got Bruno?

Now with this amazing woman lying here, knowing he had willingly pushed her away just as they'd both been starting to open up to each other, he had to ask himself whether all that self-preservation had really been worth it. Maybe he'd even be happier if he risked the heartbreak, embraced the potential messiness and just took a chance.

If only she wasn't still in love with Ben. That was the root of it, he thought, groaning softly to himself. It just brought all his demons to the surface. Still, he should have talked to her, explained and tried some more of that honesty he was starting to get used to.

'I'm sorry,' he whispered, taking her hand in his, tracing circles on her palm. 'I'm so sorry for pushing you away, it was stupid and selfish. I have my reasons. I promise I'll explain it all, if it will even change anything, but…at any rate we can start over, you and me. We can be friends if that's all you want. Just…make sure you come back.'

Still, she was silent; motionless.

The familiar burn of loneliness settled in his chest. With a heavy sigh, he got to his feet, giving her hand one final squeeze. He needed to clear his head, but he also needed to check on Joe.

Teddy knocked gently before stepping into the room. 'Hey, you. How're you holding up?'

Joe glanced up from his phone. He looked exhausted. 'I'm OK, I suppose. Better than I thought I'd be. How is Angel?'

Teddy felt a lump in his throat rise at her name. 'She'll be fine,' he said, hoping it was true. He leaned against the door frame, crossing his arms. 'Have you heard from your parents?'

Joe's lips twitched in a humourless half-smile. 'They're pretty busted up but nothing life-threatening.'

'Well, Bandit is with George, our pilot. You know, everyone's kind of getting used to having Bandit around now.' He paused. 'But it doesn't mean *either* of you should be here.'

Teddy watched the boy's face fall. 'I know. Mum kept

crying when she saw me, saying she was sorry for everything. But it's like…they're always fighting, Teddy. About the divorce, about me, about everything. I just couldn't take it any more, you know? I had to get out.'

Teddy stepped closer, crouching slightly so they were eye-level. 'You did what you thought you needed to do. Removing yourself from a bad situation is a very normal way of trying to protect yourself. But they're your parents. They care about you, even if they don't always know how to show it.'

Joe scoffed, but the bitterness in his expression seemed duller now. 'Yeah, well, if they care so much, maybe they should stop screaming at each other every second I'm in the room. Bandit hated it. I needed to get him away from all that.'

Teddy didn't flinch, letting the boy's well-earned frustration hang in the air before responding. 'I get it. I get why you'd want to escape, and why you'd want to help Bandit too. But your folks are just human, Joe. They're not perfect. And they're probably scared out of their minds that they're losing you. I know it doesn't make it easier to deal with, but people can't fix what's broken if they don't realise it's broken in the first place. You need to talk to them like a man. Tell them how this is really affecting you. I'm pretty sure they'll appreciate the reality check.'

Even as he spoke, Teddy realised he probably needed to start taking some of his own advice. Somehow it was always so easy to dish it out, yet so tough to take it. Joe's eyes narrowed. He studied him with the sharpness of someone who'd grown up far too fast, not unlike he'd had to at boarding school. 'I've seen how you look at Angel, by the way; have you talked to her? Have you told her you're into her?'

The question hit harder than Teddy expected. He managed a wry smile. 'Maybe you should leave the psychoanalysis to the professionals, don't you think?'

Joe laughed softly. 'You were really worried about her earlier, when that tree knocked her down; everyone saw it…'

'I'd be worried about anyone who had a tree knock them out,' he followed, but he knew his protesting was futile. 'OK, OK,' he said, looking around to see if anyone else was listening in. This was a reality check of his own that he definitely had not asked for. He straightened and patted the boy's shoulder. 'Listen, Joe. The social worker is going to see to it that you and your parents all come out of this OK. I promise you things *will* get better but you need to talk to them. And, in turn, I will talk to Angel… deal?'

Joe nodded slowly and promised him that he would talk to the social worker properly next time she called, and also that he would sit down with his parents and explain how their divorce and arguments made him feel. 'I guess I've been scared to talk to them in case it makes me look…' He trailed off, his eyes flitting away nervously. 'Weak?'

'You're not weak, kid. Lay it all out there. I guarantee you, you'll feel a million times better.'

'Maybe we both will,' Joe said.

Teddy crossed his arms, wondering how the heck he'd wound up in this situation. Maybe he should tell Angel how he felt, despite her feelings for Ben. At least then it would be out in the open, no more tiptoeing round the truth, and she could do with that what she liked. At the very least, he would enjoy an open dialogue, an emotional connection, even if it was to be purely platonic.

Joe's words echoed in his head as Teddy made his way back to Angel's room. When he approached her bedside, he was relieved to see her eyes flutter open. Those striking green orbs focused on him with confusion.

'Teddy?'

He swallowed hard, forcing a smile. 'Hey there, Sleeping Beauty. Welcome back.'

Angel gingerly attempted to sit up and he moved instinctively to help her, carefully adjusting the pillows behind her head. Suddenly she took his hand in hers, causing his muscles to tense and his heart rate to quicken. He pulled back quickly, determined to keep a professional distance between them, especially here, where anyone could walk in. But she'd thrown him completely off-balance long before that. And it was more than obvious everyone knew something had been going on all Christmas—the only person he'd been kidding was himself.

'Joe,' Angel said urgently. 'His parents. Are they…?'

'They're all OK,' he reassured her, pulling up a seat. 'Joe's fine. They're going to work through everything as a family. Turns out his parents are getting a divorce. A pretty vocal one, by the sounds of it. It all got a bit too much for him.'

Angel looked sad and Teddy sighed, rubbing his face. Even lying injured, her first thought was for others. It was one of the things he loved about her.

'I'm sure they will find a way,' she replied, just as a wince of pain took over her face, and he adjusted her bed slightly to help her get more comfortable.

He took a deep breath, steeling himself for what he knew he had to find a way to say. 'Listen, Angel, I… I wanted to apologise for New Year's Eve. I shouldn't have ditched you like that.'

Angel's brow furrowed. 'Teddy, you don't have to—'

'No, I do,' he interrupted, dragging his hands through his hair. 'It was a crappy thing to do. I know you're still… you know…working through stuff with Ben. I guess I was processing that internally, instead of talking to you about how I felt.' The name of her ex felt bitter on his tongue, but he was determined to be the person Joe wanted him to be, and the person he wanted to be for himself and Angel. 'The bottom line is, I don't want to lose your friendship over this, Flores. It means a lot to me.'

Angel stared at him, blinking rapidly, as if his words made no sense. 'It means a lot to me too, Teddy,' she began slowly. 'I really think we…'

Before she could finish, however, the same nurse as before poked her head into the room. 'Sorry to interrupt again, Teddy,' she said, smiling a private smile at him that made a flush of heat creep up his neck like fire yet again. OK, now everyone was going to talk about this. 'I need to check Angel's vitals.'

'Yup.' Teddy stepped back. 'Of course,' he said. 'I should get going anyway. Rest up, Angel. I'll check on you later.'

He turned around, his mind churning. He couldn't believe he'd just told her he didn't want to lose her friendship, when friendship was literally the last thing he wanted going forward, but it was in his best interests just to let her go. Just as he made to step towards the door, however, Angel's small but determined voice called out from behind him.

'Teddy, wait.'

CHAPTER FIFTEEN

ANGEL REACHED OUT QUICKLY, knocking a blanket off the bed. Her fingers grazed Teddy's arm, stopping him in his tracks. 'Wait,' she said again, her voice coming out as a croak. 'Don't go.'

Teddy turned around again, his dark eyebrows furrowed as he glanced between Angel and the nurse and she knew what he was thinking. He was concerned about what people thought. And so should she be, but somehow it didn't even matter any more.

'Just...wait outside until the nurse is done, OK?' she managed. What was the point of holding it all back? Life was short; she might even just have lost hers, thanks to that tree!

Teddy nodded, his eyes softening at the look on her face. His eyes lowered to her hand, now clutching his arm with some degree of desperation. 'Of course. I'll be right outside.'

She nodded and released him, and just as he stepped away his phone started buzzing. Teddy glanced at the screen. His jaw tightened almost imperceptibly before he slid the device away, ignoring the call.

The nurse made cheerful small talk as she checked Angel's vitals. But Angel's focus refused to leave the frosted glass of the door, where Teddy's silhouette paced back and forth. She would know that silhouette anywhere now, she thought. How quickly she had got to know him. Well, as much as he'd decided to show her while she'd actually been awake, she thought, realising the nurse was frowning at her heart rate. It had definitely sped up, the more she'd focused on Teddy. But, now that she was fully conscious, Teddy's whispered words flooded back, bringing a flush to her cheeks at the same time.

I'm sorry, he had said, all the while letting his fingers trace those gentle circles on her palm. *I'm so sorry for pushing you away, it was stupid and selfish. I have my reasons. I promise I'll explain it all, if it will even change anything...*

She'd heard and felt it all from somewhere outside herself. It had felt like a dream but she knew it wasn't. She had known that the second she'd opened her eyes and seen his face—the relief. The emotion in his voice echoed in her mind even now. She had spent so long guarding her heart, making up all these new rules around love, romance and Christmas, determined never to be hurt again. But Teddy's words, his unwavering presence throughout it all over the holidays, had made her reevaluate everything.

And still he still wanted to be friends. It just didn't make sense.

'Your heart rate is still a bit elevated,' the nurse commented now, still peering at the monitor. 'Everything alright?'

Angel nodded, forcing a smile. 'Just a bit anxious to get out of here,' she lied smoothly. She needn't have bothered. The nurse followed her eyes to Teddy's silhouette and smiled softly. Shifting on the bed, she thought of all the times she had pushed him away over the last few days, no doubt mirroring his own attempts at distance. She had a feeling she knew some of his reasons—his family being one. It was terrifying how fast she had fallen, but what they had was special. There was no way in hell they would ever just be friends; he must know that.

The nurse's voice cut into her thoughts. 'OK, Angel. All done here. You're doing well, considering. I'll let the doctor know.' She paused in the doorway. 'Want me to send Teddy back in?'

'Um…yes please, would you?'

The woman stepped outside, closing the door with a soft click, but not before shooting her a knowing glance. She was sure she saw a smirk there, too. Angel's cheeks flushed, even though she was by herself. Everyone would talk about them even more now and speculate about Teddy and her. But she had spent too long telling herself that what everyone else thought mattered. It was time to remember that life was all about taking risks. Heck, she'd taken the biggest risk of all not long ago, setting up a Christmas wedding! Just because it had never happened didn't mean she had to stop believing in herself or her own ability to make magic happen. And Teddy was very good at making magic happen too. She just had to be honest with him about what really happened with Ben, so she could put it behind her and move on, no matter how he really felt, or didn't feel, about her.

The door opened again slowly. Teddy peered in, then closed it behind him and moved straight to her bedside, his strong fingers enveloping her hand. Even exhausted, with dark circles under his eyes and his usually tame hair all mussed up from the wind and rain, he was achingly good-looking. Angel's breath caught as she met his gaze.

'So, do we think you're going to live to try and fell another tree with your bare hands?' he asked. OK, so he was attempting humour, but she could feel how tired he was, probably from worrying about her and their so-called friendship.

Angel swallowed hard. 'Teddy, I…' She paused, gathering her courage. 'I need to tell you something.'

His brows met in the middle as he studied her questioningly and she took a deep breath. 'I like you. I never told you that outright. Gosh, I sound like I'm back in school or something, but if I don't tell you it will just fester inside me with everything else—and the thing is, Teddy, I haven't been entirely honest with you.'

Her voice trembled slightly as his eyes scanned her face, but she pressed on. 'I know you have your reasons for pushing people away; from what you've told me, your family aren't that fun to be around.'

Teddy stiffened suddenly. She felt his hand tighten around hers.

'No, please,' she insisted. 'Let me finish. I understand because…because I've been doing the same thing to my family. They're no fun to be around when all they do is question me about how I am, after what happened to me.'

The words hung between them, heavy with implication. The room seemed to hold its breath, as if it were waiting for his response. Teddy's brows furrowed in concentration, his hand still tightly holding hers. 'What do you mean?'

'There's something I've never told anyone here,' she began, her voice barely above a whisper. 'About why I hate Christmas. About… Ben.'

Teddy leaned closer, his eyes never leaving her face, though he looked strangely wary now, just at the sound of her ex's name. 'What about Ben?'

Angel looked away for a second. She had promised herself she wouldn't do this but suddenly she was fighting back the sting of a pool of tears. 'Ben and I were supposed to get married on Christmas Day last year. It was supposed to be a dream wedding, although admittedly I did most of the planning. But that's not the point.'

She saw Teddy's jaw clench, but he waited for her to continue.

'I was there, in my dress, at the church. Everyone was there. My family came from Scotland and the Philippines; everyone came from both sides. We were thrilled to get the celebrations going—a huge Christmas party, a band, fizz to last a week. But Ben…he just…he never showed up.'

The words tumbled out of her now, as if a dam had broken somewhere inside her. 'He left me standing at the altar, basically—no explanation, no nothing; he just disappeared. I thought he was dead! Then he sent a message to say he was sorry, but he just couldn't do it. He'd flown to Marrakech.'

'Marrakech?'

'Yes. On Christmas Day, of all days. He knew it was my favourite day. He knew he would be ruining it for me for ever, but he did it anyway. I mean, he was right to do it, if he didn't want to marry me, but he had a million chances to tell me sooner. He just…didn't.'

Teddy's hand tightened around hers and she realised his knuckles were slowly turning from pink to white. Angel couldn't bear to look at his eyes.

'I've never been so humiliated in my life,' she continued. 'And, ever since, my family…they won't stop asking if I'm OK, if I've heard from him. It's like they're always just waiting for me to announce that all is forgiven and we're getting back together.' She let out a shaky breath. 'That's why I came here—to escape all of that. That's why I didn't want to celebrate Christmas with my family. I didn't want to celebrate it at all.'

When she finally looked up, the intensity in Teddy's eyes

took her breath away. His face was a mask of barely contained fury, and his body was all tense, as if he was waiting to spring into action.

'How could he…?' he started, his voice low and dangerous. He took a deep breath, visibly trying to calm himself. 'Angel, I can't believe you went through all that. I can't believe that anyone would do that to you!' His free hand clenched into a fist at his side. 'How can you possibly still be in love with someone who treated you like that?'

'What?' Angel felt a sudden, inexplicable urge to laugh. Of all the things she'd expected Teddy to say, that most certainly was not one of them. 'You sound like one of my cousins—the one who was probably always secretly in love with Ben.'

Angel shook her head. 'As if I'm still in love with him after that!' Then she narrowed her eyes at him. 'Wait. You thought…'

Teddy swept a hand through his messed-up hair and she watched more confusion replace the anger in his eyes. 'I thought there must be something going on.'

'Not that,' she said adamantly. 'I mean, it took time, yes, but I have maintained some element of self-respect, Teddy! I've moved on. What happened hurt like hell, maybe more than that tree just now, but it also taught me a lot about myself.'

She watched as Teddy processed her words, his thumb absently tracing circles on the back of her hand. He cleared his throat, looking slightly uncomfortable. 'I saw a photo of you and Ben on the table at your place,' he admitted. 'I thought maybe our little, whatever it was, had got you missing him, or hoping you could get back together with *him*.'

Angel's eyes widened in surprise. 'Oh, *that* photo,' she said, remembering the framed picture she'd forgotten to put away before he'd showed up at her place. 'I should have got rid of it ages ago. I think I was testing myself, keeping it there, seeing how long it would take for me to be able to look at it and not let what he did affect me. Turns out what he did doesn't affect me any more, not like it used to. I'm not even angry. It led me here.'

Her pulse quickened at the way his hand tightened more around hers, and the heart monitor sped up just enough to give her away. 'I'm sorry for assuming,' Teddy said. 'I should have asked you about it instead of jumping to conclusions.'

Angel squeezed his hand gently. 'It's OK. I understand why you might have thought I was still pining for him.' She paused, gathering her courage. 'We were together for a long time. But the truth is, maybe he wasn't as perfect for me as I thought he was.'

She swallowed as she met Teddy's intense gaze. His blue eyes held more vulnerability now than she had ever seen.

'You've taught me how to laugh again, how to have fun. And you've reminded me why I always loved Christmas so much…' She paused. 'I thought I'd never enjoy it again, but I've had a surprisingly amazing time with you, even when you've pushed me out of my comfort zone. *Especially* when you've pushed me out of my comfort zone! The way you love Christmas, the way you've wanted to share it, it's infectious. Your excitement, your joy…it's all exactly why people love you, Teddy. And I want that. Not just for the holidays, but…all the time.'

She watched as Teddy's expression shifted, myriad emotions playing across his features. For a moment, he looked almost overwhelmed, and Angel's heart clenched with fear. Had she said too much?

Teddy drew a deep breath. His grip on her hand tightened. 'Angel, I…' He trailed off, seeming to struggle with his words. 'I've never… This is all new to me.'

The beeping of the hospital machinery seemed to fade into the background as she looked at him.

'I've always been on my own, you know?' he said, his voice rougher than usual. 'Relying on myself, not letting anyone get too close. And my family…' He shook his head, a flash of pain crossing his face. 'Well, I think you've gathered by now that they've never really understood what I do, why it matters so much to me.'

Angel's heart ached for him. She'd seen glimpses of this before—the loneliness hidden beneath Teddy's confident exterior. 'It must be hard,' she murmured, gently encouraging him to continue.

Teddy nodded, lowering his gaze to their intertwined hands, and Angel felt a surge of protectiveness wash over her. She wanted to shield Teddy from that pain, to show him how incredible he truly was.

'Your work is important, Teddy,' she said firmly. 'You save lives every single day; you show people that life is worth living. That matters. And you deserve people to love you for that, and for everything else you do too.'

A small, grateful smile pulled at his lips. 'Thanks, Angel,' he murmured, his thumb resuming its gentle circles on her hand. 'That love thing you just mentioned…. I've just never really known it, or what it feels like.' He paused, letting his gaze drift to hers, sending goose bumps up her arms. 'But you make me want to do things, and share things I've never shared with anyone, actually. And not just for Christmastime.'

Angel's breath caught in her throat. Their lips were mere inches apart when with a loud click the door swung open. Angel jerked back, startled, just as the doctor strode in.

'Good news, Ms Flores,' he announced, oblivious to the moment he'd interrupted. 'Your tests look good. We can discharge you tonight.'

Angel blinked, trying to process the information through the haze of emotions swirling around in her head. 'Tonight?' she repeated.

Teddy cleared his throat. 'That's great news, doc. What time can we expect the discharge papers?'

As the doctor rattled off instructions, Angel found her gaze drawn back to Teddy. He was listening intently, but she noticed the slight flush on his cheeks, the way his hand still rested close to hers on the bed. When the doctor left, Teddy turned to her. Something in his eyes sent a thrill through her. 'If it's alright with you,' he said softly, 'I'd like to take you home. Make sure you're settled in.'

Angel felt a swarm of butterflies flocking to her stomach, just as the heart monitor gave her away. She didn't care—so what? This time was different. She could see it in the tenderness of his gaze and feel it in the way he gently squeezed her hand again. 'I'd like that,' she whispered.

Just then, Teddy's phone buzzed. He glanced at it, frowning slightly before answering. 'Hello?'

Angel watched as surprise flickered across his face. He listened intently, occasionally murmuring, 'Yes,' or 'I understand.' When he hung up, he looked slightly dazed.

'Everything alright? What happened?'

He nodded slowly. 'It was my mother,' he said, sounding bewildered. 'She saw on the news about a tree falling on a flight paramedic. When I didn't answer her call earlier, she called the base and George told her what happened.'

Angel's eyes widened. 'Is she angry that you didn't answer, or tell her you were alive?'

'No, that's the thing,' he said, shaking his head in disbelief. 'She called me a hero. She actually said she was proud of me for rescuing Joe twice.' He looked at Angel, almost laughing now. 'She actually cares…'

Angel reached out, cupping Teddy's cheek. 'Of course she cares, Teddy. How could anyone not see how amazing you are? Maybe she's just always had a problem knowing exactly how to show it, because you haven't been around.'

'How did you get so wise?' he said, leaning into her touch. When he took her face and kissed her, Angel felt the heat blooming from around her heart, spreading through every bone in her aching body, and she kissed him back. Who cared who saw them now? This was a new beginning for both of them; she could feel it.

EPILOGUE

SNOWFLAKES DANCED AND swirled outside the frost-rimmed windows, but inside the Flores' cozy Scottish cottage, the crackling fireplace radiated nothing but blazing heat through Teddy's bones and it felt as if his heart was about to burst.

So much for not liking Christmas. Just one year after announcing how much she loathed it, thanks to her ex, here Angel was, laughing with her family, hanging shiny ornaments on a giant tree, wearing a Christmas jumper.

He caught her eye from across the room, where he nursed a spiced cider in his favourite slippers, sending messages back and forth with Joe. He promptly switched on the lights on his jumper and quirked an eyebrow at her. She laughed and stuck out her tongue, then did the same to her own jumper, making a flock of sheep start blinking in red and green flashing sparkles, even brighter than his own. They had challenged each other—who could find the ugliest, brightest flashing jumper. She had definitely won, and she looked gorgeous in it too, of course.

How was it that this woman could be so damn sexy in any setting? he thought to himself, watching her long hair gleaming in the soft glow of the overhead twinkling lights as she reached up to hang a delicate glass ornament on the tree. Her eyes sparkled with pure delight over every single decoration she pulled out of the box, and so did her mother's, her father's, her sister's, her brother's and her aunt's… To be honest, he had lost count of the number of relatives who'd flown in from the Philippines for their first Christmas in Scotland. But seeing Angel so happy, surrounded by her family, made him fall even more in love with her than he'd already been. This was a far cry from the guarded, wary woman he'd met a year ago. But then, he was different now too.

'Careful with that one, love,' Angel's mother cautioned suddenly, waggling her glass of sherry at her. 'It's been in the family for generations, that one. Granny bought it from Kerala…'

Angel rolled her eyes good-naturedly. 'Mum, I'm a paramedic. I think I can handle a bauble.'

Teddy chuckled, drawing their attention his way, and Angel shot him a playful glare. 'Don't you start. Come make yourself useful instead of lounging about like a lazy dog.'

'I was messaging Joe,' he protested, setting down his mug and crossing the room. And, as if he thought he was the lazy dog in the room, Bruno shot up from his place by the fire and padded over too. He looked adorable in the Christmas jumper Angel's sister had given him, complete with glittery bones on it.

'As my lady commands,' Teddy teased her, brushing a kiss against her cheek as he passed, then plucking a shiny red ball from the box.

'And how is Joe doing?' she asked him, hanging a small gingerbread man next to his red ball, then pinging it with her finger, making Bruno jump up and try to eat it. The small room was so noisy with everyone talking around them, but somehow, they managed to create their own little world in it.

'He's having a great time. He got a BMX from his dad, and his mum… I guess he'll find out tomorrow when he goes to her place. He's splitting Christmas between both their houses, so he's happy to get two gifts.'

Angel laughed, fending Bruno off the stack of gingerbread decorations. 'Well, that's the way it's meant to work, I suppose. I'm so glad he's getting on better with them both since their divorce. They all seem happier.'

'His parents are even better friends now than when they were married, so Joe says.' Teddy smiled, suddenly catching sight of her ring. The red Christmas tree lights glinted off the diamond on the platinum band, almost blinding him. He caught her hand in his and brought it to his lips, dropping a kiss on the back of her fingers.

'I still can't believe you're my fiancée now,' he said quietly, completely unable to hide the pride in his voice. They'd been engaged for roughly four months and strangely, the longer they waited to get married, the more he just wanted to march to that church and sweep her off her feet at the altar, kiss her and make her his wife. But they were planning a summer wedding and hoped that Yorkshire would provide the sunshine.

The scent of pine and cinnamon enveloped him as he hung more ornaments, savouring the unfamiliar feeling of belonging in this huge, extended family. His own childhood Christmases had been pretty lonely affairs at times—but then, on reflection, maybe he had chosen to remove himself from more situations than he should have, instead of just discussing how he felt around his family, as he was able to now.

A chirping sound from the couch interrupted his bauble-hanging. Teddy picked up his phone again, expecting to see a message from Joe. He and Joe had become unlikely pals over the last year, with Teddy adopting a kind of mentor status, taking him out onto the moors, showing him new paths and biking trails, always with Bandit close by. Joe was determined to become a helicopter pilot, no thanks to George's enthusiastic encouragement.

It wasn't Joe, though. 'It's my parents,' he announced.

Angel crossed to him and squeezed his hand. 'Answer it,' she encouraged softly.

Teddy swiped to accept the video call, angling the phone to include Angel and her parents in the frame just behind him. 'Merry Christmas!' he greeted them, forcing cheer into his voice that he still didn't quite feel. At least he could answer these days without feeling the dread creep up his spine.

'Teddy, darling!' His mother's face filled the screen, her perfectly coiffed hair at odds with the casualness of the Flores gathering here in the cute but over-stuffed living room. 'Oh, and hello to you all! What a fabulous tree you have there.'

Teddy panned the camera around the room, showcasing the decorations and the gentle snowfall outside, and introducing Angel's family members one by one. They were staying at a B&B down the street and had pretty much filled every room there. 'It's beautiful up here,' he said. 'How's the weather down there?'

His father's gruff voice chimed in. 'Wet and dreary, as usual. But never mind that. You look…happy, son. Happier than I've seen you in years, actually.'

The unexpected observation caught Teddy off-guard. He pulled the phone back to himself and glanced at Angel, who was still smiling encouragingly. 'I am happy, Dad,' he admitted slowly. 'Happier than I've ever been.'

There was a moment of loaded silence before his father cleared his throat. 'Well, good. That's good. Listen, Teddy…maybe next year you can finally come home and spend Christmas with us instead. We'd love to have you and Angel here for the festive period; it's been a while since we've seen you at Christmas.'

Teddy felt his shoulders tense, and Angel instinctively wrapped an arm around his waist, leaning her head on his shoulder. 'That's a lovely invitation, thank you,' she replied to his father. Teddy wasn't sure what to say. The invitation, well-intentioned as it might be, felt more like a tug-of-war between his past and his future. He knew he could get through it with Angel by his side, but it wasn't as if his family issues had all just healed themselves. Not yet, anyway, but at least they were trying.

'That's…that's really nice of you to offer,' Teddy said carefully. 'We'll have to see how things go. But I appreciate the thought.'

Teddy's mother leaned closer to the screen, her eyes bright with curiosity. 'So, tell me, how are the wedding plans coming along? Have you set a date yet?'

A smile tugged at Teddy's lips as he exchanged a glance with Angel. 'Actually, we have. We're planning a summer wedding next year.'

His mother clapped her hands in delight. He was surprised by how excited she sounded, and touched. He felt his shoulders relaxing as she asked if they'd decided on a venue. 'We're still working out the details,' he replied, his hand finding Angel's. 'But, before that, we're taking some time off to visit Angel's family in the Philippines. It's important to us that both sides of the family are involved.'

He felt Angel squeeze his hand, her own silent gesture of gratitude that he had suggested this himself. Of course he had; she was always so enthusiastic about it, he couldn't wait to see it all for himself.

His father's eyebrows rose. 'The Philippines? That's quite a trip. How long will you be gone?'

'About three weeks,' Teddy explained. 'We want to make sure we have plenty of time to accept all the dinner invites everyone here is still extending, and the fishing trips, and the waterfall swimming, and—'

'The scuba diving,' Angel interrupted. 'And the volcano walk…'

'There's a lot to do,' he finished, though his mind was reeling all over again. His life had changed so much, so irrevocably, in just a year. The man who'd once lived for solitary thrills now found his greatest adventure in building a life with Angel. Who'd have thought this could ever be him?

'Well, that sounds wonderful,' his mother said, her voice tinged with wistfulness. 'You'll have to send us lots of pictures.'

'We will,' Teddy promised, feeling a twinge of guilt at the distance he still put between his family and him at times. But, before he could dwell on it, Angel gently nudged him.

'I hate to interrupt,' she said softly to Teddy before addressing his parents, 'But I think it's time we started with our duties. We have to get onto the dinner preparations. It was lovely talking to you both.'

After a round of goodbyes, Teddy ended the call. Angel tugged at his hand. 'Come on,' she said with a mischievous glint in her eye. 'Let's go grab some of those biscuits Mum made. I'm starving.'

Teddy allowed himself to be led into the kitchen, her hand in his, her jumper still doing a Christmas light festival of its own. As they stepped through the doorway, Angel paused, and a coy smile took over her mouth. She glanced upward. Teddy followed her gaze to a sprig of mistletoe hanging above them from the top of the doorway.

'Well, would you look at that,' Teddy murmured, pulling Angel close. 'I wonder who put that there.'

'Mum did,' she said, as her arms wound around his neck. 'Last year I would have torn it off the wall, but I've had a change of heart,' she whispered. 'About a lot of things.'

As their lips met, Teddy grinned under her kiss. 'I'm so glad you got over your aversion to all things Christmas.'

Angel's eyes sparkled with happiness, and a little hint of mischief. 'Well, I had a little help getting over that. And besides, some traditions are worth keeping,' she replied, looking up at the mistletoe again before pressing her lips to his in another kiss.

A snigger behind her made her pull away. Her mother and Ate were making smooching sounds, imitating them. They quickly straightened up and asked about the biscuits and Angel grabbed the plate quickly from the counter. As her family wandered back into the living room, content with their teasing, Teddy circled her waist from behind and swept her hair aside to plant a soft, warm kiss on her neck.

'I love you so much,' he said, his voice low and husky, and with the kind of sincerity that sent the butterflies raging inside her. 'But we need to talk about something.'

Angel looked around at him. 'What is it?'

Teddy turned her round and took the biscuits from her hands. 'We still need to break it to your parents that we're leaving first thing tomorrow morning.'

She pulled a face. 'Right, the skiing trip, with your mountain-rescue group.' Then she leaned in closer, and he could hear the blatant excitement in her voice. 'The forecast looks perfect for tomorrow, did you see? Fresh powder, clear skies… We can't miss it, Teddy.'

Teddy couldn't help but grin, pride swelling out in his chest. 'Look at you, Flores, talking like a pro. Hard to believe you could barely stand upright on skis a year ago.'

'Practice makes perfect, and I had a good teacher,' Angel

replied, nudging him playfully. 'But, seriously, Mum and Dad *are* going to be disappointed. They were hoping we'd stay for Boxing Day lunch.'

Teddy ran a hand through his hair, considering their options. 'We could always come back here after—make it up to them.'

Angel nodded. 'That's a good idea. I just hope they understand. You know how they can be.' She paused. 'And maybe we really should consider being with your family next year; what do you think?'

Teddy opened his mouth to object, but she kissed him again. 'Hey! Whatever happens with your parents, with my family, with anything—we've got this. Together.' She squeezed his hand. 'I love you, Teddy,' she told him, and he could see how much she meant it.

With Angel he knew even the hardest times would be a hell of a lot easier. She was the kind of woman he needed—had always needed. A woman who eagerly anticipated a challenge, and who never gave up on anything she set her mind to. She'd become his anchor, and his partner, in every sense of the word. Building for ever with Angel was already his biggest Christmas wish come true.

* * * * *

Look out for the next story in
the Royal York Hospital miniseries
Wedding Date with Dr Petrides *by Kristine Lynn*

And if you enjoyed this story,
check out these other great reads
from Becky Wicks

A Daddy for Her Babies
From a Fling to a Family
Nurse's Keralan Temptation

All available now!

MILLS & BOON®

Coming next month

EMERGENCY ROOM REUNION
Amy Blythe

He glanced at her mouth—again. And he wasn't the only one guilty of that look.

But she wasn't going to make the same mistake twice. 'We shouldn't have… That night you came in with a broken tibia, I didn't think you were staying.' Her words were running away from her, but she couldn't stop them. 'It felt like goodbye, like there was nothing to lose, but now you're *back* back, and there's something to lose. Oh god.' It hit her like a ton of bricks, the real answer to her question. 'You came back to give it another go?'

'No.'

'No?'

'I just wondered if there was still something.'

'How is that different?'

'Because there's no pressure,' he said, eyes pleading. 'Because you kissed me back and it was like nothing else.' His tone seemed to dare her to contradict him, to disagree, and she couldn't do it.

Without meaning to, without consciously making the choice to touch him, she reached out, grazed her fingertips to the back of his wrist. This was real. He was really here, really telling her he wanted her still, after all this time.